REIGN OF THE WITCH QUEEN
BOOK 3

A Crown of Fire and Ice

ANDREA ROSE

A CROWN OF FIRE AND ICE by Andrea Rose

All rights reserved.

Copyright © 2026 by Andrea Rose

First Edition.

Edited by Penny Barber

Copy Edit by Oopsie Daisy Edits

Cover design by Artscandare

Interior character art by Vivien Ginter

Special Thanks

This book was a labor of love. I'm thrilled to bring this story of Domhan's return to the light to a close. Writing a book is always a journey, and I'm thankful to a loving community of friends and family who have helped me along the way.

Dedication

A Crown of Fire and Ice is dedicated to my mother, Eleanor Fenichel, and my brother, Louis Fenichel, who have both moved on from this world. I miss them dearly and know they would have loved this series above all my others.

For Dave Mansue, my love, my friend, and my strength. I couldn't do any of this without your love and support.

Special Note to Readers

If this is the first book you are reading from the Reign of the Witch Queen series, I want to warn you that **Part Two** is riddled with spoilers for books one and two.

If you've not read *A Crown of Light and Shadow* and *A Crown of Wind and Water*, you may wish to do so before you reach that point.

Table of Contents

REIGN OF THE WITCH QUEEN

In the beginning, there were two worlds.
The human world is bound by earth, fire, water, and air.
The elven world glows with the fifth element, magic.
Over time, the sister worlds split from each other,
and humans forgot about the elves.

Centuries passed, and the elven world thrived until a beautiful and selfish witch came into power. Using her magic to dominate rather than to lead the elven people of Domhan, she cast a spell to keep men from ever assuming power. The old gods twisted her spell, and no female elves have been born since.

Darker and darker the witch queen became, until many fled the great city. Those who remained were transformed into her army of shadow demons.

Without female elves to continue their race, the elves living in fear of discovery will die out while Domhan falls into darkness. The only hope is a prophecy claiming that the human world holds the key. Only with the three earthly women and the sons of Riordan can the Watchers' Gate be opened. Inside lies the magic that can stop the witch queen.

The time has come for the three elven brothers to follow the prophecy.

Prologue
American Super Hero Combat

LAYLA

"Ladies and gentlemen, welcome to *American Super Hero.*"

The stadium shakes with applause, and my heart pounds with a surge of adrenaline. Pushing aside a lifetime of self-doubt, I focus on the clock and the first obstacle.

Don White, the former football star, continues the introductions, his voice booming in the indoor stadium. "Tonight, we have two fierce competitors who have risen through the ranks. They both finished the course during trials, but that doesn't mean anything when the pressure is on."

Spectators fill the seats on all four sides, and the noise is intense.

Breathing deep, I'm doing all I can to keep my adrenaline from taking over. The key is to stay calm. I'm ready for this. I've trained to be the best. No one will ever think of me as that poor orphan trapped in the system ever again. After today, they'll only know me as an *American Super Hero* champion.

"In red, Malinda Baker, and in blue, Layla Stark. Layla has beaten all the odds to be here. She's fought injury and circumstance and risen above it all." Don's voice carries over the cheering crowd.

Malinda's family and friends are shouting her name over and over.

I have no one, but it doesn't matter. Staring forward at the wash of red, white, and blue, I block out all the noise until even Don's voice is just a murmur.

Breathe in. Breathe out. The first obstacle is frog pads. Easy. Still, I've seen competitors fail when they get overconfident in the qualifying runs. That will not be me.

The starting bell sounds. I leap over the frog pads in a quick sequence of precise movements, from foot to foot, left, right, left, right, and dismount to the narrow platform. Using my momentum, I grab the hanging rope and swing across a wide pool. I land with two feet on the other side.

Malinda is right beside me, but I can't give her space in my head. Nothing can break my focus; that's the key.

Run your race, Layla.

The broken bridge is six trapezoid-shaped pads suspended over water by two ropes each. I must be quick and surefooted. I run through the third trick and gain a little as Malinda falters, but she doesn't fall.

On the platform, I take a breath to regain my composure. Midleap, I grab the first of a series of four swinging and spinning dumbbells. With one hand gripping the end, I spin the first disk, then swing and leap to the second. As I dismount, my biceps ache, but it's nothing to worry about.

The crowd's noise breaks through my concentration. Giving them a wave, I try to gather myself and push aside the external noise so I can focus on the salmon ladder.

Composed, I leap over the water and grab hold of the long bar. I reverse my grip on my left hand and use my legs and hips to gain momentum and thrust the bar up and into the next set of angled rungs. My arms scream with the effort, but I keep going until I reach the top, then swing myself to the soft, mat-covered surface between obstacles.

Log runner is frozen in place, but that will change the moment I hit the first cushioned log. Eight padded logs stand between me and moving past the other women in the competition. Six female competitors who came before Malinda and me didn't make it past this point.

Malinda lands next to me.

I leap and run across as fast as I can. I have to keep going or the roll will toss me into the water. I make it, and the crowd screams with joy.

There's no blocking them out anymore. They're too loud, and I'm too excited.

Giving myself a breath, I make the leap onto the spin cycle. There are three inverted basket-shaped wheels that I use my body to spin to reach the next one. I push aside the pain in my arms and legs and make it to the other side.

The warped wall looms ahead of me. The ramp is a daunting feat, and the crowd is chanting, "BEAT THAT WALL."

Three long breaths, and I hop to the ground where I'll start. I run at the wall and charge up. When gravity wants to bring me down, I leap and grip the top edge. My shoulders and arms are in agony as I pull myself up to the top of the beast.

I shake my arms out and contemplate the floating monkey bars—six spaces with only two bars that have to be moved forward to the next cradle to advance. Without looking at the clock, I feel I'm making good time. I can do this. Leaping from the platform, I grab the first bar. It wobbles in my grip. I reach out with my right hand and take the second bar. I remove the first, swing forward, and place it in the cradle. Then I repeat the process with the second bar. I miss the cradle.

The crowd gasps.

Swinging on one arm, I increase momentum and push the bar into the cradle then move to the last. I swing twice to get enough height and make the dismount.

Hands on my hips, I draw long breaths. The spider wall is two parallel walls made of glass. I stand between them, spread my legs and arms and begin shimmying up.

Malinda is only a second or two behind me.

I block her out as I make my ascent. Every six feet, I push two fifty-pound glass ceilings vertical before I continue. My arms are in agony. My back screams for rest, but I push upward one step at a time.

Malinda is gaining.

I push harder, but my body is at its limit.

At the last wall, I lose time struggling to snap the second ceiling into place.

Malinda bashes through her wall.

I drag myself onto the top platform as Melinda slams her hand down on her buzzer.

My heart sinks amid cheers and chants of "Melinda."

The world closes in around me. Still, there's a job to finish. Dejected and crushed, I press my buzzer.

Barely recognizing Malinda's arms around me, I'm on autopilot as I hug her back. Whatever consolation she tried to give me is lost in the cheering crowd and the blood rushing through my head.

Loser.

Failure.

You'll never amount to anything.

The words of a foster father who shouldn't mean anything to me scream in my head. All my attempts to banish his hateful predictions fail, and I descend the steps to the tournament floor.

Don hugs me and tells me I was amazing. I smile for the camera and congratulate Malinda. When the opportunity presents itself, I give her the stage and make my way to the locker room.

Compared to the pageantry of the arena, the locker room is quiet and drab. Blue lockers line the right, and two wooden benches run parallel to them. On the far left is a shower room with six curtained stalls. Since I was in the last group of champions, the room is empty, leaving me alone.

I open my locker and pull out my backpack. It has a change of clothes and some assorted protein bars.

The door opens, and a young woman with blond hair and gray eyes smiles at me. "Sorry, Layla. You were totally great, though. You should be really proud of yourself."

"Thanks." I can't remember her name, but she told us where to stand before we went out so that the cameras could catch any pregame jitters.

She hands me a large bottle of electrolytes. "You should hydrate, or you'll cramp up."

I take the bottle and turn the cap.

When I don't drink right away, she raises her eyebrows and waits.

After taking a long pull on the salty-sweet drink, I say, "Thank you. I'm fine. Disappointed, but fine."

With a sigh, she sits next to me. "You shouldn't be so hard on yourself. You nearly had it, and you and Malinda are the only two of eight who finished the course. That's an amazing accomplishment."

I nod because no one wants to hear my sour grapes.

"I have to get ready for the men's final. Do you need anything?" She checks her watch.

"Nah. I'm good." I drink more and cap the bottle.

Patting me on the back, she gets up and gives me another smile before heading out.

With a long sigh, I slump and wrap my arms around my bag.

A high-pitched screech fills the room, and I have to put my hands over my ears.

Looking around, I stand and back toward the showers. A black dot in the center of the lockers widens and spins. Wind sweeps through the room, spinning a stack of paper fliers.

My heart is in my throat, and I try to remember hitting my head during the competition. Backpack looped over one arm, I use my other hand to check for bruises under my hair. Nothing.

A point of light at the center of the widening hole reveals a figure coming closer. Part of me thinks *run*, but where would I go? I'm not rushing back into the stadium to face the crowds and explain why I'm freaking out. Would I say a vortex just opened up in the locker room? People would think I'm nuts, and I'm not sure they'd be wrong.

"What the hell is happening?" Maybe it's an earthquake. I've never heard of one looking like that or feeling windy, but this is California, and that's as good a possibility as any. Sensibly, I walk to the door, open it, and stand in the threshold where the structure would be safest.

The girl with the drink is on the other side, holding her phone to her ear. Her expression is worried with big eyes and a wide mouth, but she's not talking or moving.

"Hey, are you okay?"

She doesn't move or respond.

What the hell. I know I lost, but she doesn't have to pretend to ignore me. "Hey!"

Nothing.

Down the curtained area leading to the arena, two men stand by the opening. One is jumping, but his feet are off the ground, and he's just hovering in midair. The other's hands are frozen mid-clap.

The scaffold supporting the course is visible over the curtains. Three stagehands are climbing up to reset the course, but none of them are in motion. It's as if I'm the only person conscious and noticing the earthquake.

The figure in the vortex grows larger, and the hole in the lockers reveals a man with wild red hair. He jumps down to the floor, his pointed ears breaching his long, beautiful locks. Strange clothes that might have come out of a Renaissance fair's costume sales grace his tall, broad frame. With a strong jaw, carved cheekbones, and kind, almost playful eyes, he stares at me. "Layla Stark?"

I nod dumbly.

He's beautiful, otherworldly, and I'm sure I've suffered a concussion. It's not possible for anyone to be this stunning. He can't be real, so he must be a dream.

I pinch my arm, and a lash of pain proves me wrong.

His smile widens, and he holds out his hand. "The oracle gave me the song of your soul. I'm ordered to bring you to my world so that you can help to save it. You're our only hope." He looks back at the vortex and frowns.

"Save what?" I ask, trying to follow.

"My world, Domhan, is dying under the rule of an evil witch queen. You and two others have to help us, or we won't survive. You're one of the women in the prophecy." He cocks his head and stretches his hand farther.

I look back at the frozen scene and consider my unfulfilling job as an Uber driver and the other odd jobs I take to make the rent every month. I have an interview with the city to get a job driving a bus. It's not like my music career ever went anywhere. My life has turned out exactly how Buddy said it would. My last foster father collected the checks and put food on the table. He gave me a lot, but he also made sure I never thought too highly of myself. My shrink says he did the best he could and probably had a father who treated him the same way. I don't know if that's true, but he was right about me.

I just lost the competition I trained for all year. I have no family, and the few friends I made in Los Angeles will soon forget me. The dismal little apartment I live in isn't exactly home. If I'm honest, I've never had a place where I felt I belonged.

On the other hand, a gorgeous man is telling me a world

will collapse if I don't help him. At least that's a purpose. Maybe he's a madman in a costume. After all, none of what I'm seeing can be real. Can it?

If it's not real, I'll be exactly in the same place I was before this pointy-eared Adonis stepped out of a hole in the wall. If I'm not in a dream, I could help people in need and escape my miserable life.

Stepping forward, I sling my backpack over my shoulders and take his hand.

Chapter One

RAITH

I can't believe she said yes. I was sure that convincing a human woman to walk through a portal into another world would be impossible.

Layla pulled her strong shoulders back, tipped her chin up, and stepped through with me as if she saves worlds every day.

Mahogany hair pulled back from her pretty face, and lips that beg to be kissed, is not at all what I imagined in the human world. She's tall and distractingly shapely with strong, muscled arms, and the fitted blue garment she's wearing shows a midriff like I've never seen on anyone except a warrior elf. I try to concentrate on the portal and the task, but her hand is warm, and when she touches me, my pulse pounds.

When the soft oracle-created portal spins out of control, I pull her close. "Oh no." Stars blur past us, and the portal spits us out with a hard thump. I land on my back with Layla pressed to my front.

She presses her palms to my chest and pushes off me. Eyes wide, she looks around and her pretty mouth twists as if she's tasted something sour. "This is what you want me to save?"

The ground is damp, and I push to my elbows, wetness seeping through my leggings and tunic. Purple-hued land stretches across a craggy plane. We stand on a ridge of a great mountain range, but not one I've ever seen before. Leafless trees dot the bare landscape. Everything is leeched of color and life. "This is not good. This is not Domhan."

"What?" She looks at me. "What are you saying?"

Slowly turning, I take in the vastness of dry riverbeds and more dead trees. In the distance are remnants of a village, wooden structures burned, with only sticks standing among the rubble. The sky is dark, save for a few stars and a blue-and-green marble that makes my heart sink. "Raith, you've really done it this time."

"Who is Raith? What is Domhan? What have you done?" Her brows draw together. The band that held her hair must have come loose in the portal, leaving her hair hanging around her face and shoulders in waves of brown.

I wanted to impress her. I should have kept my focus. By the old gods, I can't do anything right. "I am Raith Riordan. Domhan is my world." I sigh, not wanting to answer the last question. Knowing there's no point hiding anything if we're going to survive, I point to the beautiful marble of a planet in the night sky. "That is Domhan, Layla."

She looks at the planet, then at me, before returning her gaze to Domhan. She turns to face me, her hands propped on her hips. "Are you telling me you brought me to the wrong planet?"

"I'm afraid so. I meant to keep my concentration on the portal, but you were so pretty, and your hand was soft, tough, and warm all at once. All of those things distracted me." I can't look into her eyes. She was the one person who didn't look at me with disappointment and regret. The idea of that being gone forever is too much. I stare at the ground.

A release of air follows her light laughter. "I knew it was too good to be true. What do we do now?"

Risking a look, I find her resigned, eyes wide with expectation. Perhaps the spin through the portal injured her brain. "You understand, I failed at my mission, and we're in real trouble."

"I get it, Raith. Everyone makes mistakes. How do we fix this and get to your planet?" Her brown eyes narrow, and her gaze shifts to somewhere over my shoulder.

It's in times like these that I wonder what my brothers would do. I could lie and tell her I have a plan, but that is probably not how Aaran would handle this. Of course, Aaran wouldn't ever be in this position. He'd have gotten it right. In fact, he likely brought his human back in a few minutes. There would be a parade for both of my brothers while they wait for me, all the while knowing I'll likely fail. "I don't know."

"What is that?" She points.

A mass of black cloud moves directly toward us. "Shadow demons." My heart races, and I grab her hand. "Layla, we've got to hide."

"What is it?"

There's no time to explain. I drag her down the rocky

surface of the rise with no idea what I'll find. Whatever else is in this world, it can't be worse than having our souls stolen and being forced to serve the witch queen.

"What is a shadow demon?" She pulls her arm from my hand, but thankfully keeps running behind me.

A piercing screech rends the air and stings my ears. Backing up to the sheer rock face where I've inadvertently gotten us cornered, I push Layla behind me and face the demons. Four shadow demons hover ten feet off the ground, studying us.

Maybe they're telling the witch queen, whom they serve, what they've found. I can only hope they mistake me for an Aracan elf.

Her hand on my shoulder, Layla's breath is fast, and her voice low. "What do they want?"

"Our souls."

"Mine is currently in use. Can you tell them to go away? Make them some offer?"

"I wish that were possible." I raise my hands, and when the first demon dives, I force energy through my fingertips. A wave of power flows forward, pushing them back.

"Whatever that was, that didn't work. What defeats them?"

My mind goes blank. I should know this. I'm sure someone told me at some point. I drag a long list of books long forgotten into my mind and remember page after page of theory. "No one really knows, but they are consumed by darkness, so light magic." I lift my hands again and conjure a ball of soft blue light. Reaching back, I throw it at the one in the front.

The demon erupts into ash.

"That was good." She pats my back. "Do it again."

The three remaining demons back up several feet.

"I hate this," I mutter to myself, but create another ball of light magic. "They may be demons now, but they used to be elves."

Her voice is soft and musical. "Can you save them?"

Shaking my head, I send magic into the orb I created.

Layla squeezes my shoulder. A shock of energy flows down my arm and chills my skin while it feeds my magic. She squeaks out a shocked sound and pulls her hand away.

With a deep breath, I let her magic flow into mine and throw the fortified ball of light at the shadow demons before I lose the strength of this new human magic. The light explodes, blinding me and pushing me back. I turn and shield Layla.

Black ash rains down.

"Well, that was intense," she says, looking over my shoulder. "I think you did it."

Leaning back, I look into her eyes while still pressing her against the rock wall. "I think you did it."

She shakes her head and presses her hands against my chest, backing me off her. "I'm sorry you had to kill them."

It's not as if there's another choice when it comes to shadow demons. In my mind, I can't separate them from the elves they used to be. I shrug. "They're better off." I scan the sky for any more threats. "We're too exposed here. Let's see if we can find a cave where I can think for a few minutes."

Nodding, she follows close behind me. "I have some questions."

"Of course. I'll tell you whatever I can as soon as we're relatively safe." The rock and soil are dry, but there seems to be a worn path around the base of the hills. It leads up along the dead-tree line and across the lower end of the mountains. I hope whatever uses this path is either absent or friendly. Either way, it's not a shadow demon since they don't walk.

Behind a thick stand of what were once ancient trees, a crack in the stone mountain widens into a cave mouth.

My eyes take a moment to adjust, but the cave is big enough for the two of us to rest, and the cover should give me a few minutes to try to figure out how I'm going to fix the mess I've made. We could go deeper, but if animals are using this place for shelter, they may be inside, and I don't want to have to kill an animal unless it's something we can eat. One mortal danger moment is enough for today.

Layla's warm, sun-kissed skin looks a bit ashen as she wraps her hand around her abdomen and stares into the darkness. "What lives on this planet besides the demons?" She swivels back to look outside.

"The elves that inhabited this planet are thought to be either dead or changed to shadow demons in service to the witch queen. We should be safe here for a little while." I sit with my back against the wall.

"What do you think happens to the shadow demons when they die?" She slides down the wall and sits. Digging into her pack, she pulls out a white-and-pale-blue striped shirt and pushes her arms through the sleeves before tying the long front at her waist.

I sigh. "I hope they go where all elves go when they die. I pray they find peace away from the rule of Vanora Braddish." I spit out her name.

"Is that the queen you want to dethrone?"

Nodding, I push down my rage at being forced to kill.

"She's a fiend that uses dark magic to control her armies, both demon and elven."

With her eyes closed, Layla shakes her head as if to clear it. "And your magic is different?"

I never needed to explain magic before. It's part of every Domhan elf's life. "Light magic is part of everything on Domhan. We live with it, and we die with it."

"But it can kill." She sits opposite me and wraps her arms around her knees.

Nodding, I sigh. "Yes. Light magic can be as deadly as dark in many ways."

"How do I know I've picked the right side?" She says it in a voice that might have been meant only for her own response.

"I guess you'll have to determine that for yourself?" I can't take my eyes off her. She's so beautiful, and her eyes seem filled with constant consternation. "Why didn't you tell me no when I asked you to come and help me?"

Her chest rises and falls with a long breath. "That's part of the very long and complicated story of my life, Raith. I'm not ready to share it all just yet."

Why would she tell me her deepest secrets? I'm no one to her. Yet I hear the song of her soul, and it's precise and beautiful in my heart. "Can you tell me about the strange room where I found you?"

A dry, humorless laugh pushes from her full, red lips. "It was a locker room. That's where we change and prepare for competition or sport. I had just finished losing the finals of a huge competition that was broadcast across the world."

"You lost?" It's hard to imagine her failing at anything. She's like a bright, life-giving light in my heart.

"By 1.2 seconds. That's practically an eternity in *American Super Hero* combat." She picks up a small black pebble from the cave floor and rolls it between her fingers.

"The clothes you're wearing are specific to that?"

She nods.

"What kind of sport is it?"

"The kind where you can get injured by ten different gauntlet-type tasks." She describes a few of the tasks she overcame.

My mind reels with the image of her leaping across water and muscling her way hand over hand across bars. "I assume this is not a common pursuit of humans."

"No. Most people have regular jobs where they climb a corporate ladder rather than a literal one." She stares at her open palms and shakes her head.

"Why did you take another path?" I'm driven to know more about my human.

She rolls her eyes. "You're determined to get it out of me. Okay. Fine." She stands and stares into the darkness beyond the cave opening. "I was orphaned at birth, a foundling, which means my mother left me where she hoped someone would find me. In my case, it was at the door to a hospital emergency room. During my youth, I lived in fifteen different foster homes. No one wanted me. The last of them was a couple in a dingy part of Los Angeles." She shrugs when I cock my head. "It's a big city near the ocean."

"I see." I don't want to say more until she seems ready to continue. It takes a lot to keep quiet, as I can't believe any parent would abandon Layla. She must have been as perfect at birth as she is right now. Anger at her mother and father, whom I'll never know, rushes through me.

"That couple wasn't the worst I ever lived with. They didn't beat me, and they made sure I had clothes and food. My foster father, Buddy, was a hard man. He fixed cars, but his bad attitude meant he got fired a lot, and he wound up working from his own garage at the back of the house. They needed the money that foster services gave them for taking on kids like me. I was fifteen when I got there and pretty much sure life was a terrible thing that had been forced on me. I probably could have been nicer. Buddy told me on the first day that I'd never amount to anything.

"It was as if he issued me a challenge. If I brought home a bad grade, he'd say it was to be expected. Then I'd work to prove him wrong. I even got a scholarship, but since I'd aged out of the foster system, I had to work to find a place to live, and couldn't afford to go to college. So at eighteen, I started driving people for money. I make enough to live and train. I just wanted Buddy to see that I could win. I didn't need him any more than he needed me." She dashes a tear away before looking at me with clear, determined eyes.

"I think you're the bravest person I've ever met. You jumped through that portal as if you did such things every day." I mean every word. I keep my other thoughts about her beauty and soul song to myself.

She shrugs. "I had nothing better to do, Raith."

"I'm sorry that I lost concentration, though, I should tell you it's not unlike me. I'm not known for getting things right the first time." I laugh at the understatement.

With a shrug, she sits back down. "Can you make one of those portals here?"

Shaking my head, I say, "If we can find an existing portal, I can open it, but I can't make a portal without that magic already existing. The oracle made the one I brought you through."

"What's an oracle?" She touches the rock behind her, then presses her fingers to her tongue.

My body instantly responds to the sensual sight, but I focus on her question. There's nothing like thoughts of the oracle to calm a raging attraction. "The oracle is my world's highest level of wisdom. They are elves who are elevated both mentally and magically. They live longer and are extremely learned."

"Why did they send you to find me?"

Good question. "My mother is the rightful queen. She has three sons, and each of us was sent to find a particular human woman that the prophecy claims can save our world and break the curse."

She taps the stone wall. "This is water. At least we won't die from dehydration." She smiles, and her eyes light up. "What's the curse?"

The way she looks when something makes her happy sends a jolt of joy through my heart, and I nearly miss her question. *Get it together, Raith.* "When Mother was dethroned, and we had to flee, Vanora cast a spell to keep men from ever ruling Domhan. Somehow, the spell back-fired, and the result was that no females have been born in thirty suns. In twenty or so more, we won't be able to recover, and elves will die out. Mother prayed I'd be a girl. She won't admit it, but I know she did. She was already pregnant with me when the curse was cast."

"Thirty years. How can you ever recover from that?" She stares at my ears. "How long do elves live? How old can your people conceive?"

Her eyes narrow, and I begin to realize this is a sign she is calculating a problem and how to solve it. "Longer than humans. Two hundred suns is not unusual. Women have conceived into their seventies, though it's less common."

"And you're thirty." She keeps her gaze on the ground. "I'm only twenty-five. What do you do when you're not finding human women?"

"I help..."

Meeting my gaze, she raises her eyebrows. "It felt like there was more. Who do you help, and with what? You're a prince, so no like, day-in, day-out type job?"

"I'm not really a prince because my mother is no longer queen. She governs the new capital city and leads an army, though my father usually handles those matters. My brother Aaran helps Mother, and Liam is a soldier. I help with whatever they ask of me. If new elves come to the city and need housing, I'll help them get settled. I'm always in attendance for feasts and balls to charm whoever needs charming." The more I speak, the less I like what I'm saying.

She cocks her head, and a soft smile plays across her lips. "I'm guessing there's more to it, but you don't have a defined job description."

"I'm the family disappointment, Layla. I'm sorry you didn't meet one of my brothers. They would have impressed you and done everything right." I get up and search the night for some bit of wisdom. "If I could take you back right now, I would do it."

"Then who would save your world?"

She's the most amazing person I've ever met. Maybe all humans are sweet, strong, and forgiving, but my gut tells me that's not true. Layla is extraordinary.

Before I can turn to tell her how amazing she is, something moves in the darkness. I back up a step and nearly trip over Layla's legs.

Six Aracan elves with sharpened stones and spears step out of the shadows and begin talking in their language. I catch a word or two and put my body between Layla and the pointy ends of their rough weapons. Raising my hands, I try to show them we're not a danger, but I can't understand them, at least not while they're all talking the old language at once. It sounds like gibberish. Two of them carry torches, and they push them out in front to get a better look at us.

It's tempting to draw the sword from my back, but these elves look as if they've been through too much.

Layla presses her front to my back and peers around me. "Who are they? What are they saying?"

I call my magic forward and let a ball of energy form in my hand.

The Aracans back up with wide eyes filled with fear. They cower from me but don't run.

"These are the lesser elves who inhabit this planet. I guess reports that they were all taken or killed were exaggerated."

Taking my wrist, she lowers my hand so the magic in my palm isn't as threatening. "I don't think they're dangerous, Raith. They look terrified and dirty, like refugees I've seen in the news. Maybe they can help us." She steps around me and smiles. Holding her hands out in a peaceful, open-palmed gesture, she says, "We won't harm you. We're lost."

"They don't speak the common tongue." I hold Layla's shoulders and pull her a few steps back.

"Then you talk to them and tell them we won't hurt

them and ask if they can help you find one of those portal things." She speaks through a forced smile, maintaining eye contact with the central Aracan.

The male Aracan elf who stands in the center is too thin, but his shoulders are broad. They all look as if they could use a month of good meals, a long bath, and some serious rest, but they also appear to be strong, and most importantly, they've survived.

"I don't speak the old language. At least, it's been a long time since my lessons."

"Did you understand anything they said when they first saw you?"

I dig into the memories of those old texts from my schooling. Each one is embedded in my mind, though long pushed aside. "I heard 'go away' and 'kill.'"

"That's not what I was hoping for." She turns her attention to a female who is staring at Layla's ears. Layla pushes her hair back and touches her round ear. She laughs, and the Aracan does too. "Raith, can you say 'help' in their language?"

"Maybe, but they might think we're going to help them rather than them helping us." I search those old scrolls like pictures in my mind with the ancient language and look for vocabulary, and all I find are words I don't know.

"It doesn't matter. Maybe we can help them. Right now, we need shelter, food, and a portal, and we're not getting any of that while they're holding pointy Stone Age weapons at us." She says all of this while still making fun of her rounded ears.

Even the stern leader smiles.

I push aside the mental scrolls and think about the

parchments where I wrote my lessons. I find words I translated. Skimming the page, I find *peace*. "Sith." Then I find *help*. "Cuidich." And finally, *gate*. "Geata."

The six of them gasp at my use of language they understand. The leader steps forward and eases Layla aside more carefully than I would have expected. He speaks in a rush of old language, and I catch the word *dachaigh*, or home, and he pokes me in the chest.

Stepping around him, I walk outside the cave and point to Domhan, where it's rising in their sky. "Dachaigh." I point to my chest. "Cuidich."

Chapter Two

LAYLA

I have no idea what words Raith used, but they have done the trick because the leader of the Aracan elves nods and pushes past while indicating that we should follow.

With three elves in front and three in back, we have little choice but to go with them through the tunnels of the cave, leading deeper into the mountains. The hilt of a sword pokes out from a scabbard strapped to Raith's back, and I'm glad he never drew the blade. I don't feel like these elves are dangerous.

"Where are they taking us?" I whisper to Raith.

"I don't know specifically, but I think they live inside these caves, and they're bringing us home." He wraps his hand around my upper arm, and his warmth seeps through my shirt.

"It's better than pointing weapons at us," I say.

"Or me having to harm them. They look like they've been through enough."

Their clothes are tattered and dirty, and they're far thinner than Raith. I'm guessing that whatever this witch queen has done to their planet has made hunting and gathering difficult, and any farms they might have had are long abandoned in favor of the safety of these caves.

I like that Raith doesn't want to hurt these elves. In fact, he didn't like killing the shadow demons, even though I get the feeling that was a kindness in a way. There's something about him that is very alluring, and it's more than how gorgeous he is. I mean, there's no denying that part, but it's as if there's more pulling me toward him.

The cave slopes down, and I brush aside other thoughts and concentrate on keeping on my feet and avoiding whatever might jump out of the crevices. The only light comes from two torches held by elves, and then a dim light appears ahead.

Raith's hand tightens slightly as if letting me know that he sees it too. "I think we're arriving."

I nod without any idea if he can see me clearly enough to notice.

The tunnel ends at a cliff that looks down into a wide, open area filled with several hundred elves huddled around a central campfire. The scent of meat cooking fills the cavernous space, along with other smells that accompany large groups of confined people.

It is not the best combination of odors, but I can understand how it's come to be this way. They remind me of news reports about war refugees—too thin, hollow eyes, and slow to react.

Someone coughs at the other side, and the sound echoes with crying and soft voices, as well as voices raised in argument.

"It's an entire village." Wonder fills Raith's voice. "This is unexpected."

The leader calls out something, and all eyes turn toward us.

We're nudged to the left along a ledge that slopes down to the cavern floor. People rush from below and gather at the bottom, happy to see the elves leading us. There are hugs, and the crowd brims with excitement. The leader wraps his arms around a woman and kisses her forehead.

Relief washes over her face at the sight of her man returning unharmed from wherever he and the others were.

They see me, and the joyous reunion goes silent. A woman touches my hair. Another tugs at my shirt. Someone pulls my ponytail.

I yelp.

They all holler different things all at once, and the crush tightens around us. The joy at seeing their friends shifts to anger and hostility. My skin tingles with it, and my mind shifts back to Buddy and the way his mood could change without notice. When I was six, the woman who fostered me had a nasty temper when she drank, which was often. I could feel the shift in her an hour before it happened and quickly learned to hide rather than take a beating.

The hair on my arms rises with the rage of the elves. I step back, ready to run and hide.

Raith calls out something in their language and pulls me into his arms, with one arm around my head and face and the other around my upper back. He's protecting the most essential parts of me so that if things turn violent, I won't be seriously injured.

I freeze, not sure how to react. His woodsy scent fills my senses. My fear eases, and my sense of danger subsides with his protection. The idea that he'd take a beating for me is new.

Whatever he yells, the leader repeats louder and more forcefully.

The crowd falls silent and steps back, forming a wide circle around us. Their faces are like Raith's, long and attractive, but in their tired eyes, there is pain as well as innocence. They're tall and lean with hair of every color but cropped to the chin rather than long and flowing. Their skin tones are as varied as their hair color, though perhaps none so fair as Raith. They are a beautiful people.

The leader speaks gently as he points to us and tells them something. Some nod in response.

Raith says, "He's telling them that we come from the blue planet, if my translation is right. That we need their help to get home."

"You understand them now?" How is that even possible?

Shrugging, Raith says, "We learned the ancient language in school. They're speaking in an old dialect. I had to search my memory for some vocabulary. I'm still working on remembering grammar."

The leader turns to Raith. He points to his own chest. "Tog."

Simple enough.

Raith gives his name while pressing his hand to his chest, then pats my head and says, "Lay-La" in a way that emphasizes each syllable.

Tog nods in approval, then points to each of us. "Rats. Layla."

"Close enough." Raith laughs as he releases me. His cheeks flush. "I think you're safe now."

The group listens as Tog speaks.

Leaning close, Raith says, "He's telling them something about us in the cave. I think they may have seen us kill the shadow demons from a distance." His brows pull together as if he's straining to understand. "They followed us when we hid in the cave opening, not sure if we would kill them with our bright magic."

Many elves are wide-eyed and nod.

Tog continues, and Raith translates. "This part is strange. He says, the dark fell and bright won. The fire burned into the bright from round ears." He shrugs. "Maybe that's you?"

"I would guess so, but what do they mean about fire?"

"I think when you gave me your magic."

Stepping back, I stumble into the elves behind me and rush forward again. "I don't have any magic. Humans don't have magic. You killed those things in the sky. I...I..." My heart pounds so loudly, it's deafening. There's no such thing as *my* magic. Well, maybe I get a sense of people's moods, and sometimes I can predict what they'll do, but fire? I have no fire. I need to run, but I'm trapped. Where would I go?

It's hard to breathe, and I drop to my knees. The stone bruises me, and I curl my hands over my head. I'll make myself small, and they'll all go away. The voice in my head is kind but urgent, as the only foster mother who ever really cared about me tells me *to never let anyone know about my abilities. Forget them. Push them as far down as you can.*

Sarah Bean's voice fades away, but I didn't follow her instructions. I can't. I need to disappear.

The elves stare, then turn away as if I'm invisible.

Raith is not fooled. He looks from them to me, and his head cocks as a thread of concern tightens the corners of his eyes. Crouching beside me, he speaks softly and gently. "We don't have to examine whatever you have inside you right now, Layla. Let them see you as I see you."

My vision blurs, and I shake my head, then let go of my held breath before I lose consciousness. My chest aches with the expansion.

The sounds of the elves return, and they look at me with kind smiles. It's the same expression as the one on Raith's face. Do they actually see me as he does? What does that mean?

Shaking off the thought, I accept Raith's offered hand and ease myself off the ground. When I expect him to pull his hand back, he keeps mine and threads our fingers together.

Rather than protest, I draw courage from the connection.

As if they never heard or saw my collapse, the elves speak conspiratorially before Tog nods and pats the air to quiet the crowd. He turns to us. "*Droch Breith.*" Tog's eyes narrow, and he points toward another opening that leads farther into the mountain. "*Droch Breith.*"

The others gesture and say the same words.

"What are they saying?" I grip Raith's upper arm. My heart is pounding at the terror in the elves' voices.

"It makes no sense." He says something to Tog in their language.

Tog insists, "*Droch Breith.*" He continues to point toward the tunnel. "*Fad cnoc.*"

Shrugging, Raith says, "They're saying 'bad birth' and 'distant mound' or 'hill.' Only I have no idea what that could mean. I suppose we should go and look down that tunnel."

I tighten my grip on his arm. "Wait. Whatever is down there is terrifying to these people. I can see it in their faces. I say we wait, rest, and then go see what bad birth means."

Raith looks around at the wide-eyed elves, who mutter *droch breith*. Some are shaking. Others seem empty, as if they've accepted that they will meet a horrible end. Raith meets my gaze, and the brightness that emanated from him has dimmed since we met. "I did use more magic than I intended." He nods and speaks to Tog.

With a smile, the Aracan elf gives a series of orders.

The entire village goes into motion, and we are shuffled toward a fire at the center of the cavern.

A central hole looks up into the night sky. I suppose that's what allows them to light fires underground. Stones circle the fire, with the scent of cooked meat making my stomach growl. Raith and I are escorted to a large flat stone and each handed a wooden bowl with some kind of meat and vegetables steaming within.

Tog points and smiles proudly at the woman who handed us the food. "Kas." He says more, but all I can understand is my name and Rats, which is what he's calling Raith, and it makes me chuckle.

"Thank you, Kas." Sitting, I take a tentative bite of the meat. It's hot, but there are no utensils, so my fingers get warmed just shy of the point of burning. The food is unseasoned and tastes like beef, with a hint of tang. It's not unpleasant, and the warmth of the fire and tiny feeling of safety is like gold on this strange planet.

The Aracans talk fast to each other. Several men and a few women speak rapidly to Tog.

"What are they saying?" It's impossible to follow the group's hierarchy. Maybe there is none, but it seems as if Tog's word is final after a vigorous debate.

With a shrug, Raith says, "I'm not following every word, but I think some are worried the queen sent us to steal them away. Others want to go to the blue planet. The woman, Kas, seems adamant that we do something about the bad birth, whatever that is."

Several children sit huddled at the far wall, and two teenage girls watch over them. I'm assuming the elves here age like me. A passel of boys of maybe ten to fifteen years sits atop a ledge looking down on us.

"They're all too thin. How long do you think they've been hiding here?"

After putting aside his empty bowl, Raith runs his fingers through his wild hair. His angular jaw ticks, and his bright eyes dim. "The information we have is unreliable regarding this world, but we think Vanora conquered here about three years ago. We believed all the Aracan elves were enslaved or turned into shadow demons." The humor in his eyes when he first walked into my world has disappeared.

"Clearly, that's not true. But it does likely mean that these people have been refugees for three years." My chest tightens, and my appetite leaves me. Still, I can't waste the last few bites of food. Who knows what they had to go through to kill and cook the meat? I finish and put my bowl with Raith's. "Maybe you can help them."

His shoulders hunch, and his jaw ticks. "My only job is to get you to Domhan. I can't lose sight of that." It sounds as if he's reciting something told to him.

Before I can contradict him, Kas comes to us and offers each of us her hand. We take them and follow her to an alcove where a few furs are laid across the hard stone floor. She smiles, showing straight but yellowed teeth. With bright eyes, she says something.

Raith nods and replies in their language. "This is where we can rest."

The makeshift bed is in a small coffin-shaped indentation in the cavern. We can both fit, but not much else. "Do you think we'll be safe here?"

He lowers and crawls inside. "As safe as anywhere else."

My pulse pounds as blood rushes through my ears. Getting to my knees, I inch into the bed. The furs give off a warm, musty scent that's pleasant enough. It's better than sleeping directly on rocks. "I don't usually share a bed with men I've just met."

When he laughs, the sound bounces around our little space. His voice is low and warm. "I promise you will always be safe with me, Layla. As beautiful as you are, I would never do anything you didn't permit and want." He laughs again. "Besides, I don't usually sleep with women I've just met either."

Pressing my back against the wall, I watch him. The light is fading from the main cavern, and the elves are quieting. I suppose they're going to bed as well.

I hug my backpack. I've been in the competition leggings and sports bra for way too long. "Um, do you think you can step out so I can change my clothes?"

Eyes wide, he stares, then nods and nearly hits his head on the low ceiling in his effort to rush out of the cave.

Once he has his back to our alcove, I dig into my bag and pull out my jeans and T-shirt that I planned to wear home from the stadium. It takes some effort to strip out of the spandex in close quarters, but I manage and pull on the baggy jeans and shirt. "You can come back in."

Eyes like saucers, he looks me up and down and smiles. "This is more normal human clothing?"

I nod as I unravel my competition wear and carefully fold it. I stuff the costume into the bottom of my gym bag. Once it's zipped, I lie down on the furs and shift uncomfortably from the hard surface beneath.

A baby cries, and a woman sings until the weeping stops.

Closing my eyes brings me no closer to sleep. I'm too filled with the events of the day. The superhero competition seems like so long ago. It feels as if I've lived a lifetime in a day. That should be exhausting, but my mind whirls and my muscles twitch to rise and run from this place. Slow, deep breaths keep me in place.

Elves whisper in their guttural language, which has an Irish lilt.

It might be any language from Earth or none at all. My own ignorance fills me with the familiar rage of being less than those around me.

As the chatter dies down, the soft sound of lovemaking filters through the cavern.

My skin heats, and I hazard a glance at Raith. His eyes are closed, and his cheeks appear red even in the dim shadows.

My heart nearly stops when his lids fly open, and his stare locks with mine.

The hard ground digs into my hips and shoulder, and I shift, searching for a comfortable position. "Even with the furs, this is not what I'm used to."

"If you can't sleep, maybe you can tell me about your magic." He raises a hand for peace when I open my mouth about to protest. "Maybe in your world, they don't call it magic. Is it instinct? Do you have visions or dreams that come to pass? You became invisible to our hosts. Not only that, it was as if they didn't even remember you were there. How did you do that?"

Sitting up, I lean against the wall. Even with the voice in my head screaming to keep it to myself, my heart pushes back. Raith is safe. I know it. This man with pointed ears is the only person who has ever protected me. "I don't know. I've always known when tempers were rising. It was a handy thing in some of the places I had to live growing up. Sometimes, if things got very violent, I could make myself small enough that everyone would forget about me. It only works for a short time. At least, I've never managed to disappear for more than an hour or so."

"Amazing."

My throat is so tight, it's hard to speak. "You saw me."

The light in his eyes brightens. "I saw you. Maybe it's because I can hear the song of your soul."

"You said that before. What is that?" My instincts want me to move closer to him, and I fight the urge by pressing my back against the rough stones.

His movements are fluid and graceful as he rises and crosses his legs. With his elbows on his knees, he leans closer to me. "The oracle gave me the song of your soul so that I would be able to find you among all the humans on Earth."

"I don't know what you're talking about." It's an internal battle to stay back and not reach out for him.

His full, beautiful lips purse, then flatten. "Everyone's soul has a song, like the prints on your fingers. The song is unique to you. I think when we move on to the afterlife, the song is how we identify each other. In life, one has to listen to hear the song."

"That's a nice idea. What does my song sound like? Is it like the music I might play on a piano?" One thing I am grateful for is Sarah Bean. She only fostered me for a year, but she insisted I take piano lessons. I loved to play and managed to keep learning during school hours throughout my education. Of course, once I graduated and aged out of the system, it was harder to find places to play. Sometimes the piano store at the mall would let me play. There's a bar a few miles from my miserable apartment that has a run-down upright. It sounds terrible, but at least I could play.

"I don't know what a piano is, but soul song is not like an instrument so much as it's harmonic. I can show you." He reaches his hand toward me.

Staring from his hand to his bright blue eyes, I'm mesmerized. Clutching my hand to my chest, I ask, "How?"

"You'll have to trust me." Within the depths of his gaze, there is desire, and a need to please me.

He wants to please *me*. My heart rises into my throat, and I have to swallow down emotion. I press my palm to his and close my fingers around his hand.

Much larger, his fingers wrap all the way around my hand. "Close your eyes, Layla. Try not to think. Just listen."

A whirlwind of thoughts sweeps through my head, and I have to push each one aside as it beats up against the new sensation of Raith's gentle prodding. It's as if there's a knock on the door of my consciousness. I focus on the knock, and a wash of calm flows through me.

His voice is just a whisper, but very close to me. His warm breath tickles my cheek. "You're safe, sweetheart. Just listen. This is you."

A vibration, then a sound, low and warm with a vibrato and a long, clear middle C repeats, rising and then falling. My mind is filled with the melodic soul that comes from me, but through Raith.

"This is me." There's a hitch in his voice.

My song stops, and a lower bolder sound fills my head. It rises and falls with deep percussions and firm rolling notes. It warms me, and my flesh tingles in places it really shouldn't. I can't want it to stop, though. It's too beautiful, too alluring.

His warm cheek presses to mine. "This is us."

The two songs come together to form a symphony of opposites. My song rises higher as if sensing his lower tones and wanting to harmonize—his softens and weaves through my vibrato as a solid foundation.

I open my eyes and pull back. Our gazes lock. It's hard to breathe with the tsunami of emotions crashing into me. "I..." I jolt away, and my head meets the hard stone wall with a sharp crack. Pain bolts through my skull, stopping the music, and I grab the back of my head. "Damn." Instinct pulls me forward, pushing me into Raith.

His hand slips easily beneath mine and over the bump forming on my skull. He presses his lips to the top of my head. "I've got you, Layla. I know I failed you so far, but I'll make this right."

Warmth spreads from his fingers and soothes away my pain—his magic tingles along my skin, down my neck to my arms.

I sit back more slowly this time and shake off his touch. "What did you do?"

"Only healed what would have been a lump on your head and probably a miserable headache." He lets his hands fall into his lap.

"You should ask me first. I don't understand your people's magic, but you shouldn't use it on me without permission." I swallow all the emotions that come with people imposing their will on me. I'm ready to fight, never to have that in my life again.

"I apologize. You're right. I should have asked." He leans back and sighs. "Forgive me?"

What is it about this man that makes me want to do more than forgive him? I want to trust him. I suppose I do trust him. After all, I walked through a portal into another world with him. I nod. "Tell me about your family."

"My mother was the queen of Domhan who ruled over all the elves. She made a mistake that cost her the throne and has put all of my world in jeopardy." He shifts his weight, and his hands fidget.

"Could she have done something different?" I want to comfort him, but I don't know enough to try.

He nods. "I'm told she could have. I wasn't born yet. She was pregnant with me when Vanora used her dark magic to steal the souls of thousands and attacked the old capital. Mother says she should have known how twisted and evil

Vanora was. She didn't believe the rumors coming from the east, where the witch queen started her evil. Then Vanora took the lives of villagers. They were given the choice to follow her or be turned into shadow demons. Half were turned, my father says. He always seems proud of that."

I can see why his father would appreciate that elves would rather be robbed of their souls than betray their beliefs. Keeping that to myself, I ask, "What are they like, though? Your parents. Are they stern? I imagine they must be with so much to worry about."

A soft smile pulls at his full mouth. "My father is the disciplinarian, at least he was when my brothers and I were young. However, he was always fair and honest. Mother is warm and kind. She is a strong ruler, but I always felt her love even though I know she wished I were a daughter."

"Because of the curse." I'm starting to understand some things about Raith.

He nods.

"What about your brothers. What are they like?" I close my eyes and lean my head back. The events of the day are starting to wear on me. My limbs feel as if they're weighed down.

"Perfect. They do everything right. I'm sorry you are burdened with the family failure, Layla. You should be in my parents' home with a large soft bed and a slew of servants to take care of you. At least until we have to go to the Watchers' Gate and save Domhan."

Opening my eyes, I stare at the pain etched in the set of his mouth and the tick in his jaw. "Maybe everything happens for a reason, Raith." I ease myself onto the furs and try to get comfortable. I shift and roll up the top end of the pelt, but my body can't find a spot that will allow me to sleep on the hard rock.

Voice raspy in the darkness, he says, "If you want, you can lean against me, Layla. I promise you'll be safe."

Sitting up, I meet his gaze and nod. I've clearly lost my mind as I push the furs next to him.

When he lies down and opens his left arm, I curl in next to him with my cheek on his chest.

Wrapping his arm around me, his hand rests on my shoulder. "Sleep. I think tomorrow will be a long day."

"Do you think they'll know where to find a portal?"

His chest rises and falls with a long sigh. "I don't even know if one exists in this world."

"If that witch queen can get from this world to yours, then so can we." I relax, his warmth like a sleeping drug.

Through the haze, his voice is filled with wonder. "That is a very good point."

Chapter Three

RAITH

Waking up with Layla snuggled against my side, her soul singing to mine, was so emotional that I needed to ease away without waking her and step outside our small sleeping cave.

Maybe she said that everything happens for a reason as an offhand comment, but the words haunted my sleep. My mother believes there is an order to everything, even when things seem chaotic, and she always accepts my constant errors and foibles. She tells me that my magic is strong and that my purpose will reveal itself at the perfect time.

If this unscheduled trip to Arcania is meant to be, then helping the elves here might be my destiny.

Insanity. I can't even save myself.

Walking up the ramp to the cave that leads outside, I'm joined by Tog and two other men. The farther away I get from the main cavern and Layla, the harder it becomes to breathe. It's as if the beating of my heart is directly linked to her now.

She's safe, I tell myself and force my attention back to the men around me.

Tog smiles and points to each man. The blond he calls "Ban," and the one with black hair is "Gaf."

I pat my chest. "Raith."

As they talk about hunting and their women, it occurs to me that the curse has not come to Arcania. There were female children. Not to say they haven't suffered; their lot has been far worse than mine, but they have young girls and women. I attempt to tell them of the curse we're dealing with on Domhan, which is again visible in the eastern sky. My use of the ancient language is far from perfect, but Tog's eyes widen when he finally understands.

He translates for Ban and Gaf, who are equally shocked. "*Chan Boireannach?*"

I nod. "No women in..." The words for numbers escape me. I hold up all ten fingers and flash them three times.

The Aracan men talk to each other so fast I can't keep up.

We move away from the cave's opening and scan the skies for shadow demons. Ban searches the land for an unknown threat. We walk to a stand of dead trees and relieve ourselves.

Before we head back down the tunnel, Gaf and Ban each take a bucket that must have been left inside the cave's mouth sometime after Layla and I found shelter here. They walk around to the right.

I follow with Tog and am amazed by a small patch of green grass at the base of the cliff. Gaf pulls aside a boulder to reveal a pool of water. They each fill a bucket and smile at me.

Tog pushes the stone back in place.

I rush to help him.

Retracing our steps to the cavern, we reach the others, and my gaze immediately falls to where Layla and Kas are stacking wood to build up the fire in the center of the encampment.

It feels as if I can breathe again after being underwater. The pressure in my chest releases, and a sharp pain takes its place. I can only imagine that being rescued from drowning has the same sensation, but that's how I feel.

Tog points at Layla. "*Boireannach.*" His voice is almost an accusation.

"*Chan Elf. Daonna. Eile Saoghal.*" I tell him, "Not elf, human, another world." I don't know why I say it in the common language. It sounded bad enough in the ancient tongue. I've really got to work on remembering more than vocabulary.

He touches his ears and stares at Layla.

For a moment, I worry that the Aracan might be xeno-phobic, but then he laughs, points to me, and then to Layla. "*Nuadh.*"

"Yes. It's all new to me, too." I smile and nod rather than attempting the translation.

As if sensing my arrival, Layla turns in her seat and meets my gaze.

Every inch of my body reacts to my human. I've got to get her to safety. Looking away, I know that's not possible. She was safe in her world. I've taken her into a war. She has no means to protect herself. What if I'm killed? How will she survive? Panic settles deep in my gut.

"Where are we going?" Layla's voice is light and full of excitement.

I don't blame her. She's been almost entirely underground since we arrived here four days ago.

"I think you should learn to shoot and fight. Tog tells me that the shadow demons don't start patrolling this part of the continent until late afternoon. That's why they mostly hunt in the morning." I hike the two bows higher on my shoulder while holding the torch that's lighting our way. I brought a bow for each of us, as I could use the practice as well.

"Oh..." Her voice trails off.

Stopping, I turn and face her. "You don't want to fight or hunt?"

She shrugs. "I think it's probably a good idea to learn."

"You sound unsure."

She steps back from the light of the torch and lets out a long breath. "I've never killed anything. I'm not certain I can."

Sometimes I forget that everyone doesn't fight a war the way my family and the army have these thirty suns. "Maybe you can, and maybe you can't, Layla. Either way, you should learn to use a bow and arrow and a sword in case you must."

"I don't want to disappoint you." Fear trembles through her words.

Closing the distance, I lift the torch high over our heads and adjust the weapon so that I can get closer and meet her gaze. "You are the most fantastic person I have ever met. It's extraordinary that the only thing that strikes fear in you is an impossibility."

She cocks her head, questions practically leaping from her wide eyes.

"You could never disappoint me, Layla Stark. I've never met anyone like you, and I've never connected with anyone the way..." How can I tell her that my feelings for her are growing with every moment we're together? She'll return to her world when this is over, and I will stay in Domhan. Of course, that's if we survive.

Cheeks flushing, she draws a shaky breath and presses her hand flat to my chest. "I feel it too."

Swallowing, I nod and bite the inside of my cheek to keep from saying more than either of us is ready to hear. It's impossible to stop staring into her deep brown eyes. The fire catches flecks of gold in her irises and blond strands in her dark hair. Nothing about her is simple. Even her looks are more than they appear. She's someone I could spend a lifetime learning new things about each and every day.

I shake my head and step back. "Come on. A little target practice will do both of us good, and if you want to go hunting with the Aracans, we can. They've been working hard to gather enough provisions for the long journey to their winter camp and to go see this 'bad birth' place. I want to help, but I don't want to leave you behind."

"I can take care of myself." She walks beside me. "You don't have to babysit me."

"What is babysit?" As we reach the mouth of the cave, I

put out the torch and search the sky and the horizon for trouble. Once I'm certain we're safe and alone, I walk toward the sadly dead forest.

Still next to me, she squints against the bright sky. "When parents go out and leave a caregiver to watch their child."

I've set up a target on one of the larger trees, where the land allows a straight shot for twenty paces. "It's not that I think you are a child who needs caring for, Layla." I put the smaller bow on the ground, sling the quiver to my back, and test the draw on the string. After nocking an arrow, I draw back to my cheek and let the arrow fly.

My arrow hits the tree, but it is about four inches from center. Definitely needs work.

"Why won't you leave me? Don't you trust the elves?" She takes the other bow from the barren ground.

"It's hard to explain." I pull an arrow out and show her how to nock it. "Two fingers to pull the string back." I show her. "Right arm straight, and draw back to your cheek as you focus down the length of the shaft and aim."

She does as I tell her and looks as if she's born to be an archer. Her back is straight and her eyes are vigilant.

"Take a breath, hold it, then let the arrow fly as if it's a surprise."

Chest rising with her breath, she lets the arrow fly and hits the tree an inch closer than mine to the mark at the center. "Why is it complicated? Either you trust the elves or you don't."

I hand her another arrow. "Not wanting to leave you has nothing to do with them."

Lowering the bow, she stares at me. "What then?" She

cocks her head, and the sun catches those flecks of gold in her eyes.

Unable to resist, I run my thumb along her jaw. "I don't know how to explain it."

"Does it feel like a hole in your chest opened up and you can't catch your breath?" She bites her bottom lip. "Is it as if you've had a part of you amputated that you didn't even know was yours?"

Her closeness is distracting in the best way; my breath catches, and I struggle to inhale fully. "You feel it too."

"When you return to the cavern, it's like I can finally come up for air. Is it magic?" The lost, helpless look on her beautiful face makes me want to be the kind of man who fixes all her troubles, even when she doesn't need me to. Only that's not really who I am. Still, maybe I could be that man for her.

I shake my head to clear it. "It must be magic, but I don't know what kind. Nothing in my past has ever felt this way."

"Do you think it's evil from your witch queen?" There's a hitch in her voice, and she backs away a step.

After taking the arrow from her hand, I press her palm to my chest. "Nothing dark brews between us. I'm certain of that. I'm not the best warrior, or the wisest elf, and I don't always do the right thing. Yet, I have no doubts about you, Layla. You're one of the humans from the prophecy, and some part of me is connected to you on a magical level."

"Does that frighten you, Raith, being connected to a stranger?"

I lift her hand to my lips and kiss her warm, soft palm. "It should, but it feels too right to spark fear. I won't let any harm come to you. I swear it."

Pulling her hand back, she makes a fist before taking the arrow from my other hand. "You shouldn't make promises that might be impossible to keep. You're at war. Bad things always happen that are out of our control, even in the best of times." She gestures to the dead planet around us. "These are not the best."

She's right, but I don't take back my vow. I'll keep her safe or die trying.

As if she's been doing so her entire life, she nocks the arrow exactly as I showed her. When she lets it fly, it hits the target dead center and quivers there. Her smile is a balm to my soul.

"You're a natural." I can't help but beam at her.

With a shrug, she says, "I'm good at training, and I did archery once at a camp when I was twelve. I liked it then, and with only a dead tree as my enemy, I like it now."

We continue practicing for half an hour, and both get better before I gather the arrows. Half a mile away, there's a small stream that's barely running, but the water is cool and clean.

I turn my back so she can wash. My body is on fire thinking of her in any state of partial dress. "I suppose you didn't have much cause to bathe in lakes and streams in your world."

She scoffs. "No. I've never even taken a luxurious bath the way they do in the movies. We take showers, and most of the foster homes I was in made sure we didn't take more than five minutes to wash. Hot water costs money." She says the last part in a deep, gruff voice.

I don't know what movies are, but whoever these foster people were, I want to find them and thrash them. She deserves love and pampering. I keep the thought to myself. "When we make our way to my home, you can try a bath and see how you like it."

"I'm done. You can turn around." Her cheeks glow pink, and her hair is damp as she braids it.

A million scenarios with her wet and in various stages of dress and undress rumble through my mind. "I will be quick."

At my obvious state of arousal, she blushes and looks away. "Take all the time you need."

The cool water would help if she wasn't only a few feet away with her back to me. There's no point in dallying. I strip and wash quickly before dressing and climbing the short embankment. "We should get back. It's getting late."

Silent during the walk, at the cave's mouth, she turns back to the open air. "Why is this planet dead?"

The forests are mostly devoid of leaves, like skeletons against a dark purple and gray background. Any blades of grass that try to surface are yellow, leaning toward brown. A few thorny shrubs with pale yellow leaves still manage some life, but it's as if the color has been leeched from this world. I let my senses flow over the ground and into the planet. Dark magic simmers at the surface, but light battles below for air. "I don't believe it's dead, but the darkest kind of magic has damaged it and pushed light down. Whatever Vanora is doing in the next mountain range must be so bad that it requires the most forbidden spells. That kind of thing leaves a mark." I gesture to the sapped land.

"How will the Aracan recover from this?" Layla takes my hand as we head inside.

I wish I knew the answer. "One problem at a time for

now. I need to get you to Domhan. The Watchers' Gate is on the northern continent, and I can't imagine it's hospitable once winter comes."

With a scoff, she asks, "What season is it now?"

It's a fair point. "It was summer when I left home. We've not seen a dragon, so I assume we're only a few days removed from that. Though it might take some time to find a way home."

"Dragons? There are dragons?" Excitement bubbles into her tone.

Stopping, I call my magic to light the torch before we run out of light from the cave opening. "Mother tells me the sky used to be filled with them on Domhan. Now there is only one, and Vanora turned him to evil."

She's quiet for so long that I think she's deep in thought. "What does the dragon have to do with what day it is compared to when you left home?"

"Dragons can shift through time." I shrug. Clearly, we've not seen a dragon.

"If the dragon is evil, can he be turned back to good?"

"No one knows that answer. We're still very focused on defeating the witch queen and surviving her curse. However, I've wondered the same thing many times. When I ask, my father says let's worry about that when we've solved our own problems." I hate it when he dismisses me that way.

"Seems to me, an evil dragon might be on the list of current problems." With a deep breath, she adds, "But what do I know?" She says what I'm thinking. She smells like heaven, even in this hell.

With only steps before we're visible in the wide cavern, I stop and pull her close. "I'd like to kiss you, if that's alright."

The right side of her mouth lifts in half a smile. "Are we talking about a peck on the cheek or a full-mouth-this-might-lead-to-more kind of kiss?"

My heart is racing, and my cock has already jumped toward the more advanced stage of her options. As a redhead, it's not unusual for heat to suffuse my neck and face as it's doing now. "I'm open to whatever you'll permit."

She takes the torch from my hand and puts it on the ground where it fizzles out. Light from the chamber leaves us in shadow, but there's enough light to see the curve of her high cheekbones and the slope of her sweet nose. She slips her hand around my neck, and her fingers thread my air, pulling it free of the leather thong. She's tall and elegant as she leans in and lifts onto her toes to press her full lips to mine.

I'm frozen in place as the warmth of the kiss floods my entire body.

A soft sigh parts her lips, and she pulls my bottom one between hers.

On fire, I wrap my hand around her waist and pull her flush against my chest. I'm sure she can feel how desperately I want her. My cock is making an effort to tear through my pants.

Pressing her weight forward, she backs me against the wall, and I grunt on impact as her tongue touches mine and sparks explode inside me. Desperate to have more of her, I grip the back of her head, and the bows slide from my shoulder to my elbow and clatter against the stone. The top end smacks against my head and then into Layla's.

She yelps and springs backward.

The hum of voices from the cavern stops.

We freeze, rubbing our respective foreheads.

Someone demands we reveal ourselves.

Layla giggles.

I look around the cave opening and wave down to the village. "All is well," I say it in the ancient language also. Blood rushes to my cheeks, which might be a good thing because I need it to rush away from elsewhere before walking through the chamber.

Blushing beautifully, Layla steps through the cave's mouth and heads down the ramp, her long legs graceful even in her embarrassment.

I force my thoughts elsewhere because thinking about any of her body parts will not help reduce the size of my cock. Taking several slow breaths, I'm finally able to make my way out of hiding.

Layla goes to Kas and sits down to help prepare the evening meal. Whatever Kas says, Layla's blush deepens even though she doesn't understand the language.

Amused and smitten, I head over to a group of men and begin to repair the arrows that were damaged as we practiced.

Gaf brings over a bundle of straight sticks wrapped with a leather tie. He says something about how good I am at arrow making and laughs.

The rest of the group laughs as well.

Before I start on the new bundle, I use a flat rock to sharpen my knife. It's meant for battle and not labor, but it will do the job. Also, it keeps me busy thinking of something other than how good Layla tasted. Not that I can wash her from my mind. She's always there, and the sound of her laughter from across the cave brings my gaze to her.

A little girl sits in her lap and toys with the human's wavy hair. As much as Layla is a distraction to all good sense, the fact that the Aracans have female children is a wonder to me. The curse didn't reach this place. Despite dark magic having ravaged Arcania, the curse is only in Domhan.

They won't survive here. This planet is all but dead. Even if we defeat Vanora and free these elves, how can they live for years on a world soaked with evil? It could take a decade for life to thrive here again.

A group of youth tosses around a ball of leather at the back. Three women tend to half a dozen babies a few feet away from the small central fire. A dozen or more prepare meats for drying while others work on meals for the entire community. Men and a few of the women practice fighting with long sticks. They aren't bad, but they'll be no match for magic.

The longer I look around the room, the more I know we cannot leave them to die on Arcania. I don't know how to fix this, but somehow, we must help them if they'll let us.

Tog crosses to Kas, and she gives him a taste of whatever is in the pot. He smiles at her and caresses her cheek with the back of his fingers. Nodding about whatever she's cooking, he kisses her forehead.

They have nothing. Their homes have been destroyed. The world that has fed them for millennia is poisoned by dark magic. Still, they find joy in the small things. They love and care for their families and community.

Gaf shoves my leg and looks at me with concern. In his language, he asks me what's wrong.

Shaking my head, I tell him I'm just worried about the future. At least I think that's what I said.

A deep frown creases his brow. He nods. "*Droch breith.*"

"That too." I nod. There are so many obstacles to getting these people to a safe place where they can thrive that I don't even know where to start. I'm no ruler or leader. I'm the third son and a poor excuse for Elspeth Riordan's child. These people deserve better. Layla deserves better.

A little voice inside my head says, *But they have you.*

Swallowing down my fears, I take a few long, deep breaths. The first step is to find out if the Aracans would leave here if I can find a way. Then we have to learn how the witch queen travels between worlds. The bad birth, Layla's safety, and probably a dozen things I haven't thought of yet are pretty high on the list, too. As for my sweet human staying safe, I'm probably the biggest threat to her right now.

"Idiot," I mutter to myself. Kissing her was a mistake. Getting emotionally attached was an even bigger one. Even if, by some miracle, we get to Domhan and save the world, if she cares for me, she'll be hurt.

More than ever, I wish I were more like either of my brothers. They would never let feelings interfere with duty.

Turning my attention to the arrows, I keep my head down and think about how my brothers would handle this. Aaran and Liam are very different, and somewhere in what I've learned from them and my parents lies the answer.

Chapter Four

LAYLA

Ever since we kissed, Raith has been avoiding being alone with me. He doesn't come to our alcove until after I'm asleep, and he leaves before I wake in the morning.

Maybe the kiss wasn't the same for him as it was for me. My entire world shifted when his lips met mine. I've never been in love. In fact, I don't think I've loved anyone in my whole life. Deep inside my dreams, I sometimes remember my birth mother and the warmth of that emotion. It's vague, but it's there. It could just be a figment of my imagination. I was a foundling, discarded like trash.

There's nothing ambiguous about my intense reaction to Raith. I want him physically, but I also want him close to me. I long to hear about his life on the planet that rises in the east and his mother who lost her crown.

Part of me, the part that always expects the other shoe to drop, thinks he might have a lover at home, and that's what keeps him away. Whatever the reason, it's clear he regrets asking to kiss me.

I brush aside an errant tear and snuggle into the furs lining our alcove.

Feet shuffle on the stone outside before Raith ducks down and crawls inside. "Are you alright?"

I sit up with my back against the wall. "Yes. Why do you ask?"

Cross-legged, he sits directly in front of me. Touching his chest, he lets out a shuddering breath. "I felt something from you."

"You used magic to read my mind?" I can't back up any farther, and I don't like feeling trapped.

His eyes widen, and he looks stricken. "I would never do that."

"But you could?" I'm not certain why I suddenly feel angry. Maybe because he abandoned me just like everyone does. It's hard to breathe. I push him aside and scramble for the opening. I need fresh air. Staring up at the hole in the ceiling, I focus on a group of stars and try to slow my pulse.

The heat of him behind me is more comforting than I like. "I will never take anything from you that you don't give, and I hope always to give more than I take, Layla. You read the thoughts of others. Why are you panicked over my sensing that you were upset?"

"I can't help it when I sense danger. It's not something I *do*. It just happens." My whispers are harsh, growing louder.

"Look at me." His voice is soft as a spring breeze.

Unable to resist, I turn.

"Why are you angry?" He tucks strands of my hair behind my ear.

His touch sends a shock of desire through me. It's such a small, innocent move, but I swear my ear must be connected to my clitoris. I suck in a quick breath. "You haven't wanted to be near me. I thought the kiss meant more than it did, obviously." I roll my eyes at the last word and skirt around him to go to sleep.

After following me inside, he waits until I'm curled into a ball at one side of the alcove. He lies behind me with only his arm touching my back. "All I have wanted is to be near you, Layla. I think of almost nothing else when there are a dozen problems to be solved. My mind is not my own because it is filled with how you look, what you think, how you smell, how your lips sent sparks of desire to every inch of my body. My heart seems to beat only for the next time I'll hear you laugh."

My face flushes with heat as the delight of his words washes over me. I roll over and lean on my elbow to look into his eyes.

Lying on his back, staring at the rough rock above us, he shifts his gaze to me. "I don't want to do anything to cause you harm."

"Harm?" I look up and down his body. I felt his hard shaft against me when we kissed. It seemed large but normal. "Are our species incompatible sexually?"

A sharp, short laugh pushes from him. "Do you always say exactly what you're thinking?"

"Most of the time, yes." I've been told to filter my thoughts but haven't had much success so far.

Rocking to his side, he faces me. "I don't know from personal experience, but my stepsister stayed in your world for the love of a human. I'm guessing we're compatible." His hand slides over my hip.

I run my fingers over the point of his ear. "I wonder how she hid her ears?"

With a shake of his head, his ears become round, and he could pass for an exquisite human. "It's a simple glamor. I'm sure Nainsi easily hides her true nature." Another shake, and his elf ears return.

If I don't push aside all the questions I have about magic, we'll be talking about that until morning. It's not my prime concern right now. "If I'm all you can think about, I don't understand how you think you might hurt me."

His bright blue eyes focus on me.

Voices in the cavern interrupt our private moment.

Holding up his hand, Raith says a few words in another language, and a shimmer covers the opening of our alcove. All sound besides our breathing ceases. "They can't hear us either."

Sitting up, I touch the shimmer. The magic tingles against my hand. "I see a shadow in the distance near the fire. "Can they see through this?"

He shakes his head as he sits up. Leaning his back against the wall, he opens his arms to me.

I crawl over, sit between his thick thighs, and lean my back against his chest.

Inhaling me deeply, he wraps his arms around me. "What will happen if everything goes perfectly and we manage to get to Domhan and save my world?"

"What do you mean?" Isn't that what we're trying to do?

"Where will you be a week or a month after the witch

queen is destroyed?" Even though his words are direct, he caresses my arm with gentle tenderness.

My heart clenches. "Home, I guess."

"Where will that leave us?" His voice hitches.

The same rage I felt every time a foster home didn't work out, or they sent me back, or someone died, rears up inside me. "Is there an us? Is this more than the desire for sex for you?"

Instead of anger or hurt, he lowers his mouth to my ear. "I think you know this is more. Somehow, we are connected. The thought of you returning to your world and leaving me on mine..." He shudders. "I've known you for eight days, Layla, and I already know that losing you will crush me."

Tears push out despite my efforts not to care. "In the meantime, we might never get off this rock. We might be turned into shadow demons tomorrow."

His arms tighten around me, and he gently rubs my arms from elbow to shoulder. "I understand that you're protecting yourself. I was doing the same, and you got angry."

"You left me for four days." My tears run freely. "You were here, but for four days, you said ten words to me. You stayed out of our bed. You refused to finish what we started. You made me feel as if you didn't want me."

"I'm sorry." His damp cheek presses to mine. "I'm so sorry, Layla. I was afraid."

Wiping my face on the shoulder of my T-shirt, I ask, "What's changed?"

"Nothing. Everything. You and I are destined for each other. I felt your sorrow, and it was as if someone drove a knife deep into my soul. I know I will lose you, and that will crush me, but it's already true, and staying away only broke my heart sooner." He kisses my hair.

Crying is something I rarely do. I can probably count on one hand the number of times I've cried since I was ten and Sarah died. She was the only foster parent I ever had who cared about me. Maybe she even loved me. Then she died, and crying didn't help. Child services came and got me. They threw all my clothes into a big black trash bag, and a few days later, I was with a couple whose name I can't even remember. I was only there for three weeks.

"Say something, Layla."

"What do you want me to say?" I'm torn between my hurt and how good it feels to be in his arms.

"Tell me you hate me and that I disappointed you. Tell me you can never forgive me. Tell me that you love me as desperately as I love you, and all my stupidity is forgiven." His tears drip onto my cheek.

My chest feels as if it might explode. "Do you love me?"

"In the eight days since I first saw you, you jumped through a portal into a world filled with evil. You never flinched. You never once made me feel as if you wished someone more capable came for you. You are the strongest, most resilient person I've ever known. I thought by putting distance between us, I was protecting you, but I was wrong. It hurt you, and it destroyed me to do it. Every day, my affection for you has grown, despite my attempts to stifle it. I love you no matter the outcome of this war or what fate has in store for us. I will always love you."

It feels as if my pulse will beat right out of me. Relaxing against him, I let go of the hurt. It's foolish to allow myself to want something pure and beautiful, knowing it will likely be ripped away. Still, I've never felt anything like this. Raising my hand, I cup his damp cheek. "I'm sorry you were torn and that we were both hurt. Maybe I should have pushed for an explanation. I'm so used to people leaving me, I accepted that it was inevitable."

He kisses my palm. "I don't deserve you." Nuzzling where my neck and shoulder meet, he whispers, "But I'm going to do whatever it takes to make myself worthy of you, Layla. I swear it."

The air vibrates with what I've come to realize is magic, as if his vow was charged with this new-to-me sense. "Did you cast a spell?"

"No, but I felt it too. My vow was charged as if the old gods were listening." He shakes his head and kisses my neck.

"Do they do that?" It's inconceivable to me that a god or a group of gods would impose their will on people.

"Not in a thousand years, but they did set this prophecy in motion, and they live behind the Watchers' Gate. That's where we have to go to defeat Vanora and break the curse." He kisses along my neck to my ear.

A soft moan escapes me. "Do you want to talk about those gods of yours?"

Sliding his hand under my breast, he caresses my abdomen, only hinting at the places I need him most. "Not just now, no."

Swallowing, I lean my head back, giving him more access to my neck, where his lips are providing the sweetest torture. "What do you want to talk about?"

"Talking is getting more difficult." He pulls me back so that my ass presses against his thick shaft. "But if you have doubts, I understand."

I'm glad to not be alone in my inability to put together a sensible thought. Turning, I straddle his hip and rock mine along the impressive bulge in his pants. "No doubts." I'm on fire from his touch and the promise of more. Stilling myself, I cup his face and meet his stare. "I don't know what will happen when we save your world. I can't promise you forever. I can only give you right now."

His Adam's apple bobs, and the shine of tears glows in his eyes, though those emotions are controlled now. "If we are separated, Layla, I will accept whatever you decide. I will never leave you, but I will let you go, taking my love with you, if that's what you want."

I've cried more in the last hour than I have in fifteen years. I brush the emotions aside. This man—this elf—says everything I need to hear, and I believe he means every word. Pressing my lips to his, everything else slips away, and our small alcove under the mountain is perfection.

Settling his hands on my thighs, he grips tighter as our tongues touch, sending a shock of lust through me. My clitoris pulses and aches.

I make love to his beautiful mouth while riding the ridge behind his trousers. I'm desperate for relief, but I don't want this to end too soon.

Raith slips his hand under the bottom of my shirt, and his warm, callused fingers trace a path up my back. Everywhere he touches burns for more, and the rest of me longs to be skin to skin. Easing back, I pull my shirt over my head and toss it aside.

My breasts bob at his eye level, and he seems mesmerized by them, which makes me laugh. "You can touch them."

He scans my face, then returns his gaze to my breasts. As

his cock hardens further, he cups one, lowers his head, and sucks my nipple into his mouth.

Gasping as pleasure shoots between my thighs, I arch my back and press my hips forward.

His cock is huge if I'm judging correctly. Reaching between us, I run my palm over his thickness. It jerks in response, and a growl rumbles in his chest. He sucks harder.

My breathing is fast, and the ache in my pussy is painful. I need more. "Too many clothes." I shift to move away and undress, but he pulls me tight, releasing my breast.

Saying something in the language that brings his magic, I feel the tingle of it as my jeans disappear and land with a rustle on the far side of the alcove.

While I'm still shocked by my own nudity, I'm just noticing he, too, is naked. His thick cock rides the wetness between my legs. Pulling me tight, he shifts and lifts me, then lays me on my back, and follows me down. When he sits back, he scans me from my head down.

His gaze is torture.

Bending one knee, I say, "I need you, Raith."

A warm smile pulls at his lips, making him even more attractive. He lies alongside me, and his hand skims along my thigh and over my hip. He touches me everywhere but where I need him most.

Still, everywhere he touches heightens my arousal. Unable to resist some relief, I press my fingers between my legs, sliding them through the wet folds. I need some relief. The need is unbearable, as if all the emotions of thinking I lost him, then realizing he was feeling so much the same, is fused in this moment.

His large hand slides over mine.

A low moan escapes my lips, and pleasure shoots through me, but it's not enough. I need more. I have to have all of him.

Taking my hand, he brings my fingers to his mouth and sucks them between his lips. His tongue tickles the pads as he releases me. "You are so sweet."

Gripping his cock, I caress up and down. "Don't tease, Raith. Not this time."

"You can't even know how good that feels." He rocks his hips, thrusting into my hand. "I'm not teasing. It's only that I want you so badly, I'm afraid this will be over in a few minutes, if I don't get myself under control." He groans and stops me from jerking him off.

"I don't care if it's quick. I need you." I touch myself again.

With a growl that's more animal than man, he presses his shoulders between my legs, cups my ass, and buries his face in my pussy.

A surge of pleasure rolls through me. I hope he's right about the magical barrier keeping the sound from traveling to the rest of the cavern because I can't help my cries. "Raith. God. That's..." I rake my fingers through his hair and lift my hips, wanting more, even as I can't take much more.

One long finger slips inside me, and he rolls his tongue around my clitoris. As a second finger joins the first, he stretches me deliciously.

I ride between his fingers and his mouth, my pleasure so close to orgasm. "I can't. I'm so..."

Raith sucks my clitoris hard, pulling me over the edge, and my body pulses around his long, thick fingers.

I shake with the pleasure and more as it ebbs.

Kissing my pussy, he rises and wraps me in his arms, holding me against his chest as the last of my climax shimmers through me.

"You're so perfect, Layla." He kisses the crown of my head.

It's impossible not to notice this hot, heavy cock resting against my hip. My body reacts as if I didn't just have the best orgasm ever. I rock so that my thigh and hip massage him. Bolstered by his moans, I repeat the movement and kiss his neck.

"I was going to be a gentleman and tell you your pleasure was enough for tonight." He caresses the side of my breast with the back of his fingers, then down along my waist.

"My pleasure is directly connected with yours. I need all of you. I want you to have all of me." I run my teeth along his jaw. When he lowers his mouth to mine and our tongues meet, a feline sound vibrates in my throat. My body is hardly under my control. It's guided by impulse and desire. I hook my leg over his, opening myself.

His cock rides my wet center, and he rolls to his back, pulling me with him.

Straddling his hips, I lift my center until he's notched at my slit, then, lowering myself, I take him in inch by inch. My body stretches, and I have to stop and adjust. "Fuck, that's good." I take more of him. My fingers are tight on his chest. I'll probably leave marks, but I can't help it. Nothing in my entire life has felt this good.

At the back of my mind, his pleasure niggles at me. His desire matches mine. His love for me pours into me like good wine, and I'm drunk with it. "I feel you everywhere."

His gaze locks with mine. "I feel you too." There's surprise and wonder in his passion-filled voice.

Impaling myself all the way, I cry his name and hold still while my pussy stretches and pleasure rolls through me.

Gripping my hips, he lifts me a few inches and rolls his body up into me, slow and steady. "You're perfect."

Every inch of me tingles from the inside out, and I'm pulled as tight as a bowstring. "Raith, I don't think I can wait. I'm. God. I'm—" My orgasm is fast and hard as my pussy grips him.

Holding me tight, he groans as if in pain. "If you keep coming like that, I won't be able to hold off." The reprimand is delivered in a delightful pleasure-pain voice.

"I can't help it. You feel amazing." Not to mention, I can feel his pleasure along with mine, and it's the most erotic thing imaginable.

He kisses my cheek and traces a line to my ear, where he licks and kisses until I'm rocking against him again. I'm ravenous for more of him. I pull away from his wicked mouth before I come again just from that naughty tongue. Rising to my knees, I ride him with a slow rhythm, then faster until I feel him losing control.

My third orgasm is just out of reach. Before I can lose hope of finding another release, Raith presses his thumb to my clitoris and circles the bud in perfect time with me.

Up and down, he fills me.

Around and around, he brings me closer.

I come in a rush with his name and names of a few deities I don't generally worship, but they flood out of my mouth.

Pulling me off, he gives a long groan and, holding me against him, he comes between us.

I suppose getting pregnant right now would be a bad idea, but I can't help missing the heat of him flooding my body. Still, it's thoughtful on his part. He's perfect. "That was amazing."

He wraps me in his arms and drags a fur over our naked bodies. "It was everything, Layla. You are everything."

"Do elves always feel each other's pleasure during sex?" I yawn and snuggle in tighter to his hard chest.

"Not always. That's reserved for true mates." He swallows hard.

"What does that mean?" I wish I could keep my eyes open. This seems like an important conversation.

He brushes my hair from my face. "Some people are destined for each other, and when that happens, there are things that are shared. Things that only happen between true mates. Some can read each other's minds. Some can talk over distances."

"No free will. We were always destined to be together." I yawn again.

His chest rises and falls with a breath. "You could have refused to walk through the portal. You could walk away right now. Free will and destiny are not mutually exclusive, *mo anam cara*."

I want to understand. I want to believe. "Let's talk about this after we sleep. Okay?"

Kissing my forehead, he says, "Sleep. I'll be here when you wake up."

That might be the nicest thing anyone has ever promised me. Sleep takes me.

Chapter Five

RAITH

Layla steps silently through what used to be dense woods, and I keep pace behind her. In Domhan, an old forest like this one would vibrate with life. The place would be teeming with animals, and the trees would be almost sentient. Here, there is silence, a retreat from the land.

The leaves are long gone, leaving dead ones under our feet. Where there was bark, smooth white trunks remain. When I touch them, there is life, but it's receded away from the evil roiling through this world.

For my entire adult life, I was dissatisfied and defiant about my place in my family. I rebuked my parents' desire for me to excel at most everything. Here, the mineral-rich purple rocks are in stark contrast to the white trees. It makes me long for the greens and blues of my home.

Some people called me a fool, and I'm beginning to believe they were correct.

The hunting party is spread out as we make our way through the skeletal remains of the trees.

Tog holds up a hand, and everyone stops in place.

A shuffle ahead lets me know a deer is close. The Aracans harvest only males, keeping the females so the deer can breed. One or two bucks can keep the species going, but if they kill off all the does for food, there'll be no food left. Though, considering how long it took us to find one of either sex, I'd say starvation will force them to change their strategy in the coming months.

For over a month, we've been hunting daily to store up food for the winter. When we travel through the mountain toward the bad birth, the village will resettle in the valley, where winter won't be as harsh.

I have seen firsthand how hard they all work to move everyone safely and have food from these better hunting grounds. I feel certain this will be the last summer they'll spend in the caves. The river is drying up more and more by the day. The spring that runs along the side of the mountain is down to a trickle.

Admiring their resiliency doesn't mean I believe they can survive here much longer.

Turning, Tog signals for Layla.

Her eyes wide, she answers his command to come closer. She's light-footed and makes no sound as she walks to the front of the line.

Easing closer, I keep silent and watch.

Tog points to a buck with good meat on him and a broken left antler. Compared to those on Domhan, the deer on Arcania are small, and they don't grow large antlers. At least, that's what's left here now.

Layla nods. Her breath is shallow, and she slows it, forcing herself to take long, even breaths. Lifting her left arm, she fists her bow and nocks an arrow.

My heart is pounding so hard that it's a wonder everyone, including the deer, doesn't hear it. Emotions run through me. She's never killed anything. I block my thoughts so they don't become a distraction to her through our link.

Slow and steady, she pulls back on the bowstring. Her thumb touches her chin, one more inch, she draws a long breath, holds, and lets her arrow fly. Her shot is true, hitting the buck in the heart and dropping him where he stood. No pain. No chase. It was one of the finest shots I've ever seen.

Tog pulls her into a fatherly hug and pats her head. Speaking in his language, he praises her.

After a month, she's learned a few words of the ancient language. Tears in her eyes, she forces a smile and nods.

Brushing the emotions off her cheeks, she walks through the edge of the woods and kneels beside the deer. Closing her eyes, she puts her hand on the deer's neck and says, "Thank you for your sacrifice. I promise your gift will be well used and nourish many."

Tog has also learned some of the common language, as have several of our new friends. He nods and gives an accurate translation for the others, who also nod.

When my father took my brothers and me hunting as children, he would pray over the animals we harvested for food. As an adult, I've rarely hunted until this past month. After watching Layla's deep gratitude, I'll never take a life given for granted again. The depth of her feelings is humbling.

Once the deer is treated and prepared for travel back to the cave, we begin our return.

Voice low, Layla says, "I didn't know if I could do it. Then I thought about how many elves need the meat to survive. If I missed, they would suffer."

"It was the best shot I've seen since we've been here. The deer didn't suffer at all." I don't want to sound condescending, but I want her to know. "I'm proud of you."

"Thank you. At least you know I won't starve if we're separated." She takes my hand, and we cross the rocky foothills below the cave. We're close to where we landed on Arcania.

The sting of dark magic vibrates the air.

"Raith?" Layla must feel it too.

Drawing my sword from the sheath on my back, I call out, "Demons. Behind me." My adrenaline pumps so high that I can't think of the words in Old Elvish.

Tog does the translation, then stands at my side, his bow loaded with an arrow.

In the place where our portal dropped us, a dozen shadow demons and two elves in black-and-red armor stand guard as if they think we'll return through another portal.

"How do they know?" Layla asks.

"The same way we feel dark magic, they or the witch queen senses the light." It's not a good sign. We could be putting the Aracans in danger.

Just as I think it, the demons turn and spot us. Their high-pitched shriek fills the air as they move as one toward us. The elven warriors follow at a run.

"This is bad." Layla lays her hand on my shoulder, and the magic she doesn't want to admit she has bubbles along my skin.

"We may need your fire, Layla. The white fire you gave me the day we came here."

She closes the distance, pressing her front to my back. She whispers, "I don't know how to make it come."

"I know, *mo anam cara*, but you can't let those things take these elves and turn them into something dark. And you are doing those poor souls a favor by releasing them to their afterlife." Maybe it's unfair of me to put so much pressure on her, but I know in my heart that Layla is the key to winning this. Just as I know she and the other two humans are the key to saving my home.

The first shadow demon reaches us.

The Aracans back away.

I draw my magic into my hand, forcing light into a ball of energy while shifting my sword to my left hand. Reaching back, I throw the magic, and it backs the demons away, but not far enough.

Loud and out of breath, the black-and-red-clad soldiers pound their way up the rocks. These are the first elves who serve Vanora that I've ever seen in person. They're thin, and their skin lacks the color of good health.

The one on the right lifts his long sword with both hands. "Join the great queen or die."

Tog lets loose an arrow, and it lands in the warrior's eye, dropping him before another word can be uttered.

The second warrior charges forward with a battle cry, heading toward Tog.

Stepping out, I block his path and his sword. All the

times I didn't want to train but wanted less to disappoint Father come rushing back as I block and counter the thin, sickly soldier. "Why do you follow a dark witch?"

"The queen is all," he gutters out and swipes at me. "Follow her or die." His eyes might have been blue once, but they are tinged with red. It might be some evil magic haunting him.

"I can help you. Stop fighting for evil, and I'll get you home."

He backs away a step before rage twists his narrow face, and he charges at me with his sword high over his head.

Standing ready, I expect he'll lower his sword, but he impales himself on my sword and then slides to the ground. The red clears from his eyes. "Thank the old gods."

The shriek of shadow demons brings me around to where the Aracan elves huddle behind Layla.

Her hands glow bright white with flames. When the demons close in, she thrusts her hands forward, and the shadow demons shift back.

My battle carried me to the edge of the rock face. It will take me too long to get to them before the shades get some or all of them. "Throw the fire, Layla. You can do it."

For the briefest moment, her eyes close and her face relaxes. When she opens her eyes, the ferocity of a champion flashes there.

A demon picks up Tog, who struggles in its grasp.

The roar that erupts from Layla's lips is filled with fear and passion. She shoots bright white arrows of fire from her fingers, hitting the one who holds Tog first.

Tog falls to the stones hard about twenty feet from me. I rush over and block him from further damage.

The shrieking gets louder as the remaining eleven thrust forward.

Layla opens her hands and shoots white fire like cannonballs, over and over.

Ash rains down over them.

Pel and San put their hands on Layla's shoulder, telling her in their language that they won and she could stop.

Staggering back, the magic fades, and she lets them support her. She searches for Tog and me. "Oh no, you're hurt." She rushes over and cradles Tog's head in her lap.

Wincing as he tries to move his awkwardly turned leg, Tog says. "Fine. Thank."

"Don't thank me. I could have gotten you killed." She looks at me with panicked eyes.

"We need to get off of this open rock before more of those things come looking." A grunt from the soldier I stabbed pulls my attention. "Layla, have them strap a few sticks to splint Tog's leg and carefully move him to the cave."

She looks from the elf soldier to me. "What are you going to do?"

My stomach roils. "Save him if I can. Get information if I can't." I squeeze her hand. "You were magnificent. Now go."

I feel her trepidation at leaving me through our connection, but she doesn't argue. She explains in broken Old Elvish to the other.

The elf holds his bleeding abdomen and looks at me. "Why don't you take the final blow?"

"I can heal you." I kneel next to him and pull at the buckles holding his armor.

Brushing my hands away, he shakes his head. "You've

already saved me. The wound is mortal." He chokes, and blood runs from the corner of his mouth.

"I'm sorry." Pressing my hand to his forehead, I ease his pain with a wash of light magic.

"She goes against every law of the old gods and nature." He chokes and coughs. "She's merging beasts, and..." With a gurgle, his eyes go dim, and his breathing stops.

My gut tightens. Liam is the soldier. He once told me you never get used to killing, and if you do, you should find another way to live. This elf is the first I've ever killed, and my heart is heavy even though he gave me no choice and was grateful for his release.

I use my magic to move the earth at the bottom of the rocks and place the bodies of the witch queen's soldiers inside before replacing the sandy soil. It should be deep enough to keep anyone from finding them, should Vanora's followers come looking.

With a prayer to the old gods, I wish these two find peace in the next life, and jog up the rock face until I reach the cave.

The tale of the day is being retold around the fire.

Layla rushes to me and hugs me around the waist. "Tog is in tremendous pain, and that leg needs to be set properly."

I take her hand. "I may need your help."

"I don't know anything about medical stuff." Still, she walks with me toward the middle of the camp where they're keeping Tog warm beside the fire.

Kas holds his hand and fights back tears.

"I may need your magic. I've used a lot, and I don't recover as quickly here as I do on Domhan." I kneel beside

Tog and grab a stick from the kindling pile. I tell Tog to put it between his teeth.

In a place like this, with limited medical knowledge and no magic, his broken leg might be fatal. At the very least, it could cripple him, which might also lead to death. Tog is the leader of these people. Without him, they could falter. Maybe not, but there's no way to know how the next leader will react to desperate times.

Not wanting to find out, I hope I have enough magic to do the job. Not knowing how human magic works, I can't gauge how much magic Layla can give me.

Breathing deep, I remind myself to take this one step at a time. I tear his trousers so I can see with my eyes before I look with my magic. His ankle is twisted in a very awkward way, and I fear his lower leg is broken as well. Meeting his gaze, I say, "This will hurt."

"*Thoir creideas.*" He trusts me. Tog's forehead is dotted with sweat, and he opens his mouth for the stick to be placed between his teeth. Releasing Kas's hand, he pats her cheek.

Kas pulls his upper body into her lap and hugs him around the chest.

Letting my magic flow through the wounded leg, I close my eyes and see the bone broken just under the knee. The bone is displaced but not as badly as I feared. Scanning lower, to where the ankle is twisted and those bones are broken as well. "Layla, I have to set these bones, then heal the bone and surrounding tissue."

"How can I help?"

Without words, I search for our connection. It's a steady flow of her heightened emotions and my own worry. I've healed people with minor wounds, but under much better conditions. Still, the theory is the same. I can do this. *Do you hear me?*

Oh my god. I do. She squeezes my shoulder.

In the same way you gave me fire when we arrived here, I need your magical energy to be able to heal Tog without harming myself. Can you concentrate on healing and send me energy? Immediately, her magic flows through me, warm and steady, like a heated pool.

Focusing on the leg, I force magic to make the bone as it was.

It's nauseating when the bone snaps into place. Tog's pain lances through me, but I push it aside. Moving to the ankle, I gently pull with my hands while letting the magic push the bones together, and the joint returns to its normal state.

The pain is almost unbearable, but I remind myself it's worse for Tog as he grunts out his agony.

Layla's voice whispers in my head, *I've got you. You're doing an excellent job.*

The way she believes in me is all the confidence I need. Healing magic flows from my fingers through Tog's swollen, bruised leg. Focusing on the bones first, I coax the magic to knit the cells together and mend the breaks one by one until the bones are strong again. The echo of pain reflects back to me. I grit my teeth.

Weariness settles deep inside me as my magic begins to wane. My muscles ache, and even breathing becomes labored.

Pressing her hands to either side of my head, her magic flows more freely. *Please let this work. Please give him the strength to heal this good man.*

Her prayers must be the source of her abilities. A surge of power rushes into me, and I control the flow as I send it to Tog's legs and ankle. Every time my energy flags, she sends me more until the leg shows only the remnants of bruising.

Layla sits back on her heels and closes her eyes.

Turning, I pull her into my arms and kiss her forehead. "Amazing." My limbs feel as if they weigh a hundred pounds each, and my bones ache, but I'm alive, and Tog is healed far beyond what I could have done without my remarkable human's help.

Rising to sit, Tog wraps his arms around both of us. "Thank you, friends."

With Kas's help, he retreats to the alcove they share.

Many members of the village pat us on the back or hug us as we struggle to stand and head to our alcove.

One of the women, Sil, brings two cups of a warm drink, similar to herbal tea. She smiles warmly and meets each of our gazes with sharp blue eyes. She's Gaf's mate, but this is the first time she's addressed us directly. As with many of the elves here, she has been wary of us even after a month.

We thank her and sit in silence while we drink the warm, earthy brew. My heart is heavy. Too tired to stay upright, I place the wooden cup just outside the alcove and lie back on the furs that have become our bed.

A moment later, Layla snuggles against my side. "It's early, but I feel as if we had more than a day already."

I nod, though she isn't looking at my face. "It will be at least another month before this village is ready to move south. Tog won't take us to whatever the bad birth is until then. I'm sure that's the direction of Vanora, or at least whatever she's doing that's killing this world."

"You think we should go without them?" She lets out a long breath but doesn't contradict.

"I think we should start learning these tunnels and what's beyond them. We've been here for over a month, and I have no lay of the land. We go hunting and to the stand of trees where I taught you to shoot. We see the ocean to the north, but what lies to the south? What are we walking into with over a hundred magicless elves?" I rein in my frustration. I'm starting to see where those strategy lessons might have been valuable.

"Then we have a month to find out."

"I could go without you. You are safer here." Saying this shoots a sharp pain just under my heart as if the muscles there are mounting a rebellion.

Rising to her elbow, she looks me in the eyes. "I'll never choose safe over being with you, so don't make me choose. We're in this together, no matter what."

Gods, I love this woman. I wrap my arm around her shoulder and pull her to my side. "I only wanted you to know you have the option, *mo anam cara*."

"If I remained here and you never came back..." She shivers. "That would not only be unbearable, but I'd be left here to die with all of the Aracans. I want to save them, but starving to death or dying from a broken leg is not how I want to end."

A shiver of dread goes up my spine. "When you put it that way, I'm sorry I mentioned it."

"What will you tell Tog?" She yawns.

"The truth. After I've rested, I'll go to him and tell him our plan to learn our way around. I'm going to suggest that if we can find a way to Domhan, he and his people come with us."

"Weapons," she says on another yawn. "Can we fashion something other than bows and arrows and staffs?"

It's a good question. "Let me think about it. Maybe we can turn some of the tools they use into weapons. They have knives and axes made from stone. With a few modifications, we could have a small arsenal."

Her breathing grows steady.

As tired as I am, these thoughts churn in my head for a long time before I can sleep, and even then, I'm restless.

Chapter Six

LAYLA

I sit just outside Tog and Kas's alcove, holding Kas's hand while the men speak in low voices. Kas understands enough to look terrified.

Raith rubs the beard that has grown since he stopped using his dagger to shave a week or so ago. The hair on his jaw is a shade brighter than his dark-red head. Since Tog has learned a good amount of English, Raith says, "This planet is going to take many years to recover, and only if we can defeat the witch queen. I would wish for you and all of these people to come to the blue and green planet with Layla and me."

Rather than becoming agitated as I would expect, Tog furrows his brow and stares at the sandy ground between him and Raith. "Curse?"

Letting out a breath, Raith nods. "My world is cursed, but at least you would have time there. Here, I fear you do not. Vegetation, animals, all scarce now."

"Soon, gone." Tog nods and meets Kas's worried gaze. In their language, he asks her what she thinks.

Kas scans the cavern filled with her family and friends. Sorrow shines in her deep blue eyes. In English, she says, "Home not place, people. Save people."

Tears spill from my eyes, and I hug this amazing woman close. I've fallen in love with Raith, but also with these elves who have taken me in and taught me more than I ever learned on Earth. "Save people."

With a nod, Tog agrees only to look at how to move to the blue and green planet. He's skeptical about magic that big, but seeing his leg fully healed, he knows magic can be good.

I don't blame him. I'm skeptical too, and I've been through a portal.

The cave we choose first is dank and inclines steadily. It's narrower than the one we use every day to reach the hunting grounds. Raith points out footprints proving that these caves are used from time to time.

Keeping my voice low as the tunnels echo, I ask, "Why do you say the elves here have no magic?"

"Aracan elves are called lesser elves by my people because they have no written language and no magic." There is no judgment in his voice. He's stating facts as he knows them.

"I'm not sure that's true." We turn a corner, and the way

gets steeper, making my thighs and backside ache. I'm out of training.

"Why do you say that?" He crouches slightly as the ceiling grows lower.

"Have you ever tried to light a fire without magic?" The wall of the cavern is damp, and I wipe my hand on my jeans. They've grown threadbare, and Kas has made me several pairs of elven trousers since I refused a dress. Still, the familiar denim is comforting.

"Not that I can recall."

"In my world, we have matches that are made with sulfur. When you strike them against something rough, the friction ignites them. It's not magic, it's science. We also have lighters, which are fuel-fed and ignite when a spark occurs. When I was at summer camp as a child, we had a workshop on how the people native to our continent lived. We had to try to make fire with leather and wood, in a way similar to how the Aracans do. It was an arduous task. Even the people who were good at it took a while to generate enough heat to catch dried grass on fire." A warmth spreads through me, thinking about those summers when I was just like all the other kids. As long as we didn't talk about our parents, everything was fine.

He cocks his head and glances my way. "What have you noticed?"

"Aracans of all ages can start a fire in seconds. I don't think it's possible to generate that kind of heat that fast without magic. Maybe they don't know they're using it. In fact, I think it's likely they don't, but it isn't science that's creating flame." I'm sure I'm right.

"Interesting. Maybe we can use that to help them

survive. I mean, if they could light their arrows on fire or superheat their axes, it might help." The cave forks, and we stop.

"Which way?" It's pitch dark in either direction.

Raith closes his eyes and takes long, deep breaths. A calm comes over him that he never used to have.

In the last few days, I've noticed it more and more. "You've changed."

When he opens his eyes, he looks at me. "I have to be better. I want to be better. It's no longer enough to be the useless third son of the great Elspeth Riordon. You and these people depend on me to save them."

The pressure he's under must be stifling. My chest aches. Cupping his cheek, I look into those beautiful blue eyes. "You are already enough, Raith. Whatever was in your past, and whatever you might think, you were chosen for this journey because you have the needed skills to succeed. If those old gods of yours are running the show, don't you think they know what they're doing?"

As he leans into my touch, his gaze softens. "I think they were mad to send me to save anyone."

With all my heart, I wish he knew how wonderful he is. "I'm sure your brothers are brilliant. Being brave and smart is probably a family gift. However, you are those things plus kind, charming, gifted with magic, and most importantly, you have an open mind. These people need us. We will get them off this dying world and keep their species from perishing into memory."

Kissing my palm, he smiles at me. "That was an excellent speech." He takes my hand and points down the tunnel to the left. "This way to the outside." He points right. "There's some kind of energy from that direction."

"I wouldn't mind some air. We can check that way when we come back." His happiness is contagious, and I know I'm grinning like an idiot.

He takes my hand and holds the torch aloft as he leads us to the left. "I never thought I would meet someone. Well, there are so few women, I never really thought any of them would bother with me."

"Did you worry about living a solitary life?" I can't even imagine a world where there are not enough men to go around. However, I can imagine not wanting any of the available choices.

"It seemed Aaran would have to get married as he's the legal heir. Though the curse makes it impossible for him to rule should anything happen to Mother." His hand tightens on mine.

Perhaps it's a reaction to thinking about his mother's mortality. I squeeze back, hoping it gives him some comfort.

"For a while, it looked as if Liam might marry Dierdre." He makes a horrible sound in his throat.

"You don't like this Dierdre?" The cave slopes upward at a steeper pitch, and I have to pay attention to my footing. I release his hand to steady myself.

"She's only interested in climbing the societal ladder. She doesn't love my brother."

"Did you tell Liam what you thought of his girlfriend?" I've had more than a dozen foster siblings, and I'm still in contact with a handful, but I'd never interfere with their personal lives. Maybe it's different with blood siblings or other families.

He shakes his head. "There was no need. He broke it off a few months ago. Still, Dierdre didn't take it well and would show up often to try to get back into his good graces. On the night before we were sent to your world, she must have crossed some line. I heard that Liam called the guards to remove her from the premises."

"What could she have done to warrant that?" What kind of world am I trying to save if they'll drag an ex away?

A rush of cool air flows down the cave.

"We must be getting close." Raith leads the way upward, keeping the torch out in front. "Liam didn't tell us what happened, but his mood took two whiskeys to brighten. If my instincts about Dierdre are right, she must have threatened one of the family—maybe my mother or Aaran. She wants to be queen. That much anyone could see."

"If that's the case, what would entice your brother to date her? Maybe you have a better instinct for people than he does."

He shrugs. "Maybe, but he came around to it eventually."

When we step through the cave's mouth onto a cliff, we're hundreds of feet above sprawling land that stretches out for miles. Every shade of purple rolls out to our left, terminating at the ocean. It's both beautiful and daunting to see so much land and so little vegetation. The water is so dark it looks black. Straight ahead in the bottom of the valley, the river still runs through, though even from this distance, the river bed extends wide on both sides. That tells the tale of a long drought. It's as if everything good is shrinking from this world.

I can't help the rush of sorrow over all the Aracan elves have lost.

Near the river lies one small pocket of green where the land hangs on for dear life.

I point to the green patch. "I suppose that's the winter camp."

Raith puts the torch on the ground, letting it gutter out. With his hands on his hips, he scans everything. He might have a photographic memory. "It's minimal. I wonder if they know how diminished that plot of land is. Surely it must have been bigger last winter. Time is running out." He continues his examination to the right.

A mountain, far larger than any in the range where we are, rises from the flat lands around it. It looks like a volcano with puffs of black smoke wafting from the peak.

"Is that active lava?"

"I don't think so. I think whatever burns there is somehow tied to the witch queen. Look how black the land is spreading out from there." His gaze continues right as far as we can see. "She has troops camped there." He points and looks back to the left of the mountain. "And there."

"Is she protecting something? Who does she think will attack? Surely not the Aracans. They have no means to defeat more than a handful of elves and seem more inclined to hide from danger." I can't imagine them going on the offensive.

Dark clouds shift above the mountain. "Shadow demons," Raith says. He frowns. "I don't know what she's doing, but she's not taking any chances with it."

"Bad birth." I shrug.

Nodding, he picks up the torch and uses his magic to

relight the flame. "Let's go back inside. We still have time to check that other cave before going back to the village."

Seeing the enemy troops and hovering demons sends a shiver up my spine. The dark magic rotting this world gnaws at my gut. I follow Raith and step carefully as we pitch downhill. "Why here? Why do you think the witch queen chose this place to do her evil? If she wants Domhan, why is she here?"

We reach the fork, and Raith takes a deep breath. "I don't think Vanora will stop at one or two worlds, Layla. She's a monster hungry for power. This world was easy to conquer, and it probably had something she needed. If she succeeds with Domhan, she'll continue to another world." He pauses and meets my gaze. "Maybe yours if she finds a way in."

The meal we had before starting our exploration curdles in my stomach. The idea of an insane witch with magic attacking Earth is enough to bring that meal back up. "Humans don't have magic. We wouldn't last long."

Pulling me into a hug, he kisses the top of my head. "One problem at a time, *mo anam cara*. She's not going to get that far. We're going to destroy her long before that can happen. Besides, the old gods protected your world before they sealed themselves behind the Watchers' Gate. Vanora would have to break through those barriers, and if she knew how to do that, she'd have gone there already to increase her army of shadow demons. Your world is safe for the moment."

Hand in hand, we head through the other cave. The tingle of magic makes the hair on my arms stand up. "What's down here?"

"I feel it too," he says. "The magic feels neutral. Not light but not dark either." Holding the torch up higher, we continue.

A hundred more feet and we step inside a more expansive space that has nowhere else to go. One wall is smooth and bulges prominently. In the torchlight, it shines like glass. "It's a dead end." I scan the grotto.

On the far side, something shines. Narrowing my gaze, I walk toward it.

Raith follows, using magic to increase the brightness of the flame. The stone shines, though it's black. He puts his hand on it, and like an old television with a weak signal, an image comes into view. A woman in a long blue dress. Her hair is blond and pulled up into a tidy bun at the back of her head. She's talking to someone. "Mother?"

"What is this?"

"Mother!" he yells. "Can you hear me?"

The woman cocks her head as if she might have heard or sensed something.

"Mother!"

The image fades.

Raith pounds his hands against the stone wall, dropping the torch on the ground.

I pick it up before it goes out. The last thing I want is to be left in total darkness.

Keeping his hands on the stone, he closes his eyes. "Mother, come back. I'm here. I'm alive. I found Layla. I need your counsel."

My heart breaks for him. She couldn't hear his calls.

When nothing else shows up in the rocks, he pounds his fists again and again until his blood marks the wall.

Carefully leaning the torch so it stays upright, I pray the fire remains. It flickers taller. I place my hand on Raith's shoulder. "Stop." I wrap my arms around him from behind. "Stop now. Be calm. We're fine." When he sits back on his heels, I kiss his cheek and say, "Heal your hands."

Dashing a tear from his cheek, he gets up and leans against the protruding rock. With a few softly spoken words, his hands stop bleeding. Eyes unfocused, he stares at the space where his mother appeared. "It must be obsidian." His voice is soft, far away, and not directed at me. "Obsidian can be imbued with scrying powers. Maybe it happens naturally? I can't remember."

"Does it matter? Could this be a way to communicate with your family?" I kneel in front of him.

Looking from me to the shining stone, his eyes narrow. "Maybe. Scrying stones are rare. They're always perfectly smooth, and making them is a difficult skill to master. It's so difficult that the last elf who made them died years ago without an apprentice."

I might be biased, but I believe Raith can do anything he sets his mind to. "How much do you need? I mean, can we break off a chunk and take it back to the cavern where you can make it into what you need?"

When he stands, his gaze is fixed on the wall. Walking over, he smooths his hand over the stone. No image appears. Leaving one hand cupped against the stone, he closes his eyes. His magic builds in the cave and tingles along my skin. It slams into the wall.

The sound of the stone cracking makes me wince. "What the fuck?"

Raith draws his sword from the sheath on his back and uses the tip to wedge into the crack and carefully pries loose a softball-size piece of rough obsidian crystal. He turns and holds it up for viewing. "I don't really have the skills, but Mother's image was shown to us for a reason, and I'll not ignore the sign. I'll try to work this into a scrying stone. It may take time. Even artisans couldn't form the right shape and shine overnight."

"We'll add it to the to-do list." My stomach grumbles.

Taking the torch, he says, "Let's get you back to the elves and a good meal."

I follow. "She's beautiful."

"Mother? Yes, she is." He lets out a long breath. "Even if she couldn't hear me, it was good to see her. Somehow knowing she's alive and well is comforting."

"Could you tell where she was? I saw a cup and dark walls." I wonder who she was talking to.

"I think she was in the dining room." He smiles. "Usually, we dress for dinner and sit together, talking about our day."

"That sounds nice." For most of my youth, dinner was where I ate fast and hoped no one would lose their temper before I had a full belly and could retreat to my bed. As an adult, dinner is a quick bite before settling on the couch to watch television. Worry floods me when I think about how his family will react to me if we ever make it that far.

"You will like it. My parents are going to love you. Before you yell at me for listening to your thoughts, you were thinking very loudly." He slows to walk beside me and nudges my arm with his elbow.

"Fine." I nudge him back. "Why do you think they'll like

me? I'm a stranger. I don't come from a fancy family or have anything to offer a prince."

Stopping, he stares at me for a long time. "You are more than I deserve and everything I need. I'm no prince. My mother lost her throne. I wasn't born yet when we were chased from the eastern continent. My family and all who survived the battle had to flee across the ocean to avoid being turned into shadow demons. My parents will love you because I love you, because you make me a better man, and because you are the bravest person I've ever met."

"Stop saying I'm brave. I'm afraid all the time." I stare down at my feet to avoid his gaze.

Raith kisses the top of my bowed head. "Courage isn't the absence of fear. It's going forward in spite of it because the goal is worth it."

"Who said that?" I can't remember where I've heard this before. School? Something close to this was on a poster.

"I said it. My father says things like this all the time. He's always good for inspiration in dire times. I sometimes wonder if that's why my mother loves him. He's very uplifting in difficult times." He laughs. "I'm pretty sure that's the first time I've quoted Father."

Raith is so good and beautiful. His garnet hair hangs loose around his angular jawline. His bright blue eyes catch the torchlight. Even his hands are big, capable, and strong.

"If I weren't so hungry, I'd suggest you strip me naked and make love to me right here."

"Fatherly quotes stimulate you, do they?" With a wicked grin, he wraps his free hand around my waist and pulls me close.

Tipping my hips forward, I rub against his growing shaft. "I find everything about you makes me hot and bothered."

He cocks his head. "Hot and bothered. Is this a human saying?"

"It is. It means—"

He presses his lips to mine, cutting off my translation. Sucking my bottom lip between his, and then the top, he vibrates with a low growl. "I understand the reference. I think I like the way humans adjust language to suit themselves."

My body curves to his as if we were made for one another. As a tall woman, it's nice to find a man—or elf—who's taller but not some muscled behemoth souped-up on steroids and conceit. Raith is perfectly fit and there's not an inch of fat on him, but he seems oblivious to his beauty. Maybe all elves lack vanity. I run my hands up his chest and thread my fingers through hair that any woman would covet for thickness and softness. "I never thought about it, but we do alter English to our liking. I'm sure you have sayings and clichés you use all the time."

"We do, but I don't find them as colorful as yours." He backs me against the wall.

My stomach growls loud enough to echo in the cave. I burst out laughing. "It must be past my dinner time."

On a groan, he steps back and adjusts his thick shaft. "Give me a minute and we'll walk back before you starve."

Laughing harder, I kiss his cheek. "I'll make it up to you tonight."

His eyes brighten, and he wraps an arm around my shoulder, pulling me close and kissing the top of my head.

These small shows of affection are everything to me. I've always admired couples who do tiny things to let each other know they care even when the situation doesn't warrant it. Who knew I'd have to go to another planet with an elf to find my person?

Chapter Seven

RAITH

After several weeks of working on the obsidian in an attempt to turn it into a scrying stone, I'm ready to give up. Frustrated with the shape and lack of shine, I lay the unfinished project on the fur in our alcove.

"Don't look so disappointed. You said it takes a long time to make one of those things work. You've only spent an hour each night on it." Layla puts aside a piece of stone she's been fitting to a shaft of wood to make an ax. She lies with her head in my lap.

"It feels as if we're not getting any closer to home." I've been gone two months. I'm sure they've given up on me ever coming home. It's likely my brothers have been back since the day we left, and now everyone is sitting around lamenting the fact that I've failed again.

She sits up and frowns at me. "We've mapped most of the tunnels, found all kinds of exits, and seen a good view of most of this dying land. We, as in the entire village, have harvested, dried, and packed enough food to last them the winter. We've even begun making tools into weapons, should we have to fight. I think a lot of progress has been made."

In reality, I should be happy I had two-plus months with this amazing woman who always sees the best in me. We're alive, and so are all the Aracans. With Layla's help to boost my magic, I've managed to heal two hunting wounds that could have become fatal.

Soon, we will start toward the winter camp. "I'll never sleep tonight. Only two weeks and no weapons that will stop magic besides you and me. As powerful as you are, we're not enough."

Her smile always makes my heart leap in my chest. It's as if each time I see it, it's the first time.

"We could make love. I promise to wear you out." She raises and lowers her eyebrows comically.

"That is a fine offer." I pull her into my lap and kiss her until we're both breathless. "May I take, what did you call it, a rain check? As much as I always want you, I'm restless. Maybe I'll explore the cave that turns south. We've not been that way."

"There's not enough air in that tunnel to sustain the torch." She straddles my hips and frowns. "How will we see?"

"We?" I don't know how I'll ever stand how much I love her. She's like pure air after being underground, and I've never needed anyone more.

"You're not going without me." Stated as a fact that brooks no argument. "Now, how will we see?"

I lift my hand between our faces and create a glowing

ball of light. It's an easy piece of magic that doesn't take too much effort. "I can sustain this for a long time without depleting myself."

Taking one of the axes she has already made and my dagger, she slips them through her belt. In Aracan clothes, she looks younger somehow. Leather pants and a matching tunic, the color of sand in Domhan. "I'm ready."

I slide my sword over my shoulder so it sits in the center of my back. "We should find a way to dye the Aracan clothes black or purple so that when we move, we can blend better into the terrain."

She considers it, and a tiny crease forms between her eyebrows. "I'll talk to Kas about it and see if she knows of something to make a dye with."

Giving my unfinished scrying stone one more look, I leave it behind and head toward the unexplored cave. Trudging through the series of caves with Layla has been more fun than it should be. We found crystals and precious jewels, including diamonds and rubies. Not that we have a need for any of those, but the diamonds are hard enough to use for sharpening and to be chiseled into points. We brought some larger ones back to see if they can be weaponized.

Whatever we find on our explorations, we've considered if and how it can help us defeat the witch queen or get us to Domhan. Every time I think about getting home, my only solution seems to be finding out how Vanora is making the journey, and using her magic to get us there.

The caves are cooling. I can see why the Aracan move out of the mountain for winter. The valley gets more sun, and the lower elevation is likely more temperate. However, they will be more exposed outside of the caves that shield them from summer heat.

Two hundred yards into the cave, and we reach the first offshoot. "Gaf told me there are many caves within this one."

Layla looks down the dark cave. Standing under my floating ball of blue-green light, she looks like a mystic from a traveling circus. "Should we start with the main cave or try each offshoot one by one?"

It's probably not useful to continue to admire her beauty, but I can't ignore the way she makes me feel. Touching the wall at the entrance, I close my eyes and search for magic. "I don't feel anything."

"But we already know that not all useful things are magical." She smiles. "Let's look."

I'd jump off the end of the world for her, so it's not much of a sacrifice to explore a cave. Sending my light to the right, I open my arm so she can precede me.

With a grin, she heads down the tunnel.

The air is thinner, but not unbreathable. We move slowly.

Layla presses her hands against the walls on either side as she walks. She has a habit of touching everything. She pulls her hand away, and studies her fingers, rubbing them together. Stopping, she stares at the wall.

I move my light closer and study the reddish stone. "This is new. We haven't seen red rock before."

She touches her finger to her tongue and cocks her head. "Metallic."

Brightening the light, I move it along the wall. A ten-inch-wide red band runs through black rock. "It could be iron." I have to think back to anything I might have learned about geology. "Iron stains the surrounding minerals red."

"Can you pull it out of there without collapsing the tunnel?"

It's a fair question. I know nothing of mining. "Let's follow the vein and see what we're looking at. Maybe this isn't iron. Even if it is, I'm not a blacksmith."

She nods, and we follow the red ribbon until there isn't enough air for us to continue. It takes a little extra magic to draw air from the main chamber, easing our return.

Once we're back to where the red starts, she presses her hand to the wall. "Do we need to know how to fold metal, or can you make a sword with magic?"

I pull my sword free of the sheath and stare at it. It was a gift from my father on the celebration of my twentieth sun. The blacksmith who made it was an artist of great talent. The blade gleams in the magic light.

She holds out the dagger I gave her. It also shines in the bluish light. The handle is carved from oak for a good grip, but the blade is polished to a silver glow. On the blade is a swirling etching of elvish words that translate to *aim true*. I bought the dagger with the only money I ever made on my own. When I was nineteen, I spent a week in Mayard Barrow's fields when three of his farmhands fell ill during harvest. It was hard work, but I liked it. It's funny that I like it even more after giving the dagger to Layla.

She smiles, her eyes bright, gazing at me as if I'm important. "Maybe try something smaller first. Don't go too deeply into the wall. We don't want to collapse this tunnel."

Dagger or sword, it's the same principle. "Normally, the iron would be mined and brought out of the mountain. Then the other elements would be taken out, purifying the metal. A blacksmith would superheat the blank and hammer it into shape before sharpening and polishing." I return my sword to its sheath and hand her dagger back.

Laying the blade over her palms, she holds it in front of me. "Don't worry about all the steps. You need pure iron from this vein; it must be strong and shaped like a dagger. That's it. We can worry about sharpening later."

"Do you think I can just ask the mountain to give me a dagger?" Frustration simmers in my tone. Even so, I consider that the blade also needs to be well-balanced with a good hilt for gripping.

Her face brightens with a wide smile. "That's exactly what you should do. When I wanted to save the Aracans from shadow demons, I prayed for whatever magic would do that."

"My magic doesn't work like that. I need to study and learn skills." No one talks to mountains. Some elves can communicate with ancient trees. Most can feel the life in things. I've never heard of anyone talking to a mountain.

"Just try, Raith. What can it hurt?" She touches my cheek with her reddened chalky fingers.

I can deny her nothing, so I press my hand to the wall and use magic to pull forth metal from the mountain. However, there is a pulse to the rock and soil that make up this place. It pulses in the bands of metal, and crystals grow and change within the pressure of this place. There's heat at the core.

Despite pouring my magic into it and sensing the mountain, nothing happens.

Just because I want to please her, and we need the

weapons, doesn't mean I can do this thing. Still, I try again. I imagine the length and shape of a dagger, the round hilt, the guard, and the blade. Closing my eyes, I can see it forming inside the wall, but with no idea if it's real or my imagination. It's heavy in my palm, and the iron is cool against my skin.

Layla presses her hand over mine. Her inner voice is clear in my mind. *Great mountain, you have given so much to us and the elves who live under your protection. Please help us protect them with this beautiful metal within you.*

Her prayer vibrates through me—the wall shimmers behind my fingers. I add the attributes of a good blade to her prayer.

Cool metal pulses against my skin, this time more than imagined. I open my eyes, and the wall in front of us glows as if heated, even though I only feel the coolness of whatever is pushing out of the rock.

Just as I sensed the life, the forming of something is tangible—metal, pure and mighty, coalescing, pushing aside the elements that will not serve as a blade. A hunk of metal falls into my hands. The dagger is ugly, dull, but clearly knife-shaped.

Releasing the magic, I stare at our creation. "We did it."

"It ain't pretty." She laughs. "But it's a knife. Well, sort of."

"It's a very good first. It can be sharpened." The amazement in my voice is exactly how I feel. Lowering the new knife, I close the distance of inches between us. Nose to nose, she leaves me breathless. "I don't think there is anything we can't accomplish together, Layla."

Pressing her forehead to mine, her skin warms to a soft

blush. She grips the front of my tunic with both hands. "I'm extremely horny right now."

My cock throbs to life. Dropping the magically forged knife with a clatter, I press my hips forward while wrapping her in an embrace. "I don't know that word, but if it means desirous, I'm in the same condition."

She wraps her calf around mine, opening herself to me and moaning at the contact. "It's what it means, and I can feel your condition." Her laugh is short and breathy.

"I wish I had you at home with a big soft bed and a dozen pillows. Then in the wide tub. You should be worshiped in an elegant room, with every comfort, not taken against a wall in a filthy cave." I wipe my hand of red dust on my tunic and cup her cheek. Lowering my lips, I halt a breath away from hers. "I can't resist you."

"I don't want you to. All those things sound nice, and when we get to your home, I'd love a long, hot bath together, but right now I need you, here, against a wall, in a filthy cave." She lifts her chin and rubs her lips across mine.

There's no force behind the kiss, still, blood rushes to my shaft at a dizzying rate. Her lips are gentle and teasing as if we have all the time in the world. She doesn't question if we'll get to my home, only when. Her belief is as arousing as the whisper of a kiss.

So much of what happened when we merged our magic should be discussed and examined, but I can't think when she is pressing her body to mine and gently exploring my mouth.

Her tongue teases, and I open. I want to give her everything. The main cavern is close enough that I call my magic to set a shield between our little cave and the larger one that leads in. The inside of her mouth is like warm satin as I sweep my tongue inside and taste her.

Clutching my hair, she moans and breaks the kiss. Her chest rises and falls fast and hard as if she ran a mile to get to this point. "I need more." She pulls the tie at the top of my tunic and presses her lips just below the hollow of my throat.

I run my fingers over the swell of her ass and down her thigh, pulling her tighter and grinding against her.

Practically climbing me, she wraps her other leg around mine and grips my shoulders.

Cupping both her ass cheeks, I tease through the fabric of her leggings. It's not enough. I'll never have enough. Lifting her away from where she clings to me, I wait for her to put her feet on the ground.

Expression confused, she opens her mouth to protest.

Before she can say anything, I drop to my knees and pull the leather bow tied below her belly button. A slight tug and her trousers slip over the swell of her hips and puddle at her feet.

Rewarded with a gasp, I press my mouth at the apex of her thighs and slip my tongue between her folds. She's slick with need and tastes like the sweetest honey. I'm ravenous for every drop of her.

Gripping my shoulders, she cries my name and widens her stance as she leans back against the wall.

Taking advantage, I lift her left leg and drag it over my shoulder, then do the same with the right. The passion in her eyes as she threads her fingers through my hair is almost my undoing.

"Raith. God, Raith."

There's no rush, and I take my time savoring her soft,

smooth folds. I tease my tongue around her clitoris and suck the sensitive bud. Lower, I slide fingers inside her, and she rocks against my face, crying out my name and senseless words along with moans and mews that bolster my need to give her release. Perfection. That's what she is. Pure and beautiful.

Her rhythm is slow and steady as she rolls her hips in time with me making love to her with my mouth. Once again, I focus on her clitoris and suck gently then hard, gentle then hard, until she loses the beat she found and jerks wildly, her thighs closing around my ears.

It's a good thing my skull is strong, or she might crack my head like a nut with her powerfully muscular legs. "Easy, *mo anam cara.*"

She relaxes. "I'm really close. I need…"

Pressing my mouth to exactly where she needs, I let the song of her soul guide me. I fill both our minds with our songs and find that perfect pace that makes her scream and rock her hips harder, faster, and her fingers tighten in my hair. Her body pulses, and she comes apart on a long keen.

I lap up every delicious drop of her essence. Her nectar is like something the old gods created just for me.

Her legs shake even as her breathing slows. "That was amazing. I could hear the songs like a symphony in my head. I always want to hear that when we make love."

Holding her leggings in place on the ground where they lay at her feet, I wait to see if she'll step out of them or if she's had enough, then I'll pull them back over her soft legs.

She steps out, and I rise. "I shall always let you hear the songs of our souls whenever you wish. Perhaps even teach you to hear them for yourself."

Pushing her hands between us, she tugs at the tie of my leggings. "I would like to learn that." The delicious fumbling against my sensitive cock forces a groan from my lips as she pulls me free and runs her fingers along my shaft.

"Gods, that's so good." I lower my head and capture her lips for a long kiss.

"I need you inside me," she says against my lips.

Gripping her ass, I press her back to the wall. "The things you say."

She wraps her legs around my hips and uses my shoulders to lift herself until the head of my cock slides through her wetness and dips into her. "I can't believe how much I want you again, even after that amazing orgasm." Letting her weight go by increments, she lowers herself onto me inch by inch.

"Layla, you are perfect. You are mine." I want to say *for all time*, but that must be up to her.

"I am yours." She tips her hips to take a bit more.

Gently, so that I don't bash her against the rock, I pull out and press inside her perfect sheath, made for me by the old gods. If I'm wrong about everything else in my life, I know I'm right about this woman and her body and soul. "Made for me. I'm made for you."

I didn't mean to say it out loud. I freeze and meet her gaze.

She pulls herself up so that I slip out of her.

I'm an idiot. "Layla. I—"

She stops me with a quick kiss. "I need more. The stone is too rough on my back."

"Of course." I really am a thoughtless fool.

Before I can tie my leggings, she turns her back to me,

puts her hands on the wall, and lowers her torso until her ass is high. Spreading her legs exposes her perfect, wet pussy. A long growl escapes me. "Layla."

With her fingers, she spreads her lips. "I was made for you."

I thrust my cock deep inside her, and when I'm fully seated, I wait for her to put both hands on the wall before I pound into her hard and fast.

She rocks back in time with me. "Fuck. Raith. Fuck."

Each time I fill her, my heavy balls slap hard against her flesh. She's so wet and tight, I'm at the edge of my own orgasm when her sheath tightens around me.

Screaming my name, she pulses with her rapture, dragging me over the edge of the cliff with her. As I come, she slaps back into me hard a few more times and cries out again and again. Her pussy tightens and releases me, bringing my pleasure higher.

My legs shake, and I grip her hips as I fill her with my seed. Leaning forward, I wrap my arms around her. "I should have pulled out, but you feel so good, I couldn't."

"I'm glad you didn't. That was the best thing I've ever experienced." She lets out a long breath. "Now I really can't wait for that tub."

I laugh. The movement makes me half hard again, and we both groan. Slowly, I pull free of her body. "I want you all over again, but maybe we should finish this after I'm washed up and we can have the relative comfort of our bed cove."

Turning into my embrace, she breathes me in. "I'm going to hold you to that."

"I'll never lie to you." It comes out more serious than I intended.

Her arms tighten around me for a moment before she lets go and reaches for her pants.

It's staggering how badly I want her back in my embrace, but I pull myself together and tuck my cock away. It's as reluctant to be anywhere but inside Layla as I am. However, I'm not letting her down. We have work to do. More pleasure can wait.

Chapter Eight

LAYLA

Carrying six daggers and three swords, we return to the cavern in time for the evening meal. It's strange how hard it is to keep up with time in the caves. At least in the central area, the oculus above shows that the light is changing.

Tog takes up a sword and studies it. "Fight?" He points to the hilt of Raith's sword sticking over his shoulder.

Sorrow clouds Raith's eyes before he nods. "I'll teach you." Once he explains that the blades need sharpening, he steps out of the main tunnel.

I watch him go and sit by Kas.

"He come back," Kas assures me as she takes my hand. She's probably not much older than me, though with elves, I have no idea. They live longer, so they age more slowly.

Still, regardless of her age, she has a motherly quality that I gravitate toward. I suppose having so little mothering growing up, I'm fascinated by the idea that anyone would want to care for me in that way.

"I know." The crazy thing is, I really do know that Raith will always come back to me. I've never felt that about anyone in my entire life. I've never dreamed that I could be that for another person. Of course, this might all be a dream.

It occurred to me a few weeks ago that I might have been knocked unconscious during the superhero competition. Maybe I'm in a coma, and all of this is the craziest, most realistic dream ever.

The thing is, if that's the case, I don't want to wake up. I know there's danger. It has not escaped my notice that I've nearly been killed on several occasions. This is still the best time of my life—the happiest I've ever been.

In my world, that would mean I should go back to therapy. Okay, maybe that's true, and I'm not opposed to talking this all through with someone who's not invested. Not that I'm in any position to find a good psychologist right now.

No one here knows that I've been unhappy in the extreme. They have no basis for comparison. To them, I'm normal. Here, I have a purpose beyond proving myself to people who probably don't even care.

I don't know if I ever want to go back to the way my life was.

Shaking off the direction of my thoughts, I take a long breath and let it out slowly. It's too much to think about in one bite. First, we have to survive and make our way to that blue and green planet of Domhan.

The sun has nearly set when Raith returns with two buckets of water for washing.

Remembering his promise, my cheeks heat.

He must sense my thoughts. Turning toward me, he smiles, and his cheeks turn pink. Unlike anyone I've ever met. Men don't blush; they preen and boast. They make conquests and move on to the next. Raith is different; he's turned my life upside down. I should thank him.

The hunt wasn't great, so the food for the night is sparse, and little was added to the stores for the journey.

Large sacks with straps have begun to be filled and placed beside the wall near the cave we'll take to the smoking mountain.

Raith sits beside me, and Tog explains, *"We need to leave in three days. That's when the days and nights are darkest. The moons do not rise, and the planet is far. We go together for a way, then split to see the bad birth."*

"I understood that." My heart is pounding with the realization that Tog spoke entirely in Old Elvish, and I didn't even think about translating. I can't even speak Spanish well enough to understand a whole conversation, and half the people I know are Latino. What is it about this place that has changed me?

Raith squeezes my hand. He hands me more food, a few pieces of meat and some leafy vegetables.

"You have to eat." It comes out more scolding than I intend.

His smile could melt the most hardened heart. "I've had enough. Eat."

"I'll split it with you." I portion what's on the wooden plate in half, and once I've eaten my side, I hand it back to him.

With a rare frown, he eats the rest.

Tog says, "No time for training."

"We will find time." Raith picks up one of the knives we made. He thrusts it forward toward the fire. *"Stick them with the pointy end."*

Tog laughs, and everyone nearby joins in. I suppose if we can't learn sword skills, that bit of advice will do.

I help clean up after the meal, then find Raith with a group of young men, showing them a few sword moves. He has their full attention.

One of the men asks about the dullness of the blade, and Raith explains that they must be sharpened on stone.

As we got better at making the blades from the mountain, they became closer to being ready to use, but still require sharpening.

When the men each take a blade and begin honing it to a sharp edge, I move to help.

Raith takes my hand. "We'll let them work. You've done enough today." Once we're near our sleep cave, he picks up the buckets. "Will you come and wash with me?"

My pulse triples, and I follow. I'm pretty sure no force of nature or magic could keep me from following him. At the front of the cavern is a small alcove where water can drain. The fissure that draws water out isn't big enough to help this place during the rainy season, but it's perfect for washing without having to go outside. Everyone in the village uses it, but tonight it is empty save for us.

Once he puts the buckets down, he creates one of his magic shields to give us privacy. Anyone looking to bathe will know something is different, but I don't protest.

Dragging his tunic over his head, he exposes not only his broad, muscular chest that looks like something out of a Hollywood movie, but also two square pieces of cloth that he has tucked into the top of his leggings. He pulls them free and drops them into the buckets, where they float for a moment before sinking.

I can hardly breathe as he steps out of his shoes and drags his leggings down his thick thighs. He places all of his clothes in a pile out of the way. Returning to me, without saying a word, he stares at me with hunger and passion. Holding the bottom of my tunic, he slowly undresses me.

I toe my shoes off and let him do the rest. It's erotic and sensual the way he's caring for me. Standing naked, I feel exposed and shy. I cross my arms over my breasts, not at all certain what my role is supposed to be.

When Raith kneels next to the buckets, he does my favorite bit of elf magic. He turns a few drops of water into a pat of soap. He explained it to me the first time he did it, as everything is made out of the same material, and you just have to manipulate it to your will. To him, it's a simple thing, but why was the same not true for making blades?

As soon as he starts soaping a cloth and looking up at me from his knees with a look that says he wants me, my cognitive abilities fail me. My mouth goes dry, and my pussy aches for his touch.

He stands and gently washes my face, then neck and shoulders.

My nipples harden to sensitive pebbles, and when he runs the soapy cloth over them, I gasp. Legs like jelly, standing takes all my concentration.

Working his way over my abdomen, then my hips, he lingers between my legs while I bite my lip to keep from crying out. My knees buckle, and I grip his shoulders for support.

With a chuckle, he kisses my belly button and continues down my legs to my feet before working his way up the back side of me. It's a rare treat to be clean from head to toe, and I'm in heaven.

Raith whispers in my ear, "Lean your head back, *mo anam cara*." He kisses behind my ear.

Complying, I lean back against his shoulder.

"Close your eyes."

Totally trusting, I comply. Water wets my hair, then his fingers caress my scalp while he lathers it. I sigh and delight in the feel of a soapy head and someone washing my hair. I can't remember when this has ever happened to me outside of a hair salon, and if it cost extra, I always just had them use a spray bottle to wet it. "This is almost as good as sex."

He lets out a short laugh. "I'm glad you added 'almost,' or I'd worry."

"Only because you don't know how good this feels." I open my eyes and look over my shoulder at him. The soap from my hair runs down his chest like a waterfall of foam and dirt since my hair should have been washed first. I follow the path, pausing at his thick erection standing out from his slim hips.

I move to turn, but he stops me.

"Let me rinse the soap." His voice is rough and so fucking sexy.

Leaning my head back, I close my eyes and, within a few seconds, water flows over my head, and Raith's hand follows, using a tingle of magic to push the soap out. He runs the cloth over my body once again after the filth of my hair marred his good work.

As soon as the water stops, I take the cloth from the second bucket. Standing, I hold out my hand.

His lips pull up into a crooked smile as he drops the soap into my palm.

"I can't do that trick with the water to wash your hair."

He does the trick, and water rushes up. I lather the soap and run my finger through the long red locks and, despite the dirt, love the feel of his thick mane. I'm careful to keep the soap from his eyes, and once I've finished, he rinses it away.

Feeling wicked, I lean over and dip the cloth in the bucket. Lingering there with my ass in the air and relishing the low, dangerous growl from my elf. When I straighten, I meet his gaze and lather up the cloth again. I wash his chest and shoulders. His hands are fisted at his sides, and I nudge them open to clean every inch of him, not missing a spot. Rounding his body, I wash his back. His wet hair clings to him.

I lather the cloth, kneel, and start at his feet. I work my way up his beautiful man legs. I haven't had many opportunities to see them, and the light from the fire barely reaches this corner, but they are muscular and dappled with hair a shade darker than on his head. I work the cloth up and down his thick cock, then over his balls before washing his ass. Letting the cloth drop, I run my hands over his body, taking in every inch as I step to his front and press against him. Slipping my hand between us, I grip his cock and slide up and down his thick shaft.

The veins in his neck are distended, and his jaw is tight. "Layla, you'll make me come right here."

"Tempting, but I'm selfish and want you inside me when you come." Lowering, I press a long kiss to the head of his cock and draw it into my mouth, swirling my tongue once before letting it pop free.

Voice strangled, he says, "The things you say." He cups the back of my head and grips under my arm as he pulls me to standing.

His chest rises and falls fast. "This teasing may have been a bad idea."

Running my hands over his chest, then down his abdomen, I grip his cock in both hands and give him a long, slow pull. "It was the best idea you've ever had as far as I'm concerned."

"You're not ready to come with a hundred elves just around that corner and nothing but a light magic shield to hide us." Even as he protests, he moves his hips in time with my hands.

Reaching for his hand, I guide it between my legs. "Don't be so sure about that."

He slides his fingers between my folds. "So wet. Gods, Layla," he growls. Stepping to the side, he moves away from me. Picking up the bucket of water, he dumps it over his head, washing away the soap, then gives his head a shake.

He's magnificent, with thick muscles and an angular jaw.

A tingle of his magic rushes over my skin, drying me, then he does the same to himself.

"Put your clothes on," he commands.

I've never seen him so forceful, and I like it. I'll have to drive him to sexual madness more often in the future. I pull on my leggings and tunic, pick up my shoes, and take his offered hand.

Pushing away his magical shield, he leads the way to our small sleeping cove.

If anyone noticed our disappearance into the washing corner, they make no comment. Most of the village has settled in for the night, and those who are still awake are gathered by the fire in quiet conversation.

At the entrance to what is essentially our bedroom, Raith stops and waits for me to enter.

It's dark within as I enter and move to one side.

On hands and knees, he crawls inside. A ball of dim blue light appears in his hand before he sends it to rest in the back corner. Muttering a few words, he magically closes off our space from the outside. "I meant to care for you and perhaps tease you to arousal, *mo anam cara*. I underestimated the fact that we have rarely seen each other fully naked outside of this small space. You are magnificent."

I drag my tunic off and wriggle out of my pants. "You're perfect." I don't just mean his body. Everything about him washing me, my hair, and the way he looks at me, is more than I've ever dreamed possible.

Also naked, he crawls forward toward me.

My heart races.

Reaching behind me, he takes the brush I had in my gym bag from where I keep it on top of a rock that juts out from the wall. He turns and leans back before pulling me between his legs with my back toward him. As if I were made of glass, he runs the brush through my hair. At every snag, he stops and eases the hairs apart. For bigger knots, he uses magic to separate the strands. Over and over, he works my damp hair through the bristles.

It's pure pleasure to have someone brush my hair. A low hum starts in my chest, and I can't stop the sighs and purrs that manifest inside me. "This comes in third on my pleasure list. Feel free to brush my hair anytime you want."

"I plan to make your list so long you will run out of numbers for them all." He moves my hair over my shoulder and presses his lips to the back of my neck. His tongue teases the skin there.

"I don't remember ever feeling so loved. I mean aroused." I remind myself this is about sex. If I get too attached, I might not survive the hurt when I have to go back home. Maybe it's already too late.

Wrapping his hand around, he cups my breast and teases the nipple as he trails kisses along my neck to my shoulder, then up to my ear. His voice is so soft it hardly sounds real. "You are loved, *mo anam cara*, my soulmate. You are deeply and completely loved and will be until the end of time. My heart beats for you. My soul sings for yours. I have been half a man without you, as if I were waiting for the rest of me to show me the way."

"You don't have to say those things. I'm not planning to deny you sex. Not tonight." Maybe not ever, if I'm being honest, at least with myself.

"Layla, I've told you that I love you, but you don't really believe me, do you?" He holds me close, his cock pressing between us, adding to my desire.

I wiggle my bottom, hoping to move things along and change the subject. "I don't think you lied to me."

"I'll never lie to you. I've sworn it." The air around us is charged with the vow. "You are my destiny, but more than that, I love you."

"Maybe it's just some kind of magic that will wear off once your witch is dead and my purpose is fulfilled." My chest tightens. Admitting my greatest fear sends a sharp pain through me, and I wince.

The only movement is the rise and fall of his chest. "Is that how you feel? Do you think what we have will disappear once the prophecy is completed?"

"I don't know. Humans don't know anything about magic." I'm ruining this perfect day and night. I feel myself doing it. I know it's a self-protection mechanism I've fallen back on all of my adult life. Still, I can't stop. It was too good, too perfect. It can only end badly. Everything ends badly.

Moving out from behind me, he sits so that I can see his face, but I keep my gaze down. "Look at me, please."

Drawing a long breath, I look into his eyes, which shine in the magical light. There is no anger, no rage, no disappointment. Raith's hurt is there but pushed aside. I can feel it there in my head and in my heart as if it were my own. Maybe it is mine.

He takes my hand. "I don't care if we solve a dozen prophesies, I shall still love and want you. Nothing will change my feelings. The old gods may have put you in my path, and for that, I'm grateful, but they can't make my heart need you."

My throat is so tight, it's hard to speak. "How...how can you know?"

Closing his eyes, he takes a long breath and lets it out in a huff. "I dream of a life beyond all these troubles. I've seen it in my mind a dozen times. I'm afraid that if I show it to you, you'll be afraid."

"I'm afraid now, Raith. You are the first person in a long time who could really hurt me. If this is only passion and sex, then I won't be vulnerable." My good sense is screaming at me to stop baring my soul, but everything about this man draws me in and holds me.

Taking my other hand, he presses both between his like a prayer. His eyes are filled with both sorrow and hope, and it's impossible to look away. "Let me show you what I see."

Unable to deny him anything, I nod.

"Close your eyes." Once I do, he leans his forehead against mine.

At first, there is only the blending of our breath and the warmth where his hands and head touch me. Light flashes behind my eyes, startling me.

"Gently, *mo anam cara*. Relax."

I try, but another flash of blue sky and fluffy white clouds shifts in the blackness behind my eyelids. Before I can stop myself, I'm searching for more of the vision.

A field of long grass sways in a breeze that tickles the hairs on my skin and brings the scent of flowers. In the distance, a great mountain range rises, snowcapped at its peaks. The grass is cool, and I brush my hand over the tops as the field rolls in the spring breeze like the ocean on a calm day.

The leggings I'm wearing are made of the softest material in a bright blue. A tunic hangs to my thighs, in a paler version of the same color. Lying back in the grass, the sun and moons are all visible as a cloud of billowy white floats past.

Something blocks the sun, leaving me in shadow.

Shielding my eyes, I stare into Raith's handsome face, smiling down at me.

A child giggles from behind him, and he turns toward the sound.

Rolling to my side, I'm filled with joy as a girl of perhaps two years toddles after a butterfly. Her bright red hair curls around her pointed ears. When I call to her, she turns, and my own eyes look back at me.

Gasping, I open my eyes. "That was our daughter. Is that real? Is she real?" My breath comes fast, in short gasps. I can't catch up with it. Panic sets in, and I cling to Raith, digging my fingers into his shoulders.

"Slow down. Just breathe. She's real, but the future is never certain. We have choices and free will. What you saw is one possible future." He drags me into his lap and holds me, kissing my hair.

"She was beautiful." Tears dampen my cheeks. "A girl. The curse was broken."

"A perfectly stunning little girl with her mother's eyes." He tips my chin up and covers my mouth with his, then sweeps his tongue inside, making love to my mouth while cupping my cheek as if I'm made of glass and might break if he's too rough.

Reaching up, I thread my fingers through his hair and slide my tongue along his for a deeper kiss that I feel down to my toes and all the places in between.

He grips my skull and ends the kiss. His loving gaze is so intense, I'm tempted to look away. His shaft presses hard and ready against my hip. "Does that future scare you?"

Oddly, it was too beautiful to stir fear. I shake my head. "It was perfect. You and our daughter were everything I could ever want." Until I saw myself in that little family, I didn't even know that was something I craved. It never seemed possible to want something I've never experienced. Now it's in my heart.

Rolling us, he eases me to my back and slides along my side. His leg covers mine, and he leans over me, keeping our connection. "I've seen that scene a few times, and every time, it's how at peace you look that strikes me in the heart. I want to make you feel safe and secure. How can I prove to you that my love will always be for you?"

I push his hair behind his ear. "Does a life with me and that little girl scare you at all?"

His cock jerks, and he presses it against my hip. Tracing a path with his fingers along my thigh to my hip, he smiles and shakes his head. "I'd like to fill a house with a dozen little girls that look just like you, Layla."

It should be shocking, but I laugh. "I'm not a broodmare, Raith. Maybe three." The fact that he's not put off or worried that forever is a long time is somehow very erotic.

I wrap my leg over his and pull him on top of me, then pull him tight with my calves around his hips.

His cock settles between my wet folds. Passion sparks bright in his eyes as he rubs along my pussy, creating the most delicious friction for both of us. "Three will be amazing," he says, as if he's ready to start making them now.

Part of me, a large part, thinks that's a great idea. "I'm trying not to worry."

Another rock and he perches at my slit. "You can worry about demons, the witch queen, and a dozen other things. You can even fuss over whether or not my parents will like you, though I'm certain they'll adore you. The only thing you are forbidden to concern yourself with is my fealty and unending love for you."

Tipping my hips brings him inside me an inch.

He shakes his head. "Tell me you believe me. Tell me you know that my love is real and not some magic trick forced on us by the old gods to be ripped away at a whim."

With a swallow and a deep breath, I stare into his eyes. His song sings to me and merges with my own. "You love me, and it has nothing to do with gods or magic. I love you, and it is real and lasting." Magic shimmers around us, and a thread appears.

Raith's eyes widen, and while he sinks deep inside me, he examines the bright white thread of light that spans from my chest around my left wrist, to his left wrist, and into his chest. "Amazing."

Unable to resist, I move beneath him by rolling my hips. "Is it good or bad?"

Chest to mine, he leans on his elbows and cups my head. Pulling back, then filling me, he moves in time with me. "It's the thread that binds us. It's good." His lips cover mine in a long, languid kiss that also takes on the cadence of our bodies connecting and separating again and again.

Breaking the kiss, he groans, rises to his knees, and cups my ass.

I stretch my legs up his torso and put my heels on his shoulders for leverage. I rise and fall, reveling in the way he fills me and the new spot deep inside me this position hits. His balls slap my ass with each thrust, adding to the sensations.

His pace quickens, drawing my orgasm closer.

I grip my breasts and tug on my nipples, heightening my sensations, trying to push myself over the edge so that I can come with him.

Meeting my gaze, his mouth opens on a moan. He presses his thumb to my clitoris and rubs the slick bud in beat with his thrusts, which are faster and faster.

The string holding me together unravels, and I come hard. My sheath clutches at his thick cock as he pounds in a last time, grunting as he fills me with his heat.

Another burst of pleasure erupts inside me, and the thread between us glows brighter, pulls tighter, and vibrates like a guitar string plucked too hard.

Raith gently puts my legs on the ground and lowers his body to mine. Weight on his elbows, he pulls my bottom lip between his, does the same with the top one, then dots kisses along my jaw, cheek, and nose. "You are everything."

I run my finger along the thread, which is not solid but has energy.

It fades and disappears, but I still feel it vibrating between us.

Chapter Nine

RAITH

It was a risk to share the dreams I'm having. But it paid off. She didn't run. Instead, she opened herself to me a little more, and when she did, the tether that connects us showed itself.

"What exactly was that?" she asks after the thread disappears from view.

"Some call it the tie that binds."

"You'll have to do better than that." Kissing my cheek, she tilts her hips, and I slip from her sweet body.

Easing to my side, I love the feel of her naked body pressed to mine. "Keep in mind that this is the first time I've actually seen a bonding ribbon. Since true mates are rare, I wasn't even sure this magical cord connecting two souls existed. My parents certainly never mentioned theirs."

"Your parents are true mates?" She turns her back to me

and snuggles against me, perfectly fitting her curves into my hard places.

I pull one of the furs over us and wrap my arm around her. "They are. Before meeting you, my parents were the only couple I ever knew to be fated for each other."

"Do you think they can see this ribbon of magic?" Her voice grows sleepy.

Hugging her tighter, I rest my head next to hers and kiss her hair. The long, eventful day is catching up with me as well. "I couldn't say, and if it only appears during lovemaking, I don't want to know."

Her light giggle is musical. "Maybe the magic wanted to prove itself to me." She relaxes, and her breathing slows and becomes even.

Holding her and barely awake, I ponder the idea that magic might have a kind of consciousness that shows itself at pertinent moments. I give in to my exhaustion.

Morning comes long before I'm ready for it. When I fell asleep, the magic shielding us from the main cave dissipated. As the village wakes, the noise grows, as does the warm woman snuggled against me.

Naked beneath the fur, it's hard to resist slipping inside her before we start the day, but the grinding of metal against stone brings my guilt over staying in bed to the forefront.

I kiss her temple. "We should get up, *mo anam cara*."

She wiggles against my extremely alert cock. "Too bad." She sighs.

Putting the shield back in place, I move out from under the fur and pull on my leggings and tunic.

As Layla dresses, my mind wanders to the scene of her in the field with our daughter. It's easy to imagine waking with her every morning. With no witch queen to defeat, we'd linger in bed, make love, talk, and bathe together. That life is so close I can taste it, and I'll do whatever I must to have that future.

"You have a very strange expression on your face." She pulls on her shoes.

"Just thinking." I let go of the magic hiding our sleeping cove. Once outside, I stretch my legs and back.

Arms above her head, Layla stands beside me and makes the most delicious sound. "That was a cryptic answer."

"Because if I show you my thoughts, we'll be naked again, and there's a lot of work to be done in a very short time." I kiss the top of her head, and her blush warms me from the inside out.

"Oh."

Taking her hand, we walk to the fire and accept the meager food to break our fast.

The elves I gave the blades to last night sit in a row, each working the knives and swords against stones to sharpen the tips and edges.

Tog nods toward the elves at work on the weapons. "You make more?"

"We will make more today." I lean into Layla. "I need to go outside and get some sun. My magic is strong, but a little sun would help our efforts."

Trepidation rushes through her to me. This connection is stronger after last night, and even after months of feeling her, I'm still getting used to the sensation. With a nod, she finishes her food and rises. "I'll go with you."

Knowing that separation, even for a few minutes, is uncomfortable for both of us, I make no protest. She'd be safer in the cave, but I don't want to leave her any more than she wants me to go. "I'll get my sword."

Each lost in our own thoughts, we walk down the main cave tunnel toward where we landed on this planet. It feels like years ago, but it was only a couple of months. Still, I should be home with Layla, safe in the castle.

She turns her gaze toward me. "Would I be safe? Wouldn't it just be the same war in a different place?"

"I shouldn't think so loudly." Taking her hand, I kiss her knuckles as we exit and the sun rises in the distance. "You're right. There is no safe place until this is finished."

"Then stop beating yourself up. We're exactly where we're meant to be, and we'll find a way to get to your home and save these elves from starvation." She looks into the distance at the ravaged world.

I sit cross-legged near the cave entrance. "When did you get to be so wise?"

She laughs. "I've always been this way, but with no one to listen to me."

Closing my eyes, I let the familiar sun warm my face and reignite my magic. "I shall always listen."

With a soft sigh, she sits silently at my side. The hum of the thread that connects us grows more constant, becoming part of this new normal we've fallen into.

Having never gone to war like my brothers, I never

needed to recharge my magic. I've always been in the sun enough to feel the whole essence of it all the time. Since landing on Arcania, it's been harder to find quiet moments to recharge. Layla's magic comes from some other source that we're yet to understand. She seems to have a bottomless well tied to her rest.

A hint of trepidation travels through our connection, and she says, "Something is coming, Raith."

Opening my eyes, I scan the horizon. Whatever it is, it's on four legs.

"Is it a dog or a wolf?" Her eyes narrow. "I think there are two."

The black beasts grow closer, and they separate so that it's clear there are two. The way they move does seem canine. "They're too big to be any wolf I've ever seen."

"Great, giant black dogs. Just what we need."

I jump to my feet. I'm an idiot. Of course. "We need to lure them away from the cave."

Feeding off my emotions, she leaps to her feet. "What is it?"

"Cú sidhe. They're not even supposed to be real, or they haven't been on Domhan in hundreds of suns. Most think they're mythological."

She gives a short laugh. "In my world, elves aren't real. Clearly, all rules have gone out the window by this point. Tell me something useful about these cú sidhe."

"They're black dogs with glowing red eyes, like demons. The books say they are the size of a small horse and are known to steal women away." I strain my memory for more of what was in those old textbooks.

"Why women? What do they do with them when they

steal them?" She takes my hand, and we run down the side of the rocks toward where we portaled here. It's a risk to be off on our own, but leading these beasts right to a cave full of barely armed elves is worse.

At a run, we dash into the open to make sure they follow and ignore the cave. "They take women who have recently given birth and use them to nurse fairy babies."

"What? You made that up."

"No, but it does sound like fiction." On the flat plane, we move to slightly higher ground and wait.

The two cú sidhe shift direction to follow us away from our village within the cave.

"Is there any chance they're friendly, and since I'm not currently able to act as a wet nurse, they'll leave us alone and go on their way?"

The beasts climb the rise a hundred yards away and bare their teeth. Saliva drips from their rotting teeth, and their red eyes glow as they fixate on us. "I'm guessing they are not friendly."

"Any idea how to fight them?" Her magic rises and crackles through our connections.

"No. The books never said anything about that. All the tales talk about is the stealing of women." I draw my sword. Nothing is taking Layla from me.

"I should have brought my bow."

"You don't need it. Pray for what you want your magic to do. It's always inside you, never external." My gut is tight as fear of losing her fills me, but protecting her is the only thing that matters. Considering the mission the oracle sent me to complete, the knowing is daunting. If it were between saving

Layla and defeating the witch queen, I would choose my mate without hesitation.

"God, stop thinking. Just do what you do. It's going to be fine." She presses her hand to her head as if my thoughts are blaring in there.

"I don't suppose I can talk you into staying behind me for now?"

"Fuck that. You die, I die." She gives me a look that leaves no room for argument.

"Do not die," I command.

Her lips twitch. "Right back at you."

Keeping the higher ground, we wait for the dogs to close the gap. As they approach, I raise my sword higher and let magic swirl in my left hand. "Stay back. You don't want us. Move along."

The hair on their haunches stands up as they lower their heads and growl. The sound is so loud it makes me flinch. These are definitely not normal dogs or wolves. These are magical beasts, but why come after us? Layla has no milk to feed fairies. Their black fur gleams, almost looking wet in the rising sun. One steps up the rock.

I hurl magic at it, hitting just in front of its long snout.

Backing up several steps, it yelps, then both look ready to leap, growling. The saliva dripping from their jaws sizzles on the ground. Cú sidhe are not a pleasant children's story, but I never read anything about them being poisonous, nor evil.

A low, hideous laugh rips from the cú sidhe's open mouth. It's female and can only come from one person. "Death is your only option, human."

I would know Vanora's voice anywhere.

"You will not succeed. You will not take this human; you will not harm her or me. All that will happen here today is that you will kill these beasts you've put under your evil black magic." It feels a bit silly speaking to dogs, even giant magical ones, but I do it anyway. We need to know what Vanora knows.

The dog on the right cocks its head while the other lies down, looking confused. The standing one opens its mouth. It doesn't speak, but Vanora's voice comes out of it. "I knew one of Elspeth's spawn had to be behind the loss of my soldiers and demons. Your brothers were harder to find. The last of the lesser elves were no match for shadows, any more than your measly family will be for what's coming for them next.

"You're the useless one. It's amusing, really. The last of the Riordan spawn, and the most disappointing, will die here in this wasteland, and your sainted mother will never know what happened to you.

"It's really too bad you never met the miserable creatures who used to inhabit this world. You would have fit right in with their backward ways and minuscule magic. They are much better off in my service. They make fine shadow demons." Her laugh, as it comes out of the dog, is obscene. "You would have been a good one, too, but I have no time for that now. My cú sidhe will rip you to bits, then bring me the human, and there's nothing you can do about it. Once I have her, I'll rip her open like I did this rock of a planet, and send her to Coire for eternity."

The dog's eyes come back into focus, and the other stands up as if it were bowing to its master and now has leave to attack. They crouch and leap.

Slashing at the lead dog, I put myself between them and Layla.

Fire flies past my shoulder, burning the second dog, who squeals and rolls to put out its flaming fur. The stench of burning hair and flesh fills the air.

My blade slashes the first dog, but it veers to the side.

They fall back a few steps, but their eyes blaze brighter as they circle—one in each direction.

"Back-to-back," I scream above the blood rushing through my head.

"I'm here," she says as her heat meets mine. Her fire reflects on the purple rocks.

The dogs leap.

I stab into one's underbelly. Blood, the color of mud, gushes from the wound. It collapses, and its claws come down across my arm, opening a deep gash.

Ignoring the pain and blood, I watch to make sure the beast doesn't rise again.

Layla's scream shakes the earth and air, making me bobble. Almost losing my footing, I turn to help. Fire flies from her hands in long spears. She hits the animal in the shoulder. The singed cú sidhe's eyes return to their earlier confusion. It gives a soft cry and limps away from us.

Unsure what else might come at us, I grab Layla around the waist and pull her up the slope.

She grabs my arm.

I wince, pulling air through my teeth.

Releasing my injured arm, she says, "You're bleeding. This is bad. Let me go, Raith."

My mind whirls with what could have been a disaster. I couldn't have fought off both dogs and protected Layla. If she hadn't used her magic, I would have lost her. The vision in my head will not go away. I can see my mate in the jaws of one of those beasts, being dragged away. It's hard to breathe.

Gripping my hand, she says softly, "I'm fine. Let me go. We need to heal this before you lose too much blood." She pulls my hand until I ease pressure on her middle. "That's it."

I tighten my hold on my sword and scan for threats. The dog I stabbed remains motionless on the rocks. The other has put distance between himself and us and is still moving away. My knees give out, and I sit on the hillside.

Layla kneels beside me, her body angled so she can see me and keep watch on the retreating dog. Until we're sure it's gone, we can't go back to the cave.

A hundred thoughts and worries spin through my head as pain throbs across my arm. My sword clatters on the stone. "She doesn't know about them."

"No. I heard. That's good." She lays my injured arm across my abdomen and presses hard with both hands. "You have to heal this, Raith. You have to do it now. I will give you magic." The ribbon that connects our hearts appears and glows like stars in the night sky. She places my other hand over my bleeding arm.

The length of my forearm is marred by a jagged cut that her hands cannot fully cover. Blood rushes from the wound at an alarming rate, seeping between and around her fingers. My vision blurs, and my head is light.

Pressing my free hand over hers, I call my magic and try healing the wound. "Why is there so much blood?"

The panic in Layla's eyes scares me more than the pain

surging up my arm. "It's a deep cut, but this seems like too much blood."

"Must be poison." My voice is calmer than I feel. Father would be proud of that. Strange, that's what I'm thinking about as my body grows weaker. My legs feel as if they've been weighted.

"Look at me, Raith." The way her voice is both stern and panicked at once draws my gaze to hers.

Out of focus, but still beautiful, I can't help feeling joy when I look at her.

Flecks of gold in her eyes sparkle like firelight. "You have to heal yourself. I will feed you my magic, but you have to funnel it to healing."

I think I nod, but there's a disconnect between my brain and the rest of me. If I don't get to healing soon, I'm certain it will be too late. Death isn't scary anymore. I'm at peace with the idea, but leaving Layla terrifies me. "I'll heal."

When she nods, it looks as if there are dozens of versions of my beautiful mate all moving at different times.

Forcing aside my drugged state of mind, I close my eyes and move my good hand under Layla's to press on the wound. The warmth and ferocity of her magic flowing through me helps clear my mind. The poison migrates through my bloodstream, toward the cut on my arm, and out.

Through our connection, white hot energy fuels me, and the speed of healing burns my arm with excruciating pain. "Easy, *mo anam cara*," I say through gritted teeth.

The power filling me slows, but it's still steady as flesh, muscle, nerves, and the vein knit back together. My vision clears, and my body lightens from the fugue.

It's easier to breathe, and in the distance, the hobbling

smudge of black dog continues to retreat. He's moving fast, even with his wounds.

The pain in my arm eases. "I'm alright." I turn my arm back and forth.

Layla sits back on her heels. Sweat dots her face, and she's covered in blood.

"Are you hurt?" I take her hands and search for injuries.

Shaking her head, she takes several long breaths. "It's all your blood. So much blood."

She's right about that. My lap and the surrounding rock are covered. It's a miracle I didn't bleed to death. "I've never read anything about the cú sidhes being poisonous. Vanora's dark magic spoiled those creatures. Both claws and teeth must be infectious. I should have been faster. Worrying about you, I lost my focus."

"Don't do it again. I love that you worry for me, but getting yourself killed won't save me." Fear and directness sharpen her tone.

Even though she's right, I don't know how I can ever release my fears of her being injured to keep myself safe. Something to work on, I suppose. "I'll try." Pushing to my knees, I test my balance as I rise to my feet. Surprisingly steady, I pull Layla into my arms. "Thank you for saving me." I kiss the top of her head.

Pressed tight to me with her arms wrapped around my waist, she steadies her breath. "We need to go inside and make as many weapons as we can, and then we need to get the hell out of Dodge."

"What is Dodge?"

"I mean, we don't have three more days to work. What if

Vanora sends more dogs?" Leaning back, she takes my hand, and we walk up the rocky hillside toward the cave.

"Or sends something worse." I let the warmth of the sun give me more magical strength. "I hope you have enough magic to do this. We don't have much time."

"At least we have one advantage. She doesn't know about our elves. She thinks she killed all the elves on this planet, and she seemed proud of that." Layla pulls a sour face. "She's a monster, far worse than those dogs."

"You'll get no argument from me. Vanora Braddish is a hideous monster who has defiled all the laws of light magic to build her army and gain control of two worlds. This one, she's already destroyed." I point to the faint outline of Domhan. It's just a blue and green orb that appears hazy through the atmosphere. "My world will be next."

"Then mine?"

We continue to climb. My legs ache from the effort and the residual effects of poison coursing through my veins. "It's possible she will continue to whatever world she can access. She knows about you and the other humans, so Earth is a logical next conquest for her."

Gripping my hand hard, she stops. "Oh my god. She said she found your brothers. Raith! Are we too late?"

A band tightens around my heart. I search the universe for my brothers' essences. Even so far away, I sense they have not moved on to the next world. My father always said my magic is strong but unfocused, yet I could always feel the people I love. "I think she lied. Besides, if she destroyed the other humans, why would she need you? Domhan needs all three of the women in the prophecy. If you were the last one, it wouldn't matter if she captured you or not." Feeling more confident in my theory, I draw a deep breath. "She lied. I'm sure of it."

Layla's shoulders relax. "I'm glad. After all this time, I can't wait to meet all the members of your family and the other two humans."

At the cave's mouth, I turn toward the fully risen sun and open my magic up to receive as much energy as I can in a minute or two.

"We need to make Tog understand what's happened and agree to move to the other camp earlier than scheduled." She rounds the side of the cave and washes blood from her hands in the trickle coming off the mountain.

I follow, and though I clean away the blood from my flesh, a long scar still mars my arm. There's also a long tear in my tunic, and both my clothes and Layla's are covered in my blood. "I think he'll see reason. If not, we'll make more weapons and pray Vanora is slow in returning."

Chapter Ten

LAYLA

While Tog readies his people, Raith and I make more weapons in the caves. "What if she sends more dogs to chase us?"

Arms full of swords and daggers, he adjusts them and drops two. I pick them up.

"Then you'll burn them."

"What if I can't get my fire to come?" The panic in my voice is embarrassing, but I'm seriously freaking out that these people might get killed because I'm not enough.

Ban, who came with us, smiles widely, though I don't think he understands my words. I'm sure he senses my doubt and fear.

"What happened to the woman who saved my life on the hillside?"

"She realized a lot of people are counting on her, and I've only been using magic for a few months." We should have practiced more. Sleep is overrated. Instead of sleeping, I should have been learning how to throw fire more accurately.

We reach the main cavern and drop the fifty or more blades we made. They're more refined than the first ones, but still need to be sharpened. There's no time for that now. I kneel beside Raith and help him strap them all together one by one until we have three bunches. They're heavy, but they'll have to be carted along.

The fire is out for the first time since we arrived. People are gathering items that must come with us. Others are storing things in the higher alcoves to keep them dry until they return. Even though they have been told this will be their last time in the cave. Even knowing that we're going to take them to the blue and green planet where food and shelter are abundant, they still prepare to come back after the rains.

I don't blame them. I wouldn't trust our plan either. It's hardly a good one. Find out how Vanora reaches Domhan and hijack her portal. This is not likely to work even if we make it past demons and dogs.

"You're going to be fine. Don't worry so much. You're the bravest person I've ever known." Raith squeezes my shoulder. "You better get your bag. It looks like Tog has them ready to go."

I take a step toward the sleep alcove that was home for the last two months. When I realize Raith is not following, I turn back. "What are you doing?"

He points to the first cave we ever explored, the one that leads to the side of the mountain facing the ocean. "I have an idea that I could leave a magical trail up that cave and maybe, anyone who chases will choose wrong and buy us some time."

"That's brilliant. Can you do that?" I immediately regret doubting him, but it's already out.

He shrugs. "We'll see. If I shroud our magic when we leave, and we brush away footsteps for the first hundred feet or so, it could work." He turns and goes to the mouth of the cave.

Watching until I don't see him anymore, I push aside my need to be near him. Through the heart-strand that connects us, I feel him, and that will have to be enough for now. Gathering my meager belongings, I'm sorry we didn't have time to get everyone's clothes dyed darker. We did manage to clothe all the children in dark purple. Kas brilliantly devised a way to pulverize stone and create dye by adding water.

All the furs are packed away for the journey, and I'm crawling out of the bare alcove when a flash of black catches my eye. Raith doesn't believe he has the skills to make the stone send word to his mother. I put the nearly smooth hand-size rock in my bag. I don't think there's anything we can't do together.

I smooth the sand with a group of twigs we've tied together for the purpose. Six men are doing the same along the ramp that comes from the main cave, and the younger people are sweeping footprints off the cavern floor as well.

Sacks of supplies are bound to every back strong enough to carry. I sling my bag across my shoulders and grab a bunch of weapons.

Raith doesn't sweep his steps as he joins me. He wants whoever comes for us to think someone is using that other cave. Hand in hand, he and I walk into the bad birth cave together. This is one of the few that we never went down. We know it's the one that leads closest to the smoking mountain.

Grinning, Ban takes the weapons from me.

I don't argue. They're heavier than they look.

Raith gives the elf, who's probably around his age, a nod of approval. Carrying both a large bundle of foodstuffs and a bunch of our magic-made weapons, Raith probably regrets he couldn't unburden me.

The six men with brooms remain at the back to brush away the footprints for a few hundred yards. Brushing sounds echo as the bulk of the group rushes through the tunnel.

When the sweepers abandon the ruse, they join the larger group. Considering we're over a hundred bodies moving down a cave three-men wide, there is minimal sound. It's as if the journey toward the bad birth has pulled all the joy from the village.

I lean toward Raith. "Do you think it's like this every year?"

"They tend to move quietly, but I think they're more fearful knowing this will be the last time they make this trek." His steps are even with mine, and his arm brushes against me. There's room to make space, but I feel better in the cave lit with only a few torches knowing he's close enough to brush against. Perhaps he feels the same.

Every time a weapon clanks or supplies shift, the sound echoes, and everyone takes a collective breath.

One of the babies cries.

A mother hushes.

Silence descends again.

The cavern was likely the center of the ancient volcano, now dormant. All of the caves were likely lava tubes made long ago, reminding me of the smoking mountain we're heading for.

I feel Raith's trepidation, and I know it's centered around taking me to a place the elves call bad birth. Even I can feel the evil from that place, and we're many miles away. However, if I want to save this race of elves, we need to see what they're dealing with. Ultimately, we have to find a portal. Ideally, we'll find a way to use Vanora's portal without anyone knowing.

Raith leans in. "It will take many days to reach our destination. If you become tired, you must tell me."

"I'll be fine." I love that he worries. "How would the portal have gotten to this world?"

"If Vanora made it, it would mean her powers have grown. I rather think the portal must have been here from the time of the old gods. Just as there are elves on both worlds, it's logical that if there are ancient portals still working on Domhan, then why not here?"

The quiet of only shuffling feet leaves my mind with too much time. I miss mobile phones and hot showers. Getting around in a car rather than hoofing it for a hundred miles to find a witch queen who wants to kill me, or worse. Even so, I wouldn't trade this found family for the life I left behind. In Los Angeles, I lived in a small apartment, always fearing a break-in, though I had nothing to lose. Now I fear evil, and every person around me is precious to me. I wouldn't go back even if I knew I could prove to every foster parent I ever lived with that they were wrong about me. I've already done that, even if they'll never know. I know.

I stumble, and Raith wraps a hand around my upper arm even though I'm an athlete and would have righted myself. The warmth of his touch through my shirt lets his abiding love seep through me like a blanket. "Thanks."

His lips twitch.

Several miles behind us, a thunderous sound fills the cave. Heavy feet on stone. The shrill of shadow demons. Another sound that grows and scrapes inside my head. The howl of those giant black dogs.

We all stop as one. The torch bearers extinguish the fires. There's a collective inhale with no release. Slowly, we sit on the floor of the cave.

Raith uses magic to dull any inadvertent sound, and the effect is a heavy shroud lying on top of us as a damper.

The growls and screeches continue echoing through the caves. It's impossible to tell if the evil beasts are coming toward us or are still in the main cavern. I expect at any moment a baby will cry or a weapon will fall, and we'll have doomed these people to a terrible fate. We should have led the demons away. They would have come for me and left the Aracans alone. They don't even know about the elves, but they will when they scream down this tunnel and attack.

My chest hurts from holding my breath. Closing my eyes, I try to decipher where the noise is coming from, but it's all bouncing around against rock, and pinpointing the location is impossible.

Raith threads his fingers through mine—his voice is soft inside my head. *We should stay behind and fight, and let them escape.*

I nod. Protecting the village is all that matters at this point.

We got these elves into this. It's our responsibility to keep them safe in every way we can.

Pride shines in his expression before he moves to the right and whispers in Tog's ear. The leader shakes his head several times, then eventually slumps his shoulders and gives a short nod.

While Raith and I move to one side, the elves quietly walk on.

The cacophony from the cavern continues long after they are out of sight, and then there is silence. Maybe they took the bait and picked the wrong tunnel.

Drawing his sword, Raith bends his knees and stands ready.

Time ticks by, and my body aches from not moving, while he seems able to hold a battle stance indefinitely. Rather than being unable to move if they come, I crouch and sit back on my heels for a while.

This cave is miles long, and from what I understand, we're not halfway. Time is all we can buy the Aracans. Maybe the battle never comes, but if it does, we have to hold the demons back by whatever means necessary. Those lovely elves took care of us when we were lost and without friends, and now it's our turn to keep them safe for as long as we can, no matter the cost.

It feels as if we've been waiting an hour or more when the first clash of metal on stone echoes down the tunnel.

I leap to my feet and draw fire without letting it spark to life. It settles in my chest like a shield.

Clashes and clangs of a war party that doesn't care if they are heard grow louder, closer.

My heart pounds against the fire inside me.

Steady, Raith's voice is like a balm to my soul. *They are far yet.*

I have no idea how he can tell the distance. To me, it's just noise banging against stone, and they could be mere feet from us.

It's not my place to fight a war. I'm just a girl from California with no training and few skills. I'm nobody. Except that here in this world and in Raith's world, I'm a human from the prophecy. Here, I have fire magic and can keep the people I love safe. The man at my side loves me without doubts or prejudices. He hides nothing from me and would die to protect me. How can I do less? I can't. I won't.

The noise of the coming battle hurts my ears. I glance at Raith.

He nods. *Close now.* Lifting his hand, he makes his magic glow so bright white that it's blue against the purple rock. He rears back and throws it down the tunnel.

Before it explodes, it illuminates the empty eyes of shadow demons, too many to count, sending my heart into my throat and making my legs feel like jelly. "My god."

Two elven men lead the way, their eyes black and devoid of reason, much like the two we killed outside the main cave that day. Bewitched. The other creature I saw must have been a nightmare. Nothing so horrible can exist in reality.

Raith conjures another ball of light magic.

The fire inside me fights to get free. I pull it from my center and send it from my fingers.

The cave heats like an inferno, forcing Raith and me to back up.

One of the elven soldiers goes up in flames. His screams fill the space while the rest of his party watches him burn.

The acrid stench makes me gag.

The other elf roars. "The queen only wants you. The Riordan can go free if you come now. Don't you want to get out of the muck and grime of life on this miserable planet, human? If you come with us, she'll take you to her palace on Domhan, where you can have all the luxury you deserve. Save that disappointment of an elf and come with us now."

Magic in hand, Raith throws it down the tunnel.

The elf steps aside, and two shadow demons burn to ash.

The creature behind them flashes red eyes and slick black teeth. The size of three men, it takes up most of the passage. Two eyes, a nose, and a mouth, but all malformed and distorted. It shifts its jaw, baring its teeth and letting out a strangled roar. With it comes another smell, not of this world.

"Brimstone," Raith tells me without my having to speak the words. "That beast is from Coire. The place where souls that have embraced the dark go to suffer for eternity."

"Hell." I'm not at all certain fighting a demon from hell was within our plan to survive this journey and get to his home, but I'm not giving up my elf for anyone. Hesitant to risk more fire in such a close space, I don't know how to help.

Your magic comes when you ask for what you need, mo anam cara.

The soldier elf watches me as if he's giving me time to decide to come with them. He knows my fire is useless unless I want to burn myself and Raith, too. It already nearly singed us, and it wasn't enough to destroy the enemy. The amount I would need to kill them all would be a fireball. I dig down, asking for help from someone I don't know. *Please. I need these evil creatures gone and for Raith to be safe. Help me.*

A chill starts in my chest where the fire was. It runs down my arms. Moisture seeps from the walls and charges through me as if I'm a sponge. My hands glow blue. I have no idea what is about to happen, but the power glows all around me. "I'm going to counter your offer. If you turn and run now, I won't destroy you right here in this cave. If you run now, you can tell your queen that she's messing with the wrong human, and I'm coming for her next."

Raith whispers. "By the old gods, Layla. You're magnificent."

"Maybe you should get behind me," I whisper back. "I have no idea what's coming."

Gaping, he gives a short laugh and does as he's told. "Concentrate on whatever that red-eyed demon is."

Shadow demons terrify me, but I don't know if my magic is going to do any good. All I know is that I asked, and something new is about to erupt from me. Taking a deep breath, I let loose this new magic.

White barbs shoot from my hands and slam the beast in the chest. Roaring, it rushes forward. Its pounding feet shake the mountain around us.

There's screaming, and I realize it's me as the cold of my ice magic runs up my arms to my elbows. I draw more water from the mountain and beyond. Water runs from outside through my feet and out my fingers, making ice daggers that pierce the beast's skin.

Reeking of brimstone, red eyes wide and fierce, it reaches for me. Its skin turns from black to blue, and it grabs my braid. The roaring stops, and it falls backward like a tree, taking my hair and me with it.

Lying across the monster's chest, I push, but my hair is trapped in its frozen fingers.

Raith leaps up next to me, wraps his arm around my waist, raises his sword and severs its fingers. They crumble, releasing me. Drawing me back and putting distance between us and the shadow demons, Raith yells, "Throw the ice at the shadows."

Barely coherent after falling into a beast from hell, I don't think. I do as he says.

A ball of Raith's light follows my ice, illuminating every shard and creating a dozen prisms.

I scream so loud that magic vibrates the shards and they explode with blinding light. The shadow demons' screams feel as if they will make my head crack open. Backing up, I hold my ears, and the ash of those demons wafts to the tunnel floor. With no idea how I knew that would succeed, I sit, and shock shakes me to my bones.

Raith steps over the frozen demon and faces the elf.

His black-and-red armor is covered in ash and the blood of his fallen comrade. Hands shaking, he raises his arched saber to defend against my magnificent elf prince. "In the name of Vanora Braddish, the true queen, I stand."

Rather than lift his sword, Raith floods the enemy with light. His magic fills the other elf's chest and pours through him until he glows with it. Raith says, "Dark magic dies in the light. Your free will is restored." He steps back and lowers his voice. "May you choose wisely."

"Eoghan." The elf says and leans against the wall. Tugging his helmet off, he tosses it to the ground. His black eyes shift to green and clear.

"Is that your name?" Raith asks.

Nodding. "It was. Before she took me away from my home, they called me Eoghan. Her soldiers have no names."

As the ice melts, the Coire demon shifts.

Raith steps to the left, lifts his sword with two hands, and removes the monster's head from its shoulders. The head rolls away, following the tunnel's natural slope.

"Don't let its blood touch you. It feeds on life." Eoghan closes his eyes and stays leaning.

My braid shifts on its own. Frozen bits of demon flesh wiggle like centipedes turning black. "Raith!" I grip a spot higher on my hair and hold it away from me.

Leaping over the demon, he pulls out a dagger and slices the bottom of my braid away. It wriggles as if it might come to life on its own. "How do we kill it and whatever is in the blood?"

"I...I don't know." He holds his head as if it might explode. "I heard her say something about the blood will consume the host. I'm not sure a bit of hair is what she had in mind."

The bit of my hair turns slimy and black, but it slows as does the flow of blood from the beheaded demon. By the time the bleeding stops, whatever was feeding on my braid is inert.

Eoghan skirts around it and looks from me to Raith. "How did she do that? I've never seen magic like that."

Before Eoghan reaches us, Raith points his sword at the center of his chest and lifts the dagger in his other hand. "You have a choice, Eoghan. You can go back to Vanora the way you came, or you can choose the light and join us." He sighs. "I suppose you might also choose to attack us, and then you will meet the same fate as the others." He lifts the tip of his sword to just under Eoghan's chin.

Pulling myself together, I stagger to my feet. Muscle memory is the only thing keeping me upright when I want to curl into a ball and sleep for a week. Well, that and the dead, headless demon crowding this part of the tunnel out.

Looking into Eoghan's eyes, I see a well of regret in the blue-white magic light from the ball Raith sent out before the fight.

"Lower your sword, Raith. I don't think we are in danger."

Eoghan's gaze shifts to mine. "You are from the prophecy."

"I'm human." I don't really know about the whole prophecy thing, but I'm not arguing that I'm human, and I have developed some crazy magic over the last couple of months. "My name is Layla. How did you come to be part of Vanora's army?"

Keeping his body between Eoghan and me, Raith lowers his sword an inch.

"I was in the fields with my brother. We had to get the grain before the winter snows fell. The shadow demons came and carried me away. I don't know where my brother is. Vanora's eyes were the next thing I saw and the last full memory I have. Though I have glimpses of death, fire, elves who died at my hands, and..." Tears stream down his face. "It would be a favor to me if you would slit my throat."

Raith sighs. "It will not lessen your guilt, Eoghan. For that, you will need to live and be redeemed in the light. Come with us." He wipes his sword on the other elf's clothes and returns it to his sheath. Taking my hand, he looks me in the eyes, searching my face for injury. "Can you run?"

"I think so." I pick up an abandoned torch and bring it back to life with my fire.

Pulling his magic back inside him, Raith smiles. "Let's catch up."

His armor heavy, Eoghan sounds like a rhino trudging along with us. "What are we catching up to?"

With a chuckle, Raith says, "Redemption."

Chapter Eleven

RAITH

It's no surprise that Layla can not only keep up with Eoghan and me, but she's barely out of breath when we're met by Tog and five Aracan elves sent to protect the others from whatever was running toward them. Meanwhile, I'm a bit winded, and it takes me a moment to catch my breath.

Tog grabs Layla by the shoulders and scans her from head to toe. "Hurt?"

"No." She accepts his embrace and relaxes. "Where are the others?"

Releasing her, Tog points down the dark cave. He looks at me and gives half a smile. Staring at Eoghan and his black armor with a blood red slash across the front of the chest, he takes a step back.

Eoghan's eyes bulge at the sight of native elves. "I thought she killed them all." He undoes the buckles on the side of his armor, leans over, and lets the symbol of the witch queen tumble over his head and land in a heap on the ground. He does the same to the leather guarding his legs. In a tattered tunic and leggings, he looks like any other elf. His braided brown hair falls to mid-back. His clear green eyes, though filled with fear, are clear of dark magic.

Stepping forward, Tog studies the newcomer. "You bad?"

Throat bobbing, Eoghan meets Tog's gaze. His voice is tight. "I don't know."

For a long moment, the two stare at each other while Tog takes his measure of the elf.

Layla steps close, as if to intervene.

I send her a quick warning to wait, and she stops, worry wrinkling her brow.

An eternity passes in a minute. Tog nods and turns back to me. "Come. Near end."

Within a quarter of a mile, fresh air filters through the tunnel. A swell of relief fills me as if the dread of a billion pounds of rock and earth falling in on us has finally been removed.

Walking with Tog, I say, "The soldiers are bespelled with dark magic."

"Yes." He nods and frowns deeply. "Bad."

I crook my thumb toward Eoghan, who walks with Ban and Gaf behind us. "How did you know?"

"Bad elf, think good. Good elf, never sure." Ever the sage, Tog never ceases to surprise me.

Nothing about the Aracan elves is what I've always been told. They may not have written language, but as Layla pointed out to me, they definitely have some rudimentary magic. They are smart and learn easily. In many ways, they are far superior to my elven people. We have isolated ourselves from other species on Domhan, using excuses. We claim centaurs are vicious, dwarves are greedy, fairies hate elves, and giants are violent, when the truth is I've never met anyone from any of those cultures. My people think Aracans are so simple that we call them lesser elves. The truth is far different. They are not less. Perhaps they are different, or maybe they have chosen a different path.

Saving these elves probably means destroying their culture. Still, there's no other choice. I've spent two months searching for an alternative where their way of life isn't eradicated. There is no choice but to get them off of this planet before they starve or Vanora turns them all into shadow demons.

Starlight beams into the cave, and we put out our torches. Villagers line the ridge that leads down the mountain. In the distance, the smoking mountain looms, but the joy at seeing them all alive and well cannot be dampened.

Kas pulls Layla into a warm embrace and mutters in Old Elvish about how she worried and prayed.

Patting her back, Layla assures her that she is fine.

Tog goes to the center, where a pile of stones has been made rather than a wood fire.

Joining him there, I crouch, place my hand on the stones, and heat them. The air grows colder, and the young and old will need warmth through the night.

Several women holding babies smile up at me, and I can't help the pleasure it gives me to do this small thing for them.

After digging through a bag, Tog hands Eoghan a piece of dried meat.

Unsure, Eoghan stares at the food, then looks at me. "They would feed me, their enemy?"

"Are you sure that's what you are? To them, you are part of the village now. You have chosen." I turn to the food stores and accept enough for Layla and me.

She's across the path, leaning against an old tree that reminds me of a yew, though without leaves it's hard to tell. Three women are around her, asking after her health and looking for whatever hurt they can help with. Assuring them that she is unharmed save for a few bruises, she smiles at me as I approach, my hands full of our evening meal.

The women rise and give me various looks of both disappointment and admiration as they pass, leaving us alone. Maybe Sil doesn't like that I allowed Layla to go into battle. There's really no help for that. I wish with all my might that it were different. She's from the prophecy, and she's here to defeat Vanora and save my world.

Sorrow settles around my shoulders like a heavy cloak of wishes that can't be granted. If we'd known the witch queen was destroying Arcania, would we have tried to save this place, or keep to ourselves as we have throughout history?

Sitting next to my human, the answer both plagues and eludes me.

She leans into my shoulder. "Stop beating yourself up. You're helping now."

It's both a blessing and a curse that she can so easily read my thoughts. I hand her the strips of dried meat wrapped in an edible leaf. "Eat. I don't know how long we'll be able to rest here, but you need food after all the energy you expended."

Letting out a long sigh, she nibbles on the deer meat. "I

don't like killing, but that thing in there, it doesn't belong in this world. It made me nauseous, like being on a roller coaster."

"I don't know what that is." Though I share her feelings about the wrongness of the Coire demon not belonging here.

"A roller coaster is an amusement ride, where you sit in a cart, and it rolls very fast around a wild track. It makes the stomach roil." Leaning back, she closes her eyes, having barely eaten her food.

"It would be interesting to explore your world one day." Maybe that's how I keep my soulmate in my life. That may be my path if we survive the war to come.

She slips her hand into her bag and pulls out the obsidian I left behind. "Don't give up on home, Raith. Maybe together..." Her eyes are filled with love and belief in me.

I hate that I will likely disappoint her at some point.

I take the cool rock in my hand. "I don't know how to force it into the scrying stone from the cave. Seeing my mother was a fluke."

"It was a sign, and now we have to stop forcing things and accept that we are better together than apart. I was just a poor orphaned woman with few friends and a chip on my shoulder. Now I'm saving lives and have found my soulmate. Whatever you were before, you are better now. You are the savior of all of these people. They need you. I need you. If we weren't supposed to contact your mother, we never would have walked into that part of the cave, the wall would never have revealed itself as obsidian, and you wouldn't have remembered some one-off bit of text you read twenty years ago." She places her hand over mine so that we're holding the stone between us.

"It wasn't quite that long ago." I kiss her fingers. "I trust you, *mo anam cara*. Do your magic, and I'll direct the stone from my memory of the scroll."

She closes her eyes, and her thoughts fill my mind as if they were my own. *Our need is great. Making this into a scrying stone so we can save these beautiful lives.* Gratitude flows through and around her, warming me from the inside out, as the beauty of who Layla is cannot be contained.

The stone brightens, making our hands glow. I grab a shirt from her pack and throw it over our hands. Light shining from the side of this mountain might call things and people we do not want to find us.

The warmth of a new kind of magic tickles my fingers and rushes up my arm and settles in my chest.

Layla's other hand presses against her breast.

Rather than disappearing, the magic settles in the crevices inside me and becomes part of me. "This is..." I have no idea what it is. "New." It's the best I can do.

Opening her eyes, she takes a shaky breath. Lifting her hand reveals the perfectly smooth obsidian. It's slightly smaller than when we started, and a thin powder catches the breeze and whisks away from my palm.

From the center, it sparks to life. The ceiling of the throne room lights with scenes of the old gods. The Dagda and his magical harp, Uaithne, come into focus as they work to put the Fomorians to sleep. This must be through Mother's scrying bowl. "Mother, are you there?"

"Do you know this place?" Layla touches the smooth obsidian, and the picture sharpens rather than distorts.

"It's my home. I think at the other end is a magical bowl where my mother can communicate long distances."

There are voices, but I can't make out what they're saying. The image fades.

"Raith?" It sounds like Mother calling my name, but an instant later it is gone. The black rock goes dark and cold again.

Frustration rushes through me. "Useless." I drop the rock.

Picking it up, she puts it in her bag. "We're tired, and maybe it's not yet time to reach your family. Don't give up hope."

Hope. Unable to form logical words, I grunt. I'm a complete idiot. Once she realizes I have no control over my magic and a terrible instinct for what to do in almost any situation, I could lose her. My chest tightens painfully. I press my hand to my heart. It shouldn't hurt so much to think of the time when Layla will look at me with the same disappointment I see in my father's eyes, and even in Mother's sometimes, before she can hide it. My oldest brother, Aaran, always shakes his head at my ineptitude. Only Liam, the middle son and closest to me in age, never loses faith in me. I've often wondered why he always believes in me when I prove him wrong over and over. Liam believes my magic is special.

I mutter an oath. "Special, my ass."

After eating a few more bites of the meat and making a terrible face when she tastes the leaf, Layla raises an eyebrow. "What was that?"

"Nothing. I was thinking about my brother." The forest, without leaves and only darkness at this time of the day, feels as if it has eyes.

"Which brother?"

"Liam."

"That's the soldier?" she asks.

"Yes. He's an excellent soldier and a thoughtful man. He's quieter than Aaran or I, but I think he sees more." I shake my head. "I'm not making any sense."

"Quiet people listen and see more because their focus is on others. At least that's what I think." She shrugs. "But what do I know?"

"You know a lot. I think you're right about Liam anyway. He's always focused on who he can save or how he can help someone else. Smart and strong, he will never be king, but that doesn't bother him. His focus is always on protecting." I miss him.

"Was that what you were thinking?" Eyebrow raised, it's clear she heard some or all of my thoughts.

"Liam always said that my magic was unique, that maybe I struggle with controlling it because the oracle and other teachers don't understand it." I shake my head at the nonsense. The oracle knows everything about magic.

"You know..." She swallows the last bite of meat and hands me the leaf with a sour expression. "I think Liam has a point. I know nothing about magic, yours or anyone's, but you have been wonderful since we got here."

"If I had been in control of my magic, you would have been in a soft bed with a hot bath months ago." My gut tightens. She should know who she's chosen.

A crease forms between her eyes and deepens. "If that had been the case, we wouldn't have known that the Aracans need us. We never would have met this village, and they would have been doomed to death or worse. Your magic did exactly what it was supposed to do. It got us here." She draws a long breath that makes her breasts rise. "And we might never have had the time to fall in love. You wouldn't have discovered that you can control your magic." She holds up a hand. "Don't argue with me. I've seen you use your magic a hundred different ways, and it's been accurate and effective. The obsidian aside, because we will still get that to work. You have saved these people. You have destroyed enemies and even forgiven them. We are moving closer to our ultimate goal with a new and wonderful family by our side. Stop beating yourself up."

She believes everything she's said. She sees me as a hero.

Funny, I see her the same way. Maybe I've changed. My magic has grown calmer. When I call it, the way is clear, where there was doubt before. "I wonder if it was the doubt that hindered me. Since I met you, I can see myself through your eyes and..." My cheeks heat. "You see me in a way I never dreamed possible."

Moving closer, she rests her head on my shoulder. "We are a good team."

I kiss her soft hair.

"How do you know what brimstone smells like?" Her voice is sleepy.

I eat the leaf she wouldn't and lean my head against the rough tree. There's no life inside, which makes me sad. "The oracle made us memorize certain scents, and brimstone is one you never forget."

"It's like burning sulfur and coal." Her nose wrinkles. "I have a bad feeling we'll be smelling it again before this is over."

Somehow, Vanora found a way for a demon to survive outside of Coire. I imagine Layla is right.

The journey is wearing on Layla. In her world, they have vehicles with combustion engines. I can't even offer her a horse. Yet, for more than two weeks, she has walked without complaint.

The bulk of the villagers left us three days ago. As we reach the base of the smoking mountain, our small party comprises Tog, Eoghen, Ban, Gaf, Dar, Layla and me.

I know it weighs on the elves to be without proof that their people arrived at their winter home unharmed. I hope they made the journey without incident, but our focus must be on the mountain and whatever is within.

Eoghen probably needed to go and rest with the others, but I need him. His skin has taken on a pasty pallor, and his eyes are bloodshot. It's as if losing the link to Vanora has left him little to survive on. "This is madness, Raith. We should join the others and leave this evil place."

"I heard you the first ten times. We need to see what's inside, and since you say you haven't been within the mountain, I have to see for myself." I pat his shoulder. "Don't let fear rule you. Even when you feel it, which is normal, you must control it and do what needs to be done." I'm sounding more and more like my father these days.

The farther we climb up the east side of the mountain, the more distressed Eoghen becomes. "This is madness."

Layla turns and presses her finger against his chest. "What is in that mountain? No one can be this nervous without knowing what we're facing." Without using any magic, she backs him against a rocky outcropping.

Ban and Dar flank her. As the only other female in our party, Dar has taken the role of Layla's protector. The tall, strong elf learns quickly and is skilled with a bow. She looms over Eoghan, ready to pounce if given the word.

Standing next to me, Tog crosses his arms. "Good woman."

She's magnificent. I nod.

Wary of the human who froze the demon in the cave, the Domhan elf holds his hands up in surrender. "The beast in the cave came from within this horrible place. The witch queen calls up things from Coire and uses the blood of elves to bring them to life here."

Stepping just behind Layla, I stare at him. "You lied. What else have you lied about?"

Shaking his head so fast his hair whips around his face, he says, "No. I have not been inside. I told you the truth. I only know she builds her army within the pit deep under this burning rock. I was assigned that creature to capture the human and kill the elf. That was the first one of the abominations I've seen." He pauses. "And the cú sidhe black dogs. They should not be here. She throws the bodies of elves she has killed to the dogs to feed on." He shivers.

Layla's eyes narrow. "How do we get inside unseen?"

"I've told you what is in there. It's madness to enter. You're walking into her hands. She's obsessed with the three from the prophecy. Once she learned you were on Arcania, she sent sentries to every corner of this place, and when those sent to the east didn't return, she sent the dogs. When she saw you through the beast, an insanity came over her.

She erupted with dark magic that killed ten soldiers. She killed her own soldiers with her unchecked rage. You must stay away from her." Tears stream down his face.

Turning to face me, Layla says, "I think we have to see what we're fighting. What do you think?"

My basest instinct is to take her far from here and keep her safe. But the truth is, whatever the viper conjures in this world is for the purpose of destroying Domhan. It's my responsibility as the son of Elspeth Riordan to protect the realm at all costs. "We need to see what she's created. We must stop her if we can. Then, when that is done, we must find the portal and a way to return to Domhan."

Eoghan leaps up from the rocks, but Dar pushes him back and away from Layla. "I can take you to the portal. I don't have the magic to open it, but it's on the western edge of the ridge that runs along the mountain where the forest ends. You needn't bother with the evil within. Just get away. Go home."

His logic is not without merit, but it is borne of fear for his own safety. I can understand it, but leaving Arcania ignorant of what happens in Vanora's lair here would be a mistake. "How can we get inside without being detected?"

Sinking into himself, he points to our left. "We need to climb around to the north side. There is a ventilation shaft. You can enter there and see the vile pit."

We pick through the dead forest, climbing and curving around the mountain. I half expect Eoghan to run away, but he remains with us, silent and sullen.

Perhaps he was so long under the weight of dark magic that none of his light has found its way to his heart.

Tog leads the way, his steps even as he moves tirelessly.

A fog settles around us, filling the space between the tree trunks. The stench of brimstone lives in the haze. "Where did this come from?"

"We're getting close to the shaft now. This is steam, not fog." Eoghan steps faster and points to our right.

A mile above us, foul mist puffs from the side of the slope. With the skeleton trees and the settling smoke of Coire, it feels as if we're all that lives in this gods-forsaken place. Maybe we are. The ground is spongy, likely from the constant moisture pushing out of that fissure.

"How can we move through that?" Layla asks. She winds what's left of her braid around her hand. When it's too short to wrap around properly, she drops it.

"We wait for the venting to stop. When it does, we'll have enough time to crawl in, and you can see what you need to." Eoghan mutters something about madness, but keeps the details to himself as he continues moving toward our goal.

Tog grabs my arm. "Look. No kill?"

Everyone stops and stares at me, waiting for the answer. "Look. At least for now." I imagine once we see what we're dealing with, we'll need a plan. I wish I'd been a better student of strategy. I miss my brother Liam more than ever.

Layla takes my hand. "We'll probably only get one shot at this. We need to see what's inside and find the portal."

I nod. "Then go to the camp and plan how to get the elves through the portal and mess up as much of Vanora's plan as we can on our way out."

Smiling at me, she nods. "It's going to be a piece of cake."

"What does cake have to do with it?" It must be another human thing.

"It means that it will be easy, but I was being a little

sarcastic." She climbs the rocks and then waits on the ledge for the rest of us to reach her.

Someday, when all of this is over, I'm going to learn all of her human colloquialisms. That thought fills me with hope as my muscles complain about the climb. It could be ten times as far. If Layla were at the top, I would find a way to reach her.

Chapter Twelve

LAYLA

One of the ways I trained for the superhero competition was rock climbing, and it's a skill that's coming in handy right now. It's a steep climb from the bare trees to the ventilation shaft.

There's not one single guard or patrol. Vanora must believe she's invulnerable. Once I reach the small shelf just above the foul steam, I wait for the others to catch up.

Raith is only a few steps behind with Dar on his heels. The rest are about thirty feet below.

Sitting with my legs hanging over the side, I take slow, deep breaths and try my best not to think about how much danger lies ahead. When I look at Raith and all my new friends, I know this is the right path. More importantly, if given the choice between the safety of my unsatisfying life on Earth or fire and ice flying from my fingers, paired with my feelings for Raith, I would choose to stay and fight every time.

Raith and Dar join me.

Dar stands behind, watching for danger. Her black hair and bright blue eyes are in stark contrast as she fists her hands, ready to defend.

"How are you?" Raith asks, brushing the dirt and grime from his hands.

"I've climbed much harder terrain than this," I assure him.

He waits for me to look at him. "That's not what I meant. I think you probably know that since you're in my head most of the time. Are you afraid?"

"Of course, I'm afraid. I'd have to be an idiot not to be. We're going to crawl through a ventilation shaft to spy on our enemy, who is using evil magic to make hell on earth." Well, not Earth, but here. I don't correct myself aloud.

With a hint of a smile, he leans in and kisses my lips. It's a quick kiss, but his love comes through like an arrow from my bow. "We should go with just Tog and Gaf. The others can wait here for us."

"Dar is not going to like being left behind." I look over my shoulder at her.

The elf stares at us as if she's ready to make her argument.

Raith explains in Old Elvish that he needs her to stay here and keep watch over Eoghan. "We may still need him, and he definitely needs us."

Tog reaches the top. He looks down at the Domhan elf and shakes his head. "He run?"

Worry reaches me through my connection with Raith.

He sighs. "Then let him go. We're not responsible for his redemption."

"Go witch?" Tog worries that Eoghan will betray us.

"I don't think so." Even so, Raith shrugs. "We have to move forward, and we can't do that if we're chasing him. Besides, he could have run already."

I'm probably the only one present who understood everything Raith said, but Tog nods and relays the information to Dar as the others reach the rock shelf.

Raith turns to Eoghan. "Stay here. When we come back, we will find a place to rest, then have a look at the portal."

Relief relaxes Eoghan's face, and he sits against the sheer wall of rock above the rough entrance to the hellish mountain.

Smoke puffing from the vent slows, then stops altogether.

"Ready?" Raith asks.

With a quick nod before my fears have time to sink in, I climb around the opening and swing inside. It's barely tall enough for me to stand up straight. "Be careful. You'll have to duck." I'm tall for a human woman, but the elves are taller, and they will have to walk hunched.

Gaf is broader than the rest, and I'm concerned he may not fit at all. However, he swings inside without any issues, followed by Raith and Tog.

Leading the way through the hole in the mountain, Gaf treads as if on air, and we follow close behind. Brimstone and death fill my nostrils, and it's all I can do not to gag. If this tunnel is like the ones where we lived before, the sound will carry, so my nausea will have to wait.

We don't have to go far. It's only perhaps a hundred yards before we reach an iron grate. Maybe it was put here to keep animals out or something in. Moving slowly, Raith puts his hand on Gaf's shoulder to stop him. He steps around the bigger elf and reaches for me. Together, we ease close to the grate. The chamber is twice, maybe three times the size of where the Aracans were living. The walls are black, covered in an oily, black substance, and the chamber glows orange. Below is a pulsating hole that emanates heat and evil. The source of the heat and light is below that.

Not sure what it is I'm seeing, my pulse triples, and my stomach tightens. It's unfamiliar, but on some base level, I know it's evil beyond anything.

At the sound of heavy footsteps on stone, we press ourselves against the walls of the vent. Tog and Gaf do the same on the other side.

There are only two caves from this chamber. The one to the west must take Vanora to the gate, and the east, I suppose, is to reach different parts of Arcania.

From the east emerge six of the beasts like the one Raith and I killed in the cave. Their black skin shines in the hellish glow, and they grunt and growl with thick saliva dripping from their deformed mouths. Between them, they drag two elves. A male and a female, both naked, and their skin tight to bone from starvation.

Everything inside me screams for us to do something to save those poor people.

Raith grips my arm and shakes his head.

I know he wants to help. We can't get past the grate, save the elves, kill the demons, and escape. It's impossible. Helplessly, we watch the female sliced in half and dumped into the pit. Her blood bubbles as her body soundlessly sinks into muck.

The male elf cries out in an attempt to reach her, but he's dragged along the landing that surrounds the pit. When they're just below us, the second elf meets the same fate.

Tears roll down my face, but I have no opportunity for grief. The roiling muck expands, and flames burst free from the edges.

Demon hands rip through the filmy surface and reach for the rock ledge. Emerging from their putrid shell, they let out screams that hurt my ears as they pull themselves up. Five in all emerge, grunting and screaming.

More march down the east tunnel hauling baskets of bloody meat that they dump on the ground before hurrying away. Even the original six who carried in the elves move as far from the newborn demons as possible.

Like starved beasts, they fight for the meat, and I try not to think about who was killed to feed these monsters.

Taking the lead, Raith leads us back the way we came. As soon as we climb out and up to the others, he pulls me into his arms.

I cry against him, wishing it were safe to scream and rage against what I was powerless to stop. The vibration of his anger and regret flows through me, easing my pain. At least I'm not alone. "How many do you think she's made, and how many elves does she keep to feed that pit?"

We turn toward Eoghan as one and wait for an answer.

He stands. "I don't know exactly. Hundreds of demons, maybe a thousand. They say are encamped in the east and will be moved to the portal when the time comes to attack Tús Nua. I was not myself. I never went to those camps, and I don't know where the elves are being held or where she stole them from. I only heard rumors that she would bring them to feed the pit. I never saw them." Fear laces every word, but I believe he's telling the truth.

"Maybe she brings them from Domhan." With his hands on his hips, Raith sighs. "When she spoke through the dog, she said there were no more elves here. She didn't know about the village in the mountain."

He's right, she must bring them from somewhere else.

Raith turns to me. "Do you think we can climb around to the west from here?"

Studying the rocky cliffs and slope, and thinking about the fact that not all of us are expert climbers, I shake my head. "Maybe in daylight, but in the dark, it's perilous. We should climb down. It's safer, and we can make our way around with the cover of the trees, such as they are."

The way down goes faster, and we head into the woods.

Only traveling by night and keeping out of sight during the shorter days, it's more than two full days before we reach the western side of the smoking mountain. We've seen several groups of soldiers, all with demons at their backs. The shadow demons stay above the smoke and float on the breezes.

There has been no sign of Vanora.

Hiding behind a wide tree trunk, Raith points to a pair of standing stones at the far side of the clearing that stretches from the western entrance to the mountain to the remnants of what must have been a great forest. "That's the portal."

It doesn't look like much. Two tall stones and a few broken ones lying in the dirt. Six demons and ten soldiers guard the area, and another four soldiers stand a football field away, guarding the entrance to the mountain and the pit beyond.

Sitting back on my heels, I lean my back against the tree. "How big is Domhan?"

"Big." He faces me in a similar position.

"Where does that gate lead? Will we land near your home?"

Raith takes a long breath and lets it out. "I doubt it. If this led to Tús Nua, someone would have noticed Vanora making the journey long before now."

"Right." Not surprising, but disappointing. "So, we find a way to get a hundred plus elves here without them being seen and trudge through that gate, which you'll have to open. When we land on the other end, we may be attacked."

"That is likely." He frowns.

"What about the elves being held for food and the thing in that mountain?" My meager dinner tries to fight its way up my throat. I swallow and wince. "Do we abandon all of that?"

"I don't think we can." He runs his fingers along my cheek. "I'd like to get you home and to safety, but we need to try to destroy her plans to make more of those things."

Leaning into his palm, I'm relieved he's not ready to jump through to keep me safe. We have people counting on us. "I agree with you. Besides, nowhere is safe. Let's get out of here and make a plan to get our elves someplace with green grass and food."

"Those she keeps in Domhan to feed that thing..." He

shakes his head, takes my hand, and we head back to where we left the others a mile away. "We'll have to find another way to save them once we're home."

"Once we destroy the witch queen, we can find and help everyone she's terrorized." Hearing myself, I can't help but think that I talk a good game. How to do any of this, I have no idea.

He nods. "One problem at a time. Destroy the pit and as many of those demons as possible, and get our elves through the portal."

Tog says that it's just a day's walk away to join the others at the winter camp. Rain starts falling from almost the moment we begin the journey, and we're soaked through. My feet hurt. My back too. I'm cold and tired, but I concentrate on how to destroy that pit and the beings that are born there.

The desire to avenge the elves fuels me to keep walking a few steps behind Tog with Raith on my heels. Hours pass without anyone speaking, and I see the first sprig of green grass. It lifts my spirits. Soon, the trees will have leaves of green and yellow. Some fall with the rain.

The camp sits on the side of a hill with the river running in the valley. The houses are abandoned and run down.

Two dozen stone-and-wood structures have been set amid the woods. If we weren't looking for them, we might miss them entirely as they're camouflaged perfectly with the terrain.

It's a small patch of green in a world nearly devoid of life. The riverbed is close, though the water is reduced to only perhaps ten feet across. Once, it might have cut a hundred-foot swath through this land. It must have been lush and filled with life when the trees had leaves, all the way to the sea and back to the mountain that now houses a pit of evil.

I shiver at the looming presence of the smoking mountain. What a spot to winter. The forest is likely used to provide some separation, but death has taken most of the trees. The small patch of green where they make camp seems inadequate.

Tog embraces Kas and points to the camp's state. "Small now."

Kas laments the river's lack of fish compared to years past.

Tog eases her worries, telling her that we won't be here long, and if need be, the stores they brought will last long enough.

Out of sorts, I wander around saying hello and catching up with the elves. We've been apart almost two weeks, though it feels much longer.

My mind is muddled with so many things, while my arms and legs feel as if they've been weighted down. I'm sitting with a group of teens, and they're telling me about how they're learning to hunt deer and fish. Even as I try to listen, my thoughts wander to the mountain.

Raith lifts me from the stump where I've perched. "You need to rest."

"I don't think I can." With my head lolling against his chest, my eyes roll back as I fight my exhaustion.

Pressing his lips to my forehead, he says, "I think you can. They've made a place for us. We'll sleep now while the others keep watch."

"This place feels too exposed. Just a day's walk from all that evil. What kept it green this long?" I doze off before he answers, then wake as he's placing me on a straw bed. "Did I sleep?"

"Only for a moment." He removes my clothes and heats a pile of rocks that have been placed at the center of the hut. Warmth fills the room and dries me while Raith hangs my sopping pants and shirt over a log serving as a crossbeam. He leaves his shoes and mine near the heat, and strips out of his wet things.

Lying beside me, he wraps his big body around me and pulls my back tight to his front. "The source of light magic that fed this world must be here or near here. Darkness is destroying it, but I think it fights to survive."

So many questions, but my eyes will not stay open, and my mind drifts. Two weeks with minimal sleep and constant danger have caught up with me.

"I see you, human. I know your nightmares, and I'm going to make each one come true." The same voice that came out of the black dog rings against the inside of my head.

There's a haze, and a woman cries out in pain. Someone is dragging her across a stone floor. Blond curls hide her face. A man's large hands have her bound, and he pushes her arm into a slimy golden pool.

She screams.

"You will be next."

The curls shift, and a very round, very human ear shows through.

"I'm coming for you, third of the prophecy."

The stench of evil permeates my dream. The room is adorned with gold and draped in black and red, yet it feels out of place. It's an island in Hell, or Coire as they call it here.

"You're in Hell and making threats."

I'm not even sure she's talking to me.

Vanora screams, but not at me. Something hurt her, and I tumble away from the scene.

I push my head out of the pile of furs covering me in the warm shelter. Light shines through the break in the leather flaps serving as a door.

The dream comes back to me in a rush. Was it a dream? I sit up too fast, and my head spins.

Out of breath, Raith pushes through the flap. "What's wrong?"

Swallowing my panic, I keep my voice soft. "I'm fine. It must have been a dream." I'm not convinced, though. It looms far more real than any dream I ever had.

"What did you dream?" He sits atop the furs next to me and brushes my hair back from my face.

"It was nothing." But I don't believe what I'm saying.

"Tell me, and then I'll get you some food. You must be starving."

There's a scratching at the leather door.

I gather the furs around me.

Raith pulls the flap back and takes a wooden bowl of food from Kas. They may say the Aracans have no magic, but I say that's not true. They sense enough that it's more than instinct.

She grins at me and backs out.

I call out a gentle, "Thank you."

Bringing me the bowl, Raith sits again. "Eat and tell me about your dream."

My stomach growls loudly enough that I flush, embarrassed by how unladylike it sounds. Stupid, after all we've been through, but there it is. "How long did I sleep?" Ravenous, I eat the stew made with rehydrated meat and some bitter leaves. I'm too hungry to mind the leaves.

"A full day and night." His eyes are filled with concern. "I worried, but you seemed fine until a few minutes ago, when I felt your distress."

"I saw your witch queen in a place that was pure evil." I tell him the rest of what I dreamed.

"The woman was human?"

I shrug. I finish the rest of the food and could easily eat another bowlful. "I haven't seen many elves from Domhan, but her ears were round."

"The Aracan elves look similar to Domhan, only our eye color varies more. The Aracan elves seem to be blue-eyed mostly."

"The woman I saw was short and curvaceous. Her face was beautiful, but rounder than anyone here. I don't think she was an elf. She was in agony, but then she hurt Vanora. I'm not sure how, but I'm sure the human injured your witch." I'm transported back into that terrible room surrounded by evil. Shaking myself back to reality, I say, "It was just a dream."

"What did she look like?" He takes the bowl from my tight grip and puts it aside.

"I told you. She was short and blond. I think her hair was curly, though she looked as if she'd been through a lot."

"Not the human. What did Vanora look like?" He brushes my knotted mass of hair away from my face. Even though in desperate need of care and brushing, it falls right back.

I suppose I've been through a lot as well. "Black hair to her waist, her eyes looked dead like a doll's, and she was pale as a sheet of paper. Tall and bony, with long clawlike fingers. Her lips looked as if they'd lost all blood."

Fear sparks in Raith's eyes. "I don't think that was a dream, Layla. You've never seen Vanora, and that was a perfect description."

"How?" I'm shaking my head even though I have no idea what I'm denying.

"A vision. Maybe a connection with the other humans sent to help Domhan."

"And Arcania." My heart tightens, and I clutch my chest. This was all for nothing. "Then she has one of the human women. We can't win."

"You say she hurt Vanora. Maybe she'll survive. If she's as strong and resourceful as you, she'll certainly give the witch queen a run." He pulls me into his arms. "If you feel up to it, get dressed. We're making plans to make our way back to the mountain with the entire village."

"I'll just be a few minutes." As soon as he takes my bowl and leaves, I grab my brush and drag it through my matted hair. It's painful and a struggle, but I manage to get out the bulk of the knots. Digging through my gym bag, I find a hair scrunchie. I make a ponytail, braid it and tie a bit of leather at the bottom. Pulling on clothes that need to be washed or thrown into a fire, I push away the thoughts. Being perfectly clean is not at the top of my list, and it won't be until I can get myself and my friends to safety.

After so much sleep, I feel better than I have in weeks. The sun is near setting, and the majority of the village is sitting in a circle at the center of the camp. A fine coating of snow has covered the ground while I slept, and the air is crisp and cold.

At least the rain has stopped.

Over my shoulder, the top of the smoking mountain looms. Even blurred by clouds and snow, it's a symbol of everything that has gone wrong in this world. Knowing what festers inside that peak makes it even worse.

My heart pounds with foreboding. The dream comes back to me, and I have to blink the images away and concentrate on the here and now.

"Layla, I think we have an idea of how to slow down the demons and soldiers while we make our escape through the portal." Raith pats the open end of the log he's sitting on.

Rubbing the chill out of my hands, I sit. "It's cold. Whatever we do, I think we'll need to do it soon."

The elves are wrapped in their sleeping furs, but they look cold as well.

With a few words, Raith sends more magic to the pile of rocks, and a wave of heat washes over me. "Better?"

I nod. "Where is Eoghan?"

"He went with a group to bring water. It's a long walk to the river, and they want to get full buckets to leave near the heat before the river freezes." Raith looks at a frowning Tog. "I'm told it's not normally this cold so early, and the river is very low."

"We don't have much time." I don't need to be magical or a genius to know that if the climate has changed, the water is nearly gone, and a witch is birthing demons in the looming volcano, we need to move fast.

"This snow is not in our favor. There's no hiding a

hundred footprints in newly fallen snow." His eyes shift to the darkness.

A moment later, I hear footsteps shuffling too. Eoghan, with seven other elves, moves into camp laden with full water buckets. They place them around the heated rocks before taking their places in the circle.

Eoghan sits across from me. He looks better. Perhaps he had a long sleep as well. "The river was frozen over. I used magic to melt the surface."

I didn't think about the fact that Eoghan is from Domhan. "What other kinds of magic can you make?"

He shrugs. "Nothing so fancy as a Riordan, but I can do most elemental magic."

"Can you turn water to ice?" Raith asks, making no show or mention of his family having greater magic than the average elf.

"Yes."

"Can you turn other things to ice?" Behind Raith's eyes, a plan is forming.

Creases form around Eoghan's eyes, and he frowns. "I...I don't know. What do you have in mind?"

A wicked grin that I haven't seen before tugs at Raith's lips, and his gaze intensifies. He picks up a stick and draws a large circle, then a smaller one to its west. Jabbing the larger one, he says, "This is the mountain..."

My pulse races. I don't know if it's the fear of the risks of whatever the plan is, or the excitement of finally getting off this dying planet.

Chapter Thirteen

RAITH

The snow is steady, and wind whips my face as we trudge through the night toward the portal. We head west to avoid passing the mountain and the pit inside.

The closer we get, the more worry shows on Layla's face. She doesn't believe in her magic, and the plan relies heavily on her magic.

I wish I understood human magic and where it comes from, but there's no time left, and if we didn't figure it out by now, we won't in another month or two. Besides, this early cold could mean that the approaching winter will claim too many Aracan lives for them to survive.

I believe, and I have some evidence, that prayer is the catalyst to Layla's magic, so she'll pray, and we'll all join in, and hope this plan of mine works. If it doesn't, a lot of elves are going to die on my watch.

We're also assuming, based on Layla's vision, that Vanora

is not on Arcania. And we're guessing that none of the soldiers can open the portal back up once I close down my magic. It's a lot of guessing and conjecture. Basically, we have to get off this planet. The portal is the only way. Everything else is unknown.

With the larger group, the journey takes longer, and we have to stop for rest a few times. It's just after dark on the second day when the heat of the mountain begins to thaw the snow before it reaches the ground.

Most elves are armed with either a sword or a knife, which I hope they won't have to use, but at least they've all been sharpened. Should battle break out, elves who have not reached maturity are charged with the safety of the young. The entire village will surround them and try to keep the bloodshed outside the circle.

Nothing in my training prepared me to go to war with a dozen elves under the age of twelve suns, or what to do with those between thirteen and eighteen. The oracle would say to use good sense, and I hope I have done that. All of their lives are in my care.

Layla takes my hand. "It's going to be alright." There's little confidence in her voice.

"Are you trying to convince me or yourself, *mo anam cara?*"

Her smile is enough to lift my spirits.

Drawing closer, we slow our approach. I raise a fist to signal we stop. Everyone crouches and waits silently.

Tog and Layla ease closer with me to get a good look at the portal's ancient stones, as well as the western tunnel entrance to the mountain.

Eoghan isn't as stealthy, but he moves more slowly to

compensate. "I don't know if my magic will reach that far." He points to the worn ground between the portal and the tunnel leading within.

My voice barely audible, I crouch nearer to him. "The ground is wet from the melting snow. Start just in front of Layla and freeze as much of that water as you can for as far as you can. As soon as you've done it, head for the portal. I'll have it opened as soon as you and Layla start your magics."

In the last week, with the kindness of the elves, he was given purpose and confidence. He wants to help. He longs for redemption even though his deeds were not his fault. Vanora used him as she likely uses many of the other soldiers. It's hard to tell if they're all bespelled, but those with black eyes certainly are not acting of their own will. I wish I could say that I'll spare them, but the Aracans must come first.

Focus. Near the mountain, a troop of six soldiers marches toward the entrance, where they relieve six others on guard duty.

Catching my breath, I tell Tog to take half the elves to the other side of the portal. I'll lead the rest to this side. We'll send the best fighters through first, then the rest. Layla, Eoghan, and I will be last. Hopefully, the fight will not follow us across worlds.

Chin high, Layla meets my gaze. "This is going to work." She sounds more convinced this time.

I force a smile. If she has faith in me, then I have to believe too. We turn back and gather our village for the biggest trip of their lives.

Creeping through the woods toward the back end of the

portal, we barely make a sound. These stones are like the ones in Domhan. They don't look like much, but they hold magic and have stood through thousands of suns. I place my hand on the standing monolith on the right, and the power inside it thrums against my palm. It's not evil or dark. It has no alliance.

Frowning and looking a bit green, Eoghan looks at me. I hope he doesn't vomit, but as long as he makes the path to the gate slick, I suppose his being sick is a secondary concern.

"Go," I whisper.

Hair flying in the steady northern breeze, and whipped by the mix of snow and rain falling in large drops, he walks around the standing stones and places himself in the center of the worn path. He waits until the only soldiers in sight are the six guards at the wide cave.

From this vantage point, it's a far bigger opening into the mountain than I thought. A legion could fit through there on horseback.

I shudder at what Vanora plans to bring out of Coire.

A guard steps out from his post. "You? Where have you been? Where are the others? Where is your armor?"

"Now, Eoghan," I call, but only so loud that he can hear me. Hopefully, the wind will carry my voice away.

Holding out his hands, he pushes his magic to the wet ground. The gravel and dirt shine and lighten in color.

Three more guards take a step forward. "What are you doing?" one shouts. They walk forward warily.

Wishing some other way would come to me, I look at Layla. "I'm ready."

"Me too." She presses her lips to mine for an instant before rushing around the portal. She stands just behind and to the left of Eoghan.

I step out as well. Going against all good instincts, I turn my back on the enemy and close my eyes. Calling old magic, I speak the words of the old gods and swing my arm in an arch.

A blast of magic hits me. Opening my eyes, I'm half amazed I actually opened the portal. With no way of knowing where it's going, I feel for something familiar within and sense my world—the green grasses, rolling hills, incredible mountain ranges, and living trees.

No longer the failed third son of the rightful queen, I wave for Tog. "I don't know where you'll land, but it will be Domhan. The blue and green planet is through here. It will hurt. Be ready in case soldiers are on the other side."

With a curt nod, he and ten others leap through.

Kas points behind me at Layla. "Help. I do." She doesn't wait for a response as she ushers her people through the portal.

Praying I haven't led them to slaughter, I turn away and draw my sword.

Shards of ice and frigid wind shoot out of Layla's open arms. She pulls the rain and snow to her and uses it to send a wave of ice and cold down the tunnel. The penetrating cold of her magic shakes the mountain. The smoke ceases its rise from the top.

"You're doing it."

Elven soldiers run from both sides of the mountain and from inside the cave. They slip and slide on the ground, slowed by Eoghan's magic. Some shoot arrows, but the wind pushes them away—the first ball of fire sails toward us.

Staying out of the line of ice magic, I draw light to me and send an orb against the fire. Both magics explode, and fire rains down. It melts the ice where it hits.

The ground rumbles, as if the earth is shifting. Demons growl and scream in deep guttural voices. In rows of six, they make their way from inside the mountain toward the mouth of the cave.

The first few rows are visible, but the stream of evil black monsters extends as far as the eye can see.

Soldiers who can wield it hurl fire at the path. Others climb over the rocky terrain to get to us.

Nearly a third of the elves are still on our side and making their way into the portal. "We need more time."

Eoghan tries to keep up with freezing the path, but there are too many fire wielders.

Rain and wind flow like a river to the sea toward Layla, who transforms it all into shards of ice that she throws at the soldiers and the mountain. "It's not enough."

"We just need a little more time." I stand beside her. "Eoghan, go through. Help the elves."

He looks at us, then back at the Aracan children and their mothers who are making their way into the portal a few at a time. "Don't wait too long." He rushes back and hurries the elves through more gently than I would have expected.

A soldier jumps down from the rocks to our right.

Layla's icy wind freezes him. His mouth open on his last cold breath, he drops in front of us.

Another gets behind me. I go sword to sword. He's

poorly trained. His eyes are blue and clear, though. No spell was put on this elf. He fights for the witch queen of his own free will.

My sword meets his with a clash of steel, and I push his back against the stones and rocks leading to the mountain. "Why?"

His eyes burn with hatred. "Vanora is the true queen. The most powerful elf alive."

"That's about to be altered." I press harder, the edge of the blade nicking his throat.

Hatred burns in his twisted mouth and fierce eyes. In a burst of strength, he thrusts me away, putting me off-balance.

He raises his sword to bring down on Layla and rage fills me. I spin back on sure feet, twist into the soldier. My sword an extension of my arms, I push magic into my blade and slice through the black armor and the man within.

He falls in a heap of flesh and blood.

Demons have reached the exit.

Fear tightens around Layla's mouth. Her eyes are wide, and her energy stings my skin.

"Another minute, and everyone will be through the portal." I stand behind her, ready to defend against whatever gets through her magic.

"But look at them! They're horrible. This is coming through that gate to your world. They will destroy every-thing beautiful just as they did here."

Time slows as I look through her eyes. Between the purple rocks and dead trees, the worn path is covered in soldiers wearing black armor with Vanora's red gash across the chest. They claw and climb over each other toward us like animals hungry for a kill. To the sides, others take the more challenging route, aiming to destroy whatever they can. No thought. No questions. They kill whatever is good in any world. At the giant hole in the mountain, hundreds of demons from the depths of Coire march toward the entrance into this world. It shouldn't be possible, but with dark magic and elven blood, the witch queen brought them. She'll bring more now that she's learned this forbidden magic.

If I destroy the portal on this side, I can't get Layla to Domhan, and Vanora wins. If I take us through now, these beasts will follow either now or later, and how we defeat an army like this, I can't imagine.

My father's voice is in my head, telling me to follow orders and bring the human to Domhan without distraction.

Layla looks over her shoulder at me. Sorrow fills her eyes and runs down her cheeks in rivulets. "I can't let that happen." She raises her hands and lets loose a scream that shakes the air, the earth beneath our feet, and the now frozen mountain.

I have to hold my ears against the power behind her rage-filled voice.

Starting between Layla's feet, the path cracks down the middle, widening away from us. The land erupts in wild vibration, the crack widens, and soldiers fall in.

I struggle to stay on my feet through the earthquake.

Demons run forward as rocks fall from the mountain—avalanches on all sides. The peak collapses inward, and pebbles and dust billow from the tunnel as it caves in, crushing soldiers and demons.

Screams and horrifying cracking sounds emanate from every direction.

The standing stones shake after millennia of stability.

"We have to go." I grab Layla around her waist and lift her as I half run, half stumble through the portal. Looking back, the last thing I see are soldiers running back to the demolished mountain. The portal collapses behind us. Holding tight to Layla, I feel as if flesh is ripped from my bones as we spiral through the gateway built by the old gods.

Layla's screams and my own are the only sounds inside the torturous void. I want to stay strong for her, but the pain is all-penetrating. All I can do is hold on.

The portal spits us out like a bad meal, and the ground rises to meet us, jarring my bones.

The crisp scent of autumn leaves and grass is tainted with the harsh stench of blood. A black-clad soldier lies to our left. His empty eyes stare into nothing.

I leap to my feet and stand over Layla.

She groans and clutches her abdomen.

Aracan elves fight with all their might all around us. Some lay bleeding on the ground. The children and their young protectors are hemmed in by two soldiers with spears, pushing them back against a lake's edge.

Eoghan and Tog battle to reach the children, but while Eoghan is a well-trained soldier, Tog has only his determination behind him as he slashes wildly.

"Layla. Get up and stay behind me." My heart races, and I draw my sword and dagger made from the metals in the Aracan cave. Its rough hilt bites into my skin, and I grip harder, relishing the bite.

My voice must have the appropriate tone for the situation as she struggles to her feet and pulls out the dagger I gave her when we arrived in Arcania. "Oh my god."

"Back-to-back." I need to get to the children and keep Layla safe.

"I don't think I have any magic left to give, Raith." Panic makes her voice higher.

"Just follow me and try not to look at the ground." I step us around the body of an elf named Ram and another named Dil. They were fine elves and deserved better. Pushing through my sorrow, I let the rage over Vanora's brutal rule flood me. Fueling my sword hand with magic, I plow forward.

Three elves are barely keeping up with a soldier whose green eyes stand out as a sign that he is not under any dark spell.

Roaring, I slice him just under his breast plate until I hit bone, and feel no remorse when he falls.

Wide-eyed elves look at me with both admiration and terror. They spare only a second before running to help their friends fight another soldier.

No time to consider which I would prefer, I check my connection with Layla, and find her still at my back. Killing two more soldiers of the witch queen, I make our way too slowly to the children.

A black-eyed soldier barrels at me with her sword raised and a battle cry on her lips.

I throw light magic at her. It explodes against her chest, staggering her.

As her eyes clear to gray, she drops the sword and gapes at the scene around her. As if all the memories of what she's become rush back, tears fill her eyes. She stares at me for a second that feels like a lifetime. Her lips tremble, and she stares at her hands as if they've done things of their own accord. Horror, anguish, and betrayal all flush through her before she opens her arms and runs into the point of my sword.

I have no time to react, to pull my arm back, or lower my blade. One moment, I had rid her of her cloak of evil, and the next, she was dead by my hand.

Blood pours from her wound, down my sword, and onto my hand.

I grip her around the back of her neck. Maybe I can save her. I need more time.

"Thank you." She slides to the ground and stares at the sky with one last gasp.

Shaking my arm, Layla screams, "You released her, Raith." She tugs me up. "The children."

The soldier herding the younger elves into a trapped position against the rocks pushes a boy, Bas, of perhaps fifteen.

Bas lifts his dagger, fear for the younger ones clear as he spreads his other arm wide to protect those in his charge.

Hate rolls off the soldier in a wave that hits me from ten feet away. Still holding the spear at the child's belly, he raises his sword and lowers it at Bas's neck.

Eoghan leaps from the left and takes the force of the blade. It cuts through his shoulder, close to his neck, and angles down several inches before he can defend himself.

The sword lodges into Eoghan's collarbone, giving me enough time to span the distance. I leap into the air, my sword high. When I come down, the soldier's head bounces several yards away.

The second soldier rears back with her spear.

Having left myself vulnerable, I steel myself to take the killing blow.

"No." Layla throws her weight against the soldier, putting her off-balance, then thrusts her dagger through the soldier's neck.

Blood spurts in a long stream from the wound. The spear drops as the light leaves the soldier's eyes.

I push past the body of the one I killed and kneel next to Eoghan. His eyes are dim as his blood runs out on the battlefield.

Behind me, Layla's soft voice. "Oh no."

"Stay with me. I will heal you." I press my hands over the wound with the sword still deep in the bone.

Softly focused on my face, Eoghan smiles. "You cannot heal this, my prince."

A murmur of voices surrounds us, replacing the noise of battle. The elves look on.

Eoghan surveys them with a look that can only be love. "I'm sorry. I should have resisted. I could have been a better man."

Brushing the damp hair from his forehead, I cup his face and look into his eyes. "You have redeemed all wrongdoing, my friend. Go to the old gods with your chin high. You are an elf of Domhan and worthy of paradise."

The light of life leaves his eyes as the last shudder of breath pushes from him. A tingle of magic spins in the air around this simple farmer who saved the lives of many good elves in his final moments.

"I will see that he is counted among the honored dead in this war." Tears clog my throat.

"We need to bury the dead and get out of here, Raith."

Layla's touch on my cheek pulls me out of the grip of profound grief, though it doesn't wash it away. This sorrow will live with me a long time, perhaps for all time.

Pyres are built across the plains with what wood we can find. A bay is to our northeast, and beyond the plains, the ocean moves. Winter is coming, and cold bites the air.

The eastern continent. An ocean away from home.

It's a problem for later. The sun is setting, and we've lost so much to get here.

Layla takes my offered hand, and we walk together to where the elves have readied the dead.

Sil's cries cut through all the other noise as he kneels beside Ban. Blond hair matted with blood, his soul already having moved on. He was placed beside Eoghan and with them, Ram, Dil, Fea, and Jar. Six good elves are gone in a bloody battle to save their people.

Beside them lay the twelve soldiers of the witch queen. My jaw clenches. "We're not mourning them." I point.

Layla pushes my arm down. "The elves feel they were either seduced or bespelled. They believe their souls have gone on to paradise and their bodies should be honored as any other dead."

"They are too good for me. I would have left those corpses for the crows to feed on." My rage is too close to the surface. Where is my balance?

Stepping in front of me, Layla cups my cheek. "Look at me."

I can't meet her gaze with all the failure burning inside me.

"Look at me, my love." She waits until I'm unable to resist and our eyes meet. "I feel everything you do. I know you regret having to kill and that you blame yourself for the death of that soldier who threw herself on your sword. You believe those of our friends who died did not deserve death."

"They did not." I bite it out in the harshest voice I've ever used toward her.

Frowning, she keeps her steady stare on me. "Do not diminish their sacrifice. They died in battle to save the elves, to save me, and to save you. They died because they believed in something bigger than themselves."

"And the soldier?" A shudder vibrates inside me, and I have to bite my cheek to keep the emotions inside.

"You freed her. She could have joined our cause, as Eoghan did. She made her choice. I don't know if it was foolish or noble, but I don't know what was in her heart, and neither do you." Rising to her toes, she kisses me. "Let's say goodbye to our friends."

Walking beside her, I say, "I'm not a soldier. These months with you are not an example of my typical life."

"I know you, Raith. Whatever you are, you are also a great leader who cares about those under your protection."

We stop next to Kas and Tog, who has a deep cut on his cheek.

Driven by the pride emanating from Layla, I pull my shoulders back. "Light the fire, *mo anam cara*."

Fire streams from her hands, across the short distance,

igniting all the wood piled beneath the bodies. Tears roll down her face, clearing paths from the dirt there.

"These souls we send on to their eternal life among the old gods. They died well on both sides. Let them all exist in the light as those gods permit." I don't bother to hide my emotions while Tog repeats my words in the old language.

Chapter Fourteen

LAYLA

Remaining with the fires until there is nothing left, we spend the night on the open plains. Raith holds me, says little, and sleeps less. Meanwhile, the visions of dropping a mountain onto elves and demons haunt my dreams. Each time I stir, Raith holds me tighter and whispers words I don't understand, but they calm me.

Before the sun breaks, we rise, and I'm happy to shed the cloak of sleep and the nightmares it brings. Finding out that we're on the wrong continent is extremely disappointing. I was really looking forward to that bathtub he told me about and a soft mattress. It feels like a lifetime ago since I was in a proper bed.

Raith points to the woods to the north of us. "There's a portal on the far side of the forest. I'm no sailor, and the sea is more treacherous than those ancient trees."

"I wish you had said that with more confidence." I take my bag from the ground and sling it over my shoulder.

Tog grins at our exchange before helping Kas with the stricken Sil.

"I'm not looking forward to another trip through a portal." The memory of that painful journey is very fresh.

"We can survive one more trip and hope it gets us home. After that, we'll have to wait a few weeks. Traveling by portal definitely takes a toll." He takes my hand and looks back at the barely smoldering remains we're leaving behind.

As we get close, something shifts in the woods. "I think I saw someone."

He cocks his head and raises his fist to stop everyone's progress. "Mother told me that elves from the Ear Talamh, the eastern continent, feared this forest because the ancient trees were hostile."

"Great, angry trees."

There's another shift near the base of a tree.

Raith draws his sword. "Come out."

Ready with my magic and my dagger, I wait, holding my breath.

An elf with dreaded hair the color of sand, blue eyes, and emaciation even worse than our elves ever were, steps into the light. He squints against the bright sunlight.

More movement behind him reveals dozens more.

The first one looks at me and points. "Queen killer?" He says it with awe, not anger, and he speaks as if the language is uncomfortable.

Tog asks him in Old Elvish who they are.

In a long string of barely comprehensible words, he tells us the witch queen used them to guard the port when a woman like me came and freed them. In fear, they ran from the water and into the woods, but as time went on, they remembered they were from the south. They considered walking home, but fear of being recaptured by Vanora kept them in hiding. His name is Gol, and he thinks he has a son who is gone.

They take us to a place where a black vein runs through the ground from the woods. "Bad. Dark."

The darker strip of ground runs across the plain to the defunct gate.

Raith kneels and places his hand on the mark. "I think she was drawing magic from here to feed the mountain on Arcania. The connection is severed." He shivers and then walks toward the trees whose leaves are brown and falling in the cold breeze. With his hand on the gnarled trunk, he slows his breathing. "Alive, but distant."

"What do we do?" I ask him, hoping he has an idea. "They're dying here." I search the horizon. "Where is the port?"

"A few days at least." Raith sighs, and through our bond, I feel the additional weight on his shoulders.

It's no wonder they're in such bad shape. "Can we help them?"

Turning to Tog, he speaks in hushed tones before nodding. "I can't bring elves whom I don't know to Tús Nua. They were Vanora's creatures. Maybe they are in the light again, and maybe not. I'm not a skilled healer in that way, but there are those who can help them. We'll go on, and when we get home, I'll ask my mother to send healers here with food and the skills to test their hearts and mend their souls."

Regret rolls off of him in waves, and I take his hand. *I understand.* It's in my mind as I say, "We should get out of the open."

His relief is immediate, and I'm glad to offer something that comforts him. It's good to be moving again. Myriad thick roots covered in fallen leaves make up the forest floor and require my full attention, keeping me from thinking about everything I've done and seen in the last day. I mean, not entirely, but enough to carry on.

The new elves follow us at a distance. They're not violent.

I can't imagine what they've suffered. "Do you think we might harvest an animal for them to eat?" I nod toward the lurking figures twenty yards away.

"We should have enough to feed them dried meat tonight, and when we leave, I'll ask Tog to leave the rest." Even though he shaved before we left the winter camp, Raith looks older than when I first saw him. His jaw is tighter and his smile slower. It rarely reaches his eyes.

"That will probably help them a great deal." I don't add that it's a Band-Aid to a bigger issue, but there's no need to say the obvious.

"This journey is farther than I expected," Raith says as the sun lowers, leaving us in shadow. "I wonder if these trees will let us make a fire."

"Can they stop you?" To me, they just look like old trees.

"The trees here are very much alive. They can help or hinder as they see fit." He reaches out for the trunk of the nearest one and presses his palm against the rough bark. Closing his eyes, he winces. When he opens them, he says,

"It's not worth the risk. They don't see elves favorably at the moment."

"This is a crazy world." I'm like Alice, and my looking glass is smashed to bits. Stepping forward, my foot slips on a root, and I stumble but right myself before hitting the ground. "If we can't have a fire, then can we at least rest for a few minutes before we trudge on through the night?"

Raith calls out for everyone to stop and rest. He warns that they shouldn't build a fire in the forest. Once everyone has stopped, he watches the new elves as they, too, sit down and keep watchful eyes on us.

Stomach growling, I accept some dried meat, then hold my breath as Tog and Gaf, laden with meat and edible leaves, cross the space to the new elves. They move slowly and carefully. Tog speaks softly, and only his soothing tone reaches me, not the words.

When Raith relaxes as they return to us, I lean back against a fallen tree trunk. Raith sits next to me and eats.

The old bark bites through the fur covering my shoulders, and I stuff my gym bag behind me. Something heats against my spine. Jerking away, I grab the bag and open it.

"What wrong?" Raith draws his dagger, ready to protect me.

"There's heat coming from inside." I search and find the scrying stone at the bottom under my tattered jeans from home. It shines as if being hit by sunlight.

"Raith? Where are you, son?" A soft feminine voice makes both our hearts race.

I hand the stone to Raith.

"Mother." He presses the stone between his hands, but the surface is still dark when he opens them.

Not quite recovered from taking down a mountain, I place my hand over his and lend heat, as it's my fire that has returned and not the ice magic. The moment I touch his hand, the oval obsidian comes to life with an image of a woman whose eyes are the brightest blue I've ever seen. Her blond hair is twisted into an elaborate style, and she looks slightly watery. "I see you. Raith, where are you? Can you hear me?"

"Mother." Tears fill his eyes. "We're on the eastern continent heading through the ancient woods toward the portal on the furthest peninsula." He speaks very fast as if worried she'll disappear as unexpectedly as she appeared.

"We've been searching." His mother's eyes well up, and she cries. She turns away and speaks to someone just out of sight. "Get Wren." Her voice is urgent.

A man says, "We should go to the oracle."

More firmly, she commands. "Wren. Now."

"Mother, I have the woman from the prophecy with me and a small loyal army. We should be closer to you soon. I'm not certain where the portal will bring us, but I hope to soon be on the same continent."

Smiling through her tears, she says, "I think we can do better than that, my sweet boy."

The familiar noise of an opening portal whooshes into existence. A pinpoint of blue light forms and spins wider.

Several elves scream.

I'm too stunned to utter any noise, but I stand and draw my dagger.

When the portal blocks the giant trunk behind it, an adorable woman with blond curls and a radiant smile steps through. She's possibly the least threatening person I've ever seen.

I lower my blade. "She's the human from my vision."

Smiling wider, she gapes when the Aracan elves all stand staring. "I'm Wren Martin. I'm here to take you home."

Raith steps in front of me, narrowing his gaze on Wren. "Where did you come from?"

She gazes back over her shoulder. "I told you he'd be skeptical."

An elf, not quite as tall but broader than Raith, steps through. His hair is dark blond and pulled into an orderly queue. In a blue uniform, he's clearly military, but the look of relief on his face and the similarity in his eyes scream Riordan. Staring at Raith, he says, "My little brother has grown cautious."

Rushing forward, Raith throws himself into his brother's arms. "Liam. I thought you were dead or worse."

Gripped in a fierce hug, Liam says, "We thought the same of you." They break apart. "Come. Let's get you and your human home."

Wren clears her throat.

A soft blush fills Liam's cheeks. "Forgive me. Raith this is Wren, my mate, and soon to be my wife."

I pick up my bag and step forward. "I'm Layla Stark, his human."

Raith lets a laugh out. "Layla, my brother Liam and Wren."

Giving each of them a nod, I say, "These Aracan elves have protected us and kept us alive. I'm not going through your portal without them."

Because he's a soldier, I expect him to growl back at me

for making demands, so I'm shocked when he laughs. He looks at his brother. "Is that your stand as well?"

"I'm afraid so. I brought them from another planet; I'm not abandoning them now." Raith stands taller and lifts his chin, still meeting his brother's sharp stare.

"Good thing I made this portal in the garden and not in the parlor." Wren takes my free hand. "Layla, we're going to be good friends. We sent a village of centaurs to the castle and then got trapped in hell for a long time."

"I saw you there. It was recently, wasn't it?" I grip her hand as if it's my lifeline.

A sadness fills her eyes, and she trembles. "We haven't been back long."

Liam slaps Raith on the shoulder. "Gather your people. The family is waiting."

"Tog!" Raith calls. "*Rach ud!*"

The elves leave the food and extra furs behind for those we cannot bring through at this time. As always, Aracan elves are intuitive and kind. Then they walk toward us with less trepidation than I would in their place. The trust Raith has cultivated with these people is so beautiful and strong.

My heart breaks a little seeing those elves left behind.

When all of our elves have gone through with Liam, Raith looks back at the Domhan-born Aracans and tells them that help is coming and not to be afraid.

Raith's sorrow runs deep. "Wren, can you leave this open to send help for them?"

"I can reopen it at will."

Nodding, he twines his fingers through mine, and we walk through the portal together.

Bracing for portal pain, we walk into a lawn in the middle of a beautiful garden as if we just stepped through a door.

Exhale.

A castle of pure white with three towers rises above, and a city spreads out like a web rolling down the mountainside in perfect symmetry. Sun gleams off the marble, and a dim purple planet sits just to the left of the tallest point.

From an expansive patio, a male elf with blond hair runs toward us with a brunette beside him. He clasps her hand as if he never intends to let go. She smiles and shakes her head indulgently.

When he reaches us, he pulls Raith into his arms. "Thank the old gods. Mother has been scrying for you for weeks, but sensed nothing until late yesterday."

"It's good to see you, Aaran. I must make sure the Aracans are cared for. They'll need a place to rest, wash, and food. Perhaps a bit of land to farm after the defeat of the witch queen." He says the last in a thoughtful but distant voice.

Aaran leans back, grasping Raith's shoulders and staring at him as if he's never seen him before. "I will see to their comfort for the time being. I look forward to hearing about your journey, little brother."

"Thank you. How long have you been home?" The strain around Raith's eyes eases.

"A few weeks. Liam only arrived days ago. His tale was

grave; I sense yours will be as well." Shaking off the fore-boding tone, Aaran introduces the human woman beside him. "My mate, Harper Craig. This is my youngest brother, Raith Riordan."

Brighter, Raith shakes hands with the woman. "Nice to meet you, Harper." Realizing I'm not at his side, he searches. His thoughts call me over.

Swallowing down the fear of his family not liking me, I walk to his side. "I'm Layla Stark. It's nice to meet you both."

Harper slips her arm through mine. "Come with me. I'm sure you're ready to have a long bath and rest, and none of that can happen until you've met the parents." Her eastern United States accent is slightly harsh, but there's humor in her tone, and understanding as well.

I'm not sure my attempt at a warm smile succeeds. "I want to make certain our friends are safe and cared for. We had to leave the others behind. They are in bad shape, and Raith is going to send food and healers. I don't want to be rude, but I'm worried for them."

She walks with me to where Kas and some of the women are sitting and running their hands over the soft green grass. Despite the cool air, the garden is still lush. "Why did you leave them?"

"These elves are friends. We've been with them for months. The others were in the great forest, and we couldn't be sure if they were light or dark." I kneel next to Kas and pull her into a hug.

When I rise again, Harper looks as if she's been hit in the gut. "Were they Aracan?"

"Yes, but from here. Not like our friends."

"What do you mean? Where have you brought these elves from?" The questions come from the stunning blond elf I recognize from the scrying stone. The displaced queen of this land and Raith's mother is addressing me, an orphan from California.

My throat tightens. I look for some courage, but land on pointing to the purple planet glowing over the castle. "There."

Here eyes go wide, and her lips flatten. "I see."

A very tall, red-haired elf, who looks like an older version of my love, frowns deeply and looks just behind me. His eyes narrow and his jaw ticks. He scolds, "Are you saying you brought these people from Arcania? Raith..."

Elspeth stops him with a hand on his arm.

Raith wraps an arm around my waist. "Mother, Father, this is Layla Stark of Los Angeles, California. She has come to help us and has suffered much on our behalf. Layla, my mother and father, Elspeth and Brion Riordan."

I have no idea how to address royalty. "Hello. Nice to meet you both, finally. I'm sorry we're late, but we ran into a few issues along the way."

My new human girlfriends both chuckle. I wish I could laugh right now. I feel as if I'm a germ under a microscope.

After the longest minute of my life, Elspeth says, "You are most welcome. I can sense you and my son are connected, as is the case with Liam and Aaran with their mates." She hugs me, then takes both my hands. "I will have these people cared for."

"Mother, we ran into a group of Aracan elves in the great woods. I suspect they were born here on Domhan. They were fragile, physically and mentally, and said Vanora bespelled them, and a human broke the spell."

Harper raises her hand with a pained expression. "They ran away before we could try to help them. I'm sure they were terrified. Hell, I was terrified."

Taking her hand, Aaran kisses her fingers. "We did the right thing at the time. Mother, can we send them help now? They should be fed, and perhaps our healers can help with the trauma."

"They worried over children left behind," I say, though where I find the courage to speak at all in this very impressive crowd of Riordans, I have no idea.

Elspeth says, "The children were brought here. If the adults are well and in the light, we'll arrange a reunion."

"Thank you. I'm relieved of that burden at least." Maybe their healers can have a look inside my head as well. I'm suddenly more fragile, and tears spring into my eyes.

A large group of elves dressed in light blue arrives in the garden. They approach slowly, but head directly for the Aracans, who cry out and back away.

Raith steps between the two parties. He speaks in Old Elvish and tells them the doctors and nurses have come to help with all their needs today.

Elspeth and Brion stare at their youngest son as if seeing him for the first time. Elspeth recovers first and orders, "Please take our guests to the ballroom. It's recently vacant and can serve as temporary housing. Marasa..." She calls a beautiful elf with honey brown skin and bright blue eyes over. "Can you arrange for food to be taken to the great forest? There are Aracan elves in need of our help. They'll need medical attention as well. When you are ready, I'm sure Wren can arrange a portal."

Wren nods.

Marasa makes a pretty curtsy and rushes to comply.

"Thank you, Mother." Raith walks into his mother's embrace. "I'm glad to be home and find you and Father well."

"I'm glad you're here. Let's get out of the public eye so we can talk." She breaks the embrace and takes her husband's arm to walk back to the castle.

Not sure what I'm supposed to do, I stare after the royal family. Raith reaches for my hand. "Come on. I promised you a long, hot bath."

Having seen the look on his father's face, I say, "I have a feeling that's going to have to wait."

Once inside, it's a series of halls and corridors before we step inside an ornate study with books and couches.

The doors are closed behind us by soldiers who remain outside.

As soon as it's just the family and the three human women, Brion turns on Raith. "Damned irresponsible." His father's eyes flash.

We all stare at Brion, who paces.

Raith draws a deep breath and widens his stance slightly as if ready for whatever barrage is about to come. "What troubles you, Father?"

Brion is as tall as Raith, and it's clear where Raith's red hair comes from. He resembles his father. However, I've never seen the stern look or judgment in the son that I see in the father now. "You ripped those people from their home with no regard for how your actions would permanently damage their culture. They should have been left to develop in their own time and on their own world."

Elspeth places a hand on her husband's arm. "We can discuss all of that after Raith has time to rest."

"Stop protecting him. He needs to take responsibility for his actions. He may well be the ruination of an entire race, Elspeth. I know he's your baby, but he has to grow up at some point, and you have to let him." Brion's words cut through me like a serrated knife.

Looking from his mother to his brothers, I realize that no one will speak up in Raith's defense. They all look uncomfortable, but their lips are tightly closed. I'm not going to stand for it. "What the fuck is wrong with you people?"

All heads turn toward me. They are all tall and strong and more intimidating than I like. Still, I'm not planning to back down. Raith deserves my support, and he'll always have it.

"I beg your pardon?" Brion narrows his gaze on me.

Maybe I'm trying to make myself bigger, but I prop my fists on my hips. "You have no idea what we've been through or what Raith has done."

Harper whispers, "Oh, shit, girl."

"Layla Stark, you are our guest, but I must ask you to stay out of family business." Brion keeps his voice low, but the vein on his forehead bulges.

As I step forward, Raith places his hand on my shoulder. He kisses my forehead, then faces his father. His voice is soft and calm. "Father, as much as I respect you, you are wrong. Vanora destroyed their world to the point where it will take years, perhaps a hundred or more, to recover. Dark magic has poisoned the earth, made the trees recede so far that their essence is barely felt. The animals are at the limit of their endurance and will be scarce at best for many years to come.

"Once Arcania was alive with elves who lived well off the land. They had small villages and traded from place to place. All that is left are just over a hundred souls, and they would not have survived the plague that we set upon them." Raith's conviction leaves no doubt that he believes he's in the right. "Leaving them behind would have meant their deaths. I could not do that, and it would not have been the right thing. Besides, without them, we never would have survived."

"We did not cause their troubles," Brion says, though his tone has changed to one of curiosity.

Raith raises his eyebrows. He looks apologetically from his mother to his father. "We failed to stop Vanora Braddish. In our failure, we allowed her to gather the magic and army she needed to invade their world and treat it as disposable. You will not convince me that I should have treated them the same.

"We should have stopped Vanora at the beginning, or sometime in the last thirty suns." He holds up a hand before his father can speak. "I know that I wasn't born when all of this started, but I've read the books and scrolls. You underestimated her, Mother. You believed she could be controlled, and you were wrong. The oracle was wrong as well. Even after you fled, you thought she would be contained to the old city, and still, you were wrong. We caused their suffering, and now we have to save what's left of them. I lost six souls in battle at the gate. Their names are burned into my heart. We'll lose many more before this is over. We will defeat the witch queen, or I will die trying. That is my vow." The air prickles with magic.

I've never been prouder of anyone. My heart is lodged in my throat, so it's a good thing that Raith needs no one's help to show he's a fantastic leader and person.

Elspeth looks as if she might need to sit. Reaching back, she grips the back of a chair. It's one of six surrounding a table.

In contrast, Brion's lips tick up a notch. "You've changed, Raith."

"I had no choice. Lives depended on me doing the right thing. That meant finding a way to get Layla and as many Aracans as possible through a portal to Domhan. While I hoped there would be another way, I had to use the witch queen's portal." He pulls his shoulders back and stares down his parents, ready for their rebuke. "Layla's vision of Coire —" He glances at Wren. "Let us know that Vanora was likely preoccupied. We made the journey and could not have succeeded without Layla bringing a mountain down on a demon army and the nest."

"What?" Aaran and Liam ask, stepping forward.

Elspeth nears and pulls him into a hug. She comes to his chin, but her hug has the strength to wash away a lifetime of doubt for Raith. "You've done very well, son. I'm prouder of you than I can put into words. The Aracans are welcome on Domhan under my protection for as long as they wish. If they want to return when Arcania recovers, we shall help them resettle. You were right to accept the blame for their situation on my behalf."

Hugging his mother, Raith relaxes. "Thank you, Mother. I could see no other way to do the right thing. Perhaps once we've regained control of Domhan, we can search Arcania for any other survivors. Vanora may also have some Domhan elves held prisoner there."

Elspeth smiles. "I shall add it to our responsibilities once Vanora is dispatched."

With a nod, Raith kisses her cheek.

Brion musses Raith's hair. "I spoke without learning the facts. I'm proud of you, Raith. Forgive me."

"There is nothing to forgive, Father. It's been a trying day for everyone. If you don't mind, I'd like to escort Layla to my room and run her a hot bath. She's been through a great deal." He takes my hand, and we walk to the door.

Getting out of that room seems almost as important as getting off of Arcania did. It's a nice room with a lot of books and some couches that look cozy for reading or chatting, but right now, I want out.

Aaran clears his throat. "Um, Raith, how did you end up on Arcania?"

Raith turns back to his family. "Initially, I thought I lost concentration and somehow redirected the oracle's portal. It wouldn't be unlike me to turn a simple thing into a mess. However, the longer we were stranded on Arcania, and the more we learned and became part of their elven culture, I knew it had not been my error. I have no idea if the oracle altered our destination or if it was the work of the old gods. However, I'm certain beyond any doubt, we were meant to save the Aracans." He squeezes my hand. "And destroy that demon nest."

"I want to hear more about that after you've rested." Elspeth's gaze is loving and kind.

We probably look as bad as I feel.

With a short nod, Raith opens the doors and leads me into a wide foyer. At some point, I want to take in the grandeur of the marble and gold, but those sweeping staircases will have to remain pedestrian for now. The weight of the journey hits me like a monsoon.

We're a third of the way up when Raith swings me into his arms. "I've got you, *mo anam cara.*"

PART TWO

Chapter Fifteen

RAITH

After a long bath that I had to command Mari, one of the household maids, not to help with, I put my sweet, beautiful, and exhausted Layla to bed. For more than an hour, I sit and stare at her sleeping in my bed like the goddess she is.

Finally, my own stench in my clean, fresh room is unbearable. I bathe, and it's hard to believe I'm home. Part of me must have thought we'd die on Arcania, because being here is wondrous. I washed Layla's hair right here, then brushed and braided it, because I can't bear for anyone besides me to care for her just yet. She's mine, and I will see to her happiness even in the small ways.

I close my eyes, and the water is cold when I open them again. Once my hair is dry, I pull it back and secure it with a leather tie.

Layla's breathing is the only noise in the dim bedroom.

Unwilling to wake her, I ease out of the room and let her sleep.

Returning to the study, I'm not surprised to find Aaran and Liam sitting on the trio of sofas with their mates at their sides.

I join them.

"You look much better. I thought you'd sleep a while." Aaran smiles and pulls Harper closer, even though she's practically sitting in his lap.

"I want Layla to rest, and frankly, I'm restless at being home again after such a long and strange journey." I lean back and breathe in the familiar scent of wood, books, and patchouli that I always associate with this room.

Liam nods. "We arrived only a few days ago. Our journey was not at all what I expected."

The doors open, and, wearing clean elven clothes, dyed heather gray, Layla steps inside. "I woke up."

I leap to my feet and cross to her. "How are you?"

She draws a long breath. "Better. Not perfect, but better."

"You are perfect." I kiss her, and everything else slips away.

She wraps her arms around my neck and toys with my hair.

Her touch sends shivers of delight through me, and then she presses her tongue against my lips, and I devour her. My body fits against hers like we were made for each other.

"Ahem." Liam clears his throat.

The other ladies' laughter fills the study.

I break the kiss and smile. I trace the soft skin along her jaw. "Come get to know my brothers and their mates."

She nods, and we walk to the empty couch. She looks left then right at our four companions. "So, is this" —she points to each of the three couples— "part of the prophecy? Does it say you three were all going to fall for the human you brought here?"

Aaran shrugs. "If it does, the oracle didn't forward the information. They said to get this human. Here's her soul song. Bring her back. Save Domhan."

"Not as easy as they made it seem." Harper grimaces and rubs her abdomen.

"Were you injured?" I ask.

"It's a long story." She pales slightly.

"I apologize. If the tale is too painful, Aaran can inform me at a later time." The last thing I want is to make either of my new sisters uncomfortable.

She shakes her head. "No. You should hear it from both of us."

"We'd like to tell you our journey as well." Liam threads his fingers through Wren's and kisses the back of her hand.

"There might be information that will help the coming war." I swallow down my desire to spare Layla.

Her voice rings in my head. *I'm fine.*

She's a warrior. How many more times will we have to tell this story? "Perhaps we need to call Mother and Father to hear all three stories told at once, and Rían as well should hear this."

"Rían has his own tale to tell." Aaran's hair hangs loose, and his mate brushes it back from his cheek, tucking it behind his ear.

"It's a good one," Harper adds.

I nod, and I'm sure curiosity is radiating from my face.

With a short kiss on Layla's cheek, I walk away from her with more difficulty than is warranted. I go to the door and ask Duncan, who's guarding in the foyer, to send for Rían and my parents.

Returning, I sit and haul Layla into my lap. "Who should begin?"

Rían Redmond, Captain of the Guard, steps inside hand in hand with a tiny woman whose wings give her away as a fairy. He smiles for half a second before restoring his serious expression and clapping me on the shoulder. "I'm glad to see you, Raith." He introduces the fairy as his mate, Princess Niamh.

"By the old gods, much has changed since I left." I lower my head in honor of the fairy princess. I should stand, but I don't want to remove Layla from her snug position.

She giggles. "No need for all of that. I've heard so much about you, I feel as if I know you."

"In time, I hope I shall share that feeling, Niamh." I offer her a seat. "Perhaps tonight will begin our friendship. This is my mate, Layla."

Aaran opens his mouth to begin. Harper touches his hand. "The short version, Aaran. Layla and Raith have been through an ordeal and have had little to no rest. They'll never make it through if you tell every detail."

Rather than be offended or put out, Aaran grins at her. "You'll help me, *mo chroí*?"

"Of course." She changes from scolding to swoony in an instant and looks at my oldest brother as if he's all the stars in the night sky.

"I arrived in the human world and demanded Harper come with me to Domhan. She refused, and with good reason," he adds before the lady can comment. "We encountered wolves controlled by the witch queen while still in that world. But that also led to our discovery of Harper's magic.

"Since I lost the oracle's portal, once Harper agreed to help, we had to drive to the one on the island off the Labrador Coast. It was there, in a small village, that I found Nainsi."

My heart leaps at the thought of seeing our adopted sister again. "Our Nainsi?"

Aaran nods. "She and her husband, Bert, helped us get to the portal and came back with us to help battle the curse."

Shaking her head, Harper says, "We arrived through that miserable portal, went to Clandunna, where Vanora found me, the trees saved the village, and I was captured and tortured. Aaran and the warriors from the village found Fancor and came to save me. I burned Vanora, though she escaped, and we left the old city with quite a few elves who had been enslaved."

"Who is Fancor?" It's not an elvish name.

"He's a dwarf," Aaran says as if we have dwarves to supper daily. "You are oversimplifying, Harper."

"Maybe, but your way will take all night." She cups his cheek, and he takes her hand in his.

"Then tell it your way, and if my brother has questions, he'll have to stop your rant."

"I never rant." Facing Layla and me again, Harper continues. "I was in pretty bad shape, as were some of the elves, but we managed to defeat a slew of creatures poisoned by dark magic. At the ocean, we encountered the Aracan elves, and my magic exploded with a prayer to get out of the situation without anyone getting hurt. The spell on the elves was lifted, and they ran away, but when we arrived at the ship, we found they had left their children behind. We brought them with us." Her eyes grow distant, shining with unshed tears.

Aaran pulls her tight and slips his hand over her knee. "The sea voyage was arduous, marked by sea monsters and Coire demons. Still, most of us survived." Sorrow fills my oldest brother's eyes. "Not all, though, and I nearly died. Then, as we escaped, we lost several elves and some of the children to Vanora. She captured them through portals in the ground while she tried to get to Harper."

He pauses for a long moment. "Harper and I separated from the group, and eventually, we made it to Tús Nua in battered shape."

I blink and look around the room. There are more people than when the story started. A bearded dwarf with a sharp gaze stands just inside the doorway with his thick arms crossed over his barrel chest.

My parents sit in chairs just outside the conversation area.

I turn back to Aaran. "I have too many questions to ask any. I'd like to hear the other stories before I ask anything."

Sitting forward, Layla asks, "Did you go and find the children?" There's panic hiding under her stern tone.

The fairy clears her throat. "I think that is where our story begins." Her iridescent wings flutter, lifting her from Rían's lap.

He draws her back down. I've never seen any softness or tenderness from him in my life. He's a soldier through and through, but with the fairy, with whom he has clearly mated, he is warm and loving.

Trying not to stare, I'm glad for the distraction when I'm introduced to Fancor. "I'm very pleased to meet you, sir. You are the first of your kind I've had the opportunity to speak to."

His grip is like a vise, but there's mirth in his brown eyes. "You're not nearly as frivolous or lacking in attention span as I was told. You sat through the tale of our coming here without being distracted." He laughs.

I do too. "They weren't wrong in how they described me, Fancor. I've had a life-changing few months."

The angry wave coming off of Layla warms my heart. She does not like the way my family views me, but she has minimal experience with the frivolous man I was before we landed on Arcania. *I'm* still getting used to the way I deal with and react to everything and everyone around me.

Letting his amusement die, Fancor grips my shoulder. "These quests you were tasked with can change anyone's countenance."

"That's for sure." A human woman with blue eyes and blond hair dappled with gray steps into the study. She looks at me, and tears spring to her eyes before she drags me into a hug. "We've been so worried for you and your lady."

I have to lean down to hug her properly. I pat her back. "I thank you for your concern, madam."

She steps back. "Where are my manners? I'm Birdie Martin, Wren's momma."

Layla stands as if she doesn't know what to do with herself. "You brought your mom with you?"

"As if I could keep her from coming along." Wren laughs and tucks her curls behind an ear.

"It's nice to meet you, Lady Martin." I bow.

"Oh, lord above. I'm no lady. You call me Birdie, son." She cocks her head and looks at Layla. "You poor thing." She rushes around the couches and pulls Layla into a tight hug, rubbing her back and telling her that everything is going to be okay.

Layla bursts into tears. "I'm sorry. I don't even know why I'm crying."

"Because you've had an ordeal. It's alright, you're safe now." Birdie continues to hug and reassure Layla.

I drift closer, not sure what to do. My warrior soulmate's tears are precious and rare. I've seen her cry, but never weep and let someone comfort her like this.

The room, now filled with friends and family talking in soft tones among themselves, politely ignore Layla's outburst.

My father produces a handkerchief from inside his coat and hands it to my mate.

She blushes and thanks him. "Sorry, everyone. I never cry like that. I suppose the idea of Birdie coming along with Wren seems so sweet. I've never really had a mother." Letting out a humorless laugh, she looks at Wren through red, swollen eyes. "Thank you for the loan."

"Momma has that effect on people. No apology needed."

In her dinner dress, my mother looks like the queen she is. Her gown is the deep blue of our family, and her hair is in an elaborate braided bun. "I think I'll ask the kitchen staff to bring the dinner in here. We can make our own plates and continue the stories of the past few months. This is cozier. Don't you think so, Brion?"

Father nods and pulls off his dinner coat. "It's a fine idea, Elspeth. No one needs to change as we have, and we can all relax in each other's company."

Mother pulls the cord, and a moment later, Lila, the head housemaid, steps inside the study. They speak in hushed tones near the door.

Rían clears his throat. "The food will take a little while. Shall I tell you about our quest, Raith?"

I sit and pull Layla into my lap. Caressing her soft hair, I send her calming thoughts, and our songs merge to soothe her. "Yes. I can't wait to hear how you came to be mated to a beautiful fairy princess, my friend."

"At the stern request of Harper, I embarked with a small party, including Fancor, to recover the elves and children lost in the marshes when Aaran and Harper made their journey home." He levels his gaze on Harper.

Without any sense of fear or remorse, Harper shrugs. "The need was urgent, and you are Captain of the Guard."

"Indeed." Rían lowers his head in deference. "We traveled by portal near the old city and prepared to invade when a tiny little fairy, no bigger than a fly, told us we were in the wrong place."

Niamh shakes her head. "I made myself bigger so you would pay attention to me."

"I could hardly ignore you, princess." His smile speaks volumes about his love for the fairy.

"I'd already found the prisoners at the cloisters. I was watching with my father's magic." She flutters her wings and her lashes with eyes only for her mate.

With a long inhale, Rían says, "We followed our guide to the cloister and managed to get the prisoners out. I won't drag out that part as we lost two elves to darkness, and that was disappointing. We escaped to the centaurs' forest."

"Centaurs." It comes out on a gasp. "Forgive me. Go on."

"They actually protected us as best they could, but Vanora's vile man, Ciaran, came with a battalion and attacked us. I lost Donald. Then Niamh gave her life to portal us to a safe place. With her father's help, she used her magic and transported us to a new fairy glen."

"Donald was a good man." The lives I lost along the way rush back, and I wonder if I could have done better.

"No," Layla whispers for my ears only.

"He was, and he died protecting those who could not protect themselves."

Brion says, "No nobler way for a soldier to die."

No one speaks for a long moment.

Finally, Layla says, "I don't understand. You said Niamh gave her life to save you."

Wrapping his arms around his mate, Rían nods. "I did, and she did. She died in the fairy glen she created. Her father, King Muiredach, came and led the party out of the glen to Tús Nua. I remained with my Niamh. I couldn't leave her all alone."

With her head resting on his shoulder, Niamh says, "I was elsewhere, but my essence hadn't finished its journey when Rían's love pulled me back into the glen. We don't know how it happened, but I suspect the old gods granted us a gift."

"Love really can conquer all." Layla brushes a remaining tear from her eye.

Harper and Wren nod.

The kitchen and dining room staff enter carrying platters of food, wine, water, ale, plates, and silver. They clear the large desk and spread a cloth over the top. Lila commands everyone to place their burden here and there until she shoos them from the room. "My lady, if you require anything else..."

"This looks perfect. Thank you," Elspeth says.

My stomach growls loudly.

Aaran chuckles and rises. "At least our little brother's appetite hasn't changed. Come, bring your mate, and let's get you both fed. If you're up for Liam's story and your own tonight, then we'll talk as long as you can manage." He softens and looks at Layla. "If you wish to take to your bed at any point, little sister, you should let us know, and we'll continue tomorrow."

"Thank you." Layla's voice is tight. "I'm hungry too."

Taking that as my cue, I offer her my hand and escort her over to the buffet table. "Tell me what you would like."

A large platter of cut-up roasted pheasant and a boat of gravy sit beside sliced lamb, bread, butter, beans in mustard sauce, and creamed greens. There's a large platter of fruits, berries, and nuts on the card table near the window.

"Just the bird, whatever it is, and some greens. Maybe I'll try that fruit. It looks like grapes." She puts her hand on the plate as if to take it from me.

I kiss her forehead. "Go and sit, *mo anam cara*. I'll make a plate for you."

For a moment, she looks as if she might argue, but then she kisses my cheek and returns to the couch.

Waiting for her to sit, I control my worry. She needs rest, but I feel her mind reeling from everything we've been through and all we've heard tonight. Honestly, I feel much the same.

When I turn to the food, where everyone is chatting and

making up plates, Mother watches me with a soft smile. "You hear her mind?"

"Yes. Almost from the beginning." I make my way to the fruit platter since so many are still serving themselves the meat and vegetables.

My mother follows. "I knew you would find your way home with your human, Raith. I always knew."

A lump fills my throat. "Thank you, Mother. I'm surprised you believed that, but I appreciate your confidence, even if it was misplaced. It was more likely that Father would have been right about my abject failure."

She grins. "And yet, here you are, and there she sits." She points to Layla.

I shrug and fill a corner of the plate with different fruits and nuts that I think my mate will enjoy. "I'm relieved not to have let you down."

Looking as if she has more to say, Mother nods and concentrates on her own plate.

Once I've filled Layla's plate, I bring it to her, then fill one for myself before joining her on the couch.

The conversation is lively throughout the meal, and for the first time in my life, I feel outside the central group. Perhaps it's a consequence of my need for several days' sleep. Maybe, because I've changed, I don't know how my brothers see me.

It's a relief that Layla is eating. I've devoured my plate and could go back for more, but I put the plate aside and listen to the banter around the room. It's good to be home even if I feel out of place.

Liam, who is always attuned to those around him, puts his empty plate on the low table. "Raith, how did you scry if you were in the great forest? I doubt the Aracans have such magic."

"I wondered that too." Mother has barely touched her food.

"Layla and I made a scrying stone from a piece of obsidian I drew from a tunnel under the mountain where we lived with the Aracans. I saw you on the wall of that underground chamber, Mother. I couldn't hear you, but for a moment, I saw you there on the wall. I pulled the rock to me with magic and then spent a great deal of time trying to forge it into something useful. I had given up, but Layla helped, and with our joined magic, we were able to make it work." My pride in the woman I love swells inside me. She's made me a better man, of that I have no doubt.

"Obsidian," Father says in a low voice, mostly to himself. "I would like to see the stone. It's a rare gift to make such a thing."

"Born out of need," Mother says. "Anything is possible if the need is great enough." She looks at me with pride, which fills me. "Is that how you armed the Aracans as well?"

"Yes. Layla and I drew the metal from the mountain in the basic shapes of swords and daggers, then the village sharpened them, and we did what we could for training in a short time."

"They are not violent in nature." Layla's gaze grows distant. "I think they had a lovely agrarian existence before the witch queen started turning them into shadow demons."

"You obviously have grown fond of the lesser elves, Miss Stark." Father narrows his gaze, studying my mate for flaws in the same way he's searched for them in me all of my life.

Before I can react, Layla's tone sharpens. "They are far

from lesser, sir. They are full of joy and life. They lived through hell, accepted strangers and magic, and they may not have a written language, but they most definitely have magic. I would very much prefer it if you would call them Aracan elves."

Father's frown deepens. He's not used to being contradicted or put in his place, and Layla has done so twice in her first day in Tús Nua. "I shall be more respectful of your friends, Miss Stark."

Her lips tip up gently. "Thank you. Please, my name is Layla."

Lowering his head, Father bows.

I wish I could have learned to handle him so well twenty years ago, and my mate has him tamed in one day. "The Aracan elves are bright and learn quickly. Layla is correct. They have magic, though they don't realize they use it every day. They make fire, are empathic to a fault, and can find water in the driest terrain. They managed to hide from Vanora's army for three suns after they saw what she did to their neighbors."

"They will be welcome here, Raith. We will find a home for them to thrive, and if someday they wish to return to Arcania, we'll find a way to send them home." Mother's steady assurance eases my worries. "For now, they are in the ballroom and have what they need to regain their strength."

"Thank you, Mother."

Chapter Sixteen

LAYLA

I should be asleep, but I can't get enough of these stories. I'm surprised when Raith's parents listen to me about the elves and even more so when they consider their son's thoughts on the matter.

Wren and her mother are carbon copies of each other. Birdie is the parent I always dreamed of. She's loving and kind.

It's embarrassing that I cried all over her, but no one seems to mind.

"Liam, start the story of our journey," Wren urges him.

The way he looks at her with such devotion and admiration tightens something in my chest.

His eyes shine with love. "You should tell the start. After all, you had the advantage." He winces.

Wren blushes. "You were unbearable and got what you deserved."

"Perhaps," he concedes.

Without making him admit more, Wren sits back and leans against his side. "Momma and I were on vacation in London, and I broke a tooth. While I was in the dentist's chair, Liam froze the world and stepped out of a portal, demanding I come with him. When he grabbed at me, I did what any self-respecting Texas woman would do."

"I would have kicked him in the balls," I think out loud.

Everyone laughs.

"Right." Wren claps happily. "Then I ran, but Momma was frozen, and I wasn't leaving her behind with a mad elf."

"If not for Birdie, I might have failed in my duty." Liam nudges Wren's hip. "Birdie let me follow along during their vacation."

Birdie's laugh is addictive. "I can't resist an adventure. Though I'll admit I didn't count on everything that was to come."

Leaning over, Wren takes her mother's hand. She draws a deep breath. "I eventually agreed to come to Domhan. But during the journey, a dragon transported Liam and me back in time while Momma was left on her own.

"By the time we arrived, she was gone. Centaurs found us and told us that she had traded herself to Vanora in exchange for several of their young who were captured."

The rest of the fantastic tale comes out in a rush of demons, wolves, crows, and a white raven who saved Liam with a magic berry. By the time Wren and Liam are sucked into Coire, my head is spinning.

Liam says, "Coire was everything one might expect and far worse. Vanora was feeding off the evil there. She has some kind of pool where she can revive herself."

Wren shivers. "It was filled with horrible pain."

"I saw you there." My heart speeds up. "I dreamed of you. Someone had your arm pushed into the pool. I heard your screams."

Agape and eyes wide, Wren nods. "Ciaran is Vanora's lover, and he held my arm in the pool. They tortured me, thinking it would break me, but it was the push I needed to find portal magic."

Liam wraps his arm around her. "We went to the fairy glen, a few hours' walk from here. That is where Niamh found us and brought us home." Gazing into Wren's eyes, he waits for some sign and must get it, because he nods. "There are a lot of details left out of our story, but that's basically how we arrived, months later than planned."

I'm sure every elf in the room can hear my heart pounding. These stories are more terrible than I could have imagined. I know Raith didn't expect his brothers to have struggled through a journey as difficult as ours. He thought he was deficient in some way, but he was wrong. We're here.

Leaning into him, I begin our story from the moment Raith stepped into the women's locker room at the arena where I competed and lost the *American Super Hero* competition.

The memory of going to bed is so vague, I'm startled awake by the sun streaming through the windows. The large room has very little furniture, aside from an oversized bed. Cool air floats in, and cream-colored curtains billow inward. The walls are painted off-white, and dark-wood bookshelves cover the wall in front of me. Between the bed and the library is a wide space that seems to be waiting for furniture, but it is bare save for a blue rug.

The fireplace in the corner is dark despite the approaching winter.

Raith rolls toward me and wraps his arms around my waist, pulling me back to the mattress. "It's too soon to rise, *mo anam cara*. Stay in bed a while."

"Why don't you have a fire or furniture?" I don't resist his cuddle. In fact, I wiggle my ass against him, and my reward is a low growl.

"I broke too many chairs, and I'm rarely cold. Also, I burned the curtains once and haven't been allowed a fire since." He cups the underside of my breast and kisses my back. His thick cock presses against my ass, and he rolls his hips.

Pushing back with equal desire, I don't bother to stifle my moan. "I think you'll be more careful now. A chair to read in and a fire to sit by in the evening would be nice."

He slides his hand up and worries my nipple between his thumb and forefinger. "Yes. I'll arrange it."

His touch shoots delight straight to my clitoris. I could adjust my body and take him inside me, but we have a bed and sheets, not to mention being clean. Rolling toward him, I feel wickedly aroused and press my hands to his bare chest. "I'm glad we didn't die before we made it to this bed."

Grabbing my hips, he jerks me forward, and his shaft rides along my pussy, making it difficult to concentrate. "You're the first woman I've had in my bed."

"And the last." Determined, I throw off the covers and admire his broad shoulders, slim hips, and thick, muscular thighs. His cock stands perpendicular to the rest of him, and before he can grab me, I crawl away and kneel between his legs.

"Layla?" Passion burns in his eyes.

I wrap my hands around the base of his shaft, lower my head, and take him inside my mouth. Drawing him deep, I run my tongue around his tip, and the taste of precum makes me moan as I release him with slow suction. Drawing him deep again, I open my throat and take an inch more while caressing his balls.

His deep guttural moan is more like a growl as he threads his fingers through my hair.

Up the length of his chiseled body, my gaze meets his, and the feral way he stares back forces all the blood to my clitoris, which throbs. As I take him all the way to the back of my throat, a strangled cry pushes from me. I release his cock and reach between my legs to slide my fingers through my slick folds.

"You smell so fucking good, Layla. I need to taste you." He pulls my hair gently but firmly until his shaft pops from my mouth. "That was amazing, but I need all of you." Releasing my head, he grabs my waist and lifts me until I'm sitting with my knees spread on either side of his head, and his mouth is an inch away from my slit.

I nearly lose my balance and grip the dark-wood headboard to steady myself.

Raith wraps his hands around my thighs and pulls me until his tongue laps along my pussy to my clitoris.

I scream.

He sounds like he's lapping up ice cream.

His lips and tongue focus on my sensitive bud, and I rock against his face. My body shakes as I clutch the bed and fuck his mouth harder and faster. "Raith. Fuck." I come in a tidal wave of pleasure and emotion. Pleasure explodes between my legs, my womb contracts, my legs shake, and I hold on to the bed for dear life.

As he waits for my orgasm to ebb, he presses soft kisses all around my center, licking up my cum and making the most delicious sounds. "You're magnificent, *mo anam cara*. I could survive a lifetime just on the sweet taste of you."

The truth of his need for me and love for me comes through our bond and ignites my passion anew. "I need you inside me, Raith, my love. It's terrifying how much I want you."

Rather than maneuver me or wait for me to gather my wits and move myself, he slips from between my legs. A moment later, he's behind me with his hands on my hips. "I am always yours, in this life and all the lives to come." The head of his cock presses against my pussy.

I walk my hands down the headboard, and when I'm on all fours on the mattress, I lower my chest and raise my ass high. "Every lifetime." I reach between my legs and grip his shaft, guiding him deep inside me.

We both cry out as he fills me.

Clutching the sheets, I slam back into him with every thrust. The sounds of our joining and the slap of flesh on flesh fill the chamber.

His pace quickens, and he wraps one arm around me, then teases my clitoris with two slick fingers, circling the bud in time with his thrusts until I tense and pulse around him.

Screaming his name, I collapse on the soft mattress as he fills me and pushes another round of pleasure through me. Flat on my stomach, I shiver with the pure joy of making love with Raith. "That was amazing."

Slow and steady, he pulls back and slips from me with a low groan. He kisses my cheek. "Don't move. I'm going to run us a hot bath."

The bed shifts. Water runs.

All my muscles seem to sigh, relieved to fully relax at last.

It feels like a second has passed when Raith lifts me in his arms. "Maybe I should let you sleep."

"A bath sounds nice." I run my fingers over his brow and along his sharp jaw. "I suppose all elves are beautiful. At least all the ones I've seen are. But when I look at you, I see more. You're everything to me, and it has nothing to do with being displaced." I press my hand to my chest where the invisible thread connects us. "I don't think there is me without you anymore. What happens when we defeat Vanora?"

He lets out a soft breath as he lowers me into warm rose-scented water. Leaning over the side of the deep tub, his face is an inch from mine. "I'll never give you up. I'll never leave you. Where you go, I go. Nothing and no one will separate us, Layla. Only you can keep me away. Only you have that power."

Staring into his eyes, I can't find words. Would he live in California if I asked him to? I think he would. I lean forward and kiss him. "I'll never send you away from me."

Forehead to forehead, he says, "I don't know if I could bear it if you did."

"Never." As he stands, I slide forward, allowing him to get into the tub behind me.

His legs settle on either side of mine while his cock presses against my ass, at the ready as if we didn't just release all our desire a few minutes ago. Taking the soap and cloth from a small table to our left, he soaps the cloth and washes my neck and shoulders before making his way down my body.

I gasp when he washes between my legs, and I'm disappointed when he continues down my legs.

It's even more erotic than the washing room in the cave. Surrounded by gold fixtures and polished marble, this bathroom is the most elegant place I've ever seen, yet it would be nothing without Raith with me.

He washes his arm.

Taking the washcloth from him, I turn to face him and take over the job of cleansing him from head to toe. I abandon the washing and slide my hands over his thick cock under the soapy water.

"Layla, you are everything, but this is not necessary." His voice is deeper and full of the agony of need.

I rise to my feet and step over his thighs so I'm straddling him before I sit back down and impale myself on him. "Fuck. So. Good." I clutch his shoulders as the pleasure of him stretching me nearly makes me come before either of us has moved.

Anchoring us with his legs, Raith grips my ass with both hands. His fingers tease my asshole, and it heightens my pleasure.

He lifts me a few inches, then fucks me from below.

Water sloshes over the sides of the tub with each move, like the tide ebbing and flowing.

My body was made for his. I clutch his hair and pull his face against my breasts.

As he turns his head, he takes my nipple into his mouth and sucks hard.

Pleasure shoots through me to my clitoris, and my scream echoes against the stone floor. It nearly pushes me over the edge.

Raith fills me again, jerking as his orgasm crashes. Before I can settle back, he lifts me to standing, slides two fingers inside me, and thrusts his tongue between my folds. Sucking and licking, he presses those fingers in and out.

My legs shake, and I'm not sure I can keep my footing.

Banding an arm around me, he hums against my pussy. "Come for me, *mo anam cara*. I need to taste you again." His mouth covers my bud and sucks hard.

I come in a rush, and if not for his steadying embrace, I would fall over from the coursing pleasure that engulfs me.

As promised, Raith licks up every drop of my juices before finding the cloth and carefully rewashing me.

When we return to the bedroom, thankfully wrapped in a towel, Lila the head maid, stands near the door, tapping her foot and looking somewhere between amused and disappointed. "You two should dress and come down to breakfast. Everyone is waiting on you to begin the day."

Raith says, "I think we earned a slightly late start, Lila. Will you ask if there's any comfortable furniture in the attic that we might put in here for Layla's comfort? I think she might like a fire in the hearth in the evening as well."

He ignores his nudity when dropping his towel and pulling on a clean pair of leggings.

"I'll see what I can do, for the lady's sake. If you catch the castle on fire, I'll not be to blame." She looks at me. "Can I help you dress, Miss Stark?"

"Please call me Layla. I can manage. Thank you." I have no idea what I'm supposed to wear, and I look for some hint in the room.

"The second shelf in the dressing room has several options for comfortable day wear, and I've had several dresses hung for dinner. Since you are tall, they shouldn't need hemming. If anything is ill fitting, please let me know. It's a simple thing to make alterations." Lila smiles and opens the door to leave.

"Where is the dressing room?"

Raith shakes his head when Lila starts to return. "I will help my lady. Thank you, Lila. Tell my mother that we will be down shortly."

With a curt nod but a bit of pride too, Lila exits.

"Should I be embarrassed?" I follow him to the bathroom door, then to a walk-in closet on the right.

"Why? Because Lila knows we were making love in the bath?" He points to the shelf of elven clothes arranged for me.

"Yes." I tug a pair of soft, pale-green leggings from the second shelf and drag them over my damp legs. Dropping the towel, I pull on something like a bra but far more comfortable, and then a white tunic that hangs mid-thigh.

"No. I'm pretty sure everyone knows we're intimate since they all know about our bond as fated mates." He cocks his head. "I'm not the least bit ashamed about our intimacy. Are you?"

I turn and let out a long sigh as I return to the bathroom. At the sink, I drag a brush through my hair and pull it back into a ponytail. "I'm not ashamed. However, in my world, one's parents knowing about a sexual relationship with someone you're not married to has negative connotations."

"And even you, who has no parents, feel this shame?" He wraps his arms around me and meets my gaze in the mirror. "My parents will not censure us for our relationship." He looks as if he has more to say, and I don't quite catch the thought rolling through his head before he turns his attention to tying his own hair back and pulling on his shoes.

Once we're dressed, we head downstairs hand in hand. The castle is a maze, and it will take some time to learn my way around.

Rían stalks into the foyer from somewhere under the stairs. He's tall, dark, and handsome with his black hair shining in the sunlight streaming in through the high windows. "Good morning."

The guards open the front doors, which lead out to an expansive patio, then to a grand staircase that looks like something out of Oz. Though the steps are not made of yellow brick, they are made of a bright white stone that curves down into the city surrounding the castle.

Raith asks, "Where are you headed and where is your mate?"

"She's gone to see her father and arrange for the fairies to arrive as soon as possible. I am heading to the training grounds." He speaks in a no-nonsense tone, offering facts and nothing more.

"We've been summoned to breakfast." Raith grins. "I'm happy to be home for the summoning."

"Everyone is happy you are both here and safe." He nods to the open door. "Come outside for a moment."

We follow him through to the bright sunshine and the cool air.

There's a wide street at the bottom of the stairs, and elves are walking and riding to and fro, going about their day.

I long to explore this new, fascinating place.

"Look at what we're fighting for." Rían points to the right, above the buildings that descend the hillside and end at a field where hundreds of people are organized into groups, though I can't tell what they're doing.

Raith shields his eyes from the sun. "Are those centaurs sparring with elves?"

What I thought were horses and riders are, on closer inspection, half-horse, half-man creatures.

Nodding, Rían laughs. He moves his pointed finger slightly to the left. "And there is a battalion of dwarves doing maneuvers. Things have changed since this all began."

Raith's wonder lights him from the inside, and I experience that excitement through our bond. It's magical. He grins. "I shall join you down there as soon as my duty permits. I long to meet our new friends. Just meeting Fancor and Naimh last night was thrilling for me."

Slapping him on the back, Rían laughs. "You always were the most open to change. I'm surprised you chose duty over running to the field, but perhaps change has happened for everyone here in Tús Nua." Pride shows in the way Rían looks at Raith.

"I should always have been more mindful of my duty." A

crease forms between Raith's eyes. He brightens. "But perhaps this was all preordained to get us to this place. A place where we can defeat the witch queen."

"Perhaps, my friend. It's good to have you home. Go and see your parents, and then you will be much welcomed on the training field." The captain bows to me and hurries down the steps, then turns right on the road. He greets several people and walks out of sight.

Chapter Seventeen

LAYLA

After breakfast, we go to the ballroom, where we find our village. Everyone looks so clean, dressed in new clothes. Raith rushes to check on the children and teens who found the journey the most difficult. Tog joins him, and they begin an animated conversation, culminating in a warm, welcoming embrace.

Kas dashes toward me and wraps me in a hug. She breaks the hug first and looks at my face as if searching for something. "Well? You well?"

I nod and smile. "I'm well. It was good to sleep."

Pointing to the cots, she frowns and shakes her head. "No good."

Elspeth steps beside me, concern etched on her face despite her youthful appearance. "What would make you more comfortable?"

Confusion on her face, Kas bows her head.

Taking Kas's hand, Elspeth asks again in Old Elvish, which she speaks as if it were her first language.

Kas looks up with a spark of fear in her eye.

Rubbing her back, I tell her that she's welcome here and should tell the Riordan what the village needs.

It takes her a moment. Having learned enough English to get her point across, Kas bites her lip and says, "Land to build home. Place to hunt. Water to drink."

"So little to ask." Elspeth touches Kas's cheek. "We will find you a home." She says it again in Old Elvish. Then she suggests they stay close to the city until the witch queen is defeated. "A temporary home outside of the castle, as these accommodations are not sufficient."

I suggest the last idea in my broken Old Elvish. Turning to Elspeth, I add, "They're not accustomed to the cots and the inability to build a communal fire. I think they would be happier outdoors with some tents to keep them out of the weather."

Head cocked, Elspeth considers the problem. "I think I know a place, but we'll have to be granted permission from the oracle, as no elves have ever inhabited the lands below their caves."

"Can we go and speak to them now?" The request leaves my lips without thinking.

Elspeth calls across the room to Raith and strides toward him.

Slipping her arm through mine, Kas whispers. "Queen?"

"The would-be queen." Watching the way Elspeth speaks to the Aracans, I can see that she is a great leader. She looks every person in the eye, speaks softly yet firmly, and listens to each person's concerns or thanks as if they are the only one in her view.

Together, Kas and I go to Sil, who lies on a cot, staring at the painted ceiling that depicts some god with a harp. I kneel beside her. There are no words that will ease her pain of losing her mate, so I take her hand and let her know I'm with her, and I care.

After a few minutes, she sits up and hugs me.

Kas gathers a bowl of food, then brings it back and offers it to Sil, who takes it and nibbles while staring at nothing.

Hand in hand with a little girl, Harper joins us. "This is Tal. Her parents may be among the elves you encountered in the great forest. She wanted to meet Aracans from the purple planet."

Tal sits on the cot next to Sil. Her light-brown hair is braided at the back, and her blue eyes are full of curiosity and intelligence. She asks Sil about the purple planet. When Sil only stares, Tal continues to describe her life in the belly of a ship and how, when her parents forgot who she was, she had to care for the boys younger than she was.

Soon, tears fill my eyes.

Sil is not immune to the little girl's plight. She wraps an arm around Tal's shoulders and tells her that she will always have a home and her parents, too, once they are found.

I'm struck by the fact that these people are so much better than the humans who raised me, solely to collect a check. Some were good. I should try to remember the good ones, but there was always something that dragged me away from them. Shaking off the swell of emotions, I step away and let Sil describe what the purple planet was like before the witch queen came.

Harper sits on the floor and smiles at the exchange.

Kas takes the place on Tal's other side.

The child is lively and full of stories.

Backing away, I watch from ten feet away.

Raith steps beside me and threads his fingers through mine. "Mother wants to ride up to the oracle and look at some land for the village to make a temporary home."

"Is Tog going with you?"

"He is. Will you join us? The oracle will wish to meet you and look at your magic." He's holding his breath.

"It's the next step?" Pulse racing, I can't imagine anything worse than what I've already done and seen, yet something called "the oracle" makes me nervous.

Nodding, Raith kisses my forehead. *It will make no difference what any one parent or oracle thinks. I am yours, and you are mine for all time, mo anam cara.* "We should go."

The way he soothes worries I haven't yet put to words eases my concerns. "Then we'll go."

"Can you ride a horse?" he asks, sending a new set of worries into motion.

"No. I mean, I have been on horseback, once when I was ten, but someone held the lead." It suddenly feels as if I'm inadequate to whatever job lies ahead of me.

Wrapping me in his arms, he presses his lips to the top of my head. "Relax. You'll ride with me. When there's time, I'll teach you to ride. There is nothing you need to add to your list of worries."

And just like that, a flush of calm engulfs me. "I'll try to keep my head."

Elspeth clears her throat. "Are you ready?"

We follow her out of the ballroom, and once Tog speaks to Kas, they both join us.

We arrive at a stable where several young elves rush around to saddle the biggest horses that I've ever seen.

Raith rubs a large blond horse's nose and speaks to her in soft tones. "This is Sileadh. Her name means rainfall, because she moves in a steady stream. She has carried me for many years."

I hold my hand near Sileadh's nose. She presses her soft snout to my palm and wiggles her lips on my hand. I laugh. "She's very beautiful."

Tog pets the white star on the head of a brown horse. He explains that before Vanora, Aracans used similar beasts of burden for travel from village to village and for plowing fields. When they were forced into hiding, they freed the beasts.

Kas dashes a tear and mounts a second brown horse. "I pray they live."

With a nod, Tog swings into the saddle.

Once Raith lifts me into the saddle, he jumps up behind me and pulls my back against his chest. We take a path that leads up along the side of a mountain just north of Tús Nua. Below are rolling hills with trees and grass. A waterfall flows into a rushing stream. In the distance, a large lake and a river run south. More mountains to the far north are shrouded in mist. The forest is lush and green. Domhan is still beautiful despite thirty years of evil rule.

Maybe I can see why the elves of Domhan don't regard the Aracans as having magic. If they knew their power, perhaps they could have pushed back against the destruction of their world.

Seated in front of Raith, his arms on either side of me, I feel both protected and inadequate. I don't like lacking in an athletic skill. "I want to learn to ride as soon as possible."

His mother smiles. "There is time enough to learn. No one expects you to know all there is to know about life on a new world. You've done amazingly well. To have survived and thrived on a dying planet for months. No one doubts your abilities, my dear."

"Thank you, ma'am." I'm not comfortable calling Raith's mother by her first name. It feels disrespectful.

"You're used to those motor vehicles. Cars, I think they were called. When I was in your world, we took trains to search for clues about the prophecy. We found only one small piece of the puzzle, but it was an experience I wouldn't have missed."

"You were in my world?" It's a stupid question. She just said she was. Still, I struggle to picture the elegant elf on a train.

Smiling brightens her blue eyes. "We were at a loss for how to break the curse. It's how Nainsi met Bert. They fell in love, and she remained. Ten of your years later, they were there when Aaran and Harper needed help. I think, perhaps, it was all meant to be.

We reach a cave where we dismount. Raith and Tog tie the horses to the trees where they can reach the grass easily.

Elspeth rings a bell within an alcove, and after a few moments, a portal opens in the wall.

We are incomplete, and when I look for Tog and Kas, they are staring out at the hillside. Even with the coming winter, the land teems with life.

My heart aches for what they have lost, but I'm excited for what they may gain.

Elspeth walks to them. She speaks softly and points along the line of the hills.

Tog and Kas nod.

Wrapping his arm around my shoulder, Raith asks, "Are you alright?"

"I don't know how to answer that." My mind is so full of the wonders of this world and my life left behind. The fate of an entire species. The fact that I'm in love for the first time in my life. A witch who wants me and my friends dead. The fact that I destroyed a mountain with magic I don't understand and can barely control. "I am taking everything one moment at a time."

Kissing my head, he lingers, breathing me in. "I will help you with anything you need. You know that, right?"

"Yes. I know." The most amazing thing about this journey is not magic or strange worlds. It's the fact that I know beyond a shadow of a doubt that Raith will be there for me for whatever I need for as long as I let him. I have to choke back tears as emotions swell inside me.

I'm thankful for the distraction of Elspeth, Tog, and Kas reaching some understanding and joining us at the open portal.

There is no pain when we step through. This portal is much like Wren's. It leads us into a wide hallway, where we face a double door that rises ten feet. Having lived inside the cavern, I know the sense of having tons of rock surrounding me. I have no doubt we are inside the mountain. A female elf dressed in light-blue silk from the neck down to the floor, which shows no definition of her body beneath, but makes her look elegant and unapproachable, greets us. She's older if her eyes are any indication. Her hair shows a touch of gray, and she's the first elf I've seen look older than thirty. While I know Elspeth must be in her sixties, she appears no older than thirty.

I remind myself that these are not humans and not subject to my idea of aging.

Elspeth and Raith place one hand over their fist and bow. Elspeth says, "We come with a request of the oracle."

The woman's voice echoes oddly as if it were more than one voice. "What kind of request?"

"Our failure has injured the Aracans. They have lost their world to Vanora's evil and need a home, at least temporarily, during the time of war. I would ask the oracle to allow them to build their village on the sacred hills." Elspeth waits without adding to her request.

The urge to build a case and make it as loudly as possible burns inside me. Raith struggles to keep quiet as well.

The woman, whom I assume is part of the oracle, closes her eyes. With her hands folded at her waist, her expression is serene as if she's just dozed off. Several minutes pass.

I shift from foot to foot. This is unbearable.

Tog looks at the ceiling, the arches constructed to be both aesthetically pleasing and strong enough to hold up all the rock above our heads. He taps Kas's arm and points to the blue painting made to look like the sky. They whisper together and take in all the new sights of this world.

Opening her eyes, the oracle says, "The request is granted. Come." She turns, and we follow her as the double doors open, and we enter a dimly lit, round chamber. Ten elves sit around a circular dais. Stone sconces glow with a golden light around the room. The black floor is polished to a high shine.

One seat is empty, and the woman who spoke to us sits there. "The oracle has failed in many things over the years, as do all living beings. Our greatest failure was Vanora Braddish."

"What do you mean?" Elspeth's voice is sharp and demanding. "I let Vanora get too powerful. I underestimated her because I remembered her as a girl without friends and pitied her."

Another long silence follows before a man with dark skin and hazel eyes says, "Some of what you say is true, Elspeth Riordan, rightful queen of Domhan. But it is not the full truth. This oracle saw Vanora's power and brought her here when she was still young. She would have joined our chorus, but she chose a different path, and we didn't stop her. It is not our practice or our purpose to change the course of elven events. We were created with special magic by the old gods to advise and protect."

Fire flashes in Elspeth's eyes. "Did you know what she would become, what she would do?"

"No." They speak as one, and the sound vibrates the chamber.

Kas gasps.

I wrap my arm around her, as does Tog.

The male oracle says, "We thought she would return when she realized her magic was meant for this post, but she used the power to tap into darker magic than we could ever have imagined."

Flexing her hands, which had fisted, Elspeth nods. "Thank you for telling me, but why now, after all these years?"

The female from the corridor stands. "The oracle has too long been apart from the world of elves and the other creatures who inhabit this land. We have become distanced from those we were meant to protect." She looks at me. "Time with our human guests has taught us much these few weeks. Perhaps the greatest lesson of all is that we have more to learn. We will help the Aracans with their settlement, if the land suits them."

Bowing, Elspeth lets out a long breath. "You are welcome in my home and the city. I think the elves would be grateful to see you from time to time. You might sense their needs if you walked among them."

"This is our thought as well. It will be done." She disappears and reappears a few feet in front of me. "Welcome, Layla Stark. Your arrival is met with relief and excitement."

"Thank you." I'm not sure what to say to telepathic elves who act and speak as one. Maybe it's a committee, but the way they each have a voice that sounds like more than one voice makes me think they are more.

She approaches. "I would like to touch your forehead for the purpose of learning about your magic. May I?"

I gape, then look from Elspeth to Raith. When they both nod, I say, "I guess it's okay."

A hint of a smile almost reaches her lips as she presses

cool fingers to my forehead. The buzz of magic tingles along my skin. The mountain collapsing flashes in my mind. The screams of demons and elves ring in my ears. I try to shake away the sights of our journey, where I had to use the strange powers to protect and defend.

Raith takes my hand. "That's enough." His voice is sharp with command, very much like his mother.

The oracle's touch falls away from me, and I open my eyes. My skin is damp with sweat. "Am I a monster?" I stare into her gray eyes and wait for her to decree my sentence.

"Far from it. Your heart is kind and caring, and your instincts are beyond reproach. The quake is a magic present in all three of our humans from the prophecy. Otherwise, you all have different skills. I wish I knew what the old gods have in store, but they will make their demands known when you reach the Watchers' Gate. You and the others should prepare for your journey." She vanishes and reappears behind the dais.

"We can't leave now. Vanora will attack soon. My brothers and I can't leave our people when they are in danger." Raith's jaw ticks.

Elspeth turns to him and cups his cheek. "You really have changed, my son. I know you want to protect me and everyone in Tús Nua." She glances at Tog and Kas. "But even if war comes to our continent, and I agree, it is imminent, you must follow your destiny, and the six will breach the Watchers' Gate to gain the means to destroy the witch queen."

"What if we return and there is nothing left to save?" His voice is only a hint below what might be considered rude when speaking to a queen. The fact that she's his mother makes it both worse and better.

A soft smile eases the creases around her mouth. "We are not without strength and resources, my son. You and your brothers may find us injured, but we shall survive as a people with the help of new friends. Get your mate ready for whatever you might face. Spend a few days gathering supplies and getting to know the strengths of the other women." She looks at me. "They'll portal you to the pole where the Watchers' Gate bars the old gods from our world."

This sounds less than ideal. My Southern California upbringing is cold just thinking about going to a pole when winter is so near.

"Yes, my queen, my mother." He bows.

The oracle speaks as one. "The Riordan has spoken. We agree." Then just the woman says, "Bring the Aracan elves. Let them build their village as they please. If they need help, they need only ask."

A sharp pain hits the right side of my head at the temple. I touch the spot expecting to find blood. With the next strike, my knees slam into the stone floor. "What is this?"

"Layla?" Raith wraps his arm around my shoulders.

My head feels as if it's about to explode.

You are going to die, miserable human. Vanora's voice fills my mind like a jackhammer.

I grip the sides as if that might hold my skull together. There's a loud shriek that echoes around the chamber. My own screams feel detached.

My demons were not yours to destroy. You think you can stop me from building the greatest army anyone has ever seen? You think you are more powerful than me? Fool. I have already reformed the womb where my soldiers will be born. You cannot stop fate, and fate says I shall rule this world and the next until all the worlds bow to me.

Every word is like a bullet crashing into my brain.

Raith's voice is distant. "It's Vanora. She's in her head."

"You have to fight her." Elspeth grabs my face and stares into my eyes.

She's blurry and fading.

"You have to find a way to block her out."

The hum of the oracle surrounds me.

The only thing I can think of is the "ABC Song". I start singing it. "A-B-C-D-E-F-G, H-I-J-K-L-M-N-O-P." I sing louder. "Q-R-S, T-U-V, W-X, Y, and Z."

Your mind is mine.

"Now I know my ABCs, next time won't you sing with me. Mary had a little, little lamb, little lamb..." I keep singing as many childhood songs as I can think of. I scream them until my throat is raw.

My pain eases a fraction.

The oracle is standing around me in a circle. Their arms are linked. Their humming is words in a language I don't understand. They grow louder. Then silence.

The pain stops as if it were never there. I gasp for breath and lean into Raith's embrace. "She's gone."

Elspeth lets out a breath, lowers her hands, and stands. "How did she reach her here? This is your mountain. It should be the safest place on Domhan."

The oracle closes their eyes. After a moment, the woman who initially met us says, "She had help." She looks older than when we arrived.

"Dierdre?" Elspeth's eyes widen in horror.

Three members of the oracle turn and leave the chamber. The one who has done most of the talking says, "She allowed her body to be used as a conduit." They all close their eyes again.

"What are they talking about, Mother?" Raith presses my head against his chest and cradles me.

Kas and Tog kneel beside me.

As lovely as it is to be cared about, I pull myself out of his embrace and stand. Of course, everyone stands with me, and they surround me like a barricade.

"Dierdre has been hospitalized here with the oracle, as she tried to kill Wren. The oracle discovered that she's been working for Vanora, and there are others as well." Elspeth keeps her attention on the oracle.

They open their eyes. "Dierdre Byrne did not survive the connection."

I remember Raith telling me once that Dierdre was his brother's ex-lover. She wanted to be queen. She must have known on some level that Vanora would never let her rule. She had to have been misled. Heart aching, I say, "I'm so sorry."

Elspeth drags me into a motherly hug. "You are too precious. I see why you were chosen. It is an extraordinary person who cares about the death of a stranger who helped in an attempt on your life. She made her choices and paid the price. I'm sorry for her father and perhaps for myself as the duty of telling him his only child is dead falls to me." She also looks as if she has aged in the time we've been with the oracle.

I feel as if I have as well.

Chapter Eighteen

RAITH

While Mother goes to tell Lord Byrne, Dierdre's father, about the loss of his daughter, I seek out my brother Liam.

Layla insists on going with me. I urge her to rest, but she's determined to stay by my side, and I'm the last person to wish her away. Even better to have her tucked in front of me on Sileadh's back.

We ride to the south side of Tús Nua. The training field is like nothing I've ever seen before. Where once elven platoons marched and sparred between the woods to the west and the river to the east, now there are thousands of elves from every corner of Domhan. Among the regular army are farmers and butchers learning to fight with sword, bow, and spear. I recognize many of them from the city.

Dwarves march in perfect time, stop, and the front row

kneels and puts down a barricade of shields while the second line draws their bows. Fancor orders them to stand down their bows. Wise not to waste arrows, he commands the army of sturdy men and women to drill in the other direction.

Fairies fly above, calling out to elves and centaurs below.

Centaurs.

It's hard to believe my eyes seeing so many different species working together for a common goal.

"I thought you said centaurs were vicious, fairies only care about themselves, and dwarves are greedy and keep to their mountains." Layla's voice is filled with the same wonder I feel.

"Things have changed since I left home to find you, *mo anam cara*. I have never seen anything like this." Joy fills my heart as I realize all the lies we've believed for hundreds of years have been dispelled, along with the notion that Aracan elves are lesser in any way. If giants and dragons show themselves, I shall fall off my horse.

Scanning the field, I search for Liam and find his familiar form with the centaurs. Wrapping an arm around Layla's middle, I nudge Sileadh in to run, and we wind between platoons and companies until I'm face to face with an actual centaur who's having a conversation with my brother as if that's normal.

Liam is on foot and turns at my approach. "Raith, come and meet Corell of the western centaurs."

The centaur is magnificent with red eyes, black hair, dark skin, and his bottom half is that of a black horse. At his horse's back, he stands as tall as Liam, then several feet taller to the top of his head.

I dismount. "An honor to meet you, Corell." I help Layla down. "My mate, Layla Stark."

His voice is deep and harmonious, with a soothing quality. "The honor is mine."

"Liam, I have some news I must share with you." I try to keep my tone even, but bearing bad news is new for me, and I have no idea how he'll react.

Corell politely excuses himself and gallops toward a large group of centaurs. I'm not sure what they're doing, but they have several elves with them creating balls of light magic.

"What is it, Raith? You look as if you might be ill." Liam grips my shoulder and meets my gaze. His dark blond hair hangs loose around his face, and even in his blue military uniform, he is approachable.

My gut is in a knot, so I can't say he's wrong about my state of health. "We went to the oracle with Mother."

"Did they refuse to give the land to the Aracans?" Anger flares in his eyes. "Shall I return with you to plead the case?"

"I'm going about this wrong." I shake my head. "The land for our village was approved without need for argument."

"That's good news." He squeezes my shoulder. I can see he's proud of me, and under normal circumstances, I would relish the moment.

Layla says, "I was attacked by Vanora in the oracle's chamber."

Eyes wide, he assesses Layla's state of health. "Are you well? Should you go to a healer?"

His genuine concern for the health of my mate warms me. Though I've never doubted my brothers' love for me, and it feels right that they would extend that affection to Layla, as I do with Harper and Wren.

A loud cheer rises from the dwarves, and we all turn to see what their elation is about.

Unable to determine the reason for the glee, Liam returns his attention to Layla. "How can I help, sister?"

A small, quick smile is followed by a blush, and then Layla banishes the emotion. "I'm alright. I appreciate your concern."

He relaxes. "Thank the old gods. How could she have infiltrated the oracle's mountain? I thought that was impenetrable by dark magic."

All the air goes out of me. "She used another to gain access."

"Dierdre." He lowers his head. "I feel there is more?"

"I'm sorry, Liam. Dierdre did not survive the invasion of her mind. The dark magic needed to breach the oracle's realm killed her." Leaning in, I pull my brother into a hug. "She is a casualty of this war as much as anyone we've lost."

After a tight hug, Liam steps back. "I'm very sorry her life came to this. Should I go and speak to her father?"

"Mother and Father are with Lord Byrne now." The poor man has lost everything. His wife died in an attack twenty suns ago, and now his daughter is lost as well.

With a heavy sigh, he nods. "They are better suited to the task, and friends of Lord Byrne as well. I did not love Dierdre, but I cared for her welfare." His head hangs.

Layla says, "Maybe you should return to the castle and find Wren. I know that if I received bad news, I would want Raith nearby."

"I will take your good advice and find my mate. She will

wish to know about Dierdre." He hugs Layla. "I'm delighted you have found your way into our family, Layla. I can see that you are good for my little brother. I believe we shall be good friends as time allows us to get to know each other."

"I look forward to that and to having a family. This is a first for me."

Part of me is angry for the loss of Layla's childhood, but who would she be today if it had been different? Our experiences, both good and bad, shape us.

We ride home with Liam.

When we leave the stable, Wren is standing in the yard. "I heard about Dierdre." She wraps her arms around Liam and holds him.

Layla and I quietly make our way around them. On the path to the house, she says, "Do you think they will have a funeral? I know she went bad, but her father will want some closure. Besides, as you said, she is a casualty of war."

"It will probably be a private ceremony."

"Because she was evil?"

I open the door that leads into a side hall and wait while she precedes me inside. "In part, and because these memorials aren't fussed over anymore. We've been at war so long that death is a daily occurrence."

She stops and turns to face me. Propping her hands on her hips, she frowns, and still, she's stunning. "I think everyone who has died deserves to be regaled and mourned, even if the deaths come daily. The families and friends should be thanked for what they've given."

My pulse speeds up. Discovering new things every day is enough of a gift, but I love how passionate she is about everything, and I don't disagree. "Let's go speak to my mother about making a change."

"Just like that?" Lowering her hands, her eyes go from narrowed to wide.

Stepping forward, I hold her loosely, enabling me to continue to look her in the eyes. "My love, I am not the ruler of this land, nor do I command anyone or anything. However, I shall always listen to whatever you have to say, and together we can make a difference. Until I met you, I didn't know that was important to me, but now I see a world of possibilities. Every moment with you opens my eyes to what is good and what could be better. You have brought me hope."

"I don't know what your life was like before. I can't even imagine growing up in a place like this with a family who loves you. Even with all of that, you weren't happy." Her gaze shifts and is distant, as if she's contemplating how it was possible.

"When you put it that way, I sound like a spoiled, selfish lout." It's not far off, if I'm honest.

"No. Well, I don't know." She laughs, a short, nervous sound. "I always thought having a home and a real family would make me happy, but it wasn't that way for you."

"I am the third son. My purpose was unclear. I was not the girl my mother hoped for. I was not the warrior or diplomat that my father tried to force me to be. Maybe I've been waiting my entire life for you to complete my family, Layla. Since I met you, every moment is important and full of purpose." Lowering my head, I kiss her.

Her mouth is warm and soft, and she moans sweetly and opens willingly for me to deepen the kiss.

Breaking the kiss, she smiles. "You are definitely not a girl, for which I am grateful. The rest I don't understand. You are an excellent leader and fight well when necessary. You are a fine diplomat as well. How else could you have brought our village into a new world where it can survive? The way you handled your father when we arrived seemed to me as if you've done so a dozen times."

She cups my cheek. "Since we've been here, so many of your family and friends have said you've changed. I suppose it must be true. I know when you first brought me to Arcania, you said you made an error, and that was typical, but you've kept me alive. You kept our friends alive."

My heart sinks thinking about the loss of life suffered since we began our journey together. I lower my gaze.

Firming her touch, she forces me to look at her again. "Those who died did so in service to their people. Don't diminish their sacrifice by blaming yourself."

Wrapping her tight, I kiss the top of her head. Her hair is like silk, and the scent of lavender fills my senses. "My wise soulmate. I am a new man in many ways, but my heart has both remained the same and expanded."

The way she relaxes against me is a balm to my soul.

"Let's seek out my mother and see what can be arranged." Hand in hand, we make our way back to Sileadh, then to the castle, talking and formulating a plan of how to approach Mother with this idea. At the doors to the parlor that she and Father use as their office, we stop.

I wait for Layla to nod, then knock. Love is the only thing that could have altered my course, and now I wish never to go back to playing the fool.

Mother calls for us to enter. The guards flanking the double doors pull them open for us.

Layla and I draw breath as one and step inside.

Three days after we requested a memorial, our bags are packed for the journey to the Watchers' Gate, and we're assembled with all of Tús Nua for a ceremony to memorialize the names of everyone we've lost since this thirty-year war began. The white marble stairs that begin a thousand feet below the castle doors will be engraved with every name from every species.

The stairs gleam in the sun. The assembly is even more breathtaking with my entire family standing in a row near the castle doors. The patio is two hundred feet wide, and a hundred feet deep at the top, and elves of both worlds, dwarves, fairies, and centaurs stand shoulder to shoulder ten deep at the top, and the crowd stretches down the steps to the road below.

Directly to our right are six members of the oracle. It's the first time anyone has seen them outside of their mountain. The word *oracle* rumbles through the crowd in hushed amazement.

Mother told me, as we broke our fast, that the oracle had spent the last days spinning new magic to better protect the city and could only extend its power within the walls. It must be magic that requires a great deal of energy if they, who once kept all of the western continent safe, can only assure the protection of the walled city from dark magic.

In my entire life, I've never seen so many gathered, and to stand with the beings we so long regarded as either beneath us or with fear and malice, is nothing short of a miracle.

Aaran beams. He leans toward me and speaks for my ears only. "This is your doing, little brother. What an amazing day."

"Not me. This was Layla's idea, and she and Mother devised how to go about the thing. Father and I were only there for logistical input." I can't keep the pride from my voice.

"My new sister is remarkable. I'm not at all surprised that your mate is thoughtful and lovely. You deserve to be loved by someone as special as you are, Raith. I have, perhaps, not told you so enough."

When I meet his gaze, I'm stunned by the depth of emotion welling there. "I have never doubted your love for me, Aaran. You are a good brother and always have been. I'm happy for you as well and look forward to days when I can get to know Harper as a sister."

Mother calls for attention. She's dressed in the blue of our family. The gown reaches the ground and billows lightly in the breeze. Her hair is braided around a small diamond crown, and the rest hangs loose. She looks every bit the queen that she is.

Using magic to elevate her voice for all to hear, she addresses the assembly "I don't believe I have ever been prouder of the elven community than I have been these past months. You have risen above our erroneous assumptions to embrace our neighbors as friends.

"New friends, I'm happy to have you with us today and know that one day we will return to our normal lives with a new understanding of each other that will benefit all of Domhan for centuries and beyond."

The crowd erupts in cheers.

Her expression sobers as she waits for silence to fall. "I'm proud to announce that all three of my sons have found their true mates in the human world, and I am blessed with three daughters."

Another round of cheers.

My chest expands, and I thread my fingers through Layla's.

Layla dashes a tear away.

Birdie says, "And extended family."

Mother chuckles and nods. "One of my new daughters, Layla Stark, reminded me that we have been at war so long that our daily losses have not been mourned properly. Today, we shall remedy that. Every name spoken today will be forever etched in the marble stairs of Tús Nua for as long as the city stands. Names will be added until we have peace once again, and we as a world move past the reign of the witch queen."

I step forward and say, "Ram, Dil, Ban, Fea, Jar, Eoghan."

About ten feet in from the top step, mother's magic begins carving the names.

The crowd backs up and watches, pointing at the additions.

Lord Byrne speaks his wife's and daughter's names through a tight throat.

Liam says, "Belloc, Toball, Kieran."

Aaran steps forward next. "Lare, Cillian, Bain."

Corell's full, deep voice calls out the names of centaurs lost over the years.

Father says, "Trocar, the black dragon, may he one day have his name removed."

The fairy king, Muiredach, adds to the list.

Farmers call out the names of their sons, fathers, and spouses. The farrier lost his twin sons last autumn in a raid when they portaled east to check on family and found the village ravaged by shadow demons.

Fancor, as the son of the king of the dwarves, reads off a long list of his people who have been lost to evil over the last thirty years.

Tog's list is done from memory and is so long that many of those in the crowd begin to weep for what the Aracan elves have suffered.

When the last name is spoken and silence falls, the steps are carved with thousands of names, and as time goes on, more names will be added. Many of the soldiers are still guarding outside the walls of the city. They will come when their duty allows and speak those names as well. The magic Mother put in place here will hear them, and the tradition will continue as long as she lives or until the list is complete.

It's a brilliant piece of magic devised by Mother and Father, though it is her power that can wield a spell that requires so much finesse.

As the crowd begins to break up as the masses of Tús Nua cry, mourn, and celebrate together.

Harper gasps and holds the side of her head. "Something is wrong."

Shaking her head as if flicking a bug from her nose, Layla says, "Harper is right. I can feel it too."

Wren winces. "It's Vanora. She's close, and I feel portal magic as well."

Over the city wall, at the farthest part of the training field where the ground rises higher than the rest, a portal sized for only one purpose, to bring an army through, opens. Spinning so fiercely, it pulls the remaining leaves from the trees a hundred yards away.

Vanora's voice echoes in the valley. "You might be able to keep my magic out of the city, but you cannot stop me. I am inevitable! Kneel now, and I will call off my army. Resist and die in perpetual darkness."

Rían and Liam give orders to the armies to assemble and protect the city.

Father yells, "Get the children inside the castle."

People seem to be running in every direction, but plans for this have been in place for some time. Mothers and fathers rush their babies inside the castle doors. Those who are strong enough gather weapons and head to the city gates and join the guards on the parapets as a last line of defense should Vanora's evil get past the soldiers.

I draw my sword from my belt, where it's strapped for the formal attire.

Mother calls back to Vanora. "There will be no surrender! Domhan will never submit to dark magic."

A shadow passes over the sun as the black dragon soars above us. His magic will not breach the oracle's, but his fire and claws might.

I cast a protection spell around those in the courtyard.

The sound of thousands of demons, along with elves who have submitted or been forced to darkness, marching out of the portal is branded on my mind as the most horrible thunder I've ever heard. Their black and red emerge like a blanket of evil falling over the field of battle. They're only a few miles away.

My chest tightens, and I move with my brothers to join the fight.

Mother stops us, her expression pained. "No. This is not your battle. Take your mates, gather your supplies, and go to the oracle. They will start you on your path to the Watchers' Gate."

"Mother, you cannot ask that of us with Coire demons approaching our home and our people," Liam pleads.

She touches his cheek. "I must ask it. I know how you feel. I do. This is what you must do. If you fail, she wins."

"If she kills all of you, what will we have saved?" Aaran looks ready to come out of his skin.

Pulling her shoulders back, Mother raises her chin. "That will not happen. We are stronger now than we have ever been. Domhan is all but united. Should the giants come down from their mountain, I will beg their help as well. Go and gain what we need to destroy the darkness that has held us in stasis for thirty suns. Then, come home and fulfill the prophecy. I command it," she says, in case we had more arguments to make.

"As you command, my queen." I bow, then hug her. My brothers join the embrace.

With a last look at my mother's bright blue eyes, I smile and nod.

She returns the gesture.

Wren hugs a teary-eyed Birdie. "Stay safe, Momma."

"Be brave, baby girl."

Taking Layla's hand, I run for the castle. The six of us head for the stairs.

Father and two servants rush down with our bags and supplies. "Take the side entrance to the stable and ride hard to the oracle."

With hundreds of children being herded into the basements for safety, the castle is in chaos. Servants are armed for battle. The happy place I grew up in has a pall of the coming battle over it.

Slinging a pack over my shoulder, I make sure Layla's bag isn't too heavy for her. Once she's ready, I look at Father. "We'll see you soon."

He nods, his lips in a tight line. "I'm proud of all of you."

Emotions rise from my chest, and taking Layla's hand, I run for the passage under the stairs. The footfalls behind me tell me we are all together. Once in daylight again, the din of what's happening behind us is torture to run away from. It feels unnatural to leave our home when they need us, but Mother and Father are right; our destiny lies elsewhere.

Father must have alerted the stable because five horses are saddled and ready by the time we run down the cobbled path. My brothers and their mates leap onto their horses. I hand Layla my pack and swing into the saddle. Taking her arm, I lift her and she mounts behind me. Once she has wrapped her arms around my middle, I kick Sileadh into a gallop.

Because I'm worried that Layla might not be comfortable, we're falling behind the others.

Her arms tighten. "I'm fine. Go."

The path beneath us blurs with the pounding of hooves. I dodge a low-hanging limb. By the time we reach the oracle, Liam and Wren are dismounting while Aaran and Harper ring the bell for entrance to the mountain.

The portal opens, and two elven men exit. I've never seen them before, but they're part of the oracle. My visits to this mountain have been few, and the only place I've seen is the corridor and chamber. It's logical that they have other elves working within. One says, "We shall care for your horses. You may go through."

Another first, the doors of the oracle chamber are wide open, and all ten members stand in front of the dais. The room is brighter than usual. The rough stone walls illuminated, making the entire chamber far less mysterious and daunting.

Aaran leads the way. "Any instructions?" He makes the sign of respect with his hand over fist and bows.

A tall woman with bright green eyes and dark skin says, "Our portal will bring you to the northern isle. You must find the center where the gate watches."

"Clear as a bell." Harper's pretty lips twist with her sarcasm.

The member of the oracle sighs. "We wish we knew all, but our knowledge behind the magic of elves and prophecies is limited. You are the six chosen for this. It is our belief that the old gods would not have chosen you if you could not advance and succeed."

Wren taps the flask of water at her hip, which she can use to feed her water magic. "We're ready. I'm not letting that witch harm my momma or my new family if I can help it."

Liam smiles at her as if she were the universe in human form. "I guess that settles it." He nods at the oracle.

I know just how he feels as I watch Layla pull her bow from her pack and nock an arrow.

As one, the oracle begins chanting in the ancient language. A cold wind stirs around us before all the air is sucked from the room with a whoosh. The back wall is filled with a bright white portal.

I shield my eyes against the light pouring out of it.

Rounding the dais, we step through together.

Chapter Nineteen

LAYLA

The oracle's vortex dumps us out at the edge of what is basically the north pole. It's cold, but we're prepared for it, and pull on warmer clothes. As I button the heavy wool coat Raith brought for me, I ask, "Explain to me why Wren couldn't make one of her handy portals that take you exactly where you want to go?"

Being from Texas, Wren's teeth are chattering in time with mine. "I can't m-make a portal unless I can see the place. If Liam has been some—fuck it's cold—where, then he can show me the vision." She taps the side of her head and pulls the collar of her coat around her ears, then wraps a scarf around her head.

Liam tucks the end of the blue-and-gray scarf in, so the battering wind doesn't unwrap her protection. "No one has ever been past this point in a hundred generations. Even the oracle doesn't disturb the old gods."

The ocean behind us makes the freezing air damp and raw.

Bundled up, Raith hands me a large blue scarf.

I'm starting to get used to someone being there to take care of me. I always thought I'd never have or need anyone besides myself to survive. That's all changed now. I wrap the heavy wool around my head and neck with trembling hands. "I don't know if I can survive this kind of cold."

Raith pulls me close. "You're the strongest person I've ever known. You can survive anything."

Somehow, his belief warms me even in sub-zero temperatures.

Aaran helps Harper with her boots, holding each as she uses his back for stability and steps into them. "There's a story." He shakes his head. "I'm trying to remember it."

"What kind of story?" Raith checks my outerwear, then nods his approval.

Once Harper's boots are on, Aaran rises. He's going to be king one day, but it's clear he has no problem kneeling before his mate. "It was something about a relative of ours who traveled here and breached the Watchers' Gate, only to be sent back." He shakes his head. "I can't remember the full story. It was so long ago."

Inside my head, I feel the familiar tingle of Raith's thoughts. Nothing specific, but I sense he knows more but doesn't want to step on his brother's story. "Raith, you have a very good memory. Can you help your brother?"

The inch of his cheek showing above this scarf turns pink. "I'm sure Aaran will tell the tale."

Everyone turns to Raith.

Liam cocks his head and studies his younger brother. "If

your memory is so good, why is it you never remember anything Father asks you?"

"We should begin the journey before our mates freeze to death." Raith takes my hand and leads me inland.

The others follow, but Aaran says, "Layla, how good is his memory?"

I shrug, though it's doubtful anyone can tell under so much winter clothing. "He remembered how to speak Old Elvish after only a few days. I suspect he has a photographic memory."

"Is that so?" Liam's voice is alive with wonder and excitement.

I squeeze Raith's hand. "Tell them."

Raith lets out a long breath. "I can remember anything I've seen or read. Sometimes, I have to concentrate on where and when I read it. Then, I can find the page in my mind, and I'm able to read it as if it were still in front of me."

"Why on Domhan have you never told anyone?" Aaran sounds amazed and annoyed.

Raith shrugs while keeping me close. "With Father, it was easier to be the son he believed me to be. Now, it's different. Domhan needs me, and so do Layla and the Aracans. Previously, I was just a spare son with no purpose and little chance of being useful."

My heart is breaking. The pain in my chest from just thinking about my magnificent elf believing himself less in any way is almost too much to bear. I bite my tongue even though I know Raith can hear my thoughts.

Aaran stops and faces his youngest brother. "I have never thought you a spare, Raith. I have believed in you since the day you came screaming into the world. You may have played the fool at times, but I never thought you one. In my mind, it was always a matter of time before you found your way to something you're passionate about." He smiles at me. "I'm glad that, along with Layla, you are also passionate about our home and people."

"Domhan will always be the home of my heart. I cannot promise to remain after the witch queen is defeated, as Layla's wishes will be my first concern, but we are committed to saving our people and destroying the curse." Raith's eyes light with magic, and the air around us tingles as another vow is made.

Harper dashes a tear away. "You elves are just like human men. Stewing on a thing for years and then erupting with emotions at the last moment."

Wren and I laugh at the truth of that.

Pulling Raith into his arms. "I completely understand. We all will have to think beyond our own expectations when this is over." He pulls back and, still gripping Raith's shoulders, asks, "Now, remind us of the story about the Riordan who journeyed here before us."

The wind cuts through all my clothes, and I shiver. "Is this a myth or history?"

With a shrug, Raith says, "Patrick Salinger taught it to me when he was my tutor, as if it were history. It's the story of Dragar Riordan, and they say he lived two thousand suns ago. There are some records and writings from that time. Whether or not the tale is true, I cannot say."

Liam nods. "He was said to be the first to ride a dragon."

Nodding, Raith smiles. "He tamed the dragon Boldar and became linked with the beast. The story says they could read each other's thoughts, and in flight, Dragar could see out of the dragon's eyes."

"Oh. Like I can do with Adhar." Wren walks with her side touching Liam.

She must be as cold as I am. Harper holds Aaran's hand, but isn't chattering the way Wren and I are. "I didn't know you could see out of a raven's eyes."

"Only if I request permission, but I can, and it's amazing."

Raith resumes the story. "Dragar lived longer than any other elves, perhaps because of his connection to Boldar. He outlived his mate, their children, and their grandchildren. In his older years, he became obsessed with his own immortality and the fate of those he loved. Some say he went mad with grief and forced Boldar to fly to the Watchers' Gate, where he faced the three trials."

"Oh boy. This doesn't sound good." Harper rubs her hands together. It's the first sign that she, too, is cold.

With a grin, Raith continues. "No. It doesn't bode well if the story is true."

The snow near the water was only about two inches deep, but now it has doubled. It's good to have his deep voice to focus on, rather than how cold I am, or that there's no sign of anything but a whole lot of white.

"Dragar and Boldar landed and were met by a shadow. They fought the beast with claw and sword, but to no avail."

"Because you can't fight shadows with solid weapons." Wren shakes her head.

Raith says, "Boldar tried to send the shadow back in time, but the magic made it grow and shot pain through the dragon. Dragar flooded it with light that had no effect."

When he doesn't continue, Liam asks, "How did they defeat the shadow?"

"The story doesn't say, only that they were near madness when they moved past the first trial.

"When they reached the downward slope, a giant, Grondelforth, attacked them. Carrying a massive club—"

Before he can go on, the snow whirls all around us as if we're in the middle of a dust devil. The wind grows colder. I clutch the straps on my pack tighter as it feels as if this twisting wind might pull it from my back.

Shrill screams fill my ears and cause the elves to cover their more sensitive ones. Deaf from the noise and blinded by snow coming from every direction, it takes a moment for our senses to adjust when it all stops.

I almost wish I were still handicapped because the horror of the shadow is too much to bear. As big as a skyscraper, it looms in front of and over us. Having just heard the story of Boldar and Dragar, we don't bother with bladed weapons. "What do we do?"

Aaran creates a ball of light magic that pushes the shadow back a step. He reaches back as if to throw it.

"Wait!" Wren calls. "The story said that light magic didn't work."

Heeding her advice, Aaran holds the light and looks at Raith. "What do you think, brother?"

Pain rushes through my head as if someone has driven a spike through it. My foster fathers and mothers parade before my eyes like a river of failure. The cold ground hits my hands and knees before I even know I've fallen. Sarah, the only foster who might have cared about me, is dead, and her body lies on the kitchen floor. Her eyes stare at nothing.

The neighbor calls for an ambulance, and the police call child protective services. My meager belongings are thrown into a black garbage bag, and I'm pulled away, crying so hard I can't breathe—pain slices through my stomach. Red-faced, buddy screams that I'm worthless.

"It's not real." Raith's strained voice cuts through the horrible visions. "Push it from your minds with something else." His arms come around me. He whispers in my ear, "I thought of the first time I saw you, then the night we made love in our little alcove on Arcania. Find a thought, *mo anam cara*. Push the shadow from your mind."

I believe him, but I can't push aside this torture growing in my head.

Harper's voice sounds distant as the theme song from an old movie rings from her, with just the chorus on repeat about stayin' alive with a lot of ahs on repeat. Her singing grows louder and louder, and I focus on the song I've heard a hundred times, the one from the 80s that I remember my foster parents listening to. I let those words fill my mind like a battering ram until the pain eases.

As I open my eyes, the gorgeous vision of Raith's handsome face blinks into focus. Snow is blowing in every direction, and it's just us staring into each other's eyes. The green of his irises is bright with worry. His long, tapered fingers gently hold my head. I draw a deep breath, and the pain eases. The visions fade, and I can tuck them into the compartments where I store those memories that I don't want to focus on.

"I'm alright."

He presses his lips to my forehead and helps me get to my feet.

Aaran and Harper are in each other's arms, but both are standing.

Liam is still writhing with Wren clutching his shoulders.

Leaving me, Raith runs to his brother's side and slides to his knees. He lifts his torso out of the snow and holds him so that Liam's ear is close. "This is a mental test, Liam. You cannot fight your way out of it. Find a happy memory and focus on it relentlessly."

Liam is screaming the most terrifying sound I've ever heard. His head jerks back, his jaw so tight he might shatter his teeth. Every muscle in his body is taut.

It's unbearable to watch; I can't imagine what he's suffering. "He's too far gone to find one. Give him one. Tell him about something in the past you share."

Speaking into his brother's ear, Raith follows my suggestion. "We went to the fair that year, and they decorated everything in gold and blue feathers. Remember when we appropriated hundreds of those feathers and sent them flying with little wisps of light we conjured. We made them tickle everyone's noses in the square. They all started sneezing, and we laughed for days."

Liam's strain eases, and he draws a long breath.

"Stay focused on that day at the fair, Liam. You kissed that pig in the pen on a bet you made with Dawson Oliver and won his red cape." Raith talks about it as if it happened yesterday.

"I remember. I wore that cape everywhere for months. Dawson was miserable." Liam gasps for several breaths.

"He shouldn't have made the bet." Raith brushes damp hair from Liam's forehead despite the cold.

"Father hated that cape. He said it wasn't befitting a

Riordan to wear red or make wagers." Liam eeks out a short laugh, then takes another long inhale, which shudders as he lets it out. "I think I'm alright now."

Raith helps him stand, and as soon as he's upright, Wren wraps her arms around his waist. "I thought I was losing you."

Hugging her, he nods his thanks to Raith.

A moment later, Wren throws her arms around Raith. "You saved him. I'll never be able to thank you enough."

He pats her back gently. "I'm glad I could help." Raith's cheeks have lost their color, and he's breathing faster than usual.

As soon as Wren releases him, I slip my arm around his waist. *It's okay. You're both alright.*

"Thank the old gods," he whispers, and hugs me back.

I think he should take the credit, but I keep that to myself. These old gods are starting to annoy me with their tests and ancient stories. First, they let Vanora gather all these evil powers, then they let her cast a curse on a world they protect and the elves who still call their names in blessing. They hid for thirty years, or at least didn't reveal a prophecy that could help, sent the rightful queen's three sons to the human world, which the old gods abandoned long ago, and gave them no tools to convince three human women to travel to Domhan and fight a woman so evil, Vanora would destroy an entire planet and its peaceful people to birth demons from hell.

If that's not enough, we're trudging through the north dang pole to find a gate, and they have the nerve to make us pass tests.

Raith leans in. "You are thinking very loudly. Maybe

soften your opinion before we may possibly meet one or two of the old gods."

I humph. "I'm not wrong."

"If they had a hand in me finding you and loving you, I'll walk across a hundred tundras for the privilege." He takes my hand and kisses the gloved fingers.

"When you put it that way..."

"I think you better tell us more about that giant, Raith." Liam stops, and we all follow as we look down into an enormous crater.

Aaran points down the slope. "You better make it the short version."

The figure waiting halfway down the side of the crater is three times the size of a man or an elf. In one hand, he holds a large club reminiscent of those old images of cavemen on Earth.

The snow blurs him, but I have a feeling there's no way past him but defeating him, and we need to reach the bottom to find the gate. "Can we go around him?"

Liam shrugs. "He'll just track us, and his circumference is a shorter distance. He'll always be a few steps ahead of us."

Plus, his steps are much longer than ours. Even at a run, I doubt we can outpace the giant.

Raith picks up the story where he left off. "Grondelforth, carrying a massive club, attacked them. The dragon took to the air and tried to claw the giant but was hit by the club and lay in the snow with a battered wing. Dragar was faster and fought through both madness and years of training. After that, the story moves on to the third trial."

"Well, at least we know Grondelforth can be beaten." I pull my bow from my back and nock an arrow.

Harper draws a short sword. "And one man managed it. There are six of us."

Shaking his head, Aaran puts his hand over where Harper grips her weapon. "How about if you stay in the back line and let my brothers and I have a try at him before risking your life as well as Wren's and Layla's. We know Domhan needs the three of you. We might be expendable."

"No," I blurt before I can stop myself.

They all stare at me.

"Layla is right," Wren says. "All six of us are necessary."

I'm too wrapped up in winter clothes for anyone to see my blush, but I exchanged a look with Wren that I hope conveys my thanks.

With her hand on her hip, Harper says, "I'm with my girls, Aaran. We're all in this together. There's no way we're standing up here while you face that Grondelforth."

"I am outvoted." Aaran gives a helpless look for support from his brothers, who both decline to join his side of this argument. "Can I at least get the three of you to stand behind and use arrows and magic?"

"That's reasonable." I pull my scarf down so he can see my smile. Why I'm smiling when we're about to face an attacking giant, I can't say. Maybe it's the feeling that I'm part of something. Maybe there's a family here, and they care about me and view me as an equal. It's a first for me, and I like the feeling.

Raith whispers, "Be careful."

"You too." I walk a step behind Raith down the slope.

Losing her footing, Wren lands on her ass and slides down a few feet.

Harper and I each grab for her and lift her between us

before she slides into one of the boulders that dot the landscape in this pit. The swift move makes me lose the arrow I had ready.

Grondelforth's roar echoes against the sides of the crater. He's enormous as he lifts his club and continues to grunt out words I don't understand. Standing at least fifteen feet tall, he's dressed in a green tunic that only reaches mid-thigh. No leggings or pants, and his boots are torn at the front, exposing his toes. His hair is long and matted into dreadlocks. I think it was once brown, but dirt and grime, along with snow, have turned it black and gray. His beard is much the same and hangs to his chest. Brown wide eyes stare down at us.

It's no wonder he's cranky. He must be freezing.

"Is it bad that I'm feeling a bit sorry for the beast?" I wish I had a really large pair of wool pants for him.

Harper says, "He does seem a bit pathetic for the monster meant to test us."

"Can we reason with him?" Wren finds her footing and brushes her hair back under her shawl.

Liam has his sword raised and his knees bent, ready to attack. "Ladies, are you suggesting we talk our way through a test of strength with a raving giant whose sole purpose is to keep us from our goal?"

My fingers heat, and I sling my bow over my shoulder. "Maybe a chat isn't appropriate, but that creature must be freezing. He's thousands of years old. Do you suppose anyone has ever offered him a fire to warm himself?"

"Or a dang pair of pants." Wren cringes.

Aaran growls. "I'm not stopping to sew him trousers, and we have no wood to burn."

"Raith, do we need wood, or can you and I heat those rocks over there?" I point to an outcropping to the giant's right. "Maybe he'd welcome some kindness after a few millennia."

"I can't shoot heat; it will have to be you," Raith says with a hint of a grin and his sword ready to defend.

Grondelforth raises his club higher and swings it so close that we all have to drop to the ground to avoid being smashed. He calls out, "Dorg, dorg." He jumps up and down as if challenging us to attack.

Struggling to keep my feet as his jumping shakes the earth, I let the fire inside me come to my fingertips. Pulling off my gloves, I focus the heat into a stream and shoot it at the boulders.

"Gently, or you'll blow them up." Raith's warning is soft, yet I hear it both inside and out.

Jumping back, Grondelforth shakes the ground. He stares at the stones with his weapon in both hands. When no attack comes, he cocks his head.

"I think he's confused." Harper steps beside me. "You're doing great."

I hold back the full force of my fire and let the heat flow into the rocks until they glow. The snow around them melts enough to reveal dirt below.

Lowering his club, the giant studies the rocks. He steps closer and reaches out a hand.

"Don't touch," Wren calls out. "Hot."

He pulls back, but only a little, as he feels heat, maybe for the first time ever. "Nillet."

"Does anyone speak ancient giant?" Harper asks.

Aaran lowers his sword and steps beside her. "I'm not

even sure what he's speaking is a known language. Maybe we can slip past him while he's enamored with the heat."

Pointing to another rock, Harper says, "You could make him a blanket. Do that thing you do where you alter matter. Like with the soap you made from water."

"That was something we learn in school. It's for when no soap is available, *mo chroi*. I've never made a cloth from rock." He keeps his focus on Grondelforth, who plunks himself in front of the heat and puts down his weapon.

Holding both hands and feet close to the warmth, he grins, exposing extremely yellow and large teeth.

I stop the flow of heat and look away as the giant's short tunic leaves more than his teeth exposed. "Someone needs to give him something to cover up with."

Liam laughs. "There are some things you cannot unsee."

Shaking his head, Aaran walks to a rock about a foot across. Placing his hands on it, he mutters something. "I don't know what this will feel like."

With a few steps forward, Raith adds his magic to the heated stones so that they'll stay warm long after we're gone. My heat would have only been temporary. Once he's done, he says, "I doubt our friend will be discerning of quality."

The rock under Aaran's hands shifts and stretches. It lifts from the ground and pulls outward in all directions until it's a ten-foot-wide gray blanket lying across Aaran's arms. Walking toward Grondelforth, he looks at me. "If I'm killed for this, sister, I'm going to haunt you."

Despite his stern tone, there's amusement in his eyes, and it warms me to be called sister.

When he's a few feet from the giant, Aaran holds out the

blanket. "*Teasaich.* Stay warm." He lifts it higher and cringes as if the giant might strike him or worse.

Instead, Grondelforth takes the cloth and wraps himself in it. "Nillet."

"I guess 'nillet' is a good thing." Wren pulls her scarf tighter.

While the giant is entirely focused on his newfound comforts, we walk around him and continue toward the center of the pole.

Even with all the excitement and the fire that burns inside me, I'm cold. Raith wraps an arm around me as we trudge forward.

Liam stays at our backs to make sure the joy of a warm blanket and fire are enough to keep our new friend friendly.

Thirty minutes later, we walk out of nothing but snow and ice and step into a twenty-foot circle of green grass, and at the center stands a stone gate with strange markings carved around the frame, taller than Grondelforth and twice as wide.

Aaran turns to Raith. "Now what, little brother?"

Chapter Twenty

RAITH

Layla giggles at my brother affectionately calling me little brother when I'm three inches taller than he is. I have always felt inferior to both of my brothers, but now I can see they don't regard me that way. It's as if Aaran and Liam always knew I would find my way. Maybe they were waiting, or perhaps they didn't care either way. They love me as I am. My gratitude cannot be measured. Now that I see the benefit of using my skills to help people, it seems as if everyone sees me differently.

Never in my life would I have believed Aaran would look to me for advice, but standing in front of the Watchers' Gate, he's waiting for me to explain an old text. To me, the words on the page of that old scroll can be conjured as if I'm browsing the library in my head. Honestly, it never occurred to me that everyone couldn't recall in the same way since I chose to ignore the ability.

I hesitate, falling back on old habits. It feels instinctual to play the fool. Father's disappointed expression is branded in my mind, but when I fail, he pays attention to his spare and useless son.

Pushing away those old thoughts, I search my memory for the text about the third trial.

Layla nods, encouraging me.

The gate is bigger than I thought it would be, based on the drawings in those old scrolls. There are symbols surrounding two doors, and those weren't in the picture either. "Dragar had to solve a riddle. The final trial is that of intelligence."

Stepping close, I touch the center of the barrier between elves and the old gods. It's strange to think of this place as more than myths and stories, but everything is as it was written. The vagueness of the stories may have been intentional. If all the answers were given, then anyone could find their way inside the home of the old gods.

"How do we get the riddle?" Liam asks.

I shrug. "No idea." I run my fingers over the doors carved to look like a dragon's scales. At the place where a hinge might be, there is only a line where the door gives way to the surrounding arch of the gate. I touch a rune shaped like a bottle, and it shifts slightly. I pull my hand back. Have I broken the Watchers' Gate? No. It's stood for all time. More gently, I touch the bottle. "I think these are buttons."

Aaran studies the runes. "Push the right ones and the door opens?"

"Seems reasonable." I avoid the buttons and look for a way to find the riddle we need to solve. Maybe it's carved into the door, and time has worn it down. All I feel is the etched dragon scales.

Liam joins us as the ladies look around the grass and snow surrounding us for a clue. Magic prickles my skin.

As Liam touches the door, and all three of our hands are on the rough carvings, light blasts from the etchings and forms a golden swirl of Old Elvish words.

I step back, as do my brothers, but whatever spell unlocked continues to feed light into the clues. The air is alive with magic.

Layla rushes to my side. "You found it."

"It was a spell that triggered when all three of us touched the gate at the same time." I take her hand and kiss her knuckles. It feels like ages since we were alone, and it will be a long time. These small connections will have to be enough until this quest is over.

Aaran translates. "This gate watches but cannot open. The Tuatha de Danna behind it keep. They are locked in, and out of the worlds of man and elf. To open in not out, a joining must be there."

"What kind of joining?" Harper's voice is filled with skepticism and wariness.

"There's more." I point to the words glowing along the bottom of the gate. "First: With dark and light, they show the way. Second: North her five do light in vain. Thirdly: Seen with red and charging hooves. With the fourth, within you'll be. Black. Evil. It shakes the world, but Duine will not fall."

"What is Duine?" Layla asks.

Stunned to find the word here, I didn't translate it. My heart is pounding so fast; I think it might be hope that's gotten inside me. "Human."

No one speaks for a long moment.

Wren breaks the silence. "Our people here on these ancient carvings with this magic? It's incredible."

"That's the joining." Harper's voice is gentle. Whereas she's usually direct, she hesitates. "We are the joining that is necessary for the gate to open, human and elf."

"We need to take the riddle one part at a time." Aaran takes charge and points to the runes. "If these are buttons, they should lead to an obvious choice once we figure out the clue." He nods as if he's convincing himself as well as the rest of us.

My brother is afraid. Even more reason for me to see him as my equal. How was all of this hidden from me in the past? Maybe I was so busy trying to prove I was no good that I self-ishly ignored those around me. It's time to be more and do what is right for Domhan and my family.

Liam says, "With dark and light, they show the way."

"That sounds so random. It could be anything." Wren toes the ground as she stares at the runes. "What's dark and light?"

"I am." Harper widens her arms, then lets them fall to her sides, and Aaran wraps his arm around her shoulders. "My magic is both light and shadow, though I don't see any rune that makes me think of myself."

Most of the runes are animals: a wolf, a raven, a cougar, a swallow, a shark, but nothing that looks like a woman or that would indicate a human woman. Some of the markings remind me of Dwarvish, but I don't know that language well enough to translate if that's what they are.

Aaran points to an oval-shaped rune. "That looks a lot

like the sconces at the oracle. I've always wondered what magic powers those strange glowing stones have."

Liam's eyes widen. Stepping back, he grips Wren's hand. "The same sconces are in Vanora's chamber in Coire."

"The oracle told us that Vanora was supposed to become a member of the oracle." Layla repeats what we were told when we visited and the witch queen used Dierdre to access the chamber. "They were grooming her to take her place among them, but her desire for power pushed her to look elsewhere for magic, and she turned to darkness."

"So those can be made by light or dark and can exist on Domhan and Coire." Liam draws a long breath. "I think that's the answer." He looks to Aaran for approval, and once he gets a nod, he steps over and presses the rune with the sconce.

The grinding of stone on stone is worthy of a cringe as the button glows gold and the runes begin to move. They shift and turn until the glowing one is at the top. My heart is in my throat. We might actually do this.

Aaran speaks the second clue again. His voice filled with renewed excitement. "North her five do light in vain."

As excited as I was when the first button was correct, I am equally despondent by this second clue, which means nothing to me.

Layla says, "North. Five. Vain. There was a Greek myth about vanity and..." She shakes her head, trying to put the words together.

"Oh. I might know what you mean. The queen who boasted that her daughter was more beautiful than the goddesses or nymphs." Wren wrinkles her nose and stares into the snow. "She was punished and became a constellation."

"That's it!" Layla shrieks. "Cassiopeia, and the North Star is part of that constellation."

My brothers, Harper, and I stare at the two of them while they get excited. I wait for more, but finally ask, "How does that relate to our carvings?"

Layla looks at the runes one by one, then points to one that looks like a W that has been tipped and stretched. "That's Cassiopeia in Earth's sky." She pushes the button.

Much like before, the stones grind together as the glowing one is shifted and eventually makes its way to the top, where now two runes stand together like sentinels.

"How did Dragar know the sky in the human world?" I can't help wondering. "Had he used the portals for his own mad adventures?"

"He must have." Wren's voice is filled with wonder. "How long have elves been sneaking into the human world and for what purpose?"

Aaran says, "It's a good question, but perhaps one we can think about later. Seen with red and charging hooves must be the centaurs and their red eyes."

We all nod, and he presses the button with a centaur drawing his bow, carved across its surface. That rune joins the other two.

"That was a bit too easy." Liam shakes his head. "Maybe the old gods didn't realize that those in the light would join forces."

Harper twists her lips. "Maybe it was these old gods of yours who started the rumors that kept the races separate for so long."

The last one is a puzzle. I read the full clue aloud. "With the fourth, within you'll be. Black. Evil. It shakes the world, but Duine will not fall."

"And Duine are humans?" Layla asks again.

I nod, not sure where her thoughts are leading. So far, our mates have been clever and wise. All three have much to offer both this quest and our family.

"Why not say human, Raith?" Liam studies the glowing words, though I don't know how much of it he can read. As I recall, ancient languages were not his best subject.

"I'm not sure," I respond honestly. I read the rest in the common language. "It feels more accurate to say Duine. I suppose the translation isn't quite perfect." I shake my head. "It feels important that this word is Duine." The air around me vibrates with the rightness of it.

Wren cocks her head and studies me. "You said it's an ancient term for our people. Liam told me that long ago, humans had magic but lost it over time because they feared and neglected it."

"What are you thinking, sweetheart?"

Gaze distant, Wren's obviously putting something together. "Maybe it's a term for humans with magic rather than all humanity. Maybe Raith, with his extraordinary memory, knows that Duine doesn't encompass humanity as a whole, but only those who have the hint of magic and call it instinct or a sixth sense."

"Like the three of us." Layla stares at the symbols on the gate. "I don't see anything that looks like a person.

Harper steps beside her. "Black and evil, but can't kill a magical human." She points. "The lightning bolt." Her voice shakes. "Vanora tried to open me up with her lightning, but it didn't work. As hard as she tried, her magic couldn't reach inside me. The pain was enough to make me lose consciousness, but not kill me."

Aaran winces and rage flashes in his eyes. Maybe his anger is directed at Vanora, but I think he blames himself for what his mate suffered at the witch queen's hand. "You were stronger than her." He wraps her in his arms.

"She tried that with me, too, though I think she just wished to kill me. It was torture, but I didn't die. I sensed her frustration and the toll it took, but she couldn't kill me with that lightning." Wren places her hand on Harper's back.

As Layla stands with her new sisters, Aaran takes a step back while our three mates stand together staring at that lightning. Considering my mate never had a family, she's taken to Wren and Harper and seems glad to be part of something. At least I could give that to her.

"I didn't suffer in that way, but that button feels right. If the two of you are sure, I'm with you." Layla grips Harper's shoulder.

With her chin high, Harper presses the final button and draws a sharp inhale as the runes move. When the fourth and final piece reaches the top of the gate, the ancient doors open inward without any hint that they have been shut for thousands of suns. They move silently, releasing warmth and light.

Grondelforth roars in the distance. Maybe he's angry that he failed at his task, or perhaps he's happy for our success. It's impossible to say.

Standing together, we squint into the light. The finality of stepping through this gate is daunting.

Layla takes my hand. "Do we go in?"

"The riddle said it's not out." I hope that's true. It would be a shame to send elvenkind back to the age when the Tuatha de Danann walked Domhan.

As if by silent consensus, we step forward beyond the Watchers' Gate. Once we clear the doors, they swing silently closed with a gong of finality.

My heart gives a similar thud while my skin prickles with god magic that permeates this place. It's like walking through a million feathers—uncomfortable and addictive at the same time.

"Are we dead?" Harper asks.

A deep, steady voice replies, "No, not dead, my children. Though you are in a place where you do not belong."

The light that has kept us from seeing anything dims, and a soft glow takes its place. Standing inside a chamber with no top or sides, we are forced to shed our outerwear and drop it on a misty floor.

"But you are here now, and you have passed the trials, so come."

A female whose voice is more musical than spoken adds, "Did they truly pass?"

"In a fashion," he concedes.

She calls louder. "Why did you not strike the giant?"

Layla says, "He seemed too helpless."

"Helpless!" Our ears ring from the incredulous voice of another man. "I am certain that is the first being to call Grondelforth helpless."

The woman says, "He would have killed you if he had the chance. Is that not enough reason to attack?"

"Not today." Wren lifts her chin defiantly.

As we walk closer, the mist fades, and we step into a

circle of all white thrones in various sizes. Seated in each is a god or goddess. I recognize them all as twelve of the Tuatha de Danann. Only the central three notice us. The rest sit frozen as if in a trance. Their consciousness may be on a different plane. They are all bigger than the giant, and the six of us are like the carved soldiers I played with as a child. Perhaps that's what we are to these gods—playthings.

The largest throne is at the center, and seated in it is Dagda, the good god and father of gods. His hair is golden with gray, and his beard is streaked with red. On his right is Morrigan, goddess of war, fate, and sovereignty. Her beauty is as renowned as she is feared. To Dagda's left is Dian Cécht, the god of healing and son of Dagda. All three study us intently. The other gods continue, unmoving and uninterested in the mortals who have breached the gate.

Dagda wears a gold diadem at his brow, and at its center is an emerald. His blue eyes are full of pain, and the creases around his eyes and mouth show he is weary of ruling for millennia.

Morrigan's black hair blows in a breeze that I don't feel. Her lips are ruby red, and her gown is a soft white that hugs her curves. With stark green eyes, she looks on curiously.

I wonder if these gods recall that they summoned us with their prophesies and riddles.

Dian Cécht's stern face is weathered, and his dark eyes see all. He crosses his massive arms and meets my gaze. "We remember everything, *elfling.*"

Rather than show weakness to any god, I stare back and nod my acknowledgment that he can read my thoughts. Hopefully, it's enough to convey that I have nothing to hide.

Dagda stands. "They did not harm my giant, but in their

way, they defeated him. Rather than the sword, they used kindness to tame the beast."

"You sound amused that these mortals ruined your giant." Morrigan taps her long fingers on the arm of her throne.

"Perhaps he deserved better than I gave him out there in the cold for so long." Dagda takes a step closer. Even taller than the giant, he's a menacing figure, but something is comforting about the father of the gods. The sorrow in his blue eyes is somehow familiar. It reminds me of how my father looked when he said goodbye to his three sons. Was that today or yesterday? I feel as if we've lived an age since then.

"I'll say," Harper whispers.

With a sharp look, Morrigan narrows her gaze on Harper. "Do not forget the screaming winds." She points to Liam. "The soldier could not master his mind without help."

"I see nothing wrong with how the younger one showed them the way." Dagda continues to defend us. "They solved your riddle with ease."

I think he's teasing her.

Huffing, the goddess of war says, "I concede that they were more clever than I gave them credit for."

Dagda spreads his arms. "Do we let Domhan fall into darkness forever or fulfill the prophecy?"

Dian Cécht's voice is sharp. "All six passed through the gate as the prophecy demanded. I would give them what they came for, Father."

Morrigan says, "The elves have been entertaining in their way. The dark one should be stopped. I see a future in front of us."

Dagda smiles, showing bright white teeth. "I am pleased." He waves us forward. "Come, my children. There is not much time."

Hardly ready to defy him, we walk to the center of the circle while Dagda backs away and resumes his seat on the central throne. He waves a hand, and a large silver rock with smooth edges on eight sides appears in front of him. "This is the Stone of Lia Fal. This stone is a test of sovereignty."

Rising, Morrigan touches the stone, and it reduces its size to the palm of her hand. She steps toward Aaran, and the stone screams so loudly I have to cover my ears. "The true king." She cocks her head and steps toward Liam. Again, the stone makes a racket. With one eyebrow raised, she steps in front of me, and though I expect it to be silent, the stone screams again.

"Interesting. It would seem that any of the three born of Riordan set the Stone of Lia Fal crying."

In ancient times, this stone was used to choose a new king or queen. Lia Fal's stone legitimizes the true crown of Domhan in a way that no one can dispute. I suppose that's not true if it picks all three of us.

Dagda asks, "Will Riordan go to war with each other to decide who will rule?"

Liam and I step back and take a knee. I bow my head, showing my fealty to Aaran as the next in line to be king when the curse is broken.

Letting his voice ring out, Liam says, "There will be no war between brothers. We bow to Aaran's rule. He will be a great and fair king when the curse is broken."

Shrinking the stone and herself to human size, Morrigan silences it and hands it to me. "To break the curse, you must let Domhan see that the witch queen is a false queen. If the stone cries for her, then the curse will not be broken. No man will rule, and no woman elf will be born."

Dian Cécht clears his throat. "Forgive me, Morrigan, but that is not entirely correct." He reduces his size and circles the six of them. Closing his eyes, he cocks her head as if listening for something. "The child will not be full elf, but she will come, and this world and the other will be forever linked. More will join the first. Many more and soon after."

Wren blurts out. "Is one of us pregnant now?" She covers her mouth with her hand as if the outburst could be pushed back in.

With a smile, Dian Cécht nods.

Before we can fully process the implications, or I can ask my mate if she might be with child, Dagda reduces to our size, waves his arms, and a golden spear appears in his hand. "The second gift is the Spear of Lugh." He hands it to Liam. With this, you will strike the demons out of where they do not belong. You must send them back to Coire and seal them there."

Testing the weight of the thing, Liam nods. "How exactly do I do that?"

"Seek the first, shake the earth, and the rest will fall." Dagda gives his cryptic instructions and walks to face Aaran.

From a sheath on his back, the old god pulls the Sword of Light, Claíomh Solais. "Shed light on the darkness, Riordan. Beat back the evil that invaded your world. Strike true, and do not hesitate or seek a kinder way. She must be destroyed to fulfill the prophecy. When the deed is done, the balance will return, and the mortal world will heal."

Aaran bows. "What of those who followed the dark?"

Returning his full size, Dagda sits on his throne and looks at each of us in turn. "I cannot tell you that, my children. Use your laws and what is in your hearts to determine how to proceed after the witch queen is vanquished. Go now." He waves an arm, and the ground falls away.

I grab for Layla and find her hand before pulling her toward me while I brace for whatever we're going to hit when we land.

Chapter Twenty-One

LAYLA

At any moment, we are going to hit the ground somewhere and be killed on impact. I clutch Raith with all my might. "I love you."

"*Mo anam cara,*" he calls back to me, letting me know that I'm the other half of him.

The air gets heavy, and I hold my breath.

One moment we're falling, and the next I'm standing on wobbly legs in front of the doors to the oracle. I stumble, and Raith's arms steady me.

"What the fuck?" Harper's exclamation is what I'm feeling.

"You'd think the old gods would have a less stressful way to transport us." Wren straightens her tunic.

Aaran approaches the same two men who met us when we first arrived to go to the Watchers' Gate, where they stand near the entrance with our five horses.

One says, "There was a premonition of your arrival. The battle is not going well."

A surge of panic rushes through me, and I immediately know the feelings are Raith's and not my own. Still, my adrenaline is on high alert. We're going into a war. A few months ago, I was living in Southern California, doing odd jobs, and training for a sports television show. As Raith pulls me onto Sileadh's back, I catch a glimpse through the trees of what used to be the green fields that stretch from the city wall west to the river. Pocked with holes and strewn with bodies. "My god."

Raith searches for whatever I've seen. He kicks the horse into a gallop, and we charge down the path, pulling to a stop at a break in the trees.

The better we can see the battlefield, the worse it looks. A line of catapults throws boulders at the city wall. At that distance, they have already left several gaping holes in the outer wall. Beasts, unlike anything I've ever seen before, haul the catapults closer to the city.

The demons I hoped to destroy on Arcania spread out across the fray by the thousands. They fight with claw and spear against elves, centaurs, and dwarves. The fairies use light magic to send shadow demons to their eternal rest.

Elspeth and Brion are in the center of the battle, standing back-to-back. Brion throws balls of white light and wields his sword with the grace of a ballet. Elspeth shoots magical arrows from her fingers. All the while, they inch closer to Vanora.

The witch queen watches from the back of the fight. Standing on a berm with a blond male elf at her side, she shoots black lightning, and a fairy falls to the bloody field.

Behind her, the black dragon looks on, waiting for commands.

"We have to go." Aaran kicks his black horse into a gallop.

Following at a dangerous pace, I feel all the emotions around me. Even the horses' stress reaches me. Most of all, Raith's concerns rush through me. His need to protect his mother and father is now my own.

This is my family. I've waited my entire life to find them, and no one, not even a lightning-wielding witch, is going to take them from me. I tighten my hold around Raith's middle, and the fire and ice inside me whirl as if jostling to get out.

We will win this. There is no other option, Raith says in my head.

He already knows my heart and that I'm with him until the end of time.

At the turn that would take us to the castle and stable, we continue straight and on the heels of the other four horses. Aaran rounds the wall and leads us to the outer rear gate. Wrapping his hand around Harper's head, he pulls her close and kisses her hard. "Stay alive. Do what must be done. Keep your sisters close."

"I love you." She slides to the ground and slaps her horse's backside.

The horse runs back the way we came.

A similar scene transpires between Liam and Wren. He says, "Your mother is safe in the bottom of the castle. We will be reunited before this day is done."

After a brief kiss, she nods, likely in answer to something spoken through their connection.

Liam and Aaran ride into the battle.

Raith takes my arm and lowers me to the ground. Joining me there, he sends his horse away with Wren's. Gripping my shoulders, he says, "I must get close enough to place the Stone of Lia Fal near the witch queen." His kiss is hard and desperate. It's almost a goodbye kiss.

"We will be together again." I'm not settling for anything less.

"You are my life, Layla Stark. I will find you in this life and all the lives and worlds where souls can dwell." He steps back and looks at me, Wren, and Harper. "Stay safe. Vanora will not fall by elven hands. The three of you will have your part to play before this is over." With one last gaze into my eyes, he draws a deep breath and takes off at a run.

A demon gets in his way, and he draws his sword and slices the monster's head from its body. Staying low, he disappears into the sea of warring bodies.

A band tightens around my heart.

Wren and Harper each take my hands.

Harper speaks first. "We'll see them all again. I've always wanted a sister, and now I have two."

"We stay together," Wren says. "We fight together."

I look out over the carnage. One of the catapults, a wooden structure at least fifteen feet tall with a counterweight of purple stone, gains ground. I know those were wrought in the world of my village. "Together." I squeeze their hands and let the fire inside me push forward. Pointing to the catapult as three demons load a boulder into the bucket, I say, "We need to destroy that. It's too close. They'll reach the houses inside the city."

Harper smiles. "Burn it down, sister."

"I don't think I can shoot fire that far." I draw heat into my hands.

We run to the left, where fewer of our people are engaged in the fight.

Wind whips around our feet. Wren says, "I'll blow the fire as far as we need."

The way Harper's voice carries, you'd think she had Elspeth's magic. "Clear the way. Fire."

Elves dash left and right, leaving only demons, cú sidhe, and Vanora's soldiers in the path between us and the catapult. Some of the soldiers look around for the source of the fire. When they see nothing, they march toward the city, thinking they can take advantage of the elves backing away.

"Ready?" I ask

"Go," Wren calls back.

Praying the fire will hit none with light in their hearts, and it will destroy the implement of destruction, I make the decision that I'm a soldier in a war, just as I was on Arcania. Flames fly from my fingers in long spear shapes that arc through the air.

Wren's wind whips in the same direction, carrying the flames.

One spear runs through a demon and keeps going as the beast falls. Its black blood pools on the ground. Another falls as a fire spear hits its head. Another is sliced in two. My fire cuts down a black-and-red-clad soldier and leaves the black dog burning as it runs away.

The first fire spear to hit the catapult strikes the base. The second kills one of the demons supporting the boulder to load. The boulder rolls to the ground as the wooden frame and rope holding the counterweight go up in flames.

The three of us move back to the wall as the rope burns through and the arm swings forward without its payload, catching the demons unaware and smashing one in the head. It falls and does not rise again.

"Good work." Harper wraps her arms around both of us.

Three demons charge toward us.

Harper lets out a scream that shakes the earth and air.

The demons falter and fall.

Ten elves jump on them and slice their thick black skin with swords and knives.

"I didn't know you had that scream, too." I thought we each had different magic.

"Neither did I." Wren wraps a scrunchie around her wild curls.

"We all have it?" Harper asks.

Wren and I nod.

"Can you do the rainbow thing too?" Harper watches for danger while waiting for an answer.

The elves formed a semicircle around us in an effort to keep the demons and enemy troops from reaching us.

"What is the rainbow thing?" I try to remember her story of coming to Tús Nua.

"When I released the Aracan elves from the dark spell that tied them to Vanora, it was like a wave of rainbow." Harper's eyes go wide as a demon breaches the line.

Turning, instinct taking over, I let loose shards of ice from my fingertips, and they find their mark deep in the demon's hide. One pierces his eye, and he falls back so hard the ground shakes.

Both Wren and Harper stare at me. Wren says, "You are fierce, sister."

"I protect those I care about. No demon will reach us." When they both smile, I smile too. "Harper, can you send one of those rainbow things across the battlefield?"

She studies the scene. We can't see beyond the elves protecting us, except that there are thousands. Vanora is on high ground. The catapults are taller, so we can see them. It's a sea of lives, both good and evil, all dying. "Maybe. If my prayer was strong enough."

"I have an idea." I hold my breath for a moment while they both wait for me to go on. "It's likely that at least a portion of her soldiers are bespelled. If we could break that..."

Wren smiles. "We lose enemies and maybe even gain allies."

Excitement builds inside me. Maybe we can help save some lives. We make a plan.

RAITH

The Stone of Lia Fal weighs heavily in my pocket. Leaving Layla behind was the hardest thing I've ever done. She's in danger, and I'm running away from her to prove a point. I know it's what the old gods demanded of me, but my heart is in a war of its own.

Remembering the way she crumbled a mountain on top of a horde of demons, I run my sword through a demon and feel a bit better. Layla can take care of herself. I'm sure my brothers' mates are equally self-sufficient.

Neither soldier nor diplomat, I was trained as both. Strange, my first full battle should come on this scale, with so much to lose, but purpose and knowledge guide my actions. I dodge as many elves and enemies as I can. My job is to get the stone to a place where I can prove Vanora is not the rightful queen. As much as I want to destroy the evil with blade and strength, I must stay the course and follow my path.

The field is wet with blood that sprays up with every step I take. It reeks of death. People I've known my entire life lie dead or dying. Continuing is nearly impossible, but I must.

Screams, both of agony and victory, rise and fall all around me. There is no time to see who is winning. The sheer number of demons and dark soldiers is a bad sign. It is with pride that I note how well the elves fight for our home.

I shift to the side to avoid being trampled by a centaur with streaming blond hair and a brown horse body. He has a cú sidhe skewered through his spear and cries out his ferocity.

Foot by foot, I push through the throng, trying to reach the knoll where Vanora stands. She's stopped using her black lightning for the moment. Perhaps her strength is waning. It must have taken a lot to create the giant portal that allowed these numbers to march on Tús Nua.

Two demons run at me—their forked tongues lolling from their slime-drooling mouths filled with three-inch-long, gray, pointed teeth. No life, the way I know it, lives within those vacant eyes. Unsure if magic will harm them, I draw it into my blade instead. Layla prays for her magic, and I do the same—asking the old gods to let me strike hard and true. Leaping into the air, I wait for my descent, then cut through the beast's slick black neck.

The second demon spears my arm before I can twist out of the way. Pain lances through me, but I managed to dislodge the tip before falling back to the ground.

Lifting his crooked spear, the monster smiles as he moves to spike my chest. He jerks back, and black blood spews from his mouth.

A sword tip shoots through the demon's chest, and I roll away to avoid his heavy, disgusting body landing on top of me. When I look up, Rían is staring down at me with his hand outstretched.

I rise and stare. It's a different kind of magic that allowed me to find someone akin to a brother in this sea of life and death.

He turns to fight an enemy soldier. Swords clash.

The space between Vanora and me is thick with fighting. I search for a way through.

A tiny light flashes across my eyes, then stops, and Niamh, the size of a dragonfly, flutters in front of me. "Did you see the old gods?"

"We did." I duck a charging soldier's blade and cut him through the middle when he loses his balance. "Her soldiers are poorly trained."

Sweat and grime run down Rían's face. "Yes, but she has too many, and the demons are unnaturally strong."

"Where were you running to, Raith?" Niamh rises into the air as several more demons rush us.

Fighting back-to-back with the captain of the guard, it's

becoming clear that I'm going to need help to get through this mess, and time is running out. "I have to get to Vanora. I have the Stone of Lia Fal."

"The battle is thick, but we'll get you as close as we can." Rían begins slashing through the crowd and dashing around smaller skirmishes. "Stay low and follow me."

From above us, Niamh shouts down directions. "Right. Straight. No, left. Run hard."

If anyone gets in our way, Rían moves with magnificent speed to remove the obstacle.

As ordered, I keep close to his back and have little need for my blade. Between the fairy and my friend, we begin to make strides toward my goal. "Princess Niamh, can you see Liam and Aaran?"

She flies higher. "Liam rounds the battle to the left and Aaran to the right on horseback."

Rían picks up a dark soldier and throws him into a line of demons, who lose their balance and topple. "What is about to happen, Raith?"

"I don't know. I hope we're about to break the curse. That's the plan."

Ahead is a line of demons three deep, with shadow demons floating ten feet above them. It's obvious that they are here to protect Vanora, and between them and the dragon Trocar at her back, they are doing a good job.

I search for a break in the line. This is a terrible idea. "Rían, you know how you just threw that soldier? Do you think you can throw me between the Coire demons and the shadow demons?"

Wide-eyed, he looks from me to the line of enemies. "If I miss, your mother will never forgive me."

We shift to avoid a centaur battling one of the demon beasts that were pulling the catapult that is now on fire. Three more centaurs rush in to finish the beast.

"My mother will understand, and you won't miss." I grip his arm. "You are a brother to me. I will see you on the other side."

Emotion thick in his eyes, he nods. "Princess, we need a distraction."

Niamh rises high. "Go!" A bright light fills the area.

Crouching, Rían cups his hands.

I step in, and as he tosses me, I leap and pray for both of our strength as I fly through the air. The filthy Coire demons shield their eyes while I soar over their heads, just below the shadow demons, who are also repelled by the pure white light.

On the other side, I hit the ground rolling and end on one knee facing the witch queen with her man, Ciaran, and Trocar. Dressed in a black cape with a red interior, the cold wind makes her look like a crow in flight.

She shows her teeth in what might be a smile, but looks more like a threat. "The useless third Riordan son, I presume. Very acrobatic, but unless you are going to beg to join me, I see no use for you." She lifts her arms, and they spark with black magic. She holds, cocking her head. "You are quite pretty. Perhaps you'd like to take your place beside me and warm my bed. I would like to fuck one of Elspeth's spawn, and Ciaran has served his purpose."

"My queen?" Ciaran's eyes widen, and his already white face pales to a sickening color.

She pats his cheek. "I jest, my love."

He relaxes, but I don't think she was joking.

The caw, caw of a raven forces my gaze up. Adhar, Wren's raven familiar, circles watchfully. It comforts me to know that Wren might see what's happening, linking me to Layla in a way.

I removed the palm-size rock from my pocket. Exposed as I am to danger in front and behind, I know what must be done for Domhan. I am the first step, and I trust my brothers and our human mates will be ready. I toss it so that it lands halfway up the knoll—close enough that it should sing if Vanora were a true queen. "Let the Stone of Lia Fal show that you are a false queen."

She stares at the small black stone where it lies in the dying grass. Angling her head one way and then the other, she raises an eyebrow. "This bauble is going to stop me? You really are the useless son."

For a long moment, I think the old gods have failed me. I back away, careful not to get too close to the Coire demons, who have not yet noticed that I have breached their lines.

Using magic so that all can hear my voice. "This is the Stone of Lia Fal and the true test of Domhan's rightful ruler. If Vanora Braddish is that queen, let it sing for her now."

The stone shifts and grows to the size it was before Morrigan picked it up. Now, as big as Trocar's head, the silver rock with smooth edges on eight sides, shines with magic but makes no sound.

Glad that this wasn't a terrible miscalculation, I let go of the breath I was holding.

Magic prickles my skin. It's similar to when Layla uses her magic, but not quite the same, and a rainbow washes over the battlefield.

Baring her teeth, Vanora hisses and blocks the human magic.

Soldiers whose eyes were black with the spells that bound them to the witch queen blink away the haze and look around as if waking from a nightmare. All over the field of battle, skirmishes stop as elven soldiers regain their own minds.

The raven's caw is louder, and she flies back toward the outer wall of Tús Nua, where Wren is hopefully safe with my mate and Harper.

Awash with satisfaction, I smile and meet the witch queen's gaze. "You are a puppet master, not a ruler."

Unfortunately, Trocar's eyes are still clouded by her evil magic. Maybe we need something stronger or the proper human prayers to free the dragon. For now, he lowers his gaze to me, and I back closer to the demons, hoping my proximity will keep him from burning me or shifting me through time.

Rage darkens Vanora's eyes, and her lips open in an ear-piercing scream. She raises her hands, allowing the black lightning to come. "You cannot win this. I will destroy your entire family."

I put up a shield of white magic and brace for whatever evil burns its way through.

Chapter Twenty-Two

LAYLA

"I think we need to get to the front."

Vanora has lost her temper and is working up some of that nasty lightning, but I can only assume she's directing her rage at Raith. We heard his voice, and many stopped fighting to watch as the stone judged her unworthy of song, proving she is not the rightful ruler of Domhan.

Harper cranes her neck, trying to see more. "I agree. This waiting at the back is not for me. I can't find Aaran, and we can only ask Adhar to be our eyes and risk her life for so long."

The white raven sits on the wall behind us and gives a hearty caw.

Wren is the shortest of the three of us. She props her hands on her full hips and studies the battlefield. "I don't know how we're to get through that. Maybe if we find

Elspeth and Brion, we can all move toward the action and let the stone sing for the true queen."

Nodding, I push to the line of soldiers standing their ground around us for protection. I pick the guard in the center. "We need to find Elspeth. Can you push your way through this?"

He frowns back at me. "Our orders are to keep the three of you safe no matter what."

The female soldier next to him shifts her gaze to me, then to her comrade. "The captain also said to follow their orders, Sean."

With Wren on my left and Harper on my right, we stand together ready to do a battle of wits with the Domhan soldiers if need be.

Sean sighs, then stabs a demon as the monster tries to break through the line. "Find the Riordan, Mia." He turns his head to meet my gaze. "If we can get you to them, we will, my ladies."

Wren whispers, "Are we ladies?"

Harper shrugs. "I'm definitely not a lady, but don't tell Sean."

"I'm standing right here, my lady." Sean laughs and holds off a skirmish from trampling us.

Mia points to the west. "There."

"Form ranks around the princes' mates." Sean's command is immediately obeyed, and while five soldiers remain in front of us, five more form a line behind us. Others flank us, ready to battle any threats.

Step by painfully slow step, we march west while elves and demons fight and bleed all around us. The ground is soaked with blood, both red and black, and the smell is more horrible than anything I could ever have imagined. I gag and so does Wren, but we hold it down and grip each other's hands.

Harper makes a face, but she doesn't seem as affected by the odor. As she scans to the left, her eyes widen. "I see Aaran."

Wren jumps, trying to see. Frustration apparent in her tone, she says, "I only see Sean's back."

With a grunt, Sean strikes an enemy soldier who isn't bespelled, but a dedicated follower of the dark queen.

The enemy soldier strikes swiftly, catching Sean on the shoulder. His armor deflects the brunt of the blow, but the blade catches where the mail ends.

Blood runs from the wound at his clavicle.

The soldier on his left slices off the head of the enemy.

Sean loses a step, but rights himself and keeps moving.

Pulling a tunic from her bag, Wren cuts it with her dagger, then tears away a long strip. She hands it to me. "Press this to his wound. He needs stitches or magic, but maybe we can slow the bleeding."

I fold the fabric and press it to the two-inch cut. I wish I had the ability to heal, but that magic seems to be reserved for elves. "Hang on, Sean."

"Thank you, my lady. I'll be fine. It's just a scratch."

It's a bit more than that, and from the sound when the sword struck, I'll bet his bone is cracked. It must be excruciating, but Sean continues moving forward.

With another lost step, Sean grunts. "My ladies, please make room for me."

Harper and I separate.

Sean hollers. "Close ranks. Robyn, step up." As he moves

back a step, Mia and the rest close the gap, and another soldier, Robyn, steps up from behind us while Sean allows me to tuck the bandage under his mail. Once that's done, he steps back to protect us from behind.

Since Harper sent her rainbow wave, many of the soldiers who were under Vanora's spell have changed sides, and the fighting has lessened at the rear of the battle. Other Domhan elves, dwarves, and two centaurs join our procession.

I search the throng of horror for my elf, but I know he's too far at the head to see from here. On the far right, on horseback, Liam battles to reach the space between Vanora and a thick line of demons. "I can see Liam, Wren. He's nearly at the front."

She grips my arm. There's no way she can see over the crowd. "Is he hurt?"

"No. He looks fine. He's fighting his way through." I pray all three of our mates stay safe from harm.

Sean trudges on behind us. He's keeping up now, though I imagine that wound will limit his fighting ability, and that is likely why he gave the order to be replaced in the lead position. It's hard to say how old he is since all the elves look young to my eyes. His dark brown hair hangs to his shoulders, and his blue eyes look battlewise. I'm willing to bet he's far older than Raith. His voice is strained. "Lady Wren, do not fear. Liam is the finest soldier we've ever seen."

Loosening her grip on my arm, Wren nods. "Thank you, Sean."

"Nearly there," Mia shouts.

"What is this?" Brion demands.

Mia steps aside, leaving room for Harper, Wren, and me

to be seen by Brion and Elspeth, who are both filthy and splattered with all manner of grime.

Wide-eyed, Elspeth asks, "What are you doing? You should be safe near the wall."

A catapult lets loose and something crashes into the wall not far from where we were waiting. The sound is both terrifying and deafening.

"No place is safe." I ignore Brion's scowl. "Raith has proved that Vanora is not the true queen. You need to show the world that the Stone of Lia Fal will sing for you."

Harper adds, "We need to get to the front."

After a brief faraway look, Elspeth nods. "You're right."

"You cannot be killed, Elspeth. You should remain as far from Vanora as possible." Brion's argument is out of fear for his mate, and I understand, but he's wrong.

Touching his arm, Elspeth says, "I'm not without power, my love. She'll not defeat me a second time, and now I have my sons who can take my place should I fall."

The pain etched on Brion's face has nothing to do with the cuts and bruises he's suffered during the battle. "You will not fall."

With a swallow, she nods. "Forward." She points her sword, and all those around us who fight in the light begin moving toward Vanora and the line of demons who protect her.

RAITH

The pain when the black lightning breaches my light-magic shield is indescribable. It's as if my cells are being split apart one by one.

Something distracts Vanora, and the pain stops. Beneath a darkening sky, I can't decide if night is falling or my vision is failing. My limbs refuse to accept any commands.

To my right, only twenty feet away, demons are a wall of black against any good that survives this war. To my left, the ground rises, and Vanora calls out, her words muddled in my pain-laced mind.

Barely able to lift my head, I glimpse Liam's dark blond hair. With him, a wave of centaurs bash and stomp demons while drawing closer.

"Destroy him." Vanora orders. "Kill them all."

The demon line shifts in Liam's direction.

Pushing past bone-deep agony, I roll away from danger and strain to my knees.

From the other direction, a battle cry rises.

Aaran holds the gleaming sword high, then slices through three demons with one swing of the Sword of Light, Claíomh Solais. Not really its purpose, but he can hardly be expected to wield more than one sword or go without during a demon invasion.

"All of Elspeth's useless spawn in one place." Vanora spits on the ground. "Good. I will enjoy the horror on your mother's face when I kill all of you at once."

Liam rides in and leaps from his horse. Grabbing my arm, he steadies me. "Alright, little brother?"

"Nothing a few decades of healing won't fix." I spread

my legs and find stability. "You better send the demons back where they belong."

While Liam holds the golden Spear of Lugh high, his gleaming eyes show he wishes he could send that deadly point flying through the air and right into Vanora's heart. After what the witch did to Wren, I don't blame him. But that is not his destiny.

"Stay the course," I whisper.

"Will you strike me down and feel the heat of Trocar's magic, second son? I should have locked you in Coire away from that mongrel human of yours. I don't know how you escaped, but I know those beasts from their magicless world had some part in it. Do you think she'll shed any tears when you're burned to a crisp by my dragon?" Vanora steps back. "Use your fire, my dragon."

Trocar rears back. His slitted pupils narrow on Liam and me. Smoke puffs in long streams from his huge nostrils as his black scales gleam in the setting sun.

Aaran screams, "Harper, the dragon. Free him."

The demons are pushed to the side as Mother, Father, and our three mates breach the line. Half the army surrounds them.

Harper screams, loosing a wave of rainbow energy at Trocar. Amid the madness of war, it flows through me like peace and tranquility.

The dragon freezes. Black veins in the golden part of his eyes fade, then disappear. His pupils widen, and he stares over the battlefield.

On a long cry, Vanora shifts her magic to her largest ally. She feeds darkness into him until he roars with pain.

Wren and Layla each put a hand on Harper's shoulders.

Staring at Trocar, the three of them mutter something. They must be praying. The rainbow increases in strength and color until the black dragon is awash with pure light magic.

He beats his wings, knocking Vanora over and disengaging her magic.

Ciaran picks her up off the ground. He throws a ball of fire at Harper.

I shoot light to block the fire, and it skips away from our mates, igniting the grass.

Wren pulls water from the ground and air, dowsing the wayward flame before it can harm anyone.

Trocar stares at Vanora for a long moment, but when she raises her hands to cast another spell, he roars, knocking her and Ciaran to the ground. He beats his wings, displacing air with more force than my feet can stand.

Liam holds me in place, his own legs spread for balance.

Trocar flies up and away from battle. He must know that he is too vulnerable to the dark magic.

Hundreds of demons and the witch queen's elven followers are all around us. They seem stunned by the sudden changes in the battle's course and by the dragon's abandonment.

Elspeth steps forward. "Vanora, you cannot win. We have the old gods on our side." The Stone of Lia Fal begins singing for all to hear.

All the different people of Domhan's alliance cheer as the rightful queen is shown in the old way.

Once on her feet, Vanora screams, "Attack."

Several soldiers, including Rían, Nainsi, and Bert, surround Mother to keep her safe. Fairies fly above her to add their magic to her safety.

Liam lifts the gods-given Spear of Lugh. "By order of the old gods, I send the demons back where they belong."

Unsure what will happen next, those of us around him back away several feet.

Scanning myriad demons, Liam narrows his gaze on the largest of the horde. On its black slime-covered head is a red mark from the forehead to the back of its skull. With a long look at the spear, Liam takes a deep breath, rears back, and throws Lugh over our heads.

Watching the flight, I fear for all the possible targets the point might harm on its way into the crowded battlefield. However, my brother's aim is true, and the Spear of Lugh pierces the thick breast of the marked demon.

Dagda's words, to seek the first, shake the earth, and the rest will fall, replay in my mind "Shake the earth."

Layla's gaze meets mine. She stares for a long moment, then lifts her voice in the magical scream unique to our humans.

When Wren and Harper join her, the spear turns to white light. It swallows the demon and forms a vortex that those in the light rush away from, while the demons are drawn to it like moths to a flame. One by one, they enter the gateway to Coire as if in a trance.

"Stop!" Vanora screams. "Where are you going?" She pushes past Mother's guards and runs toward the vortex before realizing she's put herself in the middle of the battle between light and evil, and her forces are depleted as the vortex expands and swallows up every Coire demon. When it closes, not even the spear remains.

Perhaps the old gods took their weapon back.

Ciaran moves to follow, but Rían knocks his sword to the

ground and casts a binding spell to keep Ciaran's hands frozen at his sides.

Vanora looks from side to side for an escape, her remaining loyal soldiers surrounding her in much the same way ours protect Mother.

Vanora calls for shadow demons to carry her away.

The fairy king, Muiredach, flies above her and creates a spray of light that keeps the shadows from descending. His long white hair is braided for battle. His bright blue eyes narrow on Vanora. "There will be no running from this, witch."

Mother strides forward with Father to her right, and my brothers and I flanking them. "Surrender, Vanora. I promise you and those who follow you a fair trial."

"As if I would ever surrender to you. I don't care what that piece of rock whines, I am the queen of this world and Arcania. I will be queen of all the worlds." Raising her hands, she calls for her magic. A black spark lights at her fingertips, but it's slow in coming and weaker than when she attacked me.

"My son told me about your Arcania rule. You destroyed an entire planet to bring abominations into the world. You nearly drove the Aracans to extinction with your grand plan. Is that how you treat the worlds and people you rule?" Mother scans Vanora's followers, making eye contact with as many as will look at her. "Is that the kind of queen you're honored to follow?"

"Honor." Vanora spits. "There is no honor in this world or any other. There is only strength, and the power to wield it."

"You're wrong, old friend. There is honor, and there is

also love. You could have been part of something greater than yourself if you had followed the path of light. I tried to tell you all those years ago, but you would not listen." The sorrow in my mother's voice hurts my heart. Until now, I didn't realize how close she and Vanora were in their youth. Mother loved the woman who tried to destroy everything she believed in.

It's so unfair.

Who said life was fair? Layla's hand slips into mine. She squeezes then lets go, knowing that we may all need our hands for battle before this is over.

"Stay back, *mo anam cara*. When the fighting starts, stay back." I say it softly for her ears only, but I say it through our connection as well. The desperation in my voice is not lost on either of us.

"You know I cannot." Her magic simmers at the surface, tingling along my skin.

Vanora pulls her shoulders back and lifts her chin. Black lightning sparks along her arms, shoulders, and head, like a cape of evil surrounding her. "I could never be any part of your weak rule, Elspeth, any more than I could have joined those ridiculous oracles. They sit in their mountain, judging and doing nothing. They will be the first to come to their knees when I destroy you and your miserable family." She points at me. "I'll start with the useless one." She shoots pain through me.

It feels as if my gut is being torn open as I fuel my magic through sheer desperation. Pushing back, I gain ground.

Mother screams, as do my new sisters.

Layla forces her magic into me. "Her lightning can't defeat human magic."

The pain eases.

Vanora's lightning springs back, and she stumbles. She stares at me as if seeing me for the first time. "Perhaps I have underestimated you. Kneel and vow loyalty to me, and I'll make you far more important than you could ever hope to be as the third son. You know your mother wished you were a girl. She'll never love you as she does your brothers."

At that, I smile.

Vanora's gaze widens, and she frowns.

Allowing Layla's magic to strengthen me, I say, "You've miscalculated, witch. I have felt love from both of my parents all my life. Even being the third son with little to no prospects, I never doubted their love."

"I can make you head of my armies." Vanora stretches her arms out to encompass the hundreds still following her. "Or perhaps you'd like to be my consort and rule beside me."

Ciaran staggers under Rían's bind. "My queen?"

"Oh, Ciaran, you have been a good lover, but I know you've plotted against me these past years. I know of your plot to usurp me as soon as the curse is broken." With a flash of magic, she knocks Ciaran from his feet.

He lies on his back, groaning.

None of the soldiers go to his aid, but several look extremely uncomfortable.

"Kill your mother, and you can rule this world at my side."

I throw a ball of white magic at her. "Never."

She bats it aside. "Pity." Turning to Mother, Vanora attacks with her black shadow magic.

Mother falls to the ground and shakes.

Nothing, not even what we did and saw in Arcania, can

compare to the horror of watching my mother's soul being ripped from her body. I ready a ball of light magic. There is no way I'm letting her exist that way under the witch queen's command. It will haunt my nightmares for a lifetime, but I will kill my mother before I let her fall to that fate.

Father dives over her. "Do not give in to it, my love."

Layla looks at me and then at Mother. A desperate helplessness rocks her on her heels. I know exactly how she feels, but there's no other way. She screams, and the air shakes.

Wren and Harper add their voices to hers.

Even on the right side of the human magic, it's hard to stay on my feet as the earth and air vibrate with light and dark.

Losing her concentration, Vanora falters.

Her hold on Mother snaps, and Mother gasps for air as her soul snaps back into her body.

His face a mask of worry and rage, Aaran kneels beside our parents. Grasping the hilt of the Sword of Light, Claíomh Solais, he stands. "You have made your last shadow demon, Vanora Braddish." He throws the sword. It flies end over end toward Vanora, everything feeling as if it's in slow motion. If Ciaran were not still writhing on the ground, perhaps he could have batted the blade away from his queen. As she struck him down, there is no champion beside her. Claíomh Solais slices through skin and bone as it plunges through her chest.

The look of total surprise on Vanora's face, her hands still outstretched, is almost worth everything we've been through. Almost.

Light cracks her skin, radiating through breaks in the witch queen. Bit by bit, she comes apart in vulgar black threads of evil until she's nothing but black wisps that burn and sink to the ground.

Above, shadow demons wail and break apart in a much gentler fashion, their ashes floating down around us.

Rían hovers over Ciaran, ready to arrest him as soon as he recovers. "Long live the Riordan!"

The field erupts in cheers. Domhan soldiers surround elves left without their witch queen as they lay down their weapons.

Father and Aaran help Mother to her feet. Weariness and fear are pushed aside with her steady will to do right by this world, its elves, and all those who gave their lives to save the light and restore balance. She walks slowly up the side of the berm toward the Stone of Lia Fal. Now, so big it rises from the ground taller than Mother, it sings so loud it drowns out all the other noise.

She places her hand on it, and the singing stops. Her voice carries. "You have done so well, my people and my friends. You have won this world of Domhan back from the brink of destruction. We will have much rebuilding to do before we are whole again, but we are strong and will manage it together." She takes a moment to look at the centaurs, dwarves, and fairies standing side by side with Domhan elves and Aracan elves. "Never again will we allow ignorance and prejudice to tell us who to trust and where to put our friendship. I vow to work with the rulers of every community to make this world healthy and prosperous again."

Cheers and chants of "Long live Riordan" fill the air as snow begins falling.

Mother raises her hands for peace. "We will mourn our

heroic dead for half a fortnight, and then we will celebrate our victory. The prisoners will be taken to the dungeon until a more permanent solution is decided upon. Tend their wounds and feed them." She nods at Rían.

He bows and starts giving orders to move the prisoners to the dungeon and calls for the healers to follow once those in the light are tended to.

I wrap my arms around Layla. "You were magnificent."

"I couldn't let her force you to do something you'd regret for the rest of your life." She leans on me. "I need you whole for our child."

Pulling back, I stare. My entire body feels both warm and cold at once. Pure joy rushes through me like fairy magic. My voice is barely audible around my tight throat. "Child?"

A sweet blush colors her cheeks. "We've been so busy, I didn't notice my cycle was off. Also, being an athlete, I sometimes skip because of lower body fat. But after that god said what he did, I started thinking about it and noticing some changes. Still, we were in the middle of a war, and I didn't want to freak you out."

I haul her against me, nod and breathe her in. "I'm at once freaking out and have never been happier in my entire life."

"I can't promise a girl." Still in my arms, she shrugs. "Though I have a good feeling about it."

Pressing my mouth to her ear, I can hardly believe this is my mate, and our life together is about to truly start. "Boy or girl, they will be ours, and that's enough for me. I will go back to your world with you if that is what you want. I don't care where we live as long as I am with you."

"Let's do all the princely things here for the next week or so and then think about all of that." Tears rolling down her face, she kisses me. "After all, I've never had a real family. I'd like to enjoy them for a while."

The noisy post-battlefield fades away, and there is only Layla and me in a bubble I never want to leave.

Epilogue One

HARPER

As soon as the pyres have burned and elves who move rock are hard at work rebuilding the parts of Tús Nua that were destroyed by catapults, there are things I need. I've done what was asked of me; now it's time.

Aaran is in the throne room. His mother looks on as he discusses trade agreements with the dwarf king.

Fancor stands with his arms crossed over his barrel chest, his expression a mix of seriousness and confidence.

I don't care much for this room. I suppose it's what, in a large hotel, would be called a ballroom. Though at the far end, a dais rises three steps above the main floor. On either side are columns that remind me of an old church. High windows line the side walls and let in streams of light, which reflect off crystal chandeliers hanging from the center of the ceiling.

The throne is white marble, encrusted with gold and lined with royal blue cushions. It's beautiful and daunting all at once.

I lean against a column and wait for the discussion to end. The cold marble floor shines bright white, and the chill seeps through my soft elven shoes.

Nainsi steps beside me and wraps an arm around my waist. "How are things going in here?"

"Slow, from the look of it." I lean into my friend. "I'm waiting for my turn," I say, half joking.

"Oh?" She tips her head to meet my gaze. "What do you need that couldn't be discussed in the bedroom or at the dinner table?"

"I want to go home and see my mother." My heart tightens, wondering if Mom's cancer stayed away. I'm terrified of what I'll find back in New Jersey, but I have to go.

Frowning, she nods. "Why tell them in a public forum?"

"Because I'm a coward and no one will go ballistic in the throne room with so many ears and eyes." It's not an admission I'm proud of.

She chuckles. "I think they will understand. At least, I hope they will." She pauses and draws a long breath. "Bert and I will return to the Labrador Coast."

I suppose I shouldn't be shocked. "I thought you were happy to be home."

Letting her shoulders slump, she sighs. "It was good to see my aunt and uncle. I'm glad to have been here to fight for Domhan. But my life and Bert's are in the human world. I miss my bar and our little place above it. Bert needs to fish to feel alive, and I want him happy. I've spoken to Wren, and she will check in via her portal twice per sun. Elspeth has arranged for a scrying bowl in case we need to contact her or just want to visit. I won't be cut off the way I was for ten years."

"Are you sure?" My heart is breaking a little bit. I love Bert and Nainsi. "I'll miss you."

Giving me a squeeze, she smiles. "I'll miss you, too, but Bert and I belong in the human world. We have friends and a good life. Now that I'll be able to come home from time to time, it will be even better than before."

Turning, I hug her tight. "I'm happy for you and for Bert."

She hugs me back, but breaks the embrace and nods toward the dais where the dwarves are departing.

Fancor meets my gaze and winks.

I smile at my dear friend and wave as he accompanies his father, the king, down the long hall. Their boots echo against the walls and high ceilings as they depart.

"Who is next?" Elspeth turns to a young woman who reads a list of appointments from a scroll.

I shake my head. All the magic in the world, and these people still write on scrolls. It's ridiculous. "My turn, I think," I say to Nainsi.

She gives me a firm pat on the back as I step away from the pillar.

Aaran smiles at me. "*Mo chroi*, are you alright?"

With my mind blocked, I know that's why he's asking. "I will be going to see my mother in the human world." I shift my gaze to Elspeth, where she's seated on the wide throne.

Her dress is informal by her standards—a pale-blue silk that reaches her ankles. And looks very well on her. Expression stern, she stares back at me. "When do you intend to leave?"

"Tomorrow. I have done what was asked of me here, and now I have responsibilities in the human world. My mother was ill, and while Aaran healed her, anything could have happened in the months I've been away." I keep my shoulders back and my gaze fixed on the queen.

After a moment, she lowers her gaze and her expression softens. "I see. Will you return?"

"I hope so. I must speak with my mother before I know that answer." Still cut off from Aaran's thoughts, I don't need to feel them to know he's upset.

He clears his throat and steps beside me. "Mother, I think you must already know that I will go with Harper. If your rule should end, my brothers are fully capable of caring for Domhan. I will not leave my mate."

Rising, Elspeth says, "Come with me, please." She turns and walks out of the hall through a small door at the back of the dais.

We follow to a room I've never been in. About the size of one of the bedrooms in the castle, it's set up with a desk and seating area. It's informal, with leather furniture and books stacked haphazardly on shelves and tables. I suppose it's an antechamber for when Elspeth needs a break from the formality of her position.

She slumps into a chair and offers us the couch. "I have some things I want to discuss with you before you go."

"You're going to let us leave?" Aaran's surprised tone makes me angry. What did he think she would do, forbid us or restrain us?

"Domhan and its crown are not a prison, my son.

Though I'll admit that at times, the crown weighs heavily." She looks tired and somehow older since the battle.

"Of course, Mother. I didn't mean to imply..."

She holds up a hand and waves it, brushing off any insult. "Every day since the battle, I get up early and walk out to the southern field. Snow has made the bloody horror it was into a sea of white. The Stone of Lia Fal is the only gift the old gods gave you and your brothers that remains, and I go each day to see if it still sings for me."

The spear and the sword disappeared from Domhan as soon as their purposes were fulfilled. We all assume the old gods took them back. I have no idea why the stone remained, but it lies still on the side of the berm where Raith threw it, and the weight of it makes it impossible to move. Many people go to touch the iconic boulder, but I had no idea the queen visited it too.

"Why, Mother?" Aaran's expression is filled with worry that creases his brow and draws down his lips. "You are the rightful queen. No one disputes the fact."

"I have made many mistakes. While I'm grateful to have brought Domhan to peace, perhaps we are on the brink of a new Domhan where the various people of this world live and work together in harmony. It's an exciting time." She stares at her hands for a long moment. "I plan to step down after the reconstruction. My hope is that the two of you will take my place."

"Me?" I shout much louder than intended. "Sorry. I'm just...surprised. Why would you want me to be part of ruling your world? I'm not an elf."

Her eyes are so kind when she meets my gaze that my heart aches. "My daughter, I know exactly what and who you are. Fair-minded, good-hearted, strong-willed, and the love of Aaran's life. Who better to rule at his side?"

Before I can argue, Aaran says, "Are you ill?"

"No. I'm tired and unworthy. I want to enjoy my life and the grandchildren who are already on the way." She smiles, and even my heart is lighter knowing that Layla will bring a new life into the family. "Your father and I have discussed it, and once a new ruler is in place, we will retire. There is a place in the mountains where we have long planned to build a cottage, and now that dream can become a reality."

Both Aaran and Elspeth look at me, waiting for my reaction. "I want to see my mother, and if she's amenable, I would like to bring her here to our home. As far as ruling, I have no experience or training. I love the elves and people of this world, and here I have found purpose." I can't even believe I'm saying this. My heart pounds so fast and loud, I can hear little else. "If Mom is well and willing, we'll be back, and if Aaran wants to be king, I will stand at his side, as I will in all things. He is the other half of me. It wasn't easy to think about returning home without him, but I couldn't ask him to leave when there is so much to be done here."

"I'll never leave you, *mo chroi*. I'd give up a thousand crowns to stand by your side. If the human world is where you will be happy, Liam will make a fine king." Aaran takes my hand and kisses the back as if my skin were made of the most precious material.

I open our connection and let my love flow through to him. "I don't want to be without you either. It's only my mother..." Tears break through my resolve and run freely down my cheeks.

Drawing me against his chest, he says, "Let's go talk to her. Then we can decide where we'll live."

"I don't want you to give up anything for me." The ways my life has changed over the last four months are immeasurable. No one could have predicted our course from sitting in a DMV office to possibly ruling a world beside a man whose love for me is so boundless that he would follow me to New Jersey.

Aaran kisses my head. "I would die for you."

"You were born to be king." Since falling in love with Aaran, all I've wanted is to make his life better, and now the possibility of pulling him away from his destiny is like a knife in my gut.

Taking my face in his hands, he meets my gaze. "Being king of Domhan would mean nothing without you by my side. I was born to love you and nurture you for as long as we live. If you cannot be happy here, then neither can I."

"But I can be. I want to be. I don't care so much about crowns, but this world is filled with magic, and so am I. Staying in the human world means hiding my gifts from those around me. I don't want that for me, and I definitely don't want that for you." I touch his pointed ears, which he would have to hide if we remain in New Jersey.

Elspeth clears her throat.

We turn and face her.

Grinning like any proud mother, she says, "Go home to your mother, Harper. Go with her, Aaran. Stay as long as you must, and when you are ready, come back, and I will step down happily."

I rush across and hug the Queen of Domhan, a woman I have come to respect and admire. "We won't be gone long."

A hint of sorrow flashes across her eyes so fast that I might have imagined it. "We will have a large family dinner waiting when you come home."

Is this home?

My life before Aaran jumped through a portal and tried to kidnap me to save his world was mundane in the day-to-day and tragic in many other ways. My father died in a car crash, and my mother had cancer and was near death. Because I ran away from Aaran, I was able to get to know him and understand why he took such desperate steps. He healed my mother, which nearly cost him his life, and that was when I agreed to come and help his world.

In the process, has it become my world too? I have two new brothers and sisters here. That is something I never expected to find. In the short time here, I've made friends who I know will always be here for me. Fancor is at the top of that list. Between Birdie and Wren, it's hard to decide who I'll miss more. I'm just getting to know Layla, but it's clear she's fantastic, and I already think of her as a sister.

More determined than ever to speak to my mother, I can't wait for tomorrow and the journey home. It helps that Wren's portals don't feel like you're being ripped to pieces.

Hand in hand, Aaran and I say goodbye to Elspeth and walk in the snowy garden. The snow seems to falling nearly every day. It does make everything look fresh and clean, as the queen mentioned. However, I'm not sure if I can ever look at the land to the south of Tús Nua and not see it thick with blood, battle, and bodies.

Hearing my thoughts, Aaran tugs me against his side and wraps his arm around me. "You will. It will take time, but the bad will fade, and we'll remember the glory and happiness of the day rather than the horror and sorrow."

"I hope so." I snuggle against his warmth. "I love you."

"And I love you, *mo chroi*." He hesitates. "I hope you're not about to try to convince me not to go with you to see Maggie."

"Don't you think your people need you here?" I feel a bit nauseous at the idea of being away from him.

Stopping, he turns me to face him. "Whatever they need, my family will provide. I will not be a world away from you, not now, not ever." When I only nod, he smiles. "Besides, I want to see Maggie and make the case for her to live here with us."

"I wasn't sure you'd want her here." This fear pops out of my mouth before I can stop it.

"Of course I want her here. Not only in Domhan, but here at the castle. Unless she'd rather we find her a house outside. My parents are only making plans to move out because Mother feels her presence will divert attention from who the true rulers are. She's going only a thirty-minute ride up the mountain so that she can be near us, but it will also be clear that we are the highest authority in this land. That truth might become clouded if she were on-site all the time, when an important decision had to be made."

"Do you worry people won't take you seriously?" I can't imagine anyone doubting his ability to care for the elves of this world. He is magnificent in every way.

Leaning down, he presses his lips to mine, sending a spark of desire through me as if this were our first kiss.

I open for him and slide my tongue long his. A low moan rumbles in my chest.

Breaking the kiss before we end up naked in the snow, he presses his forehead to mine. "It will be *our* rule, Harper. I will not be king with you as my consort. We shall be king and queen together as equals."

"But your father was not king."

"No. Father was consort, but that will change. I have learned, as have my brothers, that to rule this land without our mates would be a disaster. If you decide that we shall return to Domhan, we will rule as equals. I already had laws and bylaws changed accordingly. Liam, Raith, and I sat down the first morning after the final battle and told Mother of our wishes. She agreed, and it is done. This way, no matter who rules in this generation, no mate will take precedence over the other. It was important to all three of us."

My mind is reeling. "I don't know what to say."

"Say that no matter what, you'll always be by my side." Worry, fear, and love mingle in his bright blue eyes. His blond hair falls loose on one side, escaping the leather holding it back.

I tuck it behind his ear. "I will be beside you. If my mom does not return here, we will make a plan that will make us both happy, Aaran."

Wrapping his arms around me, he lifts me off the ground. Joy is written in the creases around his smiling eyes and mouth.

I circle my legs around him and grip the back of his head and shoulders, kissing him as if this were the last kiss in history. The garden is suddenly entirely inappropriate.

Still locked in an embrace, our kiss not one that should be seen by anyone, let alone those we might rule one day. Aaran runs at elf speed through the garden, house, up the steps, and doesn't stop until we are safely behind the doors to our bedroom.

Placing me gently on the bed, he tears his tunic over his head and unlaces his leggings. "I would like to fill a house with babies."

My heart is near bursting. "I can't believe I'm saying this, but I want that too."

Concern tugs his beautiful lips down, and he covers me with his body, cradling my head between his hands. "We never talked about this. Did you not plan on children in your New Jersey life?"

"Honestly, I never thought about it. I never met anyone I wanted to settle down with, so kids were the last thing on my mind." I love the weight of him, and I wrap my arms around his neck and pull him down for a long kiss.

He makes love to my mouth, and my body responds as it always does. Trailing kisses along my jaw, he pauses at the pulse beneath my ear. "Now you want to settle down and make babies with me?" He holds his thick cock just below where I need him.

"Don't tease me, Aaran, or you'll be sorry. You know I always win these battles." I lift my hips and do my own teasing.

Growling, he grinds against me. "You win them all, my sweet, lovely mate."

Pleasure spreads through me like wildfire. "I want to have all the blond, pointy-eared babies we can manage."

"I can't wait for our children to run wild through the halls and drive the nannies crazy."

We both laugh. "Is that what you did?"

"We were wild, but perhaps I can tell you about those

antics another time." With a shift of his magic, my clothes are removed, as are his leggings. His cock lies heavy and urgent along my pussy.

I open for him and wrap my legs around his, and together we find an hour of pleasure before duty calls us back to the throne room.

Epilogue Two

WREN

The day after the enormous celebration that stretched through the city and the surrounding fields, I am sick. I've spent the morning bent over the side of a commode. Everything I've tried to eat has come back. I try to recall what I might have eaten that made me so sick, but there was no odd food or excessive drink.

Liam and I didn't have much at all as we moved around, trying to see as many people as possible. Momma went with us, but then stayed with the centaurs when it was time for us to move on. As far as I know, neither of them is sick this morning.

"Miss Wren? Are you alright?" Mari's sweet voice and soft knock on the bathroom door come at the same time.

"Just an upset stomach. I don't suppose you have any saltines here?"

She pushes the door open and rushes over to me. "Miss

Wren, why didn't you send for me. How long have you been ill?"

As she tries to help me up, another wave of nausea has me retching, though there's no food in me anymore.

"Just leave me here, please. I'm sure it will pass." I shrug off her hand on my arm.

"I'll fetch you some tea and toast."

It's a relief when she's gone, and I can be miserable in private. I press my forehead to the cool edge of the commode. It's not my finest moment, but I can't help it. I didn't even get good and drunk to deserve this horrible morning.

Momma's voice breaks the silence. "Baby girl?" She pushes through the bathroom door. "Of for the love of all get out. What are you doing on the floor?"

"Hoping to either die or for the bats in my stomach to die, whichever comes first." I lift my head slowly to look at her. "I swear I had two sips of some wine and nothing else but water yesterday. I don't know why I'm so sick."

Stepping out briefly, Momma returns with the footrest from near the fireplace. "Let's get you off the floor." She puts the stool behind me, and as I lift myself, she slides it under my bottom.

The soft cushion is better than the marble floor. "Thank you, Momma. I'll be fine. You shouldn't miss your breakfast."

"Don't fret. Mari will bring something for both of us, I'm sure." She goes back out and returns with the chair from my writing desk and sits beside me. "Now, baby girl, when was the last time you had your period?"

"What?" I spin to look at her. Mistake. Another retch takes hold, and I have to wait for my stomach to settle all over again.

She rubs my back in a gentle circle. Blond hair hangs around her face as she leans toward me. "Do we need to have a chat about the birds and the bees, Wren?"

"Spare me, please. It's been a few weeks since my period." I start thinking. "We were in hell or Coire, and it was very light. I suppose I hardly had anything to eat or drink in a long time, and what they fed us there was barely edible."

"You were there for two months. Do you think it was at the beginning or the end of that time?" She keeps her voice soft, as if I were a skittish horse.

"Soon after we arrived, I guess. Time was strange down there." It hits me that it would have been over two months ago, close to three, and the bleeding was so light. I had attributed it to the conditions and circumstances, but... "Good lord, I could have been pregnant before we got there." I run my hand over my stomach. Panic rushes through me. Everything that I've been through could have affected the baby. I need to see a healer. I try to rise, but my body heaves.

Footsteps in the hallway alert me Liam's arrival before he bursts through the bathroom door. "Why do I hear from Mari that you are ill? Why didn't you tell me?" He kneels next to me and runs his hand over my body.

His magic tingles as he goes. "I'm not sick, Liam." I look up at Momma.

With a nod, she stands and walks out of the bathroom.

"I can see that you are ill." His voice is filled with worry and love.

"I think I'm pregnant."

The silence that follows threatens to rip my heart out of my chest. His hand moves away from where he was touching the back of my neck, and a heaviness fills the room.

"Oh god, you don't want children." Tears sting my eyes, and panic makes me hurl again. The pain of so much vomiting fills my body from head to the backs of my thighs, and I grip the edge of the commode to bear it.

Liam presses a soft towel to my mouth and kisses my ear. "Of course I want to have children with you. I'm just overwhelmed, sweetheart. I'm going to try to ease this nausea with magic. May I?"

I nod. "It won't hurt the baby?"

"Never." The way he says it fills me with the sense that we're talking about more than magic. His hands wrap around me from behind.

His magic tingles along my skin, and the feeling of dizzying discomfort falls away. "That's better. Thank you."

He lifts me from the floor and carries me to our bed.

Momma hands me a cup of tea. "Just a sip."

Mari stands ready with a bucket should the tea come back.

However, the warm liquid slides down and stays there. I release the breath I'm holding. "I think I'm okay now."

With a nod and a smile that shows all the happiness of a woman who's going to be a grandmother, Momma says, "Mari and I are going to give the two of you a couple of minutes. We'll be in the hall, so don't get any ideas." She gives Liam a hard look. "Then we'll be back, and you're going to try some toast while we wait for the healer to have a look at you."

They go without waiting for an answer.

I take another sip of tea, suddenly feeling vulnerable. "I'm better, Liam. You can go do whatever it was you were doing before you ran back to check on me."

"Look at me, sweetheart." His voice is firm but full of love.

Ashamed of my hesitation, I meet his gaze, ready to beg forgiveness. I'm struck dumb by the love shining in the deep blue of his eyes.

Blinking back tears, he rests his head on my abdomen. "I'll never leave you, Wren. I know the men in your life before me have been unreliable, but I will never leave. If you want to go back to Texas, we'll live there. If you want to stay here, we can do that too. Tell me what you need to be happy, and I will make it happen."

How can he know all my fears and still never get angry that I push some of those old thoughts on him when he's done nothing to deserve them? I run my fingers through his hair, pulling the leather string so his soft locks lie loose and spread over my stomach. "I need you and this baby to be healthy. Maybe after a short while, we can find a house here in Domhan that isn't your mother's home. Other than that, I have never been happier in my life than I am right now."

"We'll find a home of our own and make it beautiful for our child. Birdie will be a wonderful grandmother, and my mother will be thrilled." He's quiet for a long while. "I can hear the song of her soul."

"How do you know it's a girl?" As I set my teacup on the side table, my heart skips a beat. I thread my fingers through his, where they lie on my waist. The soft sound of our child's song lilts through my mind.

"Don't you think the song sounds feminine?" He kisses my stomach.

It does sound light and airy, like a gentler version of my song. "Is that a scientific determination?"

"Maybe not, but I feel like the life inside you is a girl, though if he's a boy, we'll adore him just as much. Either way, this is a miracle." He looks up at me. Tears roll down his cheeks.

I wipe away his tears of joy. "Everything is going to be alright."

"Better than that, my sweet love."

Three Months Later

Looking up at the black tower, I can't believe what Elspeth has suggested. "You want us to live here?"

A portal opens to our left, and three members of the oracle step through.

Elspeth says, "We lived here for many years. Then, it was the white tower of Priomh Bhaile, and we were very happy here."

Harper shivers. "It's not as black as it was when I was here. The dark magic has faded."

Wrapping an arm around her, Aaran says, "The evil is gone. Only the soot remains." He looks out over the patches of grass, trying to break through the brown and gray hillside. "The light is already pushing back into the land. No one is forcing you to live here, Wren. I'm only asking that you and Liam be the stewards of the eastern continent, Ear Talamh. You can portal back and forth if that's what you prefer."

More oracle portals open, and elves walk through. Harper told me that many of the elves who came from this part of Domhan wanted to return and rebuild their homes. When they traveled in the other direction by ship, they did not look so clean or well fed.

It's a daunting obligation to care for so many who have been through so much.

Liam's voice is soft inside my head. *You have been through as much, if not more, sweetheart.*

A couple named Dorian and Cara approach. Both are blond and blue-eyed. A man behind them is darker and more serious. I'm told his name is Beran.

Cara bows. "We would apply to serve in this castle and help to cleanse the remains of the darkness." Her voice is raw, and her speech slow.

Harper told me that Vanora robbed Cara of her voice, and it only returned when the witch queen died.

"You are a healer?" I'm only repeating what I've been told. It's hard to remember everything about everyone. I know she and her mate helped Harper during her darkest moment.

With the kindest eyes I have ever seen, she meets my gaze. "I am a healer, but that is not why my voice was taken from me. The witch queen needed my healing powers and left me my hands for that purpose." She wrings her hand as if considering worse possibilities than losing her voice. "My magic can pierce the darkness, and for that, I need to be heard."

"I don't understand. Magic is still new to me." Even after all these months in Domhan, there is so much more to learn.

Momma steps through a portal and makes her way over while staring up at the gray spires of the castle where Vanora took control of Domhan. Her eyes are filled with excitement. "Corell sent word that the obelisk in the lost lands has crumbled."

Liam hugs her. "That is not unexpected, but excellent news, Birdie."

She returns her gaze to the ugly castle. "It's not much to look at. What are we doing?"

I sigh. "Cara and Dorian were offering their services to clean up this mess."

"And to be part of your household if you would have us," Dorian says.

The castle will need a staff. It's not like the two-bedroom house in Texas, which I could clean myself in an hour. "I would be honored if you would stay and help us."

Momma, who knows everything about everyone, grins. "Cara, have you shown them your special magic yet?"

"Not yet, Madam Birdie." With a bright smile, much of the lingering sorrow lifts from Cara's eyes. She turns to the ruin of a castle, closes her eyes, and begins a soft, beautiful chant in the Old Elvish language. Her voice is like a harp with perfect tone and a soft vibration. As her sound grows, the gray and black soot fades away, leaving the towers gleaming bright white.

"By the old gods," Liam breathes. "It almost looks like my last memory of it before we had to retreat."

Elspeth swipes a tear away.

I don't know what to say. "Thank you, Cara. You are amazing."

"It is only the start of a cleansing, Lady Wren. It will take much more work to make this place a home where your children will grow and play." Cara looks up at her work. "But it can be done before this princess enters the world." She looks at my round abdomen.

I caress the little elf-human growing inside me with a hand over my belly. "It seems a big job for so short a time." I should give birth in a little under four months, and I'm not keen on the filth that must be within this place for raising my baby.

Beran steps forward. "With your permission, my Lord Liam and Lady Wren, I would like to take on the task of restoring this castle. Cara can remove all remnants of dark magic, and I can, with the help of perhaps fifty good magicians and laborers, restore the rest. Perhaps not as it was, but in a new way for a new family on this continent."

Wrapping his arm around my expanding waist, Liam asks, "What do you think, Wren? Shall we live here and watch over this side of Domhan?"

I wonder what I would say if I couldn't make a portal to take us to Tús Nua whenever we want. As I can, I smile. "I think it is worth a try if Beran, Cara, and Dorian believe it is possible. After all, they likely wish to wipe away the bad by turning this into something good and happy again."

"We can always go back to Texas if castle life doesn't appeal to you, baby girl." Momma laughs. "The houses and land might be sold, but we have enough to make a life."

Smiling at her teasing, I shake my head. "Maybe for a

visit from time to time, Momma, but this is home now. Of course, if you want to return, I'll visit more often."

Her frown is epic. "If you think for one second I'm going anywhere when my first granddaughter is only months away from all the cuddles I can spare, you have plumb lost your mind."

With a laugh, I hug her. "That's what I thought you'd say."

"I could find a place nearby. I'm sure you two don't want a mother-in-law in all your business every day." She studies the terrain and the shamble of houses that surround the castle. None of them are currently livable.

"I'll not hear of it, Birdie. You'll live with us for as long as you wish." Liam really does adore my mother.

Joy washes through me, and I have to wipe tears from my cheeks. "This is all going to work out."

"Of course, it will." Harper takes my hand. "Though I'm going to miss you at home."

Squeezing her hand, I nod. "Not yet. It will take a little while before this place is livable. You'll have to put up with me a bit longer."

Liam walks with Beran along the edge of the crumbled city wall. They both point and talk about construction and repairs.

Suddenly, the image of what this ruined castle might look like flashes through my mind. It's tall white spires reaching into a cloudless sky and hills of green rolling away to the sea, where a new port boasts fishing boats tied to moorings. Houses line the streets that run in a circular pattern around the castle. Elves work and play in the prosperous city. At the gate, the stone carving says **A** *luath*. "*A luath*," I say aloud. A wave of dizziness staggers me as the vision fades.

Everyone turns to face me.

Liam rushes over and steadies me. "Are you alright?"

"I saw the city and the land around it restored. It was beautiful. I show him the image in my mind of the green hills and the white city of the east. "The sign at the gate said *A luath*."

"From ashes." He smiles. "That is what the city will be called?"

"I think so. It's appropriate, and Phoenix is already taken." I like the sound of something reborn.

Only Harper laughs at my joke.

"*A Luath*," I say again. Nodding, I give my approval to Cara and entrust her with the task.

Harper and Aaran hug me. Harper says, "I have to get back. My mother is arriving today, and I want to make sure her rooms are perfect."

"Oh geez. In all the excitement, I forgot." I concentrate on the central hall of Tús Nua and make an arch with my arm. The portal forms and the grand stairs are visible. "We'll be back for dinner. I can't wait to meet your mom."

Another hug, then Harper, Aaran, and Elspeth step through.

Momma goes over to discuss plans with Cara.

Walking hand in hand, Liam and I head north until the ocean can be spied in the distance. My feet ache, and I find a place to rest on a boulder. "I'm glad I walked through that portal in Scotland."

He kneels in front of me, and his magic tingles against my skin. My poor, swollen ankles are instantly relieved by his healing. He runs his fingers over my calves. "I thank the old gods every day for bringing you to me, Wren. There was no joy in life before you, and there could be no happiness for me without you."

"Always saying the right thing, Prince Liam. That is your special gift." I look from his deep blue eyes to the sparkling sea. "We're going to be happy here. We can visit the west often, and in the years to come, our children can grow up with their cousins."

Rising, he wraps me in his arms. "I can hardly believe there will be babies before summer's end. The old gods have blessed my brothers and me."

"And from what the healers say, they will all be girls. I also heard that the baker's wife is pregnant and that her child is a girl. Several people have been told they'll be having boys as well." Balance has returned here. That was our job, and now we're in charge of caring for the people and land. "I'm a bit overwhelmed."

He kisses the top of my head. "As am I, sweetheart. We'll make our way together as stewards and as parents. I'm glad Birdie is here. If anyone knows how to raise a perfect soul, it is her."

Tears spring to my eyes. "I'm not perfect, Liam."

"I'll not argue with you, even if you're wrong." He moves so that my bottom is pressed to his thighs and not the hard, rough boulder.

As I lean my head back on his chest, the vision of the future returns. Gripping his hands at my waist, I bring him into my mind. A lavender sky as the sun sets over the ocean. A baby gurgles behind us, and we stand on a wide terrace looking out. White sheer curtains blow in the breeze between us and our bedroom. Below, the town is quiet as people settle in for dinner hour. A centaur family gallops across the field in the distance, their hair blowing back as they go. Barely visible, a dragon flies over the ocean. "It's perfect."

Liam kisses the top of my head. "The vision was lovely, sweetheart." He squeezes me tight. "This is perfect."

In the few moments remaining before we must return to Tús Nua, I have everything I shall ever need. If my love wishes to believe I'm perfect, who am I to argue with him?

Epilogue Three

LAYLA

My growing belly will not let me do much but observe as the camp on the mountainside is dismantled for the journey. Raith has strongly suggested that I remain above and only supervise the work. He rarely gives commands, and I know he worries that the baby or I might be hurt with so much heavy work happening.

Six members of the oracle watch with me. It's strange to see them outside their mountain, but they've grown attached to the Aracan elves. I think they are sorry to see them leave.

As they do not use their given names once they join the oracle, I'm always at a loss for what to call them. The female one with dark skin is rarely seen. She has not been part of my training, but she is among the six viewing our village packing. "You will do well in your new home, Lady Layla."

"I will do my best."

The Aracans have chosen to go with us and settle farther north on the vast eastern continent. They will make a home near the town of Foiseil in the foothills where the river runs. It's not far from where we landed in Domhan.

She cocks her head. "That will be enough, I assure you. The new palace is to your liking?"

My back aches from standing. "It's very nice. Too big, but very nice. The mountains are beautiful, and there will be many Aracan elves to care for, as well as the returning population of Domhan elves to Foiseil. I'm sure I'll have plenty to keep me busy."

"I noticed you did not return to the human world as your sister did." She looks at my baby belly and narrows her gaze.

The urge to wrap my arms around my stomach is hard to resist. "I have no one there I needed to part with and no property to manage."

She nods. "It is good then that you have found a family in Domhan."

Oddly, my throat tightens with emotions. "They are the first family I have ever had." I have no idea why I told her that.

Staring at my stomach, she reaches for me. "May I check the health of the child?"

Panic hits me like a hammer to the skull. I step back. "Why? Do you sense something is wrong?"

"Wrong is not the correct word."

"What is the correct word?" Taking a deep breath, I step closer and move my hands aside for her to touch me.

"Layla?" Raith climbs up the hillside and steps alongside me. "What's happening?"

"I'm not sure." The oracle magic is subtle but strong as it flows over and through me.

She has her eyes closed, and the other members' attention shifts to us. When she looks at me again, she offers an awkward smile. It seems as if it's been a long time since she attempted the expression. "There is no danger, Lady Layla."

I lean against Raith with relief. "What did you sense?" I caress my belly.

"A second life," she says flatly.

"What?" Raith practically shouts. He crouches in front of my stomach and places both palms on me. "Twins?"

"Yes. Two lives are growing within. We are not trained as healers, but we sense that there will be a female and a male child." She attempts another smile.

Mind reeling, I wobble.

Raith leaps up and steadies me.

The oracle conjures a chair and places it behind me. "Sit. This has upset you. That was not our intention."

Pressing his ear to my stomach, Raith says, "I hear two songs. Why didn't we notice sooner?"

The oracle stands in a circle and confers. When one turns back to us, she says, "The male hid himself, we think. Perhaps to allow the joy of his sister since she will be the first female born in Domhan in so many suns."

"Are you telling me that the tiny fetus that will be our son had the presence of mind to hang back and give his sister the stage for almost six months?" It's hard to catch my breath. No wonder I'm so much bigger than Wren. I thought it was because I'm a month further along.

Harper's baby is the most recent good news, and will arrive a few months after Wren's.

Raith looks as doubtful as I am, though he's far more respectful to the oracle. "It does sound unlikely."

"I cannot say that your son did this consciously, but he has lowered his shield now and wishes to be known." She says it as if it's perfectly normal.

Horses on the path draw our attention.

Aaran and Harper ride up to the scene. Leaping from his horse, Aaran rushes to my side. "Are you ill?"

"No. I'm bowled over."

The new king looks confused.

A groom from the oracle helps Harper down from the saddle. She's barely showing her baby bump, but everyone in Domhan knows of the new queen's condition.

The oracle bows as one.

Harper acknowledges them, but kneels in front of me. "What's wrong?" She checks my feet and ankles as if I might have twisted something.

"I'm fine. It seems our son has been hiding." I'm still wrapping my head around the idea, but I can't resist watching their reaction.

She palms my stomach. "Son. I thought..." She shakes her head. "It doesn't matter. Everyone will be thrilled with a boy as much as a girl, Layla."

Aaran grips my shoulder and slaps Raith on the back. "Of course. You're not upset that the child is a boy, are you?"

Shaking his head, Raith suddenly grins. "I will love both my son and my daughter equally, just as my parents loved me despite their hope that I'd be the last girl before the curse."

Eyes narrowed with confusion, Aaran looks from Raith to me.

Harper gapes as it hits her. "Twins?"

I nod.

She wraps me in a hug and begins to speak quickly without taking a breath. "This is the most wonderful news. Should you be running off to a new house with twins on the way? Won't you stay with us until the babies are born?"

"We have a healer coming with us. Brion and Elspeth will be with us until I give birth. Unless you need us here, our place is in Foiseil." I break the hug.

Raith's pride in me is like a warm blanket. He looks at his brother and shrugs. "Twins."

Slapping him on the back, Aaran laughs. "You are finally an overachiever, little brother. I always knew you would be."

More seriously, Raith asks, "Did the transfer of prisoners go well?"

"They are underground in the cloisters with Rían and a large force to keep them there. The oracle" —he nods to those around us— "will be sending members to evaluate those who seem repentant in a few months."

"And Ciaran? Did he cause trouble?" Raith asks.

"He tried." Harper continues to kneel by my side, holding my hand.

My heart skips a beat. "Was anyone hurt?"

Aaran shakes his head. "No. Ciaran tried to use magic to alter the guards' minds. We had to render him unconscious for transport. His cell has been warded to keep his dark magic dormant."

"Do you think he can be rehabilitated?" I am doubtful, though I try to keep my opinion to myself.

"No," Aaran admits. "I think if he had the opportunity

and power, he would attempt to take Vanora's place. However, he survived the battle, and Liam has agreed that as long as he remains at the lowest level of the cloisters, he will not rip his heart from his chest."

"I'm surprised Rían didn't kill him. I wouldn't have minded that miserable ass dying," Harper admits. "After all, it was Ciaran who forced Niamh to give her fairy life to save their party. It was only Rían's love for her that brought her back."

"No one would have blamed him." I never had any contact with the horrible consort of the witch queen, but the stories from my friends and family in Domhan are enough to make him enemy number one in my mind.

"It's a far worse fate for him to have his magic bound and live out his days in a cell." Raith admires his brother for making that decision.

Aaran smiles. "Enough about that sorry creature. You are having two babies! I wish you would wait to move away, but I can understand wanting your own home."

Spring nights are cool, and the open door to our bedroom in Tús Nua brings a lovely breeze. The day went well despite the shock of learning we would be welcoming a boy and a girl in just a few months. I was just getting used to the idea of being a mother, and now learning there are two babies, I'm both thrilled and terrified.

I realize I'm smiling before the panic sets in. Family is everything.

The Aracan elves went through portals to their new home, along with several hundred Domhan elves who wanted to go back to Foiseil and begin rebuilding. Tents will serve as their shelter until the town can be restored. There is good farmland, according to Tog. Tomorrow, they'll journey to the forest and try to convince the Aracans born in Domhan to join their village by the river.

Once that is decided, Harper will bring the children they rescued back to their parents. I know she's hesitant to send them away, but they are keen to be reunited with their people despite whatever happened while Vanora controlled their minds.

Raith steps out of the bathroom wearing only his leggings and eases into bed beside me. "Our last night in this room."

"Mmm." The way both Aaran and Harper asked us to stay has been on my mind all day.

"What is it?" He snuggles against the babies, wrapping his arm around my abdomen.

"Nothing." I sigh. "Well, not nothing."

Concern draws his beautiful mouth down, and he sits up. "Tell me."

"Yours is the first family I've ever had. I love having sisters and brothers." I swallow down a sob. "And a mother."

His expression softens. "Three mothers if you count Birdie and Maggie."

"I do count them." Tears start falling before I can control them. I know it's partially hormones, but there's no help for it.

He stares at me for a long moment, panic, worry, fear,

and resignation flying across his face. "Layla, do you want to stay here until after the babies are born?" he asks in a soft, calm voice.

"The Aracans..." More tears. I gulp for breath. "They need us. We said we'd goooo."

After a long, slow breath, he cups my cheeks and stares into my eyes. "The oracle will provide transport for me to go back and forth whenever I need to until you are ready to move into our new home. They are working on new magic to have available portals between the three major cities. Tell me, *mo anam cara*, would you like to stay here with our family until after the twins are born?"

"I never had a family before, and now we're moving away, and all these hormones..." More tears come that I can't get under control.

He presses his lips to mine despite my less than sexy state. "I will speak to Aaran in the morning and let Mother and Father know we'll be remaining in Tús Nua until after the birth."

Full of joy at how much he loves me, I gulp down emotion and wipe my face. "They're going to think I'm fickle and have no business caring for a town and the Aracans."

Shaking his head, he laughs. "They will be thrilled you want to have the babies here and that you love them."

"I really do."

Raith leaps from the bed and goes into the bathroom. When he returns, he has a wet washcloth.

I wash my face and move to take it to the bathroom.

Taking it from me, he shakes his head. "Stay in bed and relax."

My aching feet and legs won't let me argue with him

about being able to take care of myself. I mean, I could, but it's nice to let him do it.

After a moment, he gets back in bed and leans against the headboard. He slides an arm behind my back and draws me against him. "I'm glad you told me what you want, Layla. I sensed some trepidation, but you'd not let me see this wish to stay with family. Why not?"

I shrug. "It seemed like I should want to be in our home before the babies came. It's what other people want when they're starting a family." I take a breath. "I wanted to be normal."

"You're extraordinary. Why would you wish to be less? You want to enjoy family, it seems perfectly natural to me, and it was more than clear today that my brother and Harper sensed your wishes." He traces a line down my arm from biceps to elbow, then along my belly, and back up again.

"Thank you for agreeing and for getting me."

"Getting you?"

"It means when you understand another person on a deep level." I settle against him and relax.

Resting his cheek on my hair, he sighs. "I get you, *mo anam cara.*"

This is precisely where I'm meant to be. Even if I hadn't spoken up, and we left for our new home tomorrow, if I'm in Raith's arms, all is well. "You are my home."

Join my Newsletter – A wonderful way to stay in touch and always know what's new and exciting in the Andrea Rose, Andie, and A.S. Fenichel book universe is to sign up for my weekly newsletter. You'll automatically receive a free book, but beyond that, you'll love all the sales, news, and book talk.

https://asfenichel.com/newsletter

Want a bit more for joining? Get a FREE novella:
https://dl.bookfunnel.com/8cs5hbl1wi

Read all about the stern Captain Rían Redman and his quest to save the captured elves and children. He'll find more than he thinks in ***A Crown of Blood and Duty***.

RÌAN

The mission is simple: rescue the elven children stolen by the witch queen before they vanish forever. Freed once by the human woman from the prophecy, then retaken, they'll be held at the black tower. Failure isn't an option.

But when a fairy steps out of the shadows to warn us that we've come to the wrong place, plans must be abandoned. Fairies never leave their island. They don't meddle in elven wars. And they definitely don't look at me the way Niamh does. She is dangerous in ways I didn't anticipate, distracting, defiant, and far too tempting. I'm here to complete a mission, not lose my heart to a fairy who doesn't belong in my world.

NIAMH

I watched Rìan Redmond long before he knew I existed. As my father studied the elven realm through his scrying mirrors, the captain of the guard was always there—steady, loyal, untouchable.

Seeing him in the flesh makes my pulse race, but this isn't a fairy tale. I left the safety of my island to help free the children trapped by the witch queen, and I won't turn back now. If fate insists on tangling my heart with a stubborn elven soldier along the way...who am I to argue?

Also by Andrea Rose

FANTASY ROMANCE

Reign of the Witch Queen Series

A Crown of Light and Shadow

A Crown of Wind and Water

A Crown of Fire and Ice

A Crown of Stars and Sea (Prequel Novella)

A Crown of Blood and Duty (Novella)

Writing as A.S. Fenichel

HISTORICAL PARANORMAL ROMANCE

Witches of Windsor Series

Magic Touch

Magic Word

Pure Magic

The Demon Hunters Series

Ascension

Deception

Betrayal

Defiance

Vengeance

🔥🔥🔥🔥🔥🔥🔥🔥

HISTORICAL ROMANCE

The Wallflowers of West Lane Series

The Earl Not Taken

Misleading A Duke

Capturing the Earl

Not Even For A Duke

The Everton Domestic Society Series

A Lady's Honor

A Lady's Escape

A Lady's Virtue

A Lady's Doubt

A Lady's Past

A Lady's Christmas

A Lady's Curves

The Forever Brides Series

Tainted Bride

Foolish Bride

Desperate Bride

Single Title Books

Wishing Game

Christmas Bliss

An Honorable Arrangement

CONTEMPORARY PARANORMAL EROTIC ROMANCE

The Psychic Mates Series

Kane's Bounty

Joshua's Mistake

Training Rain

The End of Days Series

Mayan Afterglow

Mayan Craving

Mayan Inferno

End of Days Trilogy

CONTEMPORARY EROTIC ROMANCE

Single Title Books

Alaskan Exposure

Revving Up the Holidays

Writing as Andie Fenichel

Dragon of My Dreams (Monster Between the Sheets)

Turnabout is Fairy Play (Monster Between the Sheets)

Soul of a Vampire (Brothers of Scrim Hall)

Soul of a Reaper (Brothers of Scrim Hall)

Soul of a Dragon (Brothers of Scrim Hall)

Soul of a Wolf (Brothers of Scrim Hall)

Soul of a Demon (Brothers of Scrim Hall)

Soul of a Phoenix (Brothers of Scrim Hall)

Soul of a Monster (Brothers of Scrim Hall)

The Manticore's Mate (Catskills Mountain Monsters)

Promised to the Satyr (Catskills Mountain Monsters)

Wild for the Wyvern (Catskills Mountain Monsters)

Big Enough to Bite (Harmony Glen)

Biting Bigfoot (Harmony Glen)

Bitten by Love (Harmony Glen)

Mantus

Riding With the Panther

Dad Bod Handyman (Lane Family)

Carnival Lane (Lane Family)

Lane to Fame (Lane Family)

Changing Lanes (Lane Family)

Heavy Petting (Lane Family)

Summer Lane (Lane Family)

Hero's Lane (Lane Family)

Icing It (Lane Family)

Mountain Lane (Lane Family)

Christmas Lane (Lane Family)

Texas Lane (Lane Family)

Building Lane (Lane Family)

Humbug Lane (Lane Family)

High Voltage Lane (Lane Family)

For Letter or Worse (Lane Family)

Visit Andrea Rose's website

for a complete and up-to-date list of all her books.

http://andrearoseauthor.com

About the Author

Andrea Rose is a pen name for author A.S. Fenichel. She also writes as Andie Fenichel. Andrea gave up a successful career in New York City to pursue her lifelong dream of being a professional writer. She's never looked back.

Andrea adores writing stories filled with love, passion, desire, magic, and maybe a little mayhem tossed in for good measure. Books have always been her perfect escape, and she still relishes diving into one and staying up all night to finish a good story.

With over 60 published books, Andrea Rose/Andie Fenichel/A.S. Fenichel has written historical romance, fantasy romance, contemporary romance, and mixed-genre romances. She has authored several series, including Reign of the Witch Queen, Everton Domestic Society, Witches of Windsor, and more. Strong, empowered heroines from Regency London to modern-day New York are what you'll find in all her books.

A Jersey Girl at heart, she now makes her home in Southern Missouri with her real-life hero, her wonderful husband. When not reading or writing, she enjoys cooking, traveling, history, and puttering in her garden.

Visit Andrea Rose's Website:
http://andrearoseauthor.com

Send Andrea Rose an Email:
andrearoseauthor@outlook.com

Join Andrea's Newsletter:
www.asfenichel.com/newsletter/

instagram.com/asfenichel

facebook.com/a.s.fenichel

tiktok.com/@asfenichel

bookbub.com/authors/andrea-rose

pinterest.com/asfenichel

x.com/asfenichel

amazon.com/author/andrearoseauthor

www.ingramcontent.com/pod-product-compliance
Lightning Source LLC
Chambersburg PA
CBHW071638030726
47592CB00005B/1888